The Back of Beyond

Doris Davidson is a retired primary school teacher who still lives in her native city of Aberdeen. She has been writing novels since 1984 and the first to be published was *The Brow of the Gallowgate* in 1990. Her married daughter now lives only twenty-five miles away but her son, an art teacher, also lives in Aberdeen, and he presented her with a grandson in 1987.

By the same author

DORIS DAVIDSON

The Back of Beyond

HarperCollins*Publishers*

This novel is a work of fiction. The names, characters and incidents portrayed in it are the work of the author's imagination. Any resemblance to actual persons, living or dead, is entirely coincidental.

HarperCollins*Publishers*
77–85 Fulham Palace Road,
Hammersmith, London W6 8JB

The HarperCollins website address is:
www.**fire**and**water**.com

A Paperback Original 2002

1 3 5 7 9 8 6 4 2

A catalogue record for this book
is available from the British Library

ISBN 0 00 711426 5

Typeset in Postscript Linotype Minion with
Bauer Bodoni display by
Palimpsest Book Production Limited,
Polmont, Stirlingshire

Printed and bound in Great Britain by
Omnia Books Limited, Glasgow

Like Rosie Jenkins in the story, I love my whole brood, each of them ever ready to help me with anything I need to know, or anywhere I want to go. So, my eternal thanks to Jimmy, Sheila and John, Alan, Bertha and Bill, and Debra.

Matthew, of course, deserves a special mention. At fourteen, most youngsters steer clear of elderly Grans, but he helps me in so many ways, not least by keeping my mind young, for which I am very grateful.

Then there is Susan Opie, my editor, whose patience must be stretched to breaking point with my persistence in sending her manuscripts which are far too long, and because I use too much of the Doric, a dialect which people outside Aberdeenshire find impossible to understand. At my age, however, I find it very difficult to change. Sorry, Susan! And thanks!

1929–1939

Chapter 1

'You'll have to tell her the night, Ally – we're leaving first thing in the morning.'

Alistair Ritchie gave a rueful sigh. 'I suppose I will, Dougal, but I'm dreading it.'

'You should have let her see ages ago she was wasting her time.'

'I did try, but she's got it in her head I'm the only one for her, and nothing'll shift it.'

Dougal Finnie gave an exaggerated sigh. 'I'm right sorry for you. It must be terrible to be that irresistible to women.'

Annoyed by his pal's smirking sarcasm, Alistair burst out, 'You wouldna think it was funny if it was you.'

Having arrived outside the Finnies' house, Dougal turned in at the gate, still laughing, and Alistair swung his leg over the bar of his bicycle to continue on his way home from work, his mind going over what had led to the momentous step he was to take the following day. He had made the decision when he and Dougal were propped against the back wall of the kirkyard a week and a half ago – a secluded corner where they told each other things they wouldn't, couldn't, tell anyone else – and he'd been complaining as he so often did nowadays about Lexie Fraser pestering him. 'She's been after me since we were still at school, but it's got worse since . . .'

'Some lads wouldna mind that,' Dougal had grinned. 'She's a real bonnie lassie.'

'Oh, she's bonnie enough, but since her father walked out

on them, there's been something . . . off-putting about her, like she'd smother me wi' love if she got half a chance.' He paused, then said reflectively, 'That was a funny business, wasn't it? I'd have said Alec and Carrie Fraser were a real devoted couple, and I can hardly believe what folk's saying about him, and yet . . .'

Dougal screwed up his nose. 'My Mam says there's nae smoke withoot fire. Dinna forget Nancy Lawrie left just the day afore him, and she's never come back, either. They musta been meeting someplace else to keep it secret, but folk's nae daft.'

'I canna help feeling sorry for Lexie, for she doted on her father, but it looks like she's trying to get me to make up for what he did. Every time I go out a walk wi' her, she's all over me like a rash you've just got to scratch, and I'm feared I'll give in some night and do something I shouldna.'

The twinkle in Dougal's eyes had deepened at that. 'I'm surprised you havena done it already.'

'Have *you* done it wi' somebody?'

'Dozens o' times. You dinna ken what you're missing, Ally, I bet Lexie's hot stuff.'

'I wouldna mind trying it, but nae wi' her. I feel like running the other way every time she comes near me.' He had hesitated briefly, then added, 'To be fair, though, I think she just needs . . . somebody to . . . Her Mam canna be much company.'

After a moment's silence, Dougal had looked at his friend thoughtfully. 'How would you like to be rid o' her . . . for good?'

'I'm desperate to get rid o' her, for she clings to me like a blooming leech, but I draw the line at murder. You should ken me better than that, Dougal Finnie!'

'I didna say *get* rid o' her, you gowk! I said *be* rid o' her. You see, Ally, I'm sick fed up o' working for Bill Rettie in the garage, aye clarted wi' oil and grease, and nae chance o' promotion. Any road, what he pays me hardly buys a packet o' fags, so I've made up my mind to go to London and look for a better job. What about coming wi' me?'

His first reaction, Alistair recalled, had been to say no. After two years of being delivery boy and general sweeper-up for the butcher in Bankside, the village four miles west of Forvit, he had recently been taken on as an apprentice to learn the trade. It would be a few years before he got a decent wage, but it was a steady job and he wasn't keen to give that up. On the other hand . . . he'd be well away from Lexie in London. 'When was you thinking on going?'

'As soon as you like. I could go to Aberdeen on Saturday and book our passages – the boat's a lot cheaper than the train. Are you on?'

'Um . . . um . . .' Deciding that the pros more than outweighed the cons, Alistair had given a decisive nod. 'Aye, I'm on – if my dad'll stump up the money for my fare.'

His mother hadn't been too pleased about it, though. It wasn't the money, just the fact that he was going so far away from home. 'You're only new sixteen,' she had said, sadly, 'ower young to be on your own in a place the size o' London.'

'I'll nae be on my own, Mam, I'll be wi' Dougal.'

She had shaken her head at this. 'He's never been a good example to you, aye getting you in some kind o' mischief.'

His father had come to his defence here. 'Ach, Bella, leave the laddie be! It's time he was taking a bit o' responsibility for himsel', showed some independence . . . and Dougal'll keep him right.'

Alistair smiled at the memory of this contradictory statement. Dougal had always told him what to do, not that he was a bully. Far from it. He was the best friend a boy – or man, come to that – could ever have, though he was inclined to jump first and think after. Anyway, his father had given him his fare money, and in the morning, his mother had pressed two pound notes into his hand to keep him, hopefully, till he found a job.

But he still had one thing to do before he left Forvit.

Alistair's steps were slow and reluctant as he went to meet Lexie Fraser for the last time. He dreaded the scene there was bound to be, and was afraid he might say something she could take the wrong way. If she thought for a minute that he felt something for her, she would spread it about that she was his girl, and if he *did* something he shouldn't, she might say he'd put her in the family way and he'd have to marry her. Aye, he'd have to watch his step tonight.

With Benview three miles from the village and the Frasers' house half a mile this side of it, they'd never walked in the woods between Forvit and Bankside like the other courting couples. Their trysting place was midway between their homes, where a footpath from the road led up to a tower which had been built as a look-out post during the Napoleonic Wars by the then Earl of Forvit. It was here that Alistair meant to break the news.

Although there was a track from his house diagonally up to the tower itself, he always went down to the road to meet her, and she was there first, as she always was. She hadn't heard him coming, and he wondered for the umpteenth time why he felt as he did about her. She *was* a bonnie lassie, fair-haired like himself but maybe about five feet two to his five ten, with rosy cheeks and blue eyes a shade lighter than his. She had a good figure for sixteen, her bust not too big nor yet too small, her middle nipped in by the belt of her navy trench coat, the one she had worn to school. She had once made him span her waist, and he'd nearly been able to make the tips of his fingers meet. She thought her bottom was too big, but to his mind it wasn't all that bad . . . quite neat, really.

She turned at the sound of his footsteps and tucked her arm through his when they got on to the stony track. Her chattering didn't annoy him as much as it normally did – in fact, he was glad that she didn't expect him to do any of the talking – but when they came nearer to the tower his stomach started to churn at the prospect of what he had to do.

They sat down in the small niche she had recently begun referring to as 'our special place', and when she came to the end of a long, involved story about something that had happened in the general store which she helped her mother to run since her father left, he cleared his throat nervously. 'I've something to tell you, Lexie.' His heart sank at the way her eyes lit up, and what he had planned to say died on his lips.

'Go on,' she urged. 'Say it, Al . . . darling.'

It was far worse than he had imagined – she must think he was going to say he loved her – but it had to be done. 'I . . . that is, me and Dougal . . .' Her horrified expression made him race on. '. . . we're going to Aberdeen first thing in the morning.'

The renewed hope in her eyes told that she had jumped to the wrong conclusion. She must think he was taking his friend with him for advice on buying something for her, an engagement ring, maybe. 'I'm sorry, Lexie,' he said quietly, 'we've booked our passages on the London boat.'

'You're going to London?' she gasped. 'What for?'

'To look for decent jobs. We'll never make anything of ourselves here.'

'But Al . . . you and me . . . what about us?'

Her blue eyes had dimmed, practically brimming with tears, but he had to be brutal. 'I've tried telling you before, Lexie. There's no us, not the way you'd like. I'm sorry, but that's the way it is.'

'But, Al . . . I thought . . . you felt the same about me . . .'

'I've never felt that way about you, Lexie. I like you, but that's all.'

The tears flooded out now, and he sat uneasily silent while she sobbed, 'You do love me, Al, I know you do!'

He hated her calling him Al, it reminded him of that awful gangster Capone he'd read about, but he also hated to see her crying. 'Aw, Lexie,' he muttered, sliding his arm awkwardly round her shoulders, 'you'll find somebody else.'

'I don't want anybody else!' Turning to him, she laid her head against his chest. 'I love you! I've always loved you and I always will!' Her mood changed like quicksilver, and she looked up at him accusingly. 'You're just like my father, you're deserting me and all, and you don't care what happens to me.'

He was outraged by this. 'That's not fair! I never pretended to be anything more than a friend, and at least I've told you I'm going away. Any road, it's not up to me to look after you, that's your mother's responsibility, and your father'll likely come back once he's . . . Please try to understand, Lexie. I need to get away. I want to make something of my life, and even if I don't, I won't come back here. I don't like hurting you, Lexie, but that's the way it is.'

Her eyes were beseeching now, her words a mere whisper. 'You'll surely give me a goodbye kiss?'

Feeling a proper heel, he bent his head to her upturned mouth and was immediately engulfed in a suffocating embrace. Frantically, he tried to think how to extricate himself without physically hurting her, for her passionate kisses were making an unwanted desire start in him, a desire he had no wish to fulfil.

'Stop it!' he shouted, shoving her roughly away and scrambling to his feet. 'I know what you're trying to do, but it won't work! I've told you – I don't love you and I'm leaving wi' Dougal in the morning.'

She looked at him pathetically now. 'But . . . you'll come back to me?'

'If I come back, it'll only be for a visit, to see my mother and father. Now, get up and I'll see you home.'

'Damn you, Alistair Ritchie!' she shouted. 'You've just been amusing yourself wi' me and you're abandoning me like my father, and I never want to see you again! Go away and leave me alone!'

'I can't leave you up here by yourself in the dark. Come on, Lexie, be sensible.'

'Sensible?' Her voice had risen several tones. 'How can I be sensible when you've just said you don't love me any more? You led me on, and I'll never forgive you!'

'I didna lead you on, Lexie,' Alistair said, desperately, 'I never said I loved you . . . it was all in your mind. Come on now, stand up and I'll take you back.'

She got to her feet slowly, refusing the hand he held out although she stumbled over the stones in their path when they made their way down the hill. They had almost reached the road when she murmured, with a little hiccup, 'What would you think if I killed myself? That's what I feel like doing.'

Sure that this was an attempt at moral blackmail, he snapped, 'I'd say you were mad!'

'I *am* mad . . . mad about you,' she whispered, stopping to look at him with her blue eyes wide and pleading.

'You'll soon forget me. Look, Lexie, you're just making things worse. Even if I wasn't going away, there'd never be anything between us, not on my side, any road.' In an effort to coax her out of her self-inflicted misery, he took her hand. 'Give's a smile, Lexie. I don't want us to part on bad terms.'

'But you still want us to part?'

'It's best.'

'For you, maybe, not for me.' She yanked her hand out of his. 'But have it your own way, Alistair Ritchie! Go to London and do what you like!'

'I will, then, and you can see yourself home from here!' He turned and strode back towards the track that led to his house, seething at her for being difficult yet feeling guilty for hurting her. Not that he should feel guilty, for she had done all the chasing, made all the advances. Of course, once he realized what was in her mind, he should have let her know he wasn't interested, but she likely wouldn't have listened.

Having watched Alistair stamping out of sight, Lexie walked on down to the road. She *had* felt suicidal a few minutes ago, but not any longer; she needed a man to depend on more than ever. She had often heard that jobs weren't so easy to come by in London, and he'd be back in a few months with his tail between his legs.

Her mother looked up in surprise when she went into the house. 'You havena bidden long wi' Alistair the night.'

Lexie flung her coat on a chair. 'We'd a row! Him and Dougal Finnie's going away to London in the morning.'

'That's funny. Meg Finnie was in the shop yesterday and she said her Dougal was leaving, but she never said Alistair Ritchie was going wi' him.'

'Dougal had forced him. He wouldn't have wanted to go.'

Although Carrie Fraser's interest in other people had dimmed since her husband had walked out on her, her judgement of character was still as shrewd as ever. 'I aye thought he wasna as keen on you as you was on him,' she observed.

'He was so! Dougal had got round him ... like he's aye done.'

'If you'd had ony sense, Lexie, you'd have gone for Dougal. He's more spunk in him than Alistair, and he'll do well wherever he is. Besides, Joe Finnie's a lot better off than Willie Ritchie.'

'But it's Alistair I love, Mam, and I know he'll come back to me.'

'I wouldna count my chickens if I was you, lass.'

Carrie turned things over in her mind for some time after her daughter flounced off to bed. Something worried her about Lexie these days. Of course, her father going off without a word like that was enough to knock any girl off balance, but she should be getting over it a bit – it was three months now. He must have known how badly Lexie would take it, for she'd always been a daddy's girl – and she, his wife, could still hardly believe it. What bothered her was why? If only Alec had considered them before . . .

Carrie shook her greying head despairingly. There had been a rumour – she'd just heard snatches of whispers, for folk shut up when they realized she was listening – but Alec would never have . . . he hadn't been a demanding man, not even when they were first wed. He'd never have needed another woman, but that's what they were saying. Of course, Nancy Lawrie had gone away just the day before him and never come back, and her mother had said she'd no idea where she was. That was why folk were sure she'd been expecting his bairn and he'd left to be with her – what else would they think? But Alec would never have touched a young lassie. He was a decent man, and Nancy Lawrie wasn't much older than Lexie.

Her sorrow and sense of betrayal still too raw for her to cope with, Carrie heaved a shuddering sigh. She didn't think she'd ever get over it, so why should she expect Lexie to forget? Poor lass! Alistair Ritchie could have helped her, but maybe he could see there was something not right about her nowadays. It wasn't anything her mother could put a finger on, but she was definitely different, more serious . . . over-serious, that was it . . . intense. She was young, and should be enjoying herself more, but she had likely heard what they were saying, and all, though a true family man doesn't up tail and leave his wife and daughter without a word, no matter what sort of trouble he finds himself in. He buckles to and faces up to whatever it is, but . . . fathering a bairn on a woman that wasn't his wife, a girl, really, twenty years younger than himself? In a place like Forvit, he'd have been the butt of the filthiest of crude jokes, and he wouldn't have liked that.

Running the general store and sub-post office, as well as being an elder in the kirk, he'd always held his head up, taken a pride in not going drinking with the other men, and especially not playing around with loose women, for there was a few of that kind about, even in this wee village. His interest lay in music. His father had taught him how to play their little harmonium, and he had played the pipe organ in the kirk since he was fifteen. He took the choir practice every Wednesday, the only night of the week he ever went out, and that was where he'd got friendly with Nancy Lawrie, for she was one of the sopranos.

But bad blood will out, though there had been no hint of it before! And Lexie was his daughter, so maybe there was something unnatural in her, as well? It wasn't noticeable, thank heaven, but the shock could have been enough to bring it to the surface – for just a wee while, please God! One good thing, she was coping all right in the shop, learning the postal work and all, and that could take her mind off things. And she'd find another lad. Of course she would!

* * *

Lying on top of the bedcovers, Lexie was angry at her mother for being so perceptive, but whatever she said or thought, the girl was certain that absence *would* make Alistair's heart grow fonder, and she was prepared to wait for months, even years, for him to come back to her. But suppose he kept his threat and didn't come near her when he came back to visit his mother and father? What then?

She contemplated this awful thought for some time, then decided that it would be up to her to seek him out and make him admit he loved her, as she was sure he did . . . deep down. He was the only man she'd ever want, and even if it took until they were middle-aged, till they were both grey-haired, she would get him in the end.

Chapter 2

While the Aberdeen Steam Navigation Company's 'Lochnagar' was docked at Leith, the two youths stood at the rail to watch the activity involved in the taking aboard of some twenty or so new passengers and their baggage, a welcome break from the long hours of having only seagulls and water to look at, their faces spattered by the spray sent up as the ship's prow cleaved through the angry waves.

The lengthy interlude over and on their way once more, Alistair cast a sour glance at his friend, to whom he felt somewhat less than friendly at that precise moment. 'Could you nae have got a better place for us than right up at the sharp end?'

Dougal seemed rather put out. 'What did you expect for fifteen bob? A luxury cabin? Second class return was two pounds, but single was one pound, seven and six, meals included. I ken't my mother would gi'e me enough to feed the five thousand, so I said we wouldna need meals. I saved you twelve and a tanner, and that's the thanks I get.'

'Aye, well, but I thought I'd get to London dry.'

'Ach, stop your girnin'. Tell yoursel' Lexie Fraser's getting further and further awa' every minute. Does that nae cheer you up?'

They ate their second 'meal' now, rationing their pooled resources – a crusty loaf, a hunk of cheese and a pound of cold sausages from Alistair's mother, a large meat roll, a jar of her rhubarb chutney and six hard boiled eggs from

Dougal's. Meg Finnie had also packed into the small canvas bag a flagon of home-made ginger beer to wash down the dry fare. Not long after they had packed away their remaining food, the sun peeped uncertainly through the clouds, and the sky slowly came ablaze with light.

'This is more like it,' Alistair observed, as the heat penetrated his damp clothes.

'Aye, thank goodness,' Dougal muttered. 'Maybe you'll be happy now.'

At Newcastle, while the new passengers came up the gangway, Dougal invented some reasons for their making the journey. 'See that woman wi' the red hat? I bet she's a Russian spy going to London to report to her bosses, and that man wi' the mouser's a forger, wi' his attache case full o' counterfeit notes.'

Alistair had found a new worry. 'What if the boat sinks wi' the extra weight . . . ?'

'Ach, Ally,' Dougal exploded, 'would you stop imagining things?'

Anchors up and in motion again, they decided it was time to settle for the night. The covered-in sleeping area, roughly triangular, could only be described as steerage class, but no one else was there, so it was with relief that they unfolded the bedding and made up two of the six bunk beds.

Finding it difficult to get comfortable on the lumpy mattresses and pillows, Alistair suddenly sat bolt upright. 'Did you get some place for us to bide in London?'

'We'll easy find a place.' Dougal looked sheepish for not having thought of this.

When a stocky, middle-aged member of the crew looked in some time later to check on how many had taken advantage of this basic accommodation, they were still sitting brooding, shoulders hunched, fair and dark heads bowed, blue eyes and brown staring dejectedly at the rough, grey blankets. A flat cap sitting at a rakish angle on his straggly white hair, the man regarded them speculatively. 'I hope you two aint expecting to find the streets of London paved with gold? All you Scotch laddies seem to think . . .'

'We're not as daft as that,' Dougal objected, offended by the implied slight.

'Just as well, then.' The man hesitated, then asked, 'Have you jobs to go to?'

Dougal's frown deepened to a scowl. 'Aye, we're all fixed up.'

The seaman walked away with disbelief written all over his weather-beaten face.

'Why did you tell him that?' Alistair wanted to know. 'It's a downright lie, and he didna believe you, any road.'

'He can believe what he likes. We'll easy find jobs, I can feel it in my bones.'

Alistair still wasn't convinced, but, giving his chum the benefit of the doubt, he kept quiet. Dougal had said he'd been thinking of going to London for a while, and he must have found out how the land lay as far as getting work was concerned. He would realize they couldn't live on nothing. Of course, the Finnies were well off. Joe, Dougal's father, had his own farm, and even if it wasn't the biggest in the Forvit area, it certainly wasn't the smallest, so he'd likely given Dougal a fiver at least, maybe even a tenner, to keep him going till he was earning for himself, whereas all *he'd* got was a measly two pounds, which wouldn't last long when they'd to pay for board and lodgings . . . if they ever found a place, that was.

But the Finnies' money and the Ritchies' lack of it wasn't the only difference between him and Dougal, he reflected. He was inclined to be a bit of a pessimist, whereas Dougal always found something bright about every situation, and managed to wriggle out of all the trouble he got them into with his mischievous ways.

In the morning, they made a breakfast of bread, cheese and chutney, washed down with the last of the ginger beer. The day passed uneventfully, eating when they felt the need of sustenance with only water to wash things down, taking a stroll now and then to save their legs stiffening up.

Thirty-five and a half hours after they had left Aberdeen, a movement of the other passengers told them they were nearing their destination, and they joined the line waiting to disembark, taking the opportunity to drink in the sights – the dirty buildings, the bustle of sea traffic as the boat made its way through the docks. At long last, however, they stepped shakily onto dry land, still feeling as if they were rising and falling with the tide.

'Which way do we go, then?' Alistair wanted to know, but Dougal's non-committal grimace made him burst out, 'You mean you havena found out anything aboot anything?'

'I thought . . . I thought . . .'

Seeing Dougal so obviously at a loss for words or action of any kind made Alistair more than a little frightened, as if a crutch he depended on had been taken away, but anger soon took over. 'How are we supposed to find a bed for the night, then? Or were you hoping somebody would throw a blanket over us if we lay down here?'

A heavy hand on Dougal's shoulder saved him from trying to justify himself, and he looked up into the kindly grey eyes of the seaman who had spoken to them the night before. 'I can tell by your miserable faces you're worrying about something. You said you had jobs, but it wasn't true, was it? And you've nowhere to live either, right?'

'That's about it,' Dougal muttered.

'If you wait till I get finished, I'll try to figure out something for you. I shouldn't be more than 'arf an hour, and there's plenty to see here in Limehouse.'

Trying to show that he was in no way daunted by their homeless predicament, Dougal pointed along the quay to where a few of their fellow passengers were standing. 'What are they waiting for? Are they taking another boat to somewhere else?'

'They'll be going upriver to the Houses of Parliament. Sightseers. Now, just stand there and don't wander off. I'll be back as soon as I can!'

Their waiting was lightened by the activity around them although Dougal seemed a bit preoccupied, and it didn't feel like half an hour to either of them before the seaman was with them again. He swung his seabag from his shoulder down to the ground, but before he had time to say anything, Dougal put forward the idea which had occurred to him. 'Look, we'll be OK. If you just tell us where to find the YMCA, we'll . . .'

The man's bellowing laugh stopped him. 'It don't allus do to be so independent. My trouble-and-strife's been speaking about taking in lodgers to make some extra cash, and you look like real decent boys, so why don't you come home with me? She was going to put a card in the grocer's window, but you could save her the bother, and I can guarantee she won't fleece you like some landladies.'

Alistair glanced at his pal then said firmly, 'We won't be able to pay her much . . . not till we find work.'

'My Ivy's a trusting soul. Me name's Len Crocker, by the way, and we've a two up, two down in Hackney. Oh, there's a bloke I want a word with. Hang on a minute.'

'That's a bit of luck,' Dougal smiled, when the stocky little man moved away.

'Aye, he seems real nice, but his wife mightna like us.'

'We can look for somewhere else, and the same goes if we dinna like her.'

Alistair pursed his mouth. 'You ken, Dougal, I'm having second thoughts about this.'

'We'll be fine. There's plenty of jobs in London if we look in the right places.'

'Maybe, but how'll we ken where the right places are?'

Dougal sighed and waved his hands airily. 'We'll find them.' He looked pensive for a moment, then added, 'I tell you this, if Ivy's anything like her man, we'll be in clover.'

'If she takes to us.'

'Ach, Ally, stop looking on the black side. If you turn up there wi' a sour face like that, she'll definitely nae take to you.'

Back with them, Len hoisted his seabag on to his shoulder again and boomed, 'Right, me hearties! Best foot forrard. Home James, and don't spare the horses, as they say.'

Each carrying a cardboard suitcase – containing two changes of underwear, shirts, flannels, jerseys, several pairs of hand-knitted socks, plus their Sunday suits and shoes and half a dozen well-laundered handkerchiefs – the boys had difficulty in keeping up with him as he strode out briskly to where they would get a bus to Hackney. Once seated in the double-decker, he kept up a running commentary on everything they passed, and in no time, it seemed, he said that this was where they got off. 'Just a step or two now,' he assured them, but they went through a veritable maze of identical streets before he announced, with some pride, 'This is it! Home sweet home and the fire black out.'

Alistair and Dougal exchanged alarmed glances, but his throaty chuckle let them know he was only joking. He opened the immaculately painted green door and shouted, 'I've brung two young gentlemen to see you, Ivy, love!'

They were ushered into a small sitting room and had only time to notice the brightly burning fire when a buxom woman with very blonde hair, probably in her forties, bustled in. Her slight frown vanished when she saw them. 'Well,' she simpered, 'this is a naice surprise. When you said young gentlemen, Len, I didn't expect them to be this young.' She shot her husband an enquiring look.

'That's not me usual welcome,' he grinned, grabbing her round the waist and planting a kiss on her full mouth before explaining, 'They're from Aberdeen, and they've nowhere to live, so I said you might . . .'

She jumped in quickly, addressing Alistair as she straightened her skirt. 'Ai suppose Ai *could* take you, if you're willing to share?'

At this point, Dougal thought it expedient to acquaint her with all the facts. 'We can't pay much till we're earning.'

'That's quate all right,' she smiled, not taking her eyes off Alistair, 'we can arrange all that later. Ai suppose Len told you Ai'm Ivy, so what's your name, dearie?'

'I'm Alistair Ritchie, and he's Dougal Finnie.' He felt most uncomfortable under her intense stare.

'Alistair?' she beamed, and, obviously finding the effort too much, she stopped trying to sound more refined than she was. 'I like that, so Scotch, but I expect you're hungry after coming all the way from Aberdeen. Five hundred miles anyway, isn't it? Show them up to the spare room, Len, love, and I'll rustle up something for them to eat.' She had turned briefly to her husband but directed her last words once more at Alistair. 'Just come down when you're ready, dearie.'

The upstairs room was large and airy, with a wide double bed, a wardrobe, a tallboy, a basket chair and a wooden-armed chair. Dougal grimaced. 'Nae exactly the best of hotels, is it, but it's clean, so I suppose it'll be OK.'

'There's just one bed,' Alistair pointed out. 'I've never had to share a bed before.'

'Neither have I, but ach, we'll manage. It's that big we'll have to look for each other in the mornings.'

The window, Alistair discovered when he went across to it, looked down on a small, well-tended garden at the rear of the house, a neat little patch of lawn surrounded by several flower beds which had the promise of being colourful in spring and summer. 'One of the Crockers must be keen on gardening,' he observed. 'Ivy, likely, for Len's job must take him away a lot.'

Coming up behind him, Dougal nudged his arm in a knowing way. 'She's taken a right fancy to you . . . dearie.'

'Oh, I hope no',' Alistair groaned. 'She's as old as my mother.'

'She could teach you a thing or two if you let her, you lucky devil.'

'Nae fears! I dinna want her near me, and I'm nae sure if we shoulda come here.'

'Like I said, if we dinna like it, we can look for somewhere else. Hurry up and put your things past, for my belly thinks my throat's cut.'

Agreeing that Dougal should have the top two drawers of the tallboy and Alistair the other two, they didn't take long to stow their few belongings away. Dougal was all set to go downstairs as soon as they put their empty cases on top of the wardrobe, but Alistair insisted that they should at least wash their hands before eating their meal. Luckily, Len had pointed out the doors to the lavatory and the separate bathroom, so they didn't have to ask, and some minutes later, hair slicked down with water, boyish faces shining, fingernails spotless, they went out on to the landing, where their appetites were whetted by the delicious smell wafting up from downstairs.

'Oh boy,' Dougal whispered, 'I'm going to enjoy this, whatever it is.'

They were rather taken aback by the huge amount on their plates as they sat down at the table, and they couldn't help noticing that, although they had a pork chop along with the sausages, eggs, beans, fried bread and chips, their host and hostess had not. Dougal opened his mouth to say something about this, but Alistair gave his shin a surreptitious kick under the table. It was obvious to him that the chops had been cooked for Ivy and Len's supper, and the sausages had probably been intended for their next day's dinner, but it would have been bad manners to draw attention to it.

Ivy took the opportunity now to find out more about them, her peroxided head nodding at Dougal's replies but her lipsticked mouth smiling at Alistair. She showed great surprise when she learned that Forvit village consisted of only about twenty houses, a general store which was also a sub-post office, and that butcher meat was bought from a van that came from Bankside, four and a half miles away, three times a week.

'Well!' she exclaimed. 'You're going to know a big difference here.'

'There's a kirk . . . a church, of course,' Alistair volunteered, 'and a doctor, though the chemist's in Bankside, and all, and the garage.'

'Wot about a police station?' Len put in. 'There must be police in Forvit.'

Dougal grinned now. 'There's no crime, so . . . no police. The nearest bobby's at the far end of Bankside.'

Len pursued the subject. 'Wot if 'e couldn't handle something that happened? A big robbery, say, or an assault, or . . . a murder?'

Stumped, Dougal looked at Alistair then said, uncertainly, 'I suppose he'd have to get help . . . from Huntly, that's ten mile away, and they'd likely send a squad from Aberdeen if it was a murder, but . . . that's twenty mile the other way.'

Ivy gave an exaggerated shiver. 'Stop speaking about murder, you're giving me the collywobbles.'

Laughing, Len pushed back his chair with a satisfied sigh. 'I'll soon sort you out, love. I'm off to me Uncle Ned now, so don't be long. See you in the morning, boys.'

It was only a little after nine o'clock, and Ivy giggled at the surprise on the two young faces when she explained the rhyming slang. 'My Len loves his bed, though he likes it best when I'm in there with him.' She gave a lewd cackle and dug Alistair playfully in the ribs as she stood up to clear the table.

Embarrassed, he said, 'Dougal and me'll do the dishes for you if you want to go up . . .'

She found this highly amusing. 'He can wait for it, the randy blighter.'

'We don't mind helping, honest.'

'Tell you what, then. If Dougal puts a few lumps of coal on the fire, and lays the cork mats in the left-hand drawer of the sideboard and the tablecloth, neatly folded, in the right-hand drawer, you can come and dry for me. How does that sound?'

'Suits me!' Dougal smirked wickedly, ignoring his friend's look of desperate appeal.

Trapped, Alistair helped to load the tray with dirty dishes, and carried it through to the small scullery where Ivy turned on one of the taps in the slightly chipped earthenware sink and left it running until steam billowed up from the enamelled basin nestling inside. Then she rolled up her sleeves, turned on the other tap and let the cold water run in until she could comfortably hold her hand in it.

Watching her, Alistair said, admiringly, 'You're lucky having a tap with hot water. My mother has to boil kettles on the range for everything.'

'She should get in a back-burner. That heats the tank, and in winter, when the fire's on all day, the water's still hot enough to wash next day's breakfast dishes, and once the fire's going proper, the water heats again to near boiling. In summer, of course, I don't light it at all, except on Mondays and Fridays, that's wash-day and bath night for Len and me, and I light the gas boiler for the dishes and washing faces and hands and so on.' She pointed vaguely in its direction, then picked up the bar of yellow soap sitting in a dish between the taps and swished it around in the water to get a lather.

'You're a good-looking boy,' she observed, as she wielded her dish mop. 'Do you have a steady girl back home?'

He shook his head, thankful that he could answer honestly. 'Not now.'

'I bet she didn't know the best ways to please a man, like I do.'

The colour raced up Alistair's neck. 'I wouldn't know about that . . . we never did . . .'

Ivy's smile broadened. 'Don't tell me you're a virgin, Al? I can't believe it.'

He wanted to throw the dish towel at her painted face and run out. She was being far too suggestive for his liking, and she was calling him Al, the hated name Lexie had used.

Patently enjoying his discomfiture, Ivy went on, 'I'd like to get you on your own, some time, to show you what I can do.' She fell silent, quite possibly picturing in her mind exactly what she would show him, and when she finished washing up, she squeezed past him to dry her hands on the roller towel fixed to the wall beside the pantry.

Her next move terrified him. He could feel her breasts pressing into his back, her pelvis rubbing against his backside, but he endured the unwanted, and unsettling, contact until he had dried the last plate and could sidestep away from her. At a safe distance, he turned to look at her and was disconcerted to see her eyes going straight to his crotch.

'Yes, you'll do me,' she murmured seductively, 'and you won't be shy with me for long, I swear.'

'I'm not shy,' he protested, 'but I don't think . . .'

'No, dearie, you're right. We've plenty time ahead of us and we'd better leave it for now and get back to Dougal before he starts imagining things.'

He followed her into the sitting room where Dougal looked up from the well-worn, moquette-covered armchair where he was reading the newspaper. 'All done?' he leered.

Hoping that his pal hadn't heard anything, Alistair sat down on the other easy chair, avoiding the settee where their landlady had placed herself. She embarrassed him no further, however, but kept them laughing over the next hour with stories about her neighbours and the people she met when she went shopping.

At half past ten, she suddenly said, 'Oh my Gawd, look at the time.' She stood up and stretched her arms. 'You must've been wondering if I was ever going to shut up. Len says I forget to stop once I get started, but I'm sorry for keeping you up so late, I expect you're tired out. By the way, Al, dearie, make sure all the lights are off down here when you come up. Nightie night, both.'

'Good night,' they chorused, and when the door closed behind her, Dougal looked slyly at Alistair then burst out laughing. 'I told you she fancied you.'

'Stop being so daft!'

'The walls here are paper thin, so I heard what she was saying ben there. You're in for some good times with Ivy Dearie, Ally boy.'

'Not me!' Alistair snapped. 'If you want her, you can have her with pleasure.'

'It likely would be a pleasure, and all, for I'd say she's all set for a fling, but it's not me she wants, worse luck. Now, would you say she was out of the lavvy yet?'

The two boys spent most of the following day looking for work, and returned to Victoria Park at ten past five exhausted, ravenous, and very despondent. Luckily, Ivy had a huge hotpot waiting for them, and while they ate, Len regaled them with humorous anecdotes about his time in the Royal Navy during the war. Afterwards, Dougal volunteered to help with the dishes this time, but it was Len who replied, 'Thanks, it's my turn tonight, mate, and I could do with an 'and.'

Alistair's heart sank at the prospect of being left alone with Ivy, but she said nothing outrageous, probably because Len was within earshot. Nevertheless, he still felt really uncomfortable with her.

The dishwashers completed their task in record time, and the next two hours passed with the youths answering more questions about their homes and families. Both said they had a sister, but whereas Flora Finnie, six years older than Dougal, had gone to America the year before, Alice Ritchie, three years younger than Alistair, was still at school. The evening ended with them discussing the kind of jobs they had hoped to find, but after that day's fruitless search, were far less confident of ever finding now.

Ivy commiserated profusely with them over this, but Len said, as he got to his feet, 'Ne'er mind, boys, I put word about you round the pub at lunch time, so something's bound to turn up. Me mates are a good bunch.'

In bed, ten minutes later, Dougal observed, 'We're going to be all right here, Ally. Ivy's a great cook, and that's the main thing, isn't it?'

Convinced that he had nothing more to fear from her, that she had just been testing him before, Alistair agreed. 'I just wish we could be bringing in a wage, though. She mightn't feed us so well if we can't pay our way.'

As luck would have it, he was in the lavatory the following evening when one of Len's 'mates' came to say there was a job going in the factory where he worked as an electrician. 'They're looking for a youngster to train as a clerk in the Counting House,' he told Dougal, 'and when I said I knew of a couple of sixteen-year-old Scots boys looking for work, they said to tell one of you to call first thing tomorrow.'

'That's great!' Dougal exclaimed. 'I've never worked in an office, but I always got top marks for handwriting at school.'

'There you are then,' beamed Ivy, 'it's just the job for you.'

When he came back, Alistair was honestly pleased for his friend, but found himself wishing that his bowels hadn't needed emptying at the crucial time.

Sensing his disappointment, Ivy gave his head a motherly pat. 'Don't you fret, Al, dearie, your turn'll come.'

Having to report for work the next morning, Len was up well before dawn, and Dougal also left early to find the factory and make sure he wasn't late for his interview, leaving Alistair hurrying to get out in order not to be left on his own with Ivy. She, however, had other ideas. 'There's no rush, dearie,' she purred, her hand fixing on his sleeve as he tried to take his jacket down from the peg on the hallstand in the narrow hallway. 'It's time we got better acquainted, ain't it?'

'I have to go out,' he protested. 'If I don't find work, I'll not be able to pay anything for my board.' This wasn't strictly true, but she wasn't to know that.

Her plucked eyebrows lifted. 'Haven't you never heard of payment in kind?'

'No,' he answered, puzzled. 'What's that?'

'You see me all right and I'll see you all right, savvy?' She came closer and put her hands up his pullover. 'I'm going to be ever so lonely till Len comes home again.'

Comprehending now what she was up to, he said, hastily, 'No . . . Mrs Crocker . . .'

'You'll like it, Al, I promise you.' Her hands ran over his chest, but didn't stop there, and as they continued down, he burst out, 'No, no! I can't let you . . .'

'Yes, you can, you're a big boy now.' She made a grab at him and laughed with delight. 'Yes, Al, a big boy and getting bigger by the minute.'

He'd been praying that someone would come to the door, or that there would be some kind of interruption that would let him make his escape, but he could stand no more of her caressing. 'That's it!' he shouted, shoving her away and almost knocking her off her feet. 'I'm going to look for other digs, I can't stay here! You're man mad!'

Clearly gathering that she had gone too far, Ivy stepped back. 'OK, OK, dearie, I know when I'm beat. I thought you were the answer to this maiden's prayer . . . but it seems I made a mistake. I'm ever so sorry for trying it on with you.'

She pulled such a repentant face that he had to laugh. The only way he could see of dealing with a woman like this was to make fun of her. 'A maiden?' he gurgled. 'You? It must be twenty years since you were a maiden.'

He held his breath, but she wasn't at all put out. 'Cheeky beggar,' she grinned, 'but you're right. I'd the first bite at my cherry when I was twelve . . . that's twenty years ago almost to the day.' His patent disbelief made her give a loud screech of laughter. 'No fooling you, is there, Al? All right, I'll come clean – twenty-four years ago, for I was thirty-six last month . . . and that's the Gawd's honest truth.'

He felt a sudden rush of pity for her. At first sight, he had thought she was about forty, but looking at her in the cold light of this October morning he could see the crow's feet round her eyes, the slackness of her mouth without its thick coating of lipstick, the dark roots of her bleached hair. She was fifty if she was a day, and she was likely trying to prove, to herself as much as to other people, that she wasn't past it. 'You're still an attractive woman, Mrs Crocker,' he smiled, wanting to soothe her, 'but I don't want to get involved with anybody. I want to concentrate on making a career for myself and then . . . well, I don't want to come between any man and his wife, so I'll look for a girl a bit nearer my own age. No offence intended,' he put in, quickly.

'None taken,' she assured him, although there was a touch of wistfulness in her faded blue eyes. 'I shouldn't have done what I did. I was playing a silly game and you were right to let me know how things stand. I can forget if you can, so what say we start all over? Before we leave it, though, I must tell you I admire you for the way you handled it, Al. Like a ruddy diplomat you were, and you'll make a damned good husband to some lucky gal one of these days.'

The tension having gone, he felt easy enough with her to say, 'Thank you for those kind words, Mrs Crocker.'

'Make it Ivy, for Gawd's sake, dearie, else you'll make me feel my age. Now, shall I make you another cuppa before you go job-hunting?'

'No thanks . . . Ivy, I'd best be moving.'

By three o'clock that afternoon, Alistair was wishing that he had accepted Ivy's offer of tea. His feet were throbbing from trudging through dozens of streets, each with a small scattering of shops to fulfil the needs of its denizens. In his anxiety for employment, he had even asked three butchers if they had a vacancy, though he'd have been better staying with Charlie Low in Bankside if he was going to stick to butchery, so it was just as well that there was nothing doing in any of them. He was so depressed that he was actually quite glad when it started to rain, and thankful that it was heavy enough to provide him with a good excuse for calling it a day.

Ivy tutted at his dripping clothes when he went in. 'I'm sorry I'm making such a mess of your clean floor,' he muttered, but she waved away his apology.

'It's not the floor I'm worried about,' she assured him, as she pulled off his jacket. 'You'll catch your death if you're not careful. Go up and change into something dry and I'll give you the good news when you come back.'

He couldn't for the life of him think what good news she could possibly give him, and pondered over it while he towelled his legs dry and draped his flannels over the hot tank in the cupboard at the top of the stairs. Presentable again, he ran down to hear what she had to say.

Ivy had the fire burning 'half up the lum', as his father would have said, and he stood with his back to the heat, his brows raised in question. 'You'll never believe this, Al,' she began, her voice trembling with excitement, her mascara'd eyes gleaming with satisfaction.

'Go on, then,' he said, impatiently, 'tell me.'

'I went shopping as soon as you left – I put my face on first, of course – and I got speaking to old Ma Beaton five doors down on the opposite side, and the nosy so-and-so asked me who the handsome young men were she'd seen going in and out of my house. Not a thing happens in this street without her knowing, 'cos she sits behind her net curtains all day and watches everything that goes on.'

Feeling rather let-down, Alistair muttered, 'Is that it?'

'No, it's a long story and I have to tell you everything so you'll understand.'

'I'm sorry, carry on. You were speaking to old Ma something . . . ?'

'Ma Beaton, and I told her you and your pal had come

from Scotland to look for jobs. I said Dougal was fixed up – he came back at twelve to say he starts on Monday and then went out again – but I said you were still looking and she said to try Ikey Mo. He'd been telling her he was thinking of taking a young boy on to help him. So I went and told him about you, and you've to see him tomorrow about ten.'

'B . . . but . . .' stammered Alistair, 'who's Ikey Mo, and what kind of shop is it?'

Ivy spluttered with laughter. 'That's not his real name. I can't remember what it is, but Ma Beaton calls him Ikey Mo because he's a Jew.'

'What kind of shop is it?'

'A pawnshop. I started going there when Len came out of the Navy, for he was out of work for months and I used up all our savings, but when he got a start on the North boat, I didn't need to pawn no more stuff. I used to go to Uncle – that's what most people call him – every week, and he's a nice old bloke.' Noticing Alistair's deepening perplexity, she said, 'Don't you know what a pawnshop is?'

After hearing what was entailed in the pawnbroking business, Alistair said, 'I'm sorry, Ivy, but I don't think I'm fitted for that.'

Her face darkened. 'Ain't a pawnbroker good enough for you?' she snapped. 'Is that all the thanks I get for going out of my way to ask about it for you? You think it's beneath you?'

He was quite shocked by her outburst; he had spoken without thinking and hadn't meant to offend her. 'Oh, please don't think that! I'm really grateful to you . . . and the old lady, but it's just . . . I'm worried because I don't know anything about . . . what was it you called it? Pledging things. I wouldn't know how much to give for them.'

'You'll soon learn,' Ivy smiled, her spirits restored. 'The customers'll tell you if you don't offer enough, and Uncle'll walk into you if you give too much.'

'That's what I'm worried about.'

E. D. Isaacson, as the sign under the three brass balls proclaimed the pawnbroker's name to be, was like no man Alistair had ever seen before, and because he was busy attending to a tall, belligerent woman, the boy had a chance to study him fully. He was shaped rather like a tadpole, his head big in proportion to his short body and legs. His grizzled, curly hair was quite thick, yet his crown was covered by a small skull-cap, and his long nose protruded above a bushy moustache and rounded beard, reminding Alistair of a cow looking over a dyke. Whatever his failings in appearance, however, his attitude to his customer held all the patience of a saint.

Alistair was so fascinated by the unfamiliarity of the man's physical make-up that he was unaware of the woman going out, and was startled when the old man spoke to him. 'Sorry to keep you waiting, my boy. What do you think of my little emporium, hmm?'

Having paid no attention to his surroundings, Alistair took a guilty glance round, but feeling it would be unwise to keep his prospective boss waiting for an answer, he hardly took anything in. 'It's very nice.'

'You think you could work here?' The old man's eyes held an appealing twinkle now, despite the lines of fatigue above and below them.

'I believe I could, but you'll have to learn me . . .'

'Not to worry, my boy. I shall teach you everything, but what do I call you, hmm?'

'Oh, sorry, my name's Alistair Ritchie, Mr Isaacson.'

A deep menacing rumble came from the region of the man's stomach. 'And who is this Mister Isaacson, may I ask?'

Alistair couldn't think what he had done to anger the man.

'It said ... E.D. Isaacson on the sign,' he ventured, 'and I thought that was you.' He heaved a sigh of relief when the rumbling erupted into a series of full-blooded belly laughs.

'Nobody ever calls me Mr Isaacson,' the pawnbroker said, breathless after such unaccustomed mirth and taking a handkerchief from his waistcoat pocket to wipe his eyes. 'It's sometimes Ikey Mo because I'm a Jew, although they mean no disrespect. Some call me Edie, because of my initials, but I'm Uncle to most people.' After a brief pause, he added, 'My first name is Emanuel, if you would feel happier with that.'

Alistair gave it a few moments' careful thought. 'Ikey and Edie sound disrespectful to me, but Uncle doesn't feel right, either. I'd better make it Emanuel ...'

'Shall I tell you what would give me even greater pleasure? My dear mother used to call me Manny, and no one has addressed me so since she passed away ... over thirty years ago. Do you think you could manage that? And I shall call you Alistair, a fine Scottish name for a fine Scottish boy.'

'When do you want me to start ... um ... Manny?' He found it much easier to say than he had thought.

'The sooner the quicker, hmm? What do you say to ... at this very moment, Alistair, or do you have to let your landlady know where you are?'

'Ivy knows where I am, and I'd love to start straight away.'

And thus began an unusual friendship, which deepened as the years went by and blossomed into as close a bond as any two men of different religions and generations could possibly share.

Chapter 3

❧

Alistair's uncertainties about his aptitude for the job were quickly banished by Manny's patient teaching. During slack spells, he learned how to repair clocks, large and small, and watches from the cheap to the expensive, not that many of those found their way into E.D. Isaacson's shop. Most customers wanted to pledge something, and after they went out, the pawnbroker explained why he had given what he did for the article brought in.

'Mrs Fry's husband has been unable to work since he injured his back last year,' he said, one morning. 'Sadly, she had just given birth to their fourth child at the time. They are all under school age, and she finds it extremely hard to manage on the paltry sum his employers dole out to him, less than twenty per cent of what he was earning before the accident. I suppose they are lucky, really, because his firm is one of the few who give anything at all in such cases.'

Another woman, middle-aged this time, had been widowed some months previously. 'Mrs Borland is slowly selling off all her possessions,' Manny observed mournfully, 'and goodness knows what she will do when everything is gone. She will most likely have to apply to the parish, and losing their independence is something all these women dread. It also means the loss of their self-respect.'

'So she'll never manage to redeem her things?' Alistair asked, wonderingly.

'I am afraid not, my boy. She knows that and I know that,

and I also know that they are worthless. Nothing will sell, but what can I do? I cannot let her starve, can I?'

Alistair's opinion of the elderly man rose with every day that passed, and he set out to absorb as much as he could of what he was being taught about human nature. He could not blame, any more than Manny could, the poor wives whose men drank most of their wages, or gambled them away, or refused to work at all, and admired them for struggling to keep their families fed and clad and, most importantly, together. On one occasion, however, he felt he had to comment on what seemed to him a betrayal of trust. 'The gent's watch that woman redeemed was real gold, wasn't it? How could a family as poor as that afford anything so expensive? And she didn't say anything when you let her get it back for less than you gave her for it in the first place. She's cheating you, Manny.'

'No, Alistair, never think that. All the women who come to me are as honest as the day is long. In this case, Mrs Parker's husband came from a well-to-do family, and was given the watch for his twenty-first birthday. His father, however, did not approve of the girl he wished to marry, and headstrong and deeply in love, young Parker left home in order to make her his wife. They now have three sons, and although he does not regret what he did, according to his wife, he still cherishes the watch, the one and only item of any value he possesses, and makes a point of wearing it to church every Sunday. You see, she has never told him that it languishes in my safe from Monday to Saturday each week. It is her way of proving that she can manage on what he gives her.'

'But she's living a lie,' Alistair burst out. 'She's not managing, or if she is, it's because you're helping her. She's cheating you as well as her husband.'

Manny shook his head. 'Oh, Alistair, how little you know of these people. They do the best they can with what little they have. I suppose you think Mrs Parker should *sell* the watch to me? If she did, her family could certainly live comfortably for a year or so, perhaps, but at what cost? The loss of her husband's respect, his love? Because she would never, ever, be able to buy it back for him. Can you understand that?'

The youth looked sheepish. 'Yes, I see what you mean. It must be terrible to have to live like that.'

Dougal Finnie was also having new experiences. At first, he felt as if he were caged, having to spend his entire days indoors at everyone's beck and call, but there were compensations. Apart from the cash office where he worked – they called it the Counting House – there was a despatch office and a general office, the staff of both including several girls . . . not ordinary girls, though. He had never seen such beauties, far outshining any of the girls he had known back in Forvit.

As he told Alistair one night in bed – where they exchanged stories of the events of their days – 'I'm going to be spoilt for choice, Ally, short ones, tall ones, slim, well-rounded, blonde, dark, redheads, they're all there! Would you like to make up a foursome one night? I could tell my one to bring a friend with her for you.'

Trying to imagine the kind of girls who would appeal to Dougal, Alistair said, 'No thanks, I'll find a girl of my own when I'm ready for it.'

'Och you, you're getting to be a right old stick-in-the-mud. Or are you waiting for Ivy Dearie to make another move?'

'Shut up!' Alistair grinned to show he didn't mind being teased now. Originally, he had felt cheated that nature had robbed him of the office job, but things had worked out quite well, for he was more than happy working with Emanuel D. Isaacson.

* * *

Alistair was exhausted when he finished on Christmas Eve, with dozens of mothers, and a few fathers, rushing in because they needed money, so he was glad when Manny said he was closing the following day. The Crockers' house was decorated in a manner neither of their boarders had seen before, with tinsel everywhere, holly, mistletoe (which allowed Ivy to kiss all of Len's mates who came in during the evening), and long strings of cards and paper chains stretching from wall to wall. Several cards came from Forvit to the two youths, who were deeply touched that so many people had remembered them and even felt a trifle homesick, although they pretended it was all a bore. There was no card from Lexie Fraser, however, and Alistair was relieved that Dougal didn't seem to notice his disappointment.

Ivy had provided a sumptuous meal, a whole turkey with all the trimmings, plum duff and brandy butter, mince pies, much more than they could eat, and when she was placing the covered half-empty dishes on the coolest shelf of her larder, she laughed, 'You'll be getting this left-overs for the rest of the week.' They did, and still enjoyed every bite.

No celebrations were held on Hogmanay or New Year's Day, much to the boys' surprise, especially Dougal, who had been accustomed to seeing the men of Forvit village well under the weather by midnight and continuing to bend their elbows until they dropped off to sleep where they were sitting, or ended up at the side of the road after going outside to be sick. Dougal had never understood what enjoyment they could have got from that. Alistair's father, though not exactly teetotal, only took a glass of malt whisky to see in the New Year, or on rare occasions, for medicinal purposes.

Over the following weeks, Dougal regaled his friend with tales about the girls he had chatted to in the cloakroom

– one toilet for both male and female staff – or taken for a short walk in the lunch break, or whose bottoms he had pinched in passing, all of which Alistair recounted to Manny the following day when business was over. At first, he had wondered if the pawnbroker might not be interested in such goings-on, but when the old man began to ask what Dougal had been up to the previous day, he knew that his employer was enjoying hearing about the youthful exploits and tried to inject as much humour into the telling of them as he could. One occurrence, however, was certainly not as amusing to Dougal as it was to Alistair and Manny.

They had been living in the Crockers' house for about four months and were in the middle of supper when Dougal said, with studied nonchalance, 'I'll have to get my skates on tonight. I'm meeting a girl at seven.'

A *frisson* of envy made Alistair's appetite vanish, and with it, seemingly, his power of speech, so it was Ivy who asked, 'What's her name?'

'Amy something. She works in the general office and she lives just two streets away from here, so I won't have to walk miles from seeing her home. How's that for good management?' He looked extremely pleased with himself.

'Very convenient,' she laughed.

When Dougal left the table to go and make ready for his tryst, Alistair followed him upstairs and stood in the open doorway of the bathroom while the other boy filled the basin with hot water then ran his hand over his chin. 'Um . . . do you think I should shave again? I did shave this morning, but look at me. That's the worst of having dark hair. You're lucky, being so fair. You don't really need to shave at all.'

Piqued because this was true, Alistair said nothing, and Dougal went on, 'I've been fancying Amy for days, and I met her in the corridor this morning and not a soul in sight, so I dived straight in and asked her out. I didn't think she'd come, because . . . oh, you should see her, Ally. She's a corker! Lovely blonde hair, natural, not peroxided like Ivy's, and a figure . . .' Unable to find words to adequately describe it, he sketched an exaggerated hour-glass shape with his hands. 'I'd better shave, I don't want to rough-up her soft skin.'

'When you meet her, couldn't you say something's cropped up and you'll have to make it another night?' Alistair asked plaintively. 'When Len's at home.'

'You don't need to be scared at being left on your own with Ivy.'

'I'm not scared, I just don't feel comfortable with her.'

Negotiating his safety razor round his nostrils, Dougal snorted loudly and waited until his downy whiskers were gone before lifting the towel from the rim of the bath and patting gently at his tender face. 'Shaving twice a day's a bugger!'

'You didn't need to shave again,' Alistair pointed out, sarcastically. 'I know I've only got to shave every third day, but that doesn't make me any less of a man than you.'

'No?' sneered Dougal as he made his way to their bedroom with his chum following at his heels. 'I bet I'll have more girlfriends than you, and be married first, *and* have a child first, and all. Not that I intend settling down for years. I'm going to hunt around till I find the right one.'

'We'll see,' Alistair said, darkly. 'If you go on the way you're doing, you'll end up having to marry some poor lassie before she drops your bairn. That's if her father hasn't got at you long before that.'

Still grinning, Dougal shook his head. 'Not me! I'm smarter than get caught like that. Look Ally, can you fasten this front stud for me? My fingers are all thumbs.'

When Dougal was finally satisfied with his appearance, Alistair picked up the Zane Gray he'd been reading and accompanied him downstairs, saying as Dougal went out, 'Think on me stuck here wi' Ivy when you're enjoying yourself wi' your Amy.'

He jumped guiltily when Ivy came through from the scullery, but she hadn't heard, and was regarding him apologetically. 'I'm sorry, Al, but I've to go out as well. When you were upstairs, Daisy Smith from down the street came in and asked if I'd sit with her mother to let her visit her older sister. Greta's on her own, and she fell and broke her hip, poor soul, and Daisy's going over to give her house a bit of a tidy. I'll be away for at least a couple of hours, maybe longer, but you'll be all right, won't you?'

'It'll give me a chance to finish this book. It's due back to Boots's library tomorrow.'

Alistair settled back in the most comfortable easy chair when she was gone, and was soon engrossed in *Riders of the Purple Sage*, a saga of the Wild West – so engrossed, in fact, that he did not hear the front door opening less than an hour later, and was startled when someone came into the room. 'Oh, thank God it's you, Dougal!' he gasped. 'I nearly had a heart attack. But why are you home so early? Did things not go right with you and Amy?'

'No they bloody didna! Her face was made up to the nines and she'd high heels and a tight jumper, and I thought she was sixteen, but she's just fourteen, would you believe?'

With others, they had to speak in English to be understood – although their broad vowels and guttural voices made it difficult – but when they were alone, they reverted to their native dialect, as Alistair did now. 'You didna . . . ? Nae wi' an underage quine?'

'She didna say how auld she was till I . . . I wouldna've touched her. I thought she'd give in once I got her going, you ken, but the silly bitch hadna a clue . . . about a bloody thing! God Almighty! She thought kissing would gi'e her a bairn, and I'd a helluva job convincing her it wouldna, and then, when I'd been holding myself back and kissing her as tenderly as I could, I thought I'd chance going a wee bit further. She wasna ower keen on me touching her chest, but when I tried to lift her skirt, she went bloody berserk!'

Alistair had to let his laughter out now, and it burst forth like a blast from a volcano. 'It serves you right! You went out with the intention of seducing her.'

'No, I didna! Like I said, I thought I'd work on her till she wanted it and gave in without a murmur, but . . . she went mad, raving mad!'

'She'd been terrified. She was only fourteen, you said?'

'She didna tell me afore that! She was screaming blue murder,' – here he put on a high falsetto voice – '"Don't you dare touch me! I'm only fourteen and I'll tell my father you interfered with me."' His tone deepened again. 'Then she kneed me and ran off like the wind, and I was left in absolute agony.'

Alistair was laughing fit to burst. 'I wish I'd seen it! The great ladies' man weaving his spell and getting his nuts cracked.'

'It's nae funny, Ally, it was damned painful, I can tell you, still is.'

But his friend couldn't stop teasing. 'Tell Ivy when she comes back, and she'll kiss them better.' He doubled up at the idea of this, and tears ran down his cheeks.

He had unwittingly hit the right note. Dougal's outraged expression disappeared as he joined in Alistair's laughter. 'By God, that would be a sight for sore eyes, right enough!'

When they simmered down, he said, ruefully, 'I tell you one thing, Ally, after this, I'll ask how auld a lassie is afore I ask her oot.'

When Manny was told the next morning, he thought it was the funniest thing he had ever heard. 'What a card that friend of yours must be,' he gasped, holding his aching sides. 'I wish I could have been there.'

'That's what I said, and all,' giggled Alistair, 'but it hasn't taught him a lesson. If it had been me, now, I'd never want to go out with another girl, but he's different.'

Manny nodded. 'Yes, you are as different as chalk and cheese from what you say. He is such an extrovert with the opposite sex and you seem to be timid with all females. But I can tell that you have hidden depths, my boy. There is passion lurking inside you, and when you eventually meet the right girl, love will strike you with the impact of a sledgehammer. You were born to be a one-girl man, and you will derive more happiness from that one girl, Alistair, than Dougal will from a dozen of his kind.'

Thinking about this later, Alistair decided that if everybody saw him as Manny did, they would think he didn't have much go in him. One girl? What red-blooded male stuck to one girl? If Dougal asked him again to make up a foursome, he'd damn well jump at it. How would he ever recognize the right girl if he never met any?

After this fiasco, Dougal was noncommittal about the girls he went out with . . . for at least three weeks. With his natural effervescence, he couldn't keep it up for long, so things returned to what they had been before Amy, and both Alistair and Manny, at second hand, were constantly diverted by his descriptions of what had happened on his dates.

'Fay's nice enough,' he said one night, 'if she'd just keep her trap shut. She's got a voice that would clip clouts. Like a blinking foghorn . . . and she never stops.'

'I didna ken foghorns could clip clouts,' Alistair said, trying not to laugh.

Dougal tutted his exasperation. 'Ach, you ken fine what I mean.'

After another night out, he flopped down on the bed beside Alistair. 'God, Ally,' he sighed, 'it was like pulling teeth getting anything out of Ella. The only thing she was interested in was kissing.'

'That should've pleased you,' Alistair grunted. 'That's what you want, isn't it?'

'I'd like a breather sometimes.'

Dougal's first opinion of Gladys was 'Nae bad', something of a compliment coming from him, but after their second encounter he had changed his mind. 'Why do girls aye have to go and spoil things?' he asked bitterly when he came home. 'As soon as I get my hands above their knees, they carry on like I was sex mad.'

'So you are,' laughed Alistair. 'It's all you ever think about.'

'Oh, be fair! I dinna jump on them the minute I meet them. I build up to it.'

'Well, all I can say is – you're nae a very good builder.'

'D'you think so?'

Alistair gave a serious nod, then smiled expansively. 'I'm nae expert, but to my mind you should take things as they come. Warm them up, or whatever you want to call it, and when they're ready, they'll tell you.'

'Oh, aye!' Dougal was heavily sarcastic. 'They'll say, "Please Dougal, I'm ready for it now." For God's sake, Ally, ha'e some common sense.'

'I said I wasna an expert.'

This was the pattern for several weeks until, once again, Dougal seemed to draw a veil over his activities. 'I think he's had another setback,' Alistair told Manny one morning.

'He hasn't said a word about his nights out for . . . oh, it must be a month now. Something must have upset him. Something really bad.'

'He will not keep it from you for long, Alistair. I know you are worried about him, but he is a survivor. He will get over it, whatever it is.'

Studying Dougal closely each time he came home from presumably seeing a girl, Alistair thought that he didn't look at all downcast and came to the conclusion that he had got over it, as Manny had predicted. It was strange, though, that he didn't want to discuss it. Letting another two weeks pass to see if Dougal would confide in him, give him a name and all the lurid details, Alistair finally summoned up the courage to ask.

'You're awful quiet about things these days,' he observed, as Dougal was putting on his sports jacket. 'Did you come up against another Amy, or somebody like that?'

Dougal turned and looked him straight in the eyes. 'I've turned over a new leaf.'

Watching him fold his handkerchief and place it meticulously so that only a corner was peeping out of his breast pocket, it occurred to Alistair that his chum might be speaking the truth. 'I wondered why you were keeping quiet about your conquests, but that's the third night you've gone out this week, and you've made such a fuss about shaving, and brushing your hair with brilliantine, and taking ages to make up your mind what tie to wear. Have you met somebody special?'

Dougal made sure that his Woolworth's tiepin was straight before murmuring, rather bashfully, 'Aye, this one's special.'

'Come on, then, spit it out. What's her name?'

'Marjory Jenkins, but she likes to be called Marge. She'll be seventeen in September, and we've been seeing each other for a couple of months now.'

'So she's only sixteen? I thought you'd learned a lesson about dating them so young.'

'She'll soon be seventeen and I'm nae eighteen till October, so that's just about eleven month between us. That's nae such a difference, is it? Anyway, I couldna help myself, Ally. She's perfect! She's got darker hair than mine, nearly black, and curlier, her eyes are a deeper brown, and her mouth . . . it's a Cupid's bow, perfect for kissing.' Now that he'd started, Dougal couldn't stop detailing the girl's charms. 'She's a perfect figure, and all, though I haven't laid a finger on her.' He turned to look seriously at his chum. 'Honest, Ally, I havena touched her. Oh, I've kissed her, hundreds of times, but . . . well, I think I love her. No, I *do* love her, and I'm not going to do anything to upset her.'

Alistair was on the point of saying he'd got it bad when he realized that Dougal *had* got it bad, and it wasn't fair to tease him. Instead, he said, meaning every word, 'I hope it turns out OK for you this time.'

'Thanks, Ally, but I'll have to hurry. Mustn't keep her waiting.'

'Dougal's fallen for this one,' Alistair told Ivy when they were on their own. He had survived dozens of evenings with her by this time, and although she sometimes came out with suggestive remarks, she hadn't actually done anything he could object to and he could usually laugh off what she said. 'Her name's Marge Jenkins, and she's a bit young, to my idea. She's not seventeen till September.'

'So there's not even a year between them? My Len's four years older than me, and I was seventeen when he first asked me out.'

'According to what Dougal said, Marge isn't like you. I don't mean any disrespect, Ivy, but he says he hasn't tried anything with her, so I think she's a bit prim and proper.'

'Prim and proper?' Ivy threw back her head with a loud

burst of laughter. 'You're dead right there, Al! Nobody could ever have accused me of being prim or proper, and I wouldn't have thought a girl like that would appeal to Dougal, though they do say opposites attract, don't they?'

When Dougal came in, much later, Alistair said, 'Everything OK?' Not that he needed to ask. His friend's blissful expression said it all.

'Everything's perfect.'

Alistair let this pass, although 'perfect' was the only word Dougal seemed to be able to come up with as far as Marge was concerned. 'Does she work with you?'

'Oh, no, she works in her father's hotel in Guilford Street, off Russell Square.'

This meant nothing to Alistair, who knew very little of the rest of London. 'How did you meet her, then?'

'I'd to deliver an account to her father, by hand because it was overdue for payment. It was Marge who opened the door, and I was bowled over. Just like that. Any road, she took the account to her father and came back to say he was busy and could I wait? She was standing so near me I could've reached out and pulled her against me, but I didn't dare. Do you get that, Ally? I couldn't. Anyway, there we were, looking at each other, and I thought, you've got the chance, ask her out before her father comes and throws a spanner in the works. So I blurted out, in my best English, "Would you care to come out with me some evening?" And that was it.'

'She agreed?'

'Well, her young sister came in with a signed cheque – Mr Jenkins does all the cooking and he was in the middle of doing something he couldn't leave – and Marge told Peggy to go away, and then she said, "Tomorrow at seven? At the end of the street?" I've never felt like this about any other girl, Ally. Marge is definitely the one for me.'

'I can't understand why you didn't tell me before.'

'I thought you'd torment the life out o' me, love at first sight and that sort of thing.'

'I'd like to meet her sometime, to see what she's like.'

'To give your approval? That's OK. I'll ask her tomorrow to bring her sister with her on Saturday . . . she's got two. The youngest's still at school, that's Peggy, Marge is the middle one, and I think she said the oldest, Gwen, was eighteen.'

'Maybe you'll fall for her instead,' Alistair teased.

'Never! But maybe you will.'

'Not me. I've other things to think about; I've no time for girls.'

This was perfectly true, for only that morning, Manny had given him something of a surprise. 'I have had this dream for years,' he had said while they were eating the sandwiches Ivy provided for her lodger and his boss. 'I want to put aside the pawnbroker business some day, and open a watchmaker's shop which will also offer new and antique jewellery for sale. Of course, my dream will have to wait until I can afford to get better premises, but it might be a good thing if I did a little scouting around to find some little items to start me off. Even if it could be years before I am in a position to open such a shop, I could be building up a stock for it. You are more or less confident about dealing with customers on your own, so I could start going round the markets. I am told that one can often pick up a good bargain from the stalls. What do you think, hmm?'

'You'd trust me?' Alistair gasped. 'You'd leave me here on my own?'

'Of course I trust you. Your face has been an open book to me since you first walked through that door . . . honesty, willingness to please, a wish to justify your wages by working as well as you can. In any case, I have nothing worth stealing at the moment – except the gold wrist watch Mrs Parker still brings in every Monday. But please do not think that

I am taking advantage of you. I will increase your wages by five shillings because you will be in sole charge. I wish I could make it more, Alistair, but . . . perhaps some day soon, hmm?'

On Saturday evening, on the way to Guilford Street on the underground, Alistair's stomach was churning with anxiety at the thought of meeting Gwen Jenkins. If she was anything like Lexie Fraser had been, he'd be terrified of her, and if she was as prim and proper as her sister seemed to be, he wouldn't know what to say to her, and Dougal would be too taken up with Marge to pay any attention to him.

His heart sank when he saw them – one a short but beautiful brunette who must be Marge, and the other a tall, elegant, model-like redhead who looked as if she would wipe the floor with him if he stepped out of line. God, this was going to be an evening he'd never forget . . . but not for any of the right reasons.

Before Dougal could make the introductions, Marge said, 'Gwen was sorry she couldn't come. She fell downstairs this morning and sprained her ankle. This is Petra, an old school friend I ran into yesterday, and she agreed to step in.'

The redhead inclined her head stiffly to Dougal, but when Marge said, 'Petra, this is Alistair, your date,' she turned her heavily mascara'd eyes to him, then silently slid her arm through his. They walked to Hyde Park, and because there wasn't room to go four abreast on the pavements, they split up into couples, much to Alistair's embarrassment, although he consoled himself by thinking it would be different in the Park. It wasn't. Dougal and Marge were oblivious of anyone else, strolling hand-in-hand and looking into each other's eyes so often it amazed Alistair that they didn't bump into something . . . or somebody. With Petra – it had to be a fancy name – glued to his arm, he plodded on with a heavy heart.

They took the bus back, and about two stops before they were due to get off, Petra jumped up. 'This is my stop!' She made a dive for the stairs and had jumped off the moving vehicle before Alistair took in what was happening. He turned round to Dougal in dismay. 'She should have said . . . I didn't know . . . I thought we'd all get off together.'

Marge smiled. 'Petra was always a queer fish. That's why I never kept in touch.'

'She didn't enjoy herself, that's one thing sure.'

'Don't worry about it. Gwen'll be able to come next time.'

'I don't think we should arrange a next time,' he said, looking apologetic. 'I'm not a great one for making conversation or anything like that. I'm not like Dougal.'

'I felt awful,' he told Manny the following day, 'but Petra scared the pants off me.'

The pawnbroker gave what was almost a snigger. 'A rather inappropriate turn of phrase, don't you think?'

Alistair's spells on his own extended from mornings only in the first few weeks to whole days, at the end of which Manny would return happily exhausted to show his 'manager' his latest acquisitions. Before putting them in his safe, he would spread them out on his counter and discuss each item with Alistair, asking his evaluation first and then pointing out good points or flaws in the precious stones, and soon the newly-eighteen-year-old was surprising himself as much as Manny by the accuracy of his assessments. He was also showing quite a talent for repairing even the oldest of the timepieces.

A truly sheepish Dougal broke into his self-congratulatory ramblings one night some four months later. 'I've asked Marge to marry me.'

Alistair was stunned. During the evening of the foursome with the stuck-up Petra, he had gathered that Marge wasn't the prim and proper type he had imagined, but a lively girl full of fun, and every bit as lovely as Dougal had said. 'I didn't know you were as serious as that about her,' he murmured. 'Did she say yes?'

'She did that.'

'But you can't afford to keep a wife?'

'I've been saving as much as I could since I started going with her, it's near a year now, and I think I've enough to rent a cheap flat somewhere and furnish it.'

'How the mighty are fallen,' Alistair muttered, then shook his head. 'No, don't mind me. Marge is a real nice lass and I wish you both well. Congratulations.'

After his next meeting with Marge, Dougal was not quite so elated. 'She told her family she'd accepted my proposal and her father hit the roof. He said she was far too young to think about marriage, but he might agree to it when she's eighteen – that's near a year yet – as long as I ask him for his permission properly. I'll have to ask him for her hand like he was a Victorian father. Did you ever hear the like?'

'He's making sure his daughter doesn't marry some ne'er-do-well,' Alistair pointed out, 'and I've got to admire him for that.'

Dougal snorted. 'You would. Any road, he said he'd let her get engaged, though I didn't want to have to put money out on a ring. The trouble is, if I don't, he'll think I'm a stingy blighter.'

It was Manny who solved Dougal's financial problem. After hearing of it from Alistair, he said, joyfully, 'I picked up a beautiful ring at Balham market about a month ago, remember, and I only gave thirty shillings for it, as I recall.'

Alistair was about to remind him that he had paid five pounds for it and it was worth much more, when it dawned on him that this was Manny's way of helping Dougal. 'Will I tell him to come and have a look at it?'

'I do not wish to force him into anything, Alistair, so just make the suggestion.'

Manny arranged to keep the shop open for an extra hour the next day to give Dougal time to get there after work, and during his sojourn round the stalls and second-hand shops, he picked up another two rings which he thought might be suitable.

Scarcely able to believe his luck when he saw what Manny produced, Dougal gave all three rings his deepest consideration, although he returned several times to a delicate arrangement of two emeralds and one diamond. Neither Alistair nor Manny were at all surprised, therefore, when this was the ring he finally plumped for. 'I can't believe it's only thirty bob,' he told the pawnbroker as he handed over a crisp pound note and a ten-shilling note that needed careful handling to avoid being ripped along its many creases.

'It is fairly old,' Manny replied, without a blush, 'and if your lady friend does not like it, she can come and choose for herself.' After a pause, he added, gently, 'But perhaps you would rather she did not know where you bought it?'

'I don't think she'd mind, and thank you very much for everything, Mr Isaacson. You don't know how grateful I am.'

When he and Alistair returned to the privacy of their shared room, he took the worn leather box out of his pocket to admire his purchase. 'It's lucky your boss had this ring in stock. Look at it . . . two emeralds and a diamond . . . for thirty bob!' His jubilation changed abruptly to uncertainty. 'D'you think she'll object to getting a second-hand ring? Will she think it looks cheap? Will her Dad realize . . . ?'

Alistair felt as if he were between two stools. Manny wouldn't want him to let Dougal know the real value of the ring, but he couldn't let his pal run away with the idea that it was worthless. 'It's not classed as second-hand, it's called an antique, and it's worth a lot more than thirty bob.'

Instead of soothing Dougal, this information made him scowl. 'So Manny pulled a fast one on me? Well, I'm not taking his charity, and you'd better give it back to him in the morning.'

'It wasn't meant as charity.' Alistair had to deny it. 'He buys things much cheaper in the markets because the stallholders don't know what they're worth, and even if they did, they wouldn't be able to sell them for that. You just landed lucky that Manny had got those three rings so cheap.'

'It was good of him to think of me, then,' Dougal admitted. 'I can see why you like him, Ally, he's a kind-hearted soul.'

'Have you heard from Alistair lately?'

It was a routine question, asked of Alice Ritchie almost every time her mother sent her to buy the groceries. 'Mam had a letter yesterday, and he says Dougal Finnie's got engaged, though it'll be another year before her father'll let them get wed.'

Lexie Fraser nodded pleasantly. She wanted desperately to find out if Alistair had a girlfriend, but she couldn't make it too obvious. 'Is there any word of them . . . ? It's been two years since they went away, and surely they'd get some holidays?'

'Well, I suppose Dougal's been saving his money seeing he's going to be taking a wife, and Alistair's happy enough to keep working. He says Manny, that's his boss, leaves him in full charge nowadays, and he's teaching him how to value jewellery and things like that. Besides, he's an old man, and I think Alistair feels responsible for him, in a way.'

'But he should get some time off . . . it's the law . . . all employees should get a week's holidays . . . every year.'

Guessing what Lexie really wanted to know, Alice took pity on her. 'They've good lodgings, that's one good thing. Ivy, that's their landlady, she torments Alistair it's time he got a ladyfriend and all, but he says he's not ready for that yet. He's happy the way he is.' She was glad she'd made a point of it; Lexie's relief was almost tangible.

'He hasn't got much spare cash, of course, with his lodgings to pay, and getting his washing done, and buying fags, he says he never has anything left at the end of the week. I'd better not waste any more time, though. Mam'll be wondering what I'm doing. I near forgot, how's your mother keeping?'

'She's not very great, but the doctor says there's nothing more he can do for her.'

'I'm sorry to hear that, Lexie. Tell her I was asking for her.'

'I'll do that, Alice. Cheerio just now, then.'

Lexie waited until Alice cycled off before turning the placard on the door to 'Closed', and putting the snib down. It was on one o'clock, and she knew her mother would be waiting for her dinner, though she just picked at it like a sparrow, but the girl still didn't hurry to attend to her like she usually did. Hearing about Dougal's engagement had unsettled her. Alistair had always copied his pal in everything he did, so it was a sure bet that he'd be looking for a girlfriend now.

If only he'd come back, even for a wee while, she'd do her utmost to make him see that she was the one for him, that he was the one for her. She had gone out with a few of the local lads since he'd been away, but she hadn't found one that could make her pain go away. She had loved her father so much, right up to that awful evening when he didn't come home from the choir practice. She could still hardly bear to think about it. Even when she woke in the night, she pushed it aside and dwelt only on Alistair, assuring herself that even if he had deserted her as well, *his* absence wouldn't last much longer.

When he came home, he would understand. He would sympathize, make it all right. He wouldn't be like the folk that said her father had put Nancy Lawrie in the family way then run off with her. It wasn't true! It couldn't be true, no matter what they said!

If she didn't have her mother to consider, she'd go to London to be with Alistair. His sister would give her the address of his lodgings . . . she could pretend she just wanted to drop him a friendly note, for old times' sake. But there *was* her mother to consider. She had gone steadily downhill since . . . The doctor was the only one who had done anything to help at that awful time, Doctor Birnie, that was. He had given them both sleeping pills as soon as he came, and had left a small supply to see them through the next few days as well. The police had been useless. They had sworn they were searching for her father, but as far as they were concerned he hadn't committed a crime, so they weren't really bothered.

Tam and Nettie Lawrie, Nancy's parents, had fared no better. It had been glaringly obvious that the police believed the two missing persons were together – though they'd disappeared on different days – and had likely been saying, 'Good luck to them.' Poor Nettie had been in such a state, Tam had given up his job and taken her to be beside her sister, but they'd never said where *she* bade.

They were lucky getting away from Forvit, Lexie reflected, for she was stuck here until her mother's illness took its final toll. The new doctor – he was still called new though he'd come well over a year ago – had only diagnosed the cancer last summer, and had told her, the daughter, that it was too far gone to treat. Not that there was a treatment for cancer. It was just a case of not letting a soul know what she was suffering from – there were still folk that thought it was catching – and waiting for the end.

Yet, however long it took, however much she came to resent the responsibility and drudgery of caring for her, she would never deliberately cut her mother's life short, much as she might feel tempted to stop her pain. How could God let this happen? It was a crying shame, that's what it was. As if the woman hadn't gone through enough already, with the whole village saying her man had left her for a girl young enough to be his daughter.

Shaking her head at the morbidity of her thoughts, Lexie straightened her back and went through to the house.

Chapter 4

Marjory Jenkins had been waiting, somewhat impatiently it must be said, for her eighteenth birthday, on which day her father had more or less promised, with one provision, to agree to her marriage, but time was just crawling past. One month before her dream would come true, she decided to make sure that all would run smoothly.

'I was thinking,' she said to Dougal the following evening, 'you're having Alistair as groomsman, and I'm having Gwen as bridesmaid, and they've never met yet, so why don't we get them to come out with us some time soon?'

'You're sure your father's going to let us . . . ?'

'I'm positive . . . as long as you ask him for my hand in the approved way. He's a bit old-fashioned – says a suitor should show proper respect.'

Dougal expelled a silent breath through pursed lips. 'I'm not looking forward to this, you know. I'll likely make a right muck-up of it, but I'll do my best.'

'I know you will, my darling.'

The endearment, plus the radiance of her smile, made him take her in his arms to tell her how much he loved her – serious sweet talk did not come easily to him but it was well known that actions spoke louder than words – and her earlier suggestion that they should introduce her sister to his pal was forgotten until they were saying good night some time later. 'Bring Alistair with you on Saturday,' she murmured, 'and I'll bring Gwen. The hotel's never busy at weekends – most of the reps go home to their families and we've only a couple of tourists booked for bed and breakfast – so Mum's giving Peggy the chance to be on duty on her own, to fetch drinks and things like that.'

He had to gird his senses together to take in what she was saying. 'Oh . . . yes, yes. I'll bring Alistair with me, even if I've to lead him by the nose.'

She giggled at that. 'Is he really so shy?'

'Maybe not quite as bad as that, but he *is* shy with strangers, especially girls.'

'That's funny. Gwen's the same . . . with boys, I mean. She was let down badly a couple of years ago, and she's scared to trust anybody now. Did someone let Alistair down?'

'No, it wasn't that. This girl was making a pest of herself, that's what scared him off.'

'Oh gosh, I hope they're not awkward with each other. I don't want anything to spoil our wedding day.'

'Nothing will, they won't want to upset you. No matter how they feel about each other, they won't show it.'

'Dougal, I could slaughter you for this!' Alistair fumed as they made their way to the meeting point. 'It's going to be bad enough on your wedding day, if it ever comes off, without having a rehearsal.'

'It's not a rehearsal,' Dougal soothed. 'It's just for Marge. She wants to make sure everything'll be plain sailing. Any road, maybe you'll like Gwen.'

'Have you ever met her?'

'No, but she's Marge's sister so there can't be that much difference.'

Alistair had known several instances where sisters or brothers had entirely different personalities, but he deemed it best not to argue. He didn't want to worry Dougal, whose mind was bent on making things perfect for his perfect fiancée.

It turned out that, apart from their sylph-like figures, the sisters were almost exact opposites. While Marjory was a curly-headed brunette with a creamy skin, Gwendoline had straight blonde hair and a fair skin; Marge was outgoing and bubbly, effervescent as a shaken bottle of beer, whereas Gwen was quiet and reserved. Despite this, despite his own reservations about the meeting, after five minutes in her company Alistair was talking to her as if they had known each other for years. Her friendly manner, and genuine interest in what his work entailed, encouraged him to describe his customers, give little thumbnail sketches of their lives, marvelling all the while at the compassion she showed for the poor downtrodden women and their families.

'It's a shame,' she murmured, at one point. 'People shouldn't have to live like that.'

'They're used to it,' he assured her, 'to living from hand to mouth. It's likely what their own mothers had to do, it's the only way of life they know.' Noticing that her lovely blue eyes were moist, he felt angry at himself for upsetting her, and changed to describing some of the items Manny found in the street markets.

They had been walking for almost an hour before it dawned on him that he had been doing most of the talking. 'You'll be fed up listening to me. Tell me about the hotel,' he coaxed. 'You must have some strange characters coming there?'

'Some,' she smiled, 'but not many and not too strange – most of them have been coming to us for years. It's the lady tourists who . . . they've probably never been in a hotel before and treat us like slaves.' She gave an imitation of the kind of haughty women she had to deal with, which ended with them giggling together like children.

By the time they reached the point where Dougal and

Marge were waiting for them, Alistair knew that Gwen was the only girl for him. He would gladly have lain down on the ground and let her trample all over him if that was what she wanted. Not that she would, for she wasn't that kind of person.

As he bade Gwen a cordial, and rather reserved, good night at the corner of her street, Alistair wondered if he would ever have the courage to kiss her at all, never mind in the passionate way Dougal was kissing Marge.

'That went off all right,' Dougal observed when they were walking back along Russell Square. 'I didn't see any sparks flying.'

'Gwen's really easy to get on with.'

'Oh, aye? Would I be right in thinking you've fallen for her?'

'I didn't say that.'

'You don't have to. It's written all over your face.'

'I like her,' Alistair admitted, colouring.

'Maybe you two'll be walking down the aisle a few months after us.'

'I wouldn't mind if we were, but maybe Gwen doesn't feel the same way.'

Gwen *did* feel the same way, although he didn't find out until almost two weeks later. They had been going for walks together, but on this particular night, because it was raining quite heavily, they went to a small cinema which showed, in its hour-long continuous programme, a few cartoons, an educational short, plus a roundup of world news, and because it was quite late by the time they got there, the only seats available were doubles in the back row. Sitting this close to the girl of his dreams, it still took Alistair ten minutes to slide his arm round her, and another five to pull her towards him. Then without warning, she turned to face him, and her lips were only inches from his.

For the next hour and a half, he was conscious only of her, of the whispered words of love, of the kisses that made his heart race almost out of control. The strains of 'God Save the King', heralding the end of the show, brought them both to their senses – they had sat unwittingly through forty-five minutes of repeats – and they ran, hand in hand, as fast as their legs could carry them, so that Gwen could be home before the hotel doors were locked for the night. One last snatched kiss was all they had time for, but Alistair made his way back to Hackney happier than he had ever been in his entire life.

He could hardly credit it. He wasn't handsome, nor wealthy, nor particularly clever, he couldn't make jokes like Dougal, so how on earth would a girl – the most beautiful girl in the world – be attracted to him? What could she see in him to love, for she must love him before she let him kiss her like that. He couldn't believe his luck, and he'd save every penny he could – give up smoking, buy nothing that wasn't absolutely essential – so that he could make her his wife. But maybe she didn't love him? Alistair himself could not recognize it, but, even before the kissing, he and Gwen had blossomed in each other's company, lost the apprehension of the opposite sex which their previous experiences had engendered in them.

'Good God, Ally,' Dougal teased after tea one evening, while they jostled each other for space at the bathroom mirror, 'you've been out with Gwen three times this week.'

'You've been out with Marge four times,' Alistair objected.

'That's different – we're engaged and you only met Gwen about three weeks ago.'

'And I knew right away how I felt about her.'

'You'd better warn her not to say anything about you and her to her father till after our wedding. For any sake, don't rock the boat.'

That night, as soon as Alistair met her, Gwen said, 'Dad's laying on a special meal for Marge's eighteenth birthday next Saturday, and you're invited, too. He's closing the hotel for the day, so I think he's going to give his permission for her to get married . . . but only if Dougal asks him properly. How does he feel about it, do you know?'

'He's scared stiff, but no doubt he'll do it. Um . . .' Alistair stopped, his face colouring.

'Yes? What were you going to say?'

'I was wishing . . . but it's too soon.'

'Too soon for what?'

'If I said I . . . wanted to marry you some day, what would you say?'

'I'd say that's what I wanted, too.'

'But it'll take me years to save enough, so we'd better forget about being serious for a while yet, and not show Marge and Dougal we're jealous of them.'

Ivy Crocker couldn't help teasing Dougal when the boys set off for the 'special meal'. 'You're not going to the guillotine, you're only going to ask her father one simple question. You can surely manage that?'

'Oh, Ivy, I hope I can! I feel like my mouth's full of tongue.'

She turned to Alistair now. 'It'll be your turn next, Al.'

'Not for a long time.'

On the way to Guilford Street, he muttered, 'Ach, Dougal, I'm as bad as you. I'm dreading this, for I'll feel like a fish out of water. I don't know any of them.'

'You know Marge and Gwen, and I don't know any of the rest of them either. Don't back out now, Ally, boy, I need you there to give me some self-confidence. You see, I'm worried that he never asked to meet me before this, and I'm not sure

I can pluck up courage to say what he wants me to say, but if I don't, he'll think I'm a pretty poor fish.'

'You'll manage fine without me.'

'I won't! I'll dry up, I'll stammer and stutter and look a right fool.'

'That's nothing new,' Alistair teased. 'I suppose I'd better come, to please you, but don't expect me to say anything.'

'As long as you're there, that's all I want.'

When they arrived at Jenkins' Hotel, Marge took them downstairs to the kitchen where her father, a huge white apron draped round his vast body, was sitting at a long, well-scrubbed table putting the finishing touches to a mouthwatering trifle. He did not look up until the decoration was completed, which disconcerted Dougal but gave Alistair time to study the man. He was grossly fat, his backside overlapping the stool on which he was sitting by several inches all round, his flopping belly almost covering his knees. His neck bulged red from the top of his starched collar and although his cheeks had not yet become jowls, it was a sure bet they would eventually. Because his head was bent in concentration, it could be seen that his crown was sparsely covered, yet his grey-speckled dark hair was cropped close like a soldier's.

Both youths jumped when Mr Jenkins banged down his fork and barked, 'Which of you two Jocks is after my Marge?'

It was not an auspicious opening, but Dougal managed to answer with no trace of the nerves which had been consuming him all day. 'I'm Dougal Finnie, Mr Jenkins.'

The man's eyes swivelled round. 'So you must be Alistair Ritchie?'

'Yes, Mr Jenkins.'

The man gave a sudden roar of laughter and, as they stared at him in dismay, a woman's voice said, gently, but with a hint of amusement, 'Don't tease them, dear. I'm Rosie, by the way, the girls' mother, and don't let Tiny scare you. It's just . . . it's so long since anyone called him Mr Jenkins. He was twenty-five years in the army, ending up as sergeant/cook at Aldershot, and he put on so much weight tasting everything, somebody once called him Tiny in fun, and the name stuck.'

They couldn't help but laugh at the incongruity of the nickname, and it put them entirely at ease. 'I'm pleased to meet you . . . Tiny,' Dougal said, holding out his hand.

'Ditto, my friend, but if my daughters have everything ready in the dining room, I think we should eat now. Business later,' he added, winking at Dougal, who looked at Marge and shrugged in resignation.

Whoever had taught Tiny his trade, Alistair thought as the meal was coming to an end, deserved a medal. The minestrone soup was delicious, the roast lamb was so succulent it almost melted in the mouth, the roast potatoes were crisped to a T, the other vegetables were just as he liked them, and the trifle . . . he had never tasted anything like it! And eating was clearly a serious business in this household, very little conversation had been made. Mrs Jenkins, Rosie, was dwarfed by her husband. She was slight, but obviously wiry, because she had mentioned, while the soup was being served, that she did the actual running of the hotel.

'Tiny's just the chef,' she had laughed. 'I'm clerk, treasurer – though he signs the cheques – handyman . . . the boss, in fact.'

Her husband had beamed at her, in no way put out at being relegated to the status of an employee. 'I'm boss in the kitchen, though. That's how I like it.'

Rosie's fair wavy hair had a suggestion of silver about it, yet it may have been as blonde as Gwen's when she was younger. It was drawn back off her face which was devoid of any make-up yet her cheeks were a pale shade of rose and her lips were red enough in their natural state. Her face was oval like Gwen's, and even if she looked delicate, Alistair decided, she must be a strong woman. He wondered, idly, if Gwen or Marge, or both, took after her. He had often heard it said that if you wanted to know what a girl would be like in twenty or thirty years, you only had to look at her mother. He liked Rosie, even on this short acquaintance, and he wouldn't mind if the girl he loved turned out exactly the same.

It dawned on him suddenly that there should have been a third sister, and almost as if she had read his mind, Rosie said, 'You'll have to excuse Peg. She objected to not being allowed to ask a boy to tea like her older sisters, and she's taking her dinner downstairs.'

'She'll get over it,' announced Tiny, wiping his mouth with his linen napkin and pushing back his chair, extra wide and clearly made especially for him. 'Now, Dougal,' he said, 'it's time for you and me to adjourn to the residents' sitting room to get our business done. Gwennie, you had better stay here with Alistair, and Marge and Peg'll help your mother to clear up and do the dishes.'

And before he knew where he was, Alistair was left alone with Gwen. 'I feel awful, you having to stay with me while your mother and sisters are slaving away downstairs,' he whispered. 'I could easily sit here and wait till you give them a hand.'

'You don't need to whisper, nobody'll hear us. Don't you like being alone with me?'

'I'd do anything to be alone with you . . . for ever.'

She smiled and whispered, shyly, 'Why don't you make the most of it, then?'

This made him pull her off her seat and on to his knee. It wasn't exactly comfortable, two of them on one dining-room chair, but they were making the most of it when Tiny poked his head round the door. 'So this is the way things are?' he exclaimed, giving a great guffaw of laughter at the guilty way the two young people sprang apart. 'I thought it might be, but I wasn't sure. I came to let you know that Dougal has said his piece and they're all gathered in our sitting room, but . . . Alistair, I think you and I should have a little talk, too? Off you go, Gwennie, this won't take long.'

Wishing that the floor would open up and swallow him, the trembling, scarlet-faced Alistair was sure that the man would tear him apart for daring to kiss his eldest daughter so fervently. 'I'm very sorry, Mr Jenkins,' he began, the words quavering slightly, 'I shouldn't have . . .'

'So you think I'm going to bawl you out? You look like a rookie in front of the ser'nt major. Good God, Alistair, I was young once myself, hard as it may be to believe. I took advantage of every opportunity I could to kiss a pretty girl, and, even if I say so myself, my Gwennie, like my other two daughters, is a very pretty girl. In fact, I'd go as far as say I'd have been disappointed in you if you hadn't kissed her, but there's kissing and there's kissing, if you see what I mean, and you were a bit too . . . you're serious about her, aren't you?'

'Yes, I am, Mr Jenkins . . .'

'Tiny, for goodness' sake! Mr Jenkins sounds like I'm a preacher.'

'I *am* serious about Gwen . . . Tiny. I love her, and I mean to marry her some day, when I can afford to support a wife.'

'Is money the only reason you're holding back?'

'Of course it is. I'll have to find a house and furnish it . . .'

Tiny pulled thoughtfully at his earlobe. 'I think we had better join the others. What I had planned to say to Dougal will apply equally to you, so listen carefully.'

Alistair followed him through to the back room, where a magenta-faced Dougal was standing holding Marge's hand, while Peggy and her mother, both smiling expectantly, were sitting on a long sofa with Gwen, who lifted her downcast head as the two men entered and eyed her father with some apprehension.

He let his eyes roam around them before plumping down on what was meant to be a two-seater couch but he filled it completely. 'I've just had a bit of a surprise,' he said, finally. 'I had prepared a little speech saying I was giving my blessing on a marriage between my daughter, Marjory, and Dougal Finnie, a young Scot . . .'

He was interrupted by the clamour of his family voicing their congratulations to the happy pair, and had the grace to wait until things were quiet again before he continued. 'I was going to say I was looking forward to having Dougal as a son-in-law and give him a few words of advice, but . . .' He looked round the assembly once again, stopping when he came to the nervous Alistair, who had taken up his stance beside Gwen, and letting out another of his deep belly laughs. 'I'm not a blinking cannibal, boy, so don't look as if I was ready to throw you in a pot.'

Rosie stepped in now. 'Get on with it, Tiny. It's not fair to keep them in suspense.'

'This is a moment I'm going to cherish all my life,' he told her, 'so let me proceed at my own pace.' First grinning reassuringly at Alistair, he directed his words at Dougal. 'The thing is, I cannot let Marge go. I need her here, because I would never get another girl to act as waitress-cum-chambermaid-cum-kitchenmaid as my three do. No one else would put up with me, the way I order them about, but as I always say, what's the good of keeping three dogs and barking yourself?'

Dougal was looking aghast. 'But Tiny, you said . . . you gave your permission . . .'

'And I meant it, every word, but . . . you can't take her away. You will move in here. As I see it, you'll be sharing her room without having to pay a penny for rent, getting all your meals without having to stump up for board . . .'

'What's the catch?' Dougal's eyes had narrowed. 'There must be something.'

'You will do any odd jobs that need doing, decorating, moving furniture and any heavy lifting, but only in the evenings and weekends. I'm not expecting you to give up your job. And that's it!' Tiny turned to Alistair now. 'You heard what I said to Dougal, so is there something *you* want to ask me? Or would you rather do it in private?'

Gwen's hand-squeeze was enough for Alistair. 'We don't need to do it in private. I would be grateful if you would give your permission for me to marry Gwen, maybe next year some time?'

'Next year?' Tiny erupted. 'I'm giving you the chance to make it a double wedding! It'll save putting two lots of stress on my wife and be less of a financial strain on me. We'd have everything over in one go and the hotel would get back to normal.' Noticing Alistair's sudden pallor, he said, 'You're not getting cold feet are you?'

Rosie stood up at this point. 'Give the boy a chance to get his breath back. Come on, Peggy, help me to make some coffee.'

'No, Mrs Jenkins . . . Rosie,' Alistair corrected, because of her slight frown, 'don't bother. I don't need time to think. I love Gwen, and I think she loves me . . .'

The girl blushed to the roots of her hair but said, firmly, 'Yes, Mum, I do love him.'

'And if Tiny wants a double wedding,' Alistair went on, still addressing his future mother-in-law, 'I can't see any problem . . . if *you* don't object.'

'I'm delighted,' she beamed, 'but we'll need a few weeks to prepare everything.'

Tiny took over again. 'We'll ask the vicar how soon he can fit in the wedding . . .'

'The banns'll have to be called for three weeks running,' Rosie pointed out, 'and it's too late for tomorrow to be the first time, so it'll be next Sunday and the two after that.'

'So we'll make it in four weeks, boys. That'll give us enough time . . .' His wife's frantic signal made Tiny stop to amend this. 'Five weeks from today apparently, to please my dear Rosie. Does that suit you?'

It was Gwen who made the decision. 'That's perfect, Dad. Marge and I can choose our wedding gowns together, and there'll be time for alterations if they're needed.'

'The wedding breakfast will be here in the hotel, so nothing too fancy, eh?'

'Can I go with them and get my dress, as well?' queried Peggy. 'I'll be bridesmaid for both of them, won't I, and I'll have to look nice.'

Thinking that a new dress would save her youngest daughter taking umbrage again, her mother nodded.

'How many will I have to cater for?' Tiny wanted to know. 'Just family, isn't it?'

'And Dougal and Alistair's families, as well,' Rosie reminded him.

Neither of the young men commented on this until they were on their way back to Hackney. 'I don't know what my mother's going to say about this,' Alistair declared. 'I haven't even told her I've been seeing Gwen.'

Dougal pulled a face. 'She likely knows by now. I told my Mam in my last letter and she'll likely have told yours.'

'The wedding'll not come as such a surprise, then, thank goodness.'

Manny Isaacson was delighted by Alistair's news. 'I'm so

happy for you, my boy. I was rather selfish, you know, hoping that you would not be looking for another job with more pay so that you could afford to marry your Gwen, but this seems an ideal arrangement for everyone concerned. However, there is one thing you have not touched on. Are you not thinking of giving Gwen an engagement ring? She might feel envious of her sister . . .'

'Gwen's not the jealous kind.'

'Nevertheless, I think that she should have one, and nothing would give me greater pleasure than to . . .'

'No, Manny,' Alistair interrupted. 'I won't let you *give* me one, but maybe you're right. Maybe I *should* get her an engagement ring, but I want to pay for it myself.'

The older man lifted his shoulders and turned up his palms in the expressive manner Alistair had come to recognize as a Jewish gesture. 'I do not have much of a selection at the moment, but it should not take long to pick up something decent and reasonable.'

That very afternoon, Manny returned to the shop beaming as if he had lost a penny and found a pound. 'It was like a miracle, Alistair,' he told his assistant. 'You've heard me talking about young Bill Jackson? He took over his father's stall in the Portobello Road last year, if you remember. I was telling him I was looking for an engagement ring, not too expensive but not rubbish, you know? And he said he had the very thing. It seems the nephew of an old lady who had recently died was disposing of some of her belongings, and he said he didn't need the money, just wanted to be rid of them. Young Bill, a genuine man if ever there was one, gave him ten shillings for the lot, believing that what they held would be fit only for scrap. So you can imagine his amazement when he opened the second crate, to find a jewellery box with several pieces of jewellery in it, at least two of the rings, even to his inexperienced eyes, worth more than ten pounds, never mind ten shillings, as he put it.

'He had sought out the nephew to acquaint him of this fact, but all he said was, "Keep them, and count this your lucky day." So I asked Bill what he wanted for the two rings, and he let me take them on spec. Whichever one you pick, he said he'll be quite happy if you give him ten bob for it, which is what he paid for the whole lot, remember, and I can assure you, Alistair, that each is worth in the region of one hundred pounds.'

'But are you sure you're not spinning me this yarn to make me feel . . . ?'

'No, my boy, I am telling you the absolute truth, and if you are wondering why young Bill . . .' Manny paused with a chuckle. 'I call him young Bill because I knew his father, but he must be over fifty and a dyed-in-the wool romantic. That is why he is making this gesture, and to show how much he trusts my judgement of you, he said you can let your young lady choose for herself.'

Gwen happened to be on duty that evening, and so the excited Alistair took the rings to Guilford Street to let her have her pick. She exclaimed over both of them then said she couldn't allow him to buy her anything so expensive, and was dumbstruck when he told her the story behind them. 'Take the one you like best,' he urged. 'I'll never get a chance like this again.'

Shaking her head in awe, she tried each one on the third finger of her left hand in turn and admired it from all angles, saying, 'I can't make up my mind, Alistair. I thought the solitaire diamond at first, it catches the light so well, then I wanted to have the three smaller stones . . . what do you think?'

'I'd say the solitaire looks a bit big on your finger, your hands are so dainty, but it's for you to choose.'

'Take that one back to Manny then, and thank him for thinking about us, and . . . oh, yes. Tell him to thank the other man, too . . . I can hardly believe it, Alistair. I wasn't expecting to get an engagement ring, but I adore it.'

'I'm not taking it for ten shillings, of course. I'll give him thirty, like Dougal . . .' He halted, appalled at giving away his friend's secret. 'Oh, I shouldn't have told you that, Gwen. Promise you won't let Marge know.'

'I promise, though I don't think she'd mind, any more than I do. We know you two don't get big wages, and thirty shillings is quite a lot.'

His heart aching with love for her, he had to kiss her for understanding.

'What's got into you the day, Lexie?' Her body getting frailer by the day, Carrie Fraser could still glare at her daughter. 'You've been snapping my head off ever since you came ben from the shop.'

The girl sat down at the side of her mother's bed. 'Bella Ritchie was saying her Alistair and Dougal Finnie's having a double wedding.'

Carrie frowned accusingly. 'You never said Alistair was going steady.'

'I didn't know, and neither did Bella till this morning.'

'Oh aye?' A knowing smile flitted across the invalid's pain-lined face. 'A sudden wedding, eh? A bairn on the road, likely.'

Lexie had been wrestling with this unwelcome thought ever since Alistair's mother had left the shop that afternoon, and she still refused to believe it. 'It's Dougal's girl's sister,' she muttered, miserably.

'What difference does that make?'

'Bella says the double wedding was their father's idea. He

doesn't want two upheavals in his hotel, so Alistair's been rushed into it.' Although this was not exactly what his mother had said, it was the only explanation the spurned girl could accept.

'Will the Ritchies be going to London with the Finnies, to see the weddings?'

'Bella says they've been invited but they can't afford the train fare.'

'They could take the boat, like Alistair and Dougal.'

'She says she's terrified of water. The very idea of being on a boat makes her sick.'

Carrie nodded. 'That'll just be an excuse. She likely doesna want to go. If I'd a son, I wouldna like to see him getting led up the garden path by some painted London trollop that had trapped him into it.'

The final phrase comforted Lexie. Alistair *had* been trapped into it. He would never look at another girl unless she'd put herself out to catch him, and poor Al, he didn't like hurting folk. Still, it couldn't last. A marriage without love never did, and he'd come back to Forvit ready to fall into the arms of the girl he could trust, the girl he knew did love him, the girl who would never stop loving him.

Assuring herself of this, she suddenly felt much better. 'Ach, it's his life and he'll just have to get on with it, the same as I'll have to get on with mine. Do you fancy a cheese pudding for your supper?'

Carrie slept even less than normal that night. Lexie was taking Alistair's wedding far too calmly. She couldn't still think he'd come back to her? A marriage was for life, no matter how bad it was. This was proof that Alistair had meant it when he said he was going to settle in London and Lexie would just have to accept it. He wasn't the kind of man who would break the vows he'd have to make.

Alec had stood by his vows, Carrie told herself, until the memory of what he had done hit her again, then something occurred to her that hadn't entered her head before. Had Tom Birnie told him she would never get better of what ailed her? Had he not been able to bear the thought of her dying and him having to face life without her? Aye, that was it. That was why he had run away.

The mental and physical suffering she had endured since that terrible night had made her neurotic and overemotional, and the tears of relief that burst from her now verged on the hysterical, but in no time at all Lexie was there with her, cradling her like she was a bairn, shushing her and telling her not to worry.

'If you think I'll go to pieces because Alistair Ritchie's taking a wife, you're wrong, Mam! It was a shock at first, but I'm over it, and everything's going to be all right. Shut your eyes now and sleep, like a good lass.'

Lexie lay alongside her mother for the rest of the night, assuring herself, over and over again, that everything *would* be all right for her. Alistair was being pushed into a union he didn't want but he would soon realize who he really loved. He'd come back to her within a year or two, and he'd make up for all the time he'd been away.

Chapter 5

~

'You are looking very sad today, Alistair.' Manny regarded his assistant shrewdly. 'Did you have a disagreement with your young lady last night?'

'It's nothing to do with Gwen. It's a letter I got from my mother this morning. She says they can't afford to come to our wedding.'

'Ah, that explains it! You have been so looking forward to seeing them, but do not forget that it is a long long way for them to come.'

'I know, but I thought . . .' He swallowed abruptly.

'How long is it since you left home?'

'It'll be three years come October.' Alistair knuckled his eyes as if to rid them of an irritation – an almost nineteen-year-old man dared not be seen to cry – then went on, 'But there it is . . . one of the hurdles life sometimes puts in our paths.'

'You are too young for such philosophy, my boy.' Manny felt so deeply for him that he could not concentrate on the market stalls that forenoon. He had intended to look for something unique as a wedding gift, but nothing he saw fitted the bill, and he gave up well before midday.

On his way back to his shop, however, a wonderful idea struck him. It would be a gift *par excellence*, a gift sure to please Alistair – and seeing him truly happy was certain to please his bride. But – and it was a but looming menacingly in the wings – would the boy accept it as it was meant, or would he consider it a hand-out? He was so touchy about that sort of thing.

When he entered his premises, the pawnbroker locked the door and turned the cardboard placard to 'CLOSED', saying, 'I want to talk to you without anyone interrupting us.'

Perplexed and apprehensive, Alistair followed him into the little back room – Manny's bedroom, living room and kitchen, the lavatory was in the tiny back yard – where they usually sat to have their lunch-time snack, always on the alert in case a customer walked into the shop, although there was no risk of that today.

Manny waited until a mug of tea was set in front of him. 'I have been doing some thinking, Alistair,' he began, 'and don't go jumping in bull-headed until I have finished what I have to say. Unhappiness is not a good companion, nor is it conducive to full attention to whatever work is in hand, and that applies to me as well as to you. I have been puzzling over what to give you as a wedding gift . . .'

'There's no need for you to give us anything!' Alistair butted in.

'There is perhaps no need, but it is something I want to do. When a young couple are setting up house, it is expected that relatives and friends will give bed linen, kitchen utensils, anything which would be of use in a home, but it is different in your case. You will be living in a hotel, with everything you need readily available to you, and so I have been looking for something, an antique perhaps, I was not sure what but I was sure that I would know it was right when I came across it. Sadly, I have seen nothing.'

'It doesn't matter, Manny,' Alistair muttered as the old man took a sip of tea. 'We don't need . . .'

'Let me finish,' his employer scolded. 'On the way back, it came to me – a gift without parallel! Return tickets to London for your parents and sister.'

Alistair shook his head angrily. 'No, I can't let you do that, Manny.'

'You are flinging my gift back in my face, hmm? I believe it to be the best I could possibly have thought of, and the milk has been spilt . . .' He smiled at the young man's bewilderment. 'The tickets are already bought and the seats reserved. You see, hmm? Consider, also, how your Gwen would feel if none of your family comes to your wedding. She will not want a groom standing miserably by her side wishing that his mother was there. Furthermore, so that she will not feel left out, she can come to the shop and choose a necklace or something of the kind which will be my gift to her.'

Despite his advanced age, Alistair could no longer hold back the tears, but they were tears of happiness, of gratitude, of love for this old man who had been like a father to him since the very day they met.

The twenty-eighth day of September 1932 dawned as bright and warm as a day in the middle of July, and there was pandemonium in the Crocker household as four adults made themselves ready for the big occasion – Rosie Jenkins having decided that it would be nice to invite the grooms' landlady and her husband as guests. Alistair would have loved to ask Manny, too, but he could see that it would cause difficulties, because Dougal couldn't invite all the people who worked with him. With only one bathroom – there was a dividing wall between it and the lavatory, thankfully – Len said he'd do his ablutions in the scullery, as long as nobody came in and saw him washing his 'naughty bits'.

Ivy joked that she wouldn't mind who saw her 'naughty bits', which made them all laugh, although it gave Alistair cause to worry. He knew nothing of a woman's 'naughty bits' and maybe Gwen wasn't as innocent as he thought. Hadn't

Marge told Dougal ages ago that her sister had been let down by some bloke when she was younger? But she'd have told him, wouldn't she? She wasn't the kind to hide anything as serious as that. She was bound to know he would find out . . . on their wedding night. Tonight.

Ready first and waiting, a tight bundle of nerves, for Dougal to tie a satisfactory knot in his tie, Alistair's thoughts strayed to the previous evening, when they had met their families at King's Cross – the better-off Finnies had been quite happy to spend money on fares to see their son being married. The reunions had been very emotional after such a long separation, hugs and kisses (unusual for Scots) exchanged tearfully on the platform, and then they all piled into a large hackney carriage to be transported to Guilford Street, where Rosie had seen to making rooms ready for the important visitors.

The meeting of relatives and soon-to-be-in-laws had gone off very well, Alistair recalled, everyone taking to everyone else, and his mother had even found an opportunity to whisper that she was pleased he was marrying such a nice girl. 'She'll make you a good wife,' she had added, 'so you make sure you treat her right.' He would have married Gwen supposing the verdict had gone the other way, of course, but it was better that it was so favourable.

He was brought back to the present by Dougal's loud sigh of satisfaction. 'Thank the Lord, that's it straight now. You know this, Ally, I'm in a right old state! I don't know how you can look so calm.'

'Maybe I *look* calm,' Alistair mumbled, 'but I don't *feel* calm.'

The last five minutes, waiting for the cab which would convey them to the Register Office where the ceremony was to take place, seemed an eternity to both young men, but Ivy, looking very smart in a midnight blue grosgrain suit and matching straw hat, stopped nerves getting the better of them. 'I don't know what I'm going to do without you two handsome blokes,' she giggled. 'I'll have nobody to share my bed now when you're away, Len.'

Knowing his wife's propensity for exaggeration, he gave a hearty guffaw. 'They wouldn't have come anywhere near you, Ivy, and . . .' he pretended to scowl, 'if they had, I'd have knocked their ruddy blocks off.'

Ivy chuckled again. 'A girl can dream, can't she?'

The arrival of the taxi put an end to the conversation, and they were soon being borne as swiftly as possible through London's rush-hour traffic.

Breakfast was an embarrassing time in the hotel for at least four of the people round the table the following morning. As Dougal confided to Alistair on their way back from seeing their families off that evening, 'I didn't think it would bother me, but I felt awful sitting there with them all knowing what Marge and me had been up to. Oh boy, what a time we had, hardly a wink of sleep all night. How did you get on?'

'We were the same.' Alistair had no wish to discuss the rapturous hours he and Gwen had spent in their first taste of sexual intercourse, for he had discovered, to his infinite relief, that his bride was still a virgin.

'My Mam and Dad were really taken with Marge,' Dougal observed after a minute.

'Mine were taken with Gwen and all,' Alistair was happy to say. 'It's a pity we're so far away, though. I'd have liked to show her round the Forvit area.'

'I promised Mam I'd take Marge up for a holiday in the spring. We could all go together . . . oh no. The girls wouldn't get off at the same time, of course.'

'I couldn't afford it, any road. Gwen wants us to save

as much as we can, in case babies start coming . . . you know . . . ?'

'Oh, I see.' Dougal seemed taken aback at her planning for this at so early a stage.

'I might manage to take her away somewhere for a few days, though – Kent, maybe. I've heard it's lovely there.'

'Aye, that would be nice. Em . . . Ally, how d'you think we'll get on in the hotel?'

'What d'you mean, get on?'

'Well, we're bound to feel like two goldfish in a bowl with everybody watching us. I did tell Tiny I wanted to buy our own wee house, not too far away so Marge could still work for him, but he wouldn't hear of it.'

'Ach, we'll get used to it.'

'We'll have no privacy, that's what I'll miss.'

Alistair grinned. 'We hadn't much privacy at Ivy's, either. She always liked to know everything we were doing.'

'Aye well, but that was different. I wasn't wanting to take you to bed every spare minute you had, like I'll be with Marge.'

'You knew what you were taking on, and you'll just have to put up with it.'

'How did the wedding go?'

'It was just perfect, Lexie.' Unaware that she was turning the screws on her listener's tortured heart, Bella Ritchie gave a full description of her visit to London, breaking off if another customer came in and carrying on again afterwards as if there had been no interruption. 'It was different, wi' two brides. I thought they'd be dressed the same, being sisters, but they're nothing like each other. Dougal's wife, Marge, she's the bouncy kind, full o' life, and she's dark-haired like him, though I'd say hers is even curlier. Gwen, now, that's

Alistair's wife, her hair's a lovely blonde, natural like yours, nae like some I saw doon there, and it shines pale gold in the electric light. Her face is thinner than her sister's and she's a lot quieter, but they're real nice lassies, though I didna understand half o' what they said, they spoke that quick. Mind you, they'd a job makin' my Willie oot, for he couldna think on the English for what he wanted to say.'

'But you managed to get on with . . . Gwen?'

'Nae bother! I couldna have wished for a better . . .' About to say 'a better daughter-in-law', Bella finally remembered how attached Lexie had been to Alistair before he went away and caught her runaway tongue. '. . . a better day,' she substituted, clumsily. 'Sun shining and an awful lot warmer than it is up here. And the Jenkinses is just like ony o' us. Nae side to them though they've got a fine big hotel. There's a younger sister, and all, Peggy her name is, and the three o' them work there, waitressing, cleaning the rooms and such like, good workers, they are.'

'Oh aye?' Lexie felt obliged to make some kind of comment.

'Rosie, their mother, she's a right nice soul, slim like them and quiet, but it's my opinion she rules the roost, though her man wouldna like folk to think that. He was the biggest surprise we got. You should have seen him, Lexie . . . a great fat mountain o' a man, and he does all the cooking sitting on a stool in the kitchen in the basement. The meal – the wedding breakfast they cried it though we didna sit doon till four o'clock – oh, I canna tell you how good it was. Willie said it was the kind o' soup he likes best, the kind you can stand your spoon up in, I canna tak' him nae place, then he said the fancy stuffing wi' the roasted turkey went round his heart like a hairy worm, and I coulda kicked him, but they seemed pleased aboot it.'

'They likely took it as a compliment.'

'Aye, and so it was meant . . . if they understood it.'

'Was it a kirk wedding?'

'No, no! It was in a Register Office, then back to the hotel in taxis. Mind, I'd've been happier if it had been a kirk wedding, but . . . ach, I suppose that's the English way o' doing it, and the registrar had us a' in tears at the gentle way he advised them to respect their vows, even Tiny, that's Alistair's father-in-law . . .'

'Tiny?' Lexie gave a brittle laugh. 'That's a funny name if he's so fat.'

'It was a nickname he got in the army. To get back to my story, Gwen being the oldest daughter, her and Alistair was wed first – she'll be nineteen next month the same as him. Dougal was best man and young Peggy, I think she's fifteen or sixteen, she was bridesmaid for her two sisters, and Dougal had Alistair for *his* best man.'

'What were the brides wearing?' The poor girl couldn't help but prolong the agony; she was so anxious to know as much as she could.

'Well, Marge was in a sky-blue crepe-di-Chine dress, fitted bodice wi' a gored skirt – I was surprised she'd chose blue when her eyes are so dark brown, but it really suited her. Gwen looked a picture in a deep pink two-piece, moygashel, I think it was, and Peggy had a plain cream . . . no, darker than cream, more biscuit – plain linen kind of frock wi' a Peter Pan collar. Rosie had on a navy costume wi' a velvet collar, very smart, wi' a white blouse and a white straw hat.'

'And was there any other guests . . . besides you three and the Finnies?'

'Mr and Mrs Crocker was there, them the boys lodged wi', nice woman Ivy is, and all, maybe a bit ower much to say, but she was friendly enough. That was the lot.'

'I'd have thought Alistair would've invited his boss. Alice said it was him that paid your fares.'

'The Jenkinses just wanted a quiet family do. But Mr Isaacson – Manny, he likes to be cried – he came to King's Cross to introduce himself when we were coming hame; he's a proper gentleman. He's the first Jew I ever met, and if they're a' like him, I dinna ken where folk get the idea they're oot to rob everybody. I tried to tell him how grateful I was to him for sending us the tickets, but he said he'd bought them as a wedding present for Alistair, because he'd been that disappointed we werena going. That's the kind of man he is, like I said, a real gentleman. And Rosie and Tiny wouldna tak' onything for letting us bide there for the two nights, so we've had a right treat and it didna cost us a brass farthing.'

Having exhausted her subject, Bella said, breathlessly, 'I'm forgetting to ask. How's your Mam just now?'

Lexie shook her head and gave a dismal sigh. 'She's not good. The doctor says it's just a matter of weeks.'

'Oh, I'm sorry, lass, and me raving on like that about the wedding. Can I do anything to help you, Lexie? Would you like me to come and sit wi' her sometimes?'

'Thanks, Bella, but her sister came up from Perth on Sunday for a fortnight. I doubt if she'd know you, anyway. She doesn't know me, sometimes. I think I'll need to get somebody into the shop when my Auntie Mina goes home, so I'll have more time to look after Mam.'

'Poor Carrie. Look, I could easy sit wi' her every day to let you keep working. Me and her aye got on fine.'

'It would be too much for you, Bella, walking three miles here and three miles back every day. Anyway, I don't think she'll last much longer, to be honest.'

Thus prepared, Bella was not surprised to hear, less than a week later, that Carrie Fraser had died in the night. It was better that she was at peace, especially for Lexie's sake. And she was glad on her own behalf, and all, Bella thought guiltily. She was so easily tired nowadays she doubted if she'd have had the energy to walk to the village to sit with the poor woman, never mind walk back.

When he arrived at work about two weeks after the wedding, Alistair's solemn face prompted Manny to say, 'Have you and Gwen had words?'

'No, no. I just learned that the girl I used to go with at home . . . her mother died.'

'Ah! And you have discovered that you still feel a little something for her?'

'I . . . I feel sorry for her, that's all. Carrie Fraser was a real nice woman, and Lexie's left on her own now.'

'You are having regrets, hmm?'

'I'll never regret marrying Gwen, but . . . ach, Lexie'll be free to find somebody else now. She was a nice enough girl, just a bit overpowering, if you know what I mean?'

'She was too pushy? She wanted you to make a full commitment?'

'That's right, and I wasn't ready for it. We were just sixteen.'

'And now, at the ripe old age of nineteen, you are a happily married man.' Manny threw back his head and laughed.

'I *am* happily married,' Alistair retorted, a little put out by his employer's amusement, 'and even if I'd never left Forvit, Lexie still wouldn't have got me to marry her. She was bad enough before, but after her father walked out, she was ten times worse.'

Manny's smile vanished. 'Her father walked out? It is not surprising, then, that the girl was a little unbalanced. Why did he go? He must have had a reason, poor man.' He shook his head mournfully.

'There was rumours he'd run away with a girl he'd put

in the family way, but the folk that knew him best found that hard to believe, for he was a good-living man – elder in the kirk, trained the choir, and he'd not long taken over the treasurer's job.'

Manny stroked his beard. 'Would he have been in financial difficulties?'

'There was no money missing. They got auditors in to make sure, but it was all in order, and so were his own accounts in the shop and the post office.'

'No outstanding debts?'

'Nothing! It's a complete mystery.' Alistair's sigh was long and slightly ragged. 'Now this! Poor Lexie, I hope it doesn't push her over the edge.'

Manny hastily changed the subject. 'How is *your* dear mother?'

'She's fine, as usual, running after Dad and Alice . . .'

'As she had run after you when you were at home, no doubt?'

Alistair grinned now. 'Aye, that's right.'

Having seen her Auntie Mina on to the bus for Aberdeen where she would catch the train to Perth, Lexie lay back in her chair. She should feel utterly exhausted after the stir of the funeral, but it was as if she were floating on air. She had no one to worry about except herself now that her mother's suffering was at an end. It would be a perfect situation if only Alistair Ritchie hadn't left. He would have married her now, and they would have lived happily ever after. But Alistair had gone to London, and he hadn't had time to tire of his bride, so it would be useless to give up everything to go down there after him.

Feeling a tear trickling down her cheek, Lexie wiped it away angrily with her forefinger. Why should she cry? She hadn't given up on him yet. Give it another year or two, and things could be different.

Tiny attacked the pastry violently with the rolling pin. 'I should have known!' he stormed. 'All the ruddy Jocks I ever knew were randy buggers! The trouble was, I thought it would be Dougal who'd strike home first, but it's my Gwennie that's been nobbled and it's only nine weeks since the bloody wedding. Surely Alistair could have waited a year or two before he filled her belly.'

'Calm yourself, Tiny,' cautioned Rosie. 'Do you want the girls to hear you?'

'I don't care who hears me.' Nevertheless, he did lower his voice. 'I can't run this place without Gwennie.'

'You managed with just two before Peggy left school.'

Tiny made a rude noise. 'Gwennie's worth Marge and Peg put together, as you know perfectly well.'

'Well, it's done now and you can't do a thing about it.' Thinking that it would be wise to issue a caution, Rosie continued, 'Don't say anything nasty to Alistair, or criticize him to Gwen. At least they waited till after the wedding to start their family.'

'Good God, Rosie! You don't think he'd been at her before they were married? I'll knock his teeth down his ruddy throat if he had!'

'For heaven's sake! I don't for one second think that, so take it easy! Your face is as red as a beetroot. You'll give yourself a heart attack if you're not careful.'

'Could you blame me?'

'Yes, I'd blame you! Gwen'll be able to work practically to the time of the birth, provided you don't make her do anything strenuous. And with four women in the place, there'll be no shortage of nurses for the little one when it's born.'

Her husband glared at her in exasperation. 'You're looking forward to this . . . to being a grandma, aren't you?'

'I certainly am.' Rosie gave a rapturous sigh. 'And when you're a grandpa, you'll feel exactly the same.'

His whole attitude changed now. 'I suppose so,' he grinned. 'I can see me in a year or so, dandling a little boy on my knee . . .'

'There's no room on your knee for anything except your fat stomach,' chuckled his wife. 'You'd better stop tasting everything a dozen times, so you'll lose some of that blubber and have room for your grandchild.'

Deeming this not worth a reply, Tiny contented himself by flinging a dish towel at her.

Chapter 6

In May 1933, when Alistair received the telegram saying that his mother had died, it was so unexpected it almost tore him apart. She had never given the slightest hint in her letters that she was ill, and he hadn't suspected a thing when she was in London for his wedding. It placed him in a proper quandary. His father and Alice would expect him to go home for the funeral, but how could he leave Gwen when she was so near her time?

'Mum says first babies are usually late,' she assured him, 'and you'll only be away for a few days. In any case, if it does come early, I've all my family to look after me.'

Everyone told him he should go, but it was Dougal who clinched it, observing with his usual candour, 'What could you do even supposing you *are* here when the labour starts? You'd likely panic, and put Gwen in a panic, and all. No, Ally, that kind of thing's best left to the women, they know what to do . . . well, Rosie does. She's had three.'

On arriving in Benview, Alistair was dismayed at the change in his father. His face was drawn, his back bowed, his eyes red-rimmed and dull. 'Is Dad all right?' he asked Alice, realizing as he spoke that she, too, was looking haggard.

'He's taking it bad,' she murmured, 'though we knew it was coming, for the doctor said the bout of flu we thought she was getting over had left her so weak she couldn't fight the infection she picked up. Even if you know something's inevitable, you can't believe it's really going to happen, and when it does, it comes as an awful shock . . . like God's betrayed you. I know it sounds silly, but I'm sure Dad feels the same. And he's going to feel a lot worse after the funeral and he's left on his own.'

'Oh, my God, aye!' In the sorrow which had threatened to fell him, Alistair had given no thought to what would happen afterwards. 'Will he manage by himself?'

'He says he will.' There was a brief silence before she added, 'I said I'd forget about going to 'varsity, even if I've passed the prelims, but he wouldn't hear of it.'

'You can't do that, Alice. Mam and him wanted you to get some kind of degree, so you could have a professional career. They couldn't afford to put me through university, and in any case, it was you that was the clever one.'

'I'm not bothered about having a career. I'd rather stay at home and look after Dad. It's what I want to do, Alistair,' she said quickly as he opened his mouth to argue. 'I've no ambitions. I don't want to be a doctor or a solicitor or a teacher. I just want to get married and have a family . . . maybe two boys and two girls, and keeping house for Dad would be good practice for me.'

'But you're not eighteen yet, Alice . . .' The force of her glare stopped him telling her what a mistake she was making. It was her life to do with as she wanted. After all, hadn't he given up a steady job himself to go to London?

The ordeal of the funeral was only fractionally more harrowing than facing Lexie Fraser again. He had known she'd be there, of course – she'd always been friendly with his mother – and he had primed himself to treat her as if they'd never been anything more than school friends, but it wasn't so easy. Most of the people there believed that they had once been sweethearts if not lovers, and when he went over and shook hands with her, he could sense the knowing glances that were being exchanged behind his back. Worse still, he was so emotional anyway that his heart beat a little faster when she clung to his hand and regarded him with eyes moist with tears. Thankfully, she'd had to move away to let someone else voice their condolences and ask how he was getting on in London, and he was kept thus occupied until the minister arrived to say a prayer over the open coffin.

When the men returned from the interment in the kirkyard, Alice took her brother aside. 'Lexie's in an awful state,' she whispered. 'You'd better walk her home.'

He looked across to where Lexie was sitting forlornly in a corner, dabbing at her eyes with what looked like a sodden handkerchief, and was almost swamped by a surge of pity for her. It did flit across his mind that she could get a lift from the doctor, the one who had taken over after Doctor Birnie left, but it was really up to him to make sure she got home all right. He owed her that.

He was disconcerted by the way her face lit up when he made his offer, but once it was said, he couldn't take it back, and his father nodded gratefully as they went out.

'How's he keeping?' she asked as they set off on the three-mile walk.

'Not too good. They'd been married for nearly twenty-five years, you know, and he's going to miss her.'

'Aye, he's bound to. It's a long time.'

Their conversation, as they strolled along, revolved mainly around people they had both known, and he was thankful that she confined herself to answering his questions, and not asking him anything personal. It had to come, of course.

They were approaching the track to the tower when she looked askance at him. 'Do you remember when we used to go up there at nights?'

He didn't want to be reminded, but he couldn't tell her so. 'We'd some nice walks.'

'Nice walks? Oh, Al, you surely haven't forgotten how you used to kiss me?'

'I haven't forgotten,' he muttered. He hadn't thought about it while he'd been in London, but being with her again brought it back, the youthful, innocent kisses, given solely to find out what kissing a girl felt like, though if Lexie hadn't been so pushy, so forward, there was no saying what it might have led to. But she had spoiled it . . . and put him off girls for years.

'I never had another lad,' she said, coyly, 'not even when you took a wife.'

His wife was something he felt safe to talk about. 'I'd have liked you to meet Gwen. She was sorry she couldn't come up with me, but it was too far for her to travel. It's just a couple of weeks till our baby's due.'

'Your Mam said she was expecting.'

She stopped walking, abruptly, as if she had come to a sudden decision. 'Will you take me up to the tower again? Please, Al, just this one last time . . . for old times' sake?'

A coldness swept over him. 'I'd rather not, Lexie. I'm married now, and . . .'

'Being married shouldn't stop you from being friends with me. Come on, Al. I thought . . . you know I lost my mother, and all?'

'Yes, I know,' he replied stiffly, angry at her for taking advantage of the situation and annoyed at himself for forgetting that it was only a few months since Carrie's death.

'I need some . . . affection, Al . . . please? I don't want you to kiss me, or anything like that, just walk with me so I'll have that to remember. Or are you too high and mighty now you live in London and speak like you'd a plum in your mouth?'

There were tears in her eyes again, real tears, and he guessed that she was masking her vulnerability by being sarcastic. Poor Lexie. She was right. She had nobody now, and why shouldn't he take her up to the tower . . . for old times' sake? 'Come on then,' he said, albeit a trifle brusquely.

She walked decorously by his side, wanting to know more about his wife, about his in-laws, and he answered as best he could until she asked what they were going to call the baby. He and Gwen had not discussed the matter of names. 'If it's a boy, I'd like to call him Douglas,' he said, after a moment's consideration. 'That would be after Dougal, you see, for he's been a true friend to me all our lives. If it's a girl . . .' He paused, then shrugged. 'I haven't thought about that.'

'What about Alexandra?' she suggested, smiling.

'I don't think that'd be a good idea.'

'Why not? I've been a true friend to you, and all, more than a friend, and it would make me truly happy, Al.'

'No, Lexie, I can't. It wouldn't be fair to Gwen.'

'Haven't you told her about me?'

'There was nothing to tell, was there? It was all in your mind.'

'Oh, Al, how could you say a thing like that?' Bursting into a flood of tears, she whipped round and ran back down the hill.

He didn't chase her, but tried not to let too great a distance develop between them. He had to keep his eye on her in case she did anything silly, because she was obviously on the verge of some kind of breakdown.

It wasn't long until she slowed down to a walk and he caught up with her. 'I'm sorry, Lexie,' he said. 'I *have* always looked on you as a friend . . . just a friend, though, but Gwen might think there was more to it if I wanted to call our baby after you. Can you not understand that? How would you like it if you were married and your husband wanted to call your daughter after his old girlfriend?'

'So you still think of me as a girlfriend?'

Her voice was so low that he had to bend his head to hear. 'Well, we did go together for a good few months.' He knew he shouldn't have said it. He should have made it clear that he meant a girl friend, not a girlfriend. There was a world of difference, but now wasn't the time to be brutal.

They walked on in silence for some time, then Lexie murmured, 'I'm awful tired, Alistair. Would you mind if I took your arm?'

He did mind, but all he could do was shake his head, so she tucked her hand under his arm, hanging on as if she were totally exhausted, as quite possibly she was, he mused, compassion for her welling up in him again. His mother's funeral was bound to have distressed her by reminding her of her own mother's death, and she had nothing to look forward to when she went home except empty rooms. He had no idea how it happened, but when they reached the two-storeyed house at the rear of what had been her father's shop but which she had run for a few years now, his arm was round her waist, and she was saying, as she fitted her key into the lock, 'You'll come in for a cup of tea?'

The fire was set but not lit, and although the May evening was quite warm outside, there was a chill inside – no feeling of welcome. It was the first time he had ever been inside her home, but this room wasn't all that different from his mother's kitchen. There was an almost identical oak dresser with ornaments in its small pigeonholes, a few china plaques on the walls expressing various Victorian sentiments, several pot plants here and there, a fender round the fire with a padded stool at each end and a high-backed armchair at both sides of the hearth. There was one difference, though. Where the Ritchies had a neat tartan rug thrown over their worn couch, Carrie Fraser had used an old curtain, faded so much by the sun that it looked as if it were striped – a washed-out crimson and a pinkish white.

Flopping down on this, Lexie gave a sigh and stretched out her legs. 'Oh, Al, I'm sorry I forgot. It wasn't worth lighting the fire when I was going to be out all day, but once I put a match to it, the kettle'll not take long to boil.'

He pushed away the insidious thought that she *had* remembered that the fire wasn't lit and this was an excuse to keep him with her a little longer. She was so upset, it wasn't fair to doubt her. 'I'll light it.' He took a box of matches from his jacket pocket, struck one and held it to the paper in the grate. After blowing on it for a few seconds to make sure it was properly kindled, he turned to her again. 'Would you mind if I smoked?'

'I always loved the smell of your cigarettes,' she smiled, 'so sit down beside me and smoke as many as you want.'

Unwilling to upset her by sitting anywhere else, he edged down on the couch, lit one of his Gold Flakes and leaned back. He'd had a gruelling day himself and was glad of the rest. 'Never mind about making tea,' he told her in a minute. 'I'd better not stay, or Dad and Alice'll think I'm lost. I'll just finish this and get going.' He looked around for an ashtray but couldn't see one.

Lexie understood his predicament. 'Just put your ash in the begonia,' she told him. 'There's no rush for you to get home, is there? I'd be glad of a bit of company for a while, for I feel a bit lost.' She turned to him, appealing, 'Please, Al?'

Even in the dimness of the kitchen, he could see the anguish in her pale blue eyes. She wasn't shamming. She *was* lonely. She *did* need comfort. And he hadn't had any real comfort himself since he came back to Forvit. His father and sister were both too wrapped up in their own grief to worry about his. 'Come here,' he said, gruffly, putting his arms round her and pulling her close.

She wasn't pushy this time. She lay against him passively, the tears trickling down her cheeks until he could stand her misery no longer. 'Oh, Lexie,' he murmured, 'I know how you're feeling. It's a terrible thing to lose your mother, but we all have to go some time.' Realizing that this was unlikely to give any solace, he made up for his insensitivity by bending his head to kiss her.

On his way home on the train next day, he was beset with shame at what had happened. It had been his fault, not Lexie's, because even now he could remember how his body had responded to the arching of her back. With Gwen being so far on in her pregnancy, he hadn't touched her for weeks and Lexie's lips were so sweet, the old remembered smell of her so heady, that he'd been utterly lost.

He had unbuttoned her blouse, kissed away her faint murmur of protest and fondled her hungrily. Oh, the bitter shame of letting lust overrule sense. She hadn't encouraged him. On the other hand, she hadn't *dis*couraged him, either, and it hadn't been until he was a hair's-breadth away from the unthinkable that it seemed to dawn on her what he was doing and she started pounding at his chest. That was when his sanity had returned.

He had almost thrown her from him and, in spite of her flood of tears and bitter pleadings not to leave her like this, he *had* left her, and had run like a wild thing until a stitch in his side forced him to stop. He had leant against a tree to get his breath back and slowly slid down until he was sitting on the mossy grass at the roadside, where he had remained for well over an hour. It had taken him that long to get himself in a fit enough state to go home. His father wouldn't have noticed anything amiss if he was flushed to the gills and looked guilty as hell, but Alice would have spotted right away that something was up and demanded to know what had happened.

They were both in bed by the time he reached Benview, and, in the morning, he was able to answer his sister's query as to why he'd been so late in coming home the night before with a half-truth. 'Lexie asked me in for a cup of tea.' He had half expected her to torment him about taking so long to drink it, but she'd let it go, thank goodness.

Feeling his eyes weary – his guilt hadn't let him sleep much – he closed them for a moment, and the next thing he knew the train had arrived at King's Cross. He'd still been awake at Newcastle, but he must have dropped off and slept through the commotion of all the other stations they'd stopped at. The rest had done him good, though; he felt better now.

On the way to Guilford Street, he came to the conclusion that he had overreacted to what he had done to Lexie. He had maybe gone a wee bit further than he should have, but he'd thought it was what she wanted. It was her own fault, and she shouldn't have got in such a state, battering at him like he was trying to kill her, though it was just as well she had. If she hadn't stopped him . . . by God it didn't bear thinking about, and thank goodness there was no chance that Gwen would ever hear about it. Lexie would never belittle herself by telling anyone, for it had been a proper fiasco.

As he had done ever since he moved into the hotel, he entered by the area steps and, as soon as he went into the kitchen, Tiny said, with a touch of sarcasm, 'So Daddy's home at last?'

It was a second or two before Alistair understood. 'You mean Gwen's had the baby already? Is she all right? Is *it* all right? Is it a boy or a girl?'

Before his father-in-law could answer, Peggy walked in,

excitement making her more forthcoming than normal. 'Go up and see your daughter right this minute, Alistair. She's absolutely gorgeous.'

He took the stairs two at a time, passing Rosie without a word, his heart swelling with love for his wife when he burst into their room and saw her lying in bed looking as sweet as she always did, just a fraction paler, more fragile.

She held a finger to her lips. 'Don't make a noise, Alistair. She's asleep.'

He tiptoed across the room to kiss her. 'When was it? Was it bad? I wish I'd been here for you.'

'She was born yesterday and it wasn't too bad. Everything went as it should. Don't you want to look at her?'

Peggy hadn't exaggerated, he discovered. He had never seen such a beautiful infant before. No hair as such, of course, just a fuzz of fair down which suggested that she'd be blonde like Gwen and him, a teeny red, wrinkled face, minute hands perfectly formed and opening and closing as if searching for something to hold. She captivated him for ever by grabbing the finger he obliged with and opening her eyes. 'She looked at me,' he crowed, 'and her eyes are as blue as cornflowers.'

'All babies' eyes are blue for the first few weeks,' observed Rosie who came in at that moment with a tea tray in her hand.

'She's like a little doll,' he breathed.

'You won't think that for long,' laughed Gwen. 'Wait till you hear her bawling.'

Rosie grinned. 'She can definitely make herself heard, but you must be hungry, Alistair, and I kept some dinner for you.'

He tore himself away from his daughter to go down to the kitchen where they always had their meals, the dining room being kept for the guests, but he couldn't eat very much, he was so pleased with the tiny being he had created . . . with a little help, of course. In less than half an hour, therefore, he was racing back to see her, and his heart contracted when he saw his wife with the infant in her arms. They made a perfect picture of Madonna and Child.

'Why don't you lay her down again?' Gwen asked, holding the small bundle out to him. 'I've just fed her and she's fast asleep.'

In holding his tiny daughter, even for the short time it took to put her back in her cot, Alistair experienced an emotion like no other he had ever felt. The sheer depth of it filled him with awe. It was as if he were looking down upon the innermost part of his being.

'How did things go in Forvit?' Gwen asked, as he straightened up. 'I'm sorry, I should have asked before, but . . .'

'Don't worry about it, everything went off quite well. Dad's real down, as you'd imagine, but Alice says she wants to stay at home to look after him.'

'That's good. It'll stop you fretting about him.'

Sitting down on the edge of the bed, Alistair took her gently in his arms. 'I didn't think it would be possible to love you more than I did before, but . . . now you've given me such a lovely daughter . . .'

Her kiss stopped him, and all he could think of for some time was how lucky he was.

His wife drew away at last, stroking his cheek as she said, 'We'd better choose a name for our little one. Any ideas?'

'No, nothing. I'll leave it up to you, seeing she's a girl.'

'I'd like to give her a name to herself, not after relatives, and the midwife who attended me was really nice, so I asked her name and she said Chantal, her mother was French. It's spelled C-H-A-N-T-A-L. Unusual, but nice I think.'

After just a moment's thought, Alistair said, 'You know how folk shorten or change names, somebody might make it . . . Chanty.' He pronounced the ch as in cheese, not, as it should be, as in shell.

'What's wrong with that?'

He smiled apologetically. 'It's what folk in Forvit call a chamber pot.'

Gwen gave an embarrassed chuckle. 'That won't do, then. The only other one I thought of was one I saw in a magazine once. Leila. That couldn't be changed much?'

'I suppose somebody might say Lee, but it wouldn't matter, would it?'

'I'd prefer if they didn't, but it wouldn't be so bad. So that's settled, is it?'

'What's settled?' asked Dougal as he and Marge walked in. 'We did knock,' he added, as an afterthought.

'Your mother's name was Isabella, wasn't it?' Gwen asked then. 'So how does Leila Isabella . . . Rose strike you?'

Marge clapped her hands. 'That's great. Leila Isabella Rose. It has a ring to it.'

Dougal slapped his pal's back. 'I think we should go down and get Granddaddy to wet the baby's head with us, then we could go out for a wee stroll.'

'You've started something,' he began, when they left the hotel some twenty minutes later, Alistair having flatly refused to take more than one drink with Tiny. 'Marge has gone all broody on me.'

'Ach, your turn'll come, maybe it's better to wait, though I'm not sorry *we* didn't.'

'I'm forgetting to ask. Did the funeral go off all right? How's your father?'

'He took it bad, Dougal, but Alice is going to keep house for him.'

'That's good. Um . . . did you see Lexie Fraser?'

After an infinitesimal hesitation, Alistair nodded. 'Aye, she was there and Alice made me walk her home.'

The twinkle reappeared in Dougal's eyes. 'Did she try to get you to . . . ?'

'She didn't try anything, it was me.' He could have bitten his tongue out for the slip.

'*You* tried?' Dougal was shocked. 'But I thought you didn't even like her.'

'I never said I didn't like her, I was fed up with the way she was going on at me.'

'So she didn't go on at you this time, but you did what she's aye wanted? Good God Almighty, Ally, what were you thinking about? She'll tell the whole place . . .'

'She'll not tell anybody anything. You see, I didn't actually . . .'

'That wouldn't stop her from telling folk you did.'

'She's changed, Dougal. She's not as forward as she used to be, she wasn't forward at all. In fact, I was real sorry for her.'

'You'd a lucky escape, boy. Think what could have happened if you *had* done it.'

'I know, I know. It doesn't bear thinking about.'

'Did you get a chance to speak to my Mam or Dad?'

'Just for a minute or two. They were both looking well, I thought, and saying how pleased they were at seeing Marge at Easter.'

For the remainder of their short walk, Dougal asked after their old school friends and Alistair told him what he had learned about them, sometimes reminiscing about the exploits they and their 'chums' had got up to.

Lying beside his sleeping wife later, it occurred to Alistair that Dougal had always been the ringleader, and that he had always followed on, done what Dougal had done or told him to do. For once in his life, though, he had achieved something before Dougal managed it. He had made a daughter, the loveliest daughter any man could ever wish for. He had never knowingly felt jealous of Dougal at any time over all the years they'd been pals, yet it gave him a kick to feel that he was his own man at last.

'Congratulations, Alistair, my boy!'

Manny's welcoming words took his assistant aback. He had wanted to tell the good news himself. 'Do not look so surprised,' the old man laughed. 'I am not psychic. Your charming sister-in-law came to tell me about your daughter. Well done! But you will have to make a son before you have a gentleman's family. How is dear Gwen? I do not suppose that she is thinking, just yet, of having any more children?'

'I shouldn't think so, but she seems quite well. She said she didn't have too bad a time.'

'I believe that women usually play down what they suffer during childbirth. It is a time for the exclusion of men.'

'Did you never want children, Manny?'

'Anna and I both wanted babies, but it was not to be.' The pawnbroker averted his head for a moment, obviously to hide his sadness, but it wasn't long before he was smiling again. 'I was so pleased when Marge gave me the news that I closed the shop and went out in search of a gift for the little one. Wait and see what I found!'

He took a square wine-velvet-covered box from his safe and laid it on the counter. 'Open it, Alistair.'

Nestling amidst some pale pink cotton wool was a gold bangle which the new father removed reverently. 'Oh, Manny, you shouldn't have. I know you didn't pick this up in any of the markets. It's brand new, isn't it?'

'I have taught you too well, my boy. Yes, it is brand new, as befits a brand new baby, and when you have chosen a name for her, I will have it engraved inside. It is adjustable, and will fit her even when she is a grown woman.'

'Oh, Manny.' Alistair felt all choked up. 'The things you

think of . . . but you really shouldn't.'

'Let me know when you have chosen her name . . .'

'It's Leila. We chose it last night – Leila Isabella Rose, after the two grandmothers.'

Manny nodded his approval of this. 'Leila Isabella Rose. Yes, that rolls off the tongue very nicely. Now, when your dear wife is feeling up to it, tell her to bring little Leila Isabella Rose here to let me see her.'

It was on the point of Alistair's tongue to ask his employer to be godfather, and then he wondered how a Jew would fit into a Church of England ceremony. Come to that, he thought, how would a Church of Scotland man fit in? He knew nothing of the ways of the Episcopalian church. In any case, Gwen would likely want Marge to be godmother and Dougal to be godfather, so he had better not make any ripples by suggesting Manny.

When he went up to Gwen that night, his employer having made him swear to say nothing about the bangle, he was delighted when she said, 'I was thinking after you went to work. Manny's always been so good to us, we should ask him to the christening.'

'That's a lovely idea, my darling, and he wants to see her, as soon as you're fit to take her to the shop.'

'I'm supposed to stay in bed for ten days, so it'll be more than two weeks before I can walk as far as that. Marge could take her, though.'

'He wants to see you as well.'

'Say I'll come two weeks on Wednesday. That's not one of your busy days is it?'

'No, that'll be ideal.'

Damn Alice Ritchie, Lexie thought. She had been getting over the upset of Bella's funeral and what Alistair had done – or more like it, not done – and his sister had stirred it up again. He'd become a father while he'd been in Forvit, maybe at the very time he'd been with her, kissing her, raising her hopes that he did want her, and she had spoiled it with her stupid fear. But now, even if he could tear himself away from his wife, he wouldn't want to leave his daughter. Not for a few years.

She was still prepared to wait, though. However long it took him to realize that she was the one he really loved, she would be here for him. From what Alice had said, he was having to do odd jobs in his father-in-law's hotel after he finished work for the Jew every day, and he would soon get fed up of that. And if the bairn, as most bairns do, kept them awake at nights, that would tell on him, as well. His body would rebel; he would start to get short-tempered with his wife and fall out with her . . .

Yes, it would be worth while to wait . . . like a cat at a mousehole, like a spider in its web. He was bound to fall into her trap . . . not that she considered it a trap and nor would he by that time. His marriage would have fallen apart, his heart would be broken and she'd be there to pick up the pieces.

Chapter 7

'You're useless, Dougal Finnie! D' you know that? Absolutely, bally useless!' Marge glared at her husband. 'Gwen's had her second and you haven't even managed to make one! We've been married for two years, for goodness' sake.'

'It could be your fault.' He felt obliged to make this quite clear.

'Not mine,' she sneered. 'Nobody in my family's ever had problems having a baby.'

'Nor in mine,' he snapped. 'I've a sister in America, and Mam had another son that died when he was three, so there was three of us, the same as you Jenkinses. One thing, you can't say I haven't tried, can you?'

She gave a tight little smile. 'No, I can't say that.' Capitulating suddenly, she sighed, 'I really do wish we could have a baby, Dougal. Don't you?'

'You know I do, my darling.'

As he made ready to go down to breakfast, however, he wasn't quite sure that he did want a baby, after all. They seemed to cause an awful upheaval in people's lives. Look at Alistair. He'd had precious little sleep for months after Leila was born, she'd been a fractious wee toot, and she'd just settled into a normal routine when the new one made its debut . . . correction, his debut. Ally had never shown much sign of gumption let alone a powerful sexual drive, yet he'd put his wife up the bloody spout twice in little more than a year. He didn't need to be so cock-o'-the-walk because this one was a boy, though. He wasn't the only man on earth to make a son . . . and by God, Dougal Finnie would give his eyeteeth to be in their brotherhood. But he'd better go downstairs before Marge came up again reading the riot act.

They were all seated round the table when he entered the kitchen, and Peggy was saying, 'Thank goodness it's over! I didn't get any sleep for the noise Gwen was making. I thought she was in the throes of death.'

Dougal couldn't resist teasing her. 'I didn't know dying people kicked up a noise.'

She tossed her head, then a loud knock on the door made her jump up. 'I'll go.'

'I wonder who that can be?' Rosie remarked. 'The post came half an hour ago.'

'It's a telegram,' Peggy announced as she came in again, 'for Alistair.'

Watching the blood drain from her son-in-law's face as he read it, Rosie asked, anxiously, 'Is it your father?'

Willie Ritchie's foot had been punctured some weeks ago by one of the tines of a harrow. He had tried to kick away a stone in its path but hadn't been quick enough to get out of the way himself. The resulting wound had never healed properly, but Alice's last note, saying that he was quite poorly, hadn't prepared her brother for this. 'He died yesterday,' Alistair moaned. 'Oh, God, I should have gone home to see him when she told me about it first.'

'You weren't to know this would happen.' Rosie was always on hand to soothe and comfort her small brood if anything untoward happened.

'I should have thought,' he persisted. 'The spikes would've been coated with earth and dung, and the poison must have gone right through him.' He turned to Dougal. 'The same as old Robbie Rankin, remember, Dougal? About five years ago?' Alistair looked at Rosie in anguish. 'I can't leave Gwen just now.'

'You have to go,' she said quietly. 'You can't miss your father's funeral. Gwen's got all of us to look after her, and your sister's got nobody.'

'She's got lots of friends, and I know you're worried about Gwen.'

Rosie looked away for a moment, then admitted, 'She's not too good. The doctor's coming back today, but I'll take care of her. There's no need for you to be here . . .'

'There's every need for me to be here,' he cried. 'Good God, Rosie, if anything happened to her and I was hundreds of miles away, I'd never forgive myself.'

She met his eyes now. 'Perhaps you're right.'

Dougal offered to send a telegram to Alice, and after carrying out that duty, he went to tell Manny Isaacson that Alistair would be off work that day. 'Gwen's quite ill,' he explained. 'It wasn't such an easy birth this time. The baby's OK, but . . .'

'Oh, that poor girl. I shall pray for her speedy recovery . . .'

'And another thing,' Dougal went on, 'Alistair got word this morning that his father had died, but he's not going to the funeral . . . because of Gwen, you understand?'

The old man was obviously shaken by this further bad news, and it was only when Dougal was leaving that he rallied enough to say, 'I am so very glad that the infant is all right. Is it a boy or a girl?'

'A boy.'

'The gentleman's family . . . but the two events to occur at the same time . . . it must be a truly traumatic time for Alistair. Please convey my heartfelt sympathy for him at the loss of his father, and tell him that I shall not expect him back to work until his dear wife's health has improved.'

* * *

Tiny having put on so much weight – he was over the twenty-stone limit of their household scales – Rosie asked Dougal if he would mind doing something for her.

'Anything,' he grinned. 'Your wish is my command, madame.'

'Cheeky!' she smiled back. 'It's for Alistair really. I should have thought of it before, but with all the worry . . . You know the lumber room up on the top floor? There's an old bed-chair there. We bought it for Tiny's father when his wife was in hospital, though she was only in two weeks when she died and he went back to Swansea. That was the only time it was used. Sadly, he didn't last long himself, after that.'

'Alistair doesn't need a bed-chair,' Gwen protested weakly. 'He'll sleep with me.'

'He will not!' declared Rosie. 'You need all the rest you can get and so does he.'

But Gwen was adamant that he wouldn't disturb her, that she would prefer to feel him beside her if she woke in the night, and so the unwieldy old wooden bed-chair was left in state in the lumber room, to have further dust added to that which had already accumulated over the past fifteen years.

Despite his wife's protests, Alistair did spend a two-night vigil in a rickety basket chair by the bed, afraid to sleep, even for only a few minutes, in case she needed him. It was a full week before the doctor pronounced her out of danger and the whole household breathed a deep sigh of relief. Alistair, gaunt and hollow-eyed, cried, 'Thank God!' and bent to kiss her pale, sunken cheek before practically collapsing on to the bed at her side.

When Alistair saw his sister's writing on the envelope the following morning, he said, 'This is it! A telling-off for not going up for the funeral.' But it wasn't.

Dear Alistair,

It's a shame you couldn't get to the funeral, but I do understand and I hope Gwen's much better by now. A lot of folk turned up, for Dad was well liked, and most of them asked about you, especially Lexie Fraser. She and Meg McIntosh helped me with the funeral tea, I'd have been lost without them.

Dad has left me enough money to see me through the university, but I haven't made my mind up yet if I still want to go. I'm not really over things, for it was a bit sudden at the end. Oh, and I nearly forgot. He left the house between us but he told me he knew you wouldn't want to leave London, and I'm to stay here as long as I want. I hope that's all right with you.

You'll both be tickled pink it's a boy this time, though it's a pity Dad didn't know he had a grandson. Have you picked a name yet?

Give my love to Gwen, and kiss Leila and her baby brother for me. I hope I'll be able to see them some time soon. Your loving sister, Alice.

'Who's Lexie Fraser?' Gwen wanted to know, after she read the letter.

'Just a girl Dougal and I went to school with.'

'She didn't ask about him, though?'

'I suppose . . . I suppose she knew me best.'

'In other words, she was the girlfriend you told me about. Don't blush, Alistair, I'm not angry or jealous. Was she the only one?'

'Yes, she was,' he muttered, thinking that it sounded even more damning than if he had confessed to a whole harem.

'Ah,' his wife said, thoughtfully, 'how long were you and she . . . ?'

'It wasn't the way you think. We were still at school when we started going out for walks and there was nothing in it, till . . .' He halted, shaking his head. 'No, there never was anything in it, Gwen, darling, not on my side. She would have liked there to be, that was the trouble. I came to London with Dougal to get away from her.'

A delighted smile lit up Gwen's pale face. 'So I've Lexie Fraser to thank for having you as my husband?'

'I suppose you could put it like that. One thing's for sure. I would never have married her, whatever she thinks . . . thought.'

'You believe she might still be hoping?'

'No, of course not. I hope you don't think . . . I'd never look at another woman, ever!'

'I know that, my dear. I'm only teasing. But getting back to Alice's letter, we'll have to think of a name for our little man.'

'I used to think I'd like to call my son after Dougal,' Alistair began, but Gwen's last two words had given him a new idea. 'Back home, young mothers often spoke about a baby boy as 'my wee mannie' – it was an affectionate term, you know? – and though I know you wouldn't want to call him Emanuel, that's Manny's real name, his sign says E.D. Isaacson, so what if I ask him what the D stands for?'

The pawnbroker was so overwhelmed with emotion when he learned why he was asked his middle name that his assistant feared he might have a heart attack, but he didn't take long to pull himself more or less together. 'This is truly a great honour for me,' he murmured after a brief pause. 'No one has ever . . .' He stopped again to regain his still wavering composure, filling the awkward moments by opening his safe and taking out a gold wrist watch. 'I bought this as soon as Dougal told me that your Gwen had given birth to a son, but I wish now that it had been something more suitable for an infant.'

Alistair, too, now had difficulty in remaining calm, and his voice trembled a little as he said, 'Manny, that watch is something he can cherish for the rest of his life. You couldn't have bought him anything more fitting . . . though you shouldn't have.'

The elderly man wiped a tear from the corner of his eye with his thumb. 'You do not understand. As you know, my Anna and I were not blessed with children, and it is so long since I lost her . . . I have had no one, except you. You are the son I never had, Alistair, your Gwen is my daughter-in-law and your children are my grandchildren. You have made my life complete, so please do not be angry with me for buying gifts.'

'I'm not angry, Manny, please don't think that. I just felt it wasn't right for you to spend your money on us when you had your mind set on buying bigger premises. You'll never get your antique shop at this rate.'

'Antique shop?' Manny snapped his fingers. 'Poof! What is a shop full of the most expensive antiques in the world compared with the happiness I feel at being able to do something for your two precious little cherubs.'

And so David (Manny's middle name) William (after Alistair's late father) Trevor (after Tiny) was christened, and Manny having declined to act as godfather because of the difference in religion, Alistair paid tribute to Ivy and Len Crocker by asking them to be godparents. Both vowed to take their duty seriously, but during the meal, Ivy had them all laughing by keeping up a teasing conversation with Tiny who gave as good as he got.

At four o'clock, when Rosie, Peggy and Marge were downstairs in the kitchen tidying up, and Tiny, Dougal, Manny and Len were engaged in a discussion on politics, Gwen said, 'Shall I fetch the baby down, Ivy, so you can see him properly?'

'Ooh, yes please! I'd love to see both the little lambs.' She waited until the younger woman had left the room and then leaned over towards Alistair. 'You haven't half done well, Al, but I knew you had it in you, when you were lodging with me.' She covered her mouth momentarily to suppress a giggle. 'Oh, my Gawd! I nearly said when we were living together! Now that would have been something, wouldn't it?'

He could only respond in the same vein. 'Aye, it would that, though you were so randy you'd have exhausted me.' It was easy to laugh with her now. She couldn't help herself and she probably didn't mean half of what she said. 'I wouldn't have had enough stamina left to make any babies with Gwen.'

A wistfulness crept momentarily into her eyes, then, in a quick change of mood, she said, 'I'm really glad for you, Al, love. You deserve the best.'

'And I've got it,' he assured her, looking up as his family entered the room – his darling wife, looking radiant in a London tan woollen costume and carrying a bundle swaddled in a lacy shawl, with their beautiful daughter hanging on to her skirt. Leila was obviously newly awake, her eyes still hazy with sleep, but she soon perked up.

'She's so lovely,' cooed Ivy, who had seen her regularly since she was born. Diving into her handbag now, she extracted a small parcel which she handed to the little girl. 'I can't give your brother a present without giving you something, too, can I?'

The fifteen-month-old shook her head gravely and tore off the paper to see what was inside, then without saying anything she toddled into the hall and they could hear her feet slowly negotiating the stairs to the kitchen. 'It was only a rag doll,' Ivy said in concerned apology. 'Didn't she like it?'

'She loved it,' Gwen smiled. 'She's taken it down to let her Grandma see it.'

Ivy was reassured in a few moments when Rosie came in carrying the little girl, followed by Marge and Peggy, and for the next half hour or so, attention centred on Leila, who was adept at playing to an audience. Needing only little encouragement, she recited several nursery rhymes, missing some words and getting others wrong, sang 'Twinkle, Twinkle Little Star' – which came out as 'Tinka, tinka, icka tah' – three times and 'Umpy Dumpy satta wo', twice. To follow this, making it a mammoth production, she executed little dances her Auntie Peggy had taught her and then proved that the show was over by saying, as she climbed on to Rosie's knee, 'Aw done, Gamma.'

Baby David, as though aware that his sister was stealing the limelight although this should have been his day, slept through all her antics cradled against Ivy Crocker's ample bosom, and the party, as it had become, broke up just after five o'clock.

'Thank God that's all over!' said Marge, a little testily, after the guests had gone.

'Yes, it's been some day,' Tiny agreed.

Gwen looked keenly at her sister but said nothing until she and Alistair were in bed. 'I think Marge's jealous,' she told him. 'She's desperate for a baby.'

'So Dougal's been saying, but it's something you can't arrange to order.'

'I don't like to ask, but would he be . . .?' She paused. 'Could he have lost interest in . . . that side of things?'

Alistair had to laugh at this. 'Not Dougal, I can assure you of that.'

1935 had just begun when Tiny collapsed. The hotel had been closed on Christmas Day, but he had prepared an impressive dinner for his extended family, and despite Rosie's warnings not to overdo it at his age – 'You're sixty-seven, for goodness' sake, and would be retired if you'd been working for a boss' – he wouldn't let anyone help him. He produced another feast for New Year's Day but the upset of him being rushed to hospital as they were about to sit down to the meal banished everyone's appetite.

He hovered on the brink of death for twenty-one hours, and just when his wife and daughters thought that having survived the heart attack for so long he would pull through, he slipped effortlessly away.

Both Alistair and Dougal had their work cut out trying to comfort the three sisters, but Rosie, who had lost her partner of thirty-five years, was the calmest of them all. She told her sons-in-law to register the death and contact the undertakers so that the funeral could be arranged, then she sat dry-eyed and holding herself as erect as she had always done, seemingly impervious to her husband's demise, or more probably, unable to take it in.

The birth of Alistair's second child had made Lexie Fraser take stock of her situation. There didn't seem to be any chance of him leaving his wife, not now they had two children, and it had begun to be very painful to think of him, excruciating even to try to picture him with his expanding family. Alice had shown her a studio portrait he'd sent of his wife cuddling an infant in a christening robe, Alistair standing behind her chair with a fair-haired little girl in his arms, which had haunted her waking hours and disrupted her nights for weeks.

The pain was easing a little, but something else had reared up in her mind, something she had pushed resolutely away over the years since her father's disappearance. At the time, having been so angry and upset by the lack of interest shown by the police, she had been unable to think of anything else, yet there had always been this feeling of . . . She couldn't remember if it had been fear, or pain, or what, and she had filed it away during the years she'd had her mind on Alistair, but there was no one now to help her.

The doctor – Dr Birnie, it was, or Dr Tom as he'd affectionately been known – had done his best to comfort both her and her mother, but he had left Forvit a few months afterwards. He hadn't wanted to go, but his mother-in-law had had a slight heart attack, and his wife, the elder daughter – the younger had been working in America – had gone to Stirling to look after her. After a few days, she had told Dr Tom on the phone that she wanted them to move there permanently. He'd had to find a replacement before he could go, of course, and had been most apologetic to all his patients, more so, perhaps, to her mother and her, Lexie mused.

Because she was so young at the time he left, and hadn't yet recovered from the shock of losing her father and the stories that still circulated about him, she had fastened on Alistair with such intensity that she had scared him off, and she had blamed her heartache on his desertion of her. Just once, while she was struggling to cope with that agony, had a picture flashed through her mind.

It had been gone in an instant, and she hadn't been really sure if it was of something that had actually happened or if it had been a dream, a nightmarish dream. She didn't want to think about it. She had the feeling that it was something horrible, something so nasty it would change her life for ever, so it was probably a good thing that she couldn't recall exactly what had taken place, or when. She could remember the bobby being there, and the doctor giving her mother sleeping pills with the caution, 'They're pretty potent, so wait until you are in bed before taking them.'

She had been given two, as well, and it was just as well she'd heard that caution, because she must have gone out like a light seconds after swallowing them.

Lexie gave a shivery sigh. She didn't like dwelling on that awful time, it was too disturbing for her, so she turned her mind once again to her present circumstances. She desperately needed someone to depend on, to gather comfort from, and with there being no chance of Alistair ever coming back to her now, she had better look elsewhere. Most of the boys she had been at school with were either married or had found work in some of the big industrial cities in the south. Only two were still bachelors and still living at home – Gibby Mearns and Freddie McBain, neither particularly good-looking, but both with steady jobs in Aberdeen. Gibby, the postie's oldest son, drove a long-distance lorry for a large haulage company, and Freddie worked in the office of one of the shipyards.

Yes, one of them would be her best bet. She wasn't cut out to be an old maid.

Chapter 8

The hotel had been closed for exactly ten days when Rosie, matriarch now, the unrelieved black of her apparel emphasizing her pallor, called her family together.

'I want you to listen and weigh up everything carefully before you say anything,' she instructed them, looking at her three daughters in turn because it was from them that the inevitable arguments would come. 'I know your father only did the cooking . . .' She waved away what Marge was trying to say, and went on, '. . . but it was the meals he produced that brought people back, the kind of meals that only the top hotels could offer, and at half the price. That was why we'd a clientele of company reps and businessmen, and I can't hope to continue that. Your father was a Regimental Cook Sergeant when he married me, so he wouldn't let me do anything except serve, and even if I could probably manage to provide good plain fare, that's not what the hotel was famed for.'

The alarmed glance which passed between Gwen and Marge made her add, a little sadly, 'I see you can guess what's coming. I'm going to sell the hotel and buy a decent-sized house so we can still all be together.'

Marge could hold her concern at bay no longer. 'But, Mum, all you have to do is engage a good chef, and we'll all help you to carry on, Gwen and Peg and me. I know it won't be the same for you, but we'll manage, I'm sure we will.'

With a shake of her head, Rosie said, firmly, 'Just managing isn't enough. In any case, I couldn't afford even a mediocre chef, so it would fall to me, and if I'm tied up all day in the kitchen who'll keep account of things – what each guest is due, what we owe the tradesmen at the end of each month, order the provisions, make the guests feel at home? Who'll listen to their troubles, comfort them if their wives have been unfaithful, or left them, or died? That was a big part of what I did over the years.'

'We could do that,' persisted Marge, 'and you could show us how to do the rest.'

'I wouldn't have time, and there's something else to consider. You and Peggy will eventually have children, too, and a hotel isn't a place to bring up families . . .' She broke off, pausing long enough to compose herself, but such was the impact of what she had told them that none of them said a word.

After only a few seconds, she continued, 'What we get for it should buy a fairly big house with a garden for the little ones to play in.' She looked at her middle daughter again, waiting for further objections, but she had lapsed into silence, and Rosie hoped that she hadn't upset her by speaking about gardens for the little ones. She had thought that Marge and Dougal were purposely waiting a few years before they had children, but maybe they *had* been trying. Poor Marge! A change of home, and not having to work so hard every day, might do the trick.

Rosie felt better now. 'I think it would cheer us all up. A more modern house, with a good-sized garden, away from all the traffic and bustle. We'd need six bedrooms at least – one for Gwen and Alistair, one for Marge and Dougal, one for . . .'

'You don't have to worry about Marge and me, Rosie,' Dougal put in, as if he knew what she'd been thinking a moment or so earlier. 'I've enough laid by to put down a deposit for a nice wee place of our own. I've been thinking about it for a good while, but I didn't like to say anything in case you thought I wasn't happy here.'

'But don't you want us to stay together?' Rosie was bewildered now. She had never imagined that her attempt to keep the family round her would result in splitting it up.

'We don't need to be living in each other's pockets to be close,' Dougal persisted. 'We can still see you regularly, and you wouldn't have to buy such a big house.'

Alistair shot a silent question at Gwen and got a nodding reply. 'We were thinking of renting a place,' he told his mother-in-law, hesitantly, 'to be on our own, you know?'

This double blow left Rosie nonplussed, so it fell to Peggy to pour oil on the troubled waters. 'I think it's a good idea for us all to live our own lives. I used to get tired of you two bossing me about . . .' She gave a faint smile to show that she bore no grudge. 'Mum and I'll still be together and I can take a job somewhere to help out with expenses.'

Rosie heaved a sigh of resignation. 'I suppose . . . if that's what everybody wants?'

A sharp wail from upstairs made Alistair jump up. 'That'll be David, likely.' As he passed his mother-in-law to attend to his son, he gripped her shoulder reassuringly. 'It'll work out fine, Rosie. Dougal and I'll be masters in our own homes, and if you want us to do something for you at any time, you'll only have to let us know.'

'I feel awful,' Alistair admitted to Manny the following day after telling him what had transpired. 'Are we being selfish? Is Rosie right? Are we splitting up her family?'

As usual, Manny gave his manager's troubles his full consideration. 'It is difficult to say, my boy. From her point of view, you probably are, but you can prove it otherwise if you visit her frequently and issue an open invitation for her to visit you. From what I have seen of your mother-in-law, she is not an unreasonable woman, and she will realize that you and Dougal need to have time alone with your wives, and as long as you let her see her grandchildren as often as she wants, she should be satisfied. In any case, things may change. Tiny's death, coming when there was hope of him pulling through, was bound to have unsettled all of you, and when Rosie is able to think rationally, she may not want to give up the hotel at all.'

Alistair shook his head. 'No, her mind's definitely made up about that, and she's quite right, you know. I don't think it would be the same without Tiny in the kitchen and her at the helm, but you'd better not let Gwen or Marge know I've said that.'

The next three months were extremely busy for the Jenkins family, especially Rosie. She took to visiting estate agents with Peggy, asking to view any houses they had for sale, but found nothing that attracted her. They were all too small to her mind, although Peggy said they were big enough for the two of them.

It was Dougal who first found what he was looking for. 'One of the despatch clerks says his parents have booked one of the houses going up in Lee Green,' he told Alistair. 'It's a bit out, but I'm going to have a look at them on Sunday. Fancy coming?'

He hadn't wanted Rosie to know but Marge let it slip, and so the whole 'shebang of them', as Dougal put it, made the journey to SE 12. The neat semi-detached villas made a deep impression, each with a small patch in front for a garden, and a much larger piece at the rear. Going into the show house, completely fitted out so that prospective buyers would have a clearer picture of the possibilities, they discovered that the ground floor consisted of a square lounge at the front, a smaller living room behind it, and alongside that, a scullery with a door into the 'garden'. Upstairs were two decent-sized bedrooms, and, reminding Dougal and Alistair of the Crockers' house in Hackney, a separate tiny lavatory and a narrow bathroom.

Most of the houses in the street were finished, some actually occupied already, but two still had to be painted and the surrounding ground levelled out. 'What d'you think?' Dougal asked Marge, her smile encouraging him to ask the Site Manager for more details.

'Not bad for under £500, eh?' he observed to his wife, as they all trooped along to Hither Green to catch the train back to Russell Square. 'I've got the deposit and I should manage the mortgage, so I put my name down provisionally, is that OK with you?'

She smiled her approval. 'Perfect. I loved the house.'

'The man said I'd better make up my mind quick, because there's only two left.'

The final outcome of the expedition, however, was something Dougal was none too happy about. When he went to the builder's office on the Tuesday to sign the contract, he asked if anyone had bought the last one.

'I was hoping I could persuade you to take it,' he confided to Alistair that evening, 'but I near fell in a heap when the girl said a Mrs Rose Jenkins had been in on Monday morning and settled for it. I ask you, Ally. I thought Marge might be able to conceive once she didn't have to worry about Rosie hearing us, for I think that's what's been wrong though she never said, and now! Speak about living in each other's pockets!'

Alistair couldn't help smiling. Gwen had kept at him to make the commitment, and she'd looked disappointed when he said Woodyates Road was too pricey for him, but Rosie, bless her, had let him off the hook. 'Has she bought the house you're joined on to?' he asked Dougal.

'No, that's one thing I'm thankful for.'

'So Marge'll know her mother can't hear what you get up to in bed, not with the width of two garage runs between your house and hers.'

Rather than put a millstone round his neck, Alistair finally settled on renting an old terraced house – furnished, if a little basically – in Bethnal Green, only a short bus run from Manny's shop. Like Dougal, he had been worrying about furniture, and had warned Gwen that she'd have to put up with second-hand for a while, so all that concerned them now was buying essential household items. Then Rosie told them that there was enough furniture, bed and table linen, dishes and cutlery in the hotel to equip all three houses and still leave enough for the new owners to start off with.

Now came a time of frantically begging for tea chests and crates to pack things in, the three young women making sure that everything was fairly divided and each item marked with its proper destination. Of course, with the amount of upheaval going on, it was not surprising that Leila and David were fretty, and Ivy's offer to keep them from the day before the removals until the day after was gratefully accepted. It certainly wasn't a time to have small children running around under everybody's feet disrupting things.

The more time Lexie Fraser spent with Ernie Gammie, the more she came to like him. He was thoughtful, asked no questions of her and, most important, he was courting her – the only way to describe it – in the good old-fashioned way. He hadn't kissed her until the fourth or fifth time he saw her home, and he hadn't tried anything else even yet, and they'd been keeping company for almost eight weeks now.

Remembering, how that had come about, she gave a satisfied little smile. Over the past six or so months, she had gone out with three other men before Ernie, but once was enough with each of them. As soon as they got her where nobody would see them, she'd had to fight them off, even Gibby Mearns, who had known her since she was five and should have known her better than try. Davie Lovie, the van driver who delivered newspapers to the shop, hadn't been quite so bad, but he hadn't asked her out a second time – probably because she wouldn't let him do what he wanted – and although Freddie McBain had waited until he took her home, he was as determined as the other two to get her flat on her back.

But Ernie wasn't like that. She had been surprised when he walked into the shop that day; and even more astonished when he asked her out; he'd never shown any interest in her before. 'Somebody told me you were married,' she'd replied, to let him know that she knew. It was why he had never entered into her plans.

'Cathy died two years ago.'

'Oh, Ernie, I'm sorry. I could kick myself for . . .'

'No, you were right to say it, and you're the first one I've . . .' He paused, uncertainly, then ended, 'I haven't looked at anyone else since I lost her.'

She learned on their first date that he had joined the Aberdeen Fire Service, that he and his late wife had had no children, and that he was still living in the house in King Street that he had rented when he got married. 'I've been thinking about emigrating,' he had told her, 'to get a new life somewhere different, but I can't make up my mind – especially now things are starting to look up for me again.'

This small compliment – she was sure it was a compliment – was all she had needed to accept his invitation to see a show in Aberdeen, and that had been the first of many truly enjoyable evenings, though it had always been the first house of the Tivoli or the early showing of a film so that they could get a bus back to Forvit.

On their first date, she had said, 'I'll easy manage home on the bus myself.'

He had taken her hand and squeezed it. 'No, I'll see you home. I wrote to my mother to say I'd need a bed there tonight – tomorrow's my day off.'

She was grateful that he had made this arrangement, his father's farm was only a mile and a half off the main road, so he didn't have far to go after he'd seen her inside. And it saved her from worrying whether or not she should ask him to stay over at her house.

She was certain she was doing the right thing at last, and she wished that she had known much earlier that he was free . . . and how nice a man he had turned out to be. Take tonight, for instance. After meeting her at the bus terminus, he had suggested taking a tram to the Bridge of Don and walking along the prom. 'It's too fine a night to be sitting inside a picture house,' he had smiled, and then his expression had changed. 'That's if it's OK with you?' he had asked, anxiously.

'I'd love it,' she had told him, and so she had.

On their stroll, they had talked of this and that, and she'd been tempted to ask about his wife, what kind of woman she was, what she looked like, how she had died, but it was too early yet to be so openly inquisitive. If he felt like telling her, he probably would, though maybe he didn't like to mention what had caused her death. It could have been cancer, and that wasn't something people liked to speak about, though she wouldn't have minded – she'd had long enough experience of it with her mother. It was just another illness, an illness that couldn't be cured, and dying as a result of it was nothing for the family left behind to be ashamed of.

They sat down for a while on one of the benches overlooking the wide expanse of calm sea, dotted here and there with homecoming trawlers making their slow way into the harbour, but one much larger ship made Lexie ask, curiously, 'Why's that big one not moving?'

'It'll be sitting at anchor waiting for the pilot to come and lead it in,' Ernie told her. 'You see, there's all sorts of currents and things that captains from other places have to beware of.'

'Where would that one have come from?'

'It's definitely a foreigner because of the flag, but it's too far out for me to make out which country's it is.'

In another twenty minutes, they were treated to the spectacle of the tiny pilot boat shooting into sight from behind the harbour wall and then turning round to escort the visitor to its allocated berth. Having watched until both vessels were out of sight, Ernie said, 'I think we should make tracks again. We don't want to miss the last bus.'

They walked smartly along to the Bathing Station where they would catch a tram into town, and the air having grown a little colder, he put his arm around her waist as they waited. 'I've been thinking on buying a second-hand car,' he said. 'It would be a lot handier than having to depend on public transport like this. What d'you think?'

'It's not up to me. Can you afford it?'

'Just about, but we could go anywhere and stay out all night if we wanted, too.'

She had nearly said he could stay *inside* all night with her, but she still didn't feel free enough to let him do what he wanted . . . if he wanted it. She would be better to wait to see what developed before making any rash commitments.

Alistair could see that Gwen wasn't happy in their new abode. Even after two months, she was missing her mother and her sisters. 'I didn't realize how much work the children were,' she wailed one evening, while she was washing out the clothes their offspring had been wearing that day. 'Mum or Marge or Peggy always saw to them if I was busy, but now I've got to do the cooking, the washing and ironing, make the beds and do all the cleaning, as well as look after the kids all day.'

Alistair pushed aside the thought that she was blaming him – she knew that they couldn't afford a mortgage like Dougal was paying – but he still felt a wave of indignation at the thought of her lack of effort. 'You've been blooming lucky, you know,' he said, brusquely. 'Not many young mothers have built-in nursemaids like you had at the hotel.'

Noticing her bottom lip trembling, he regretted his brutality. She was right – two infants must be an awful handful, and other mothers would have learned from looking after their first before a second came along, whereas Gwen had been thrown in at the deep end, so to speak. 'I'm sorry, darling. It must be terrible for you on your own all day, but I have to work. I can't leave Manny in the lurch, and we need the money.'

'I know it's not your fault, but I get so tired, and . . .'

'Come here,' he said, gruffly, reaching out and taking her in his arms. He hated to see her crying, especially when he looked at the situation from her side. He was blaming her for not making an effort, but he was just as bad. If he'd really wanted to, he could have bought the house Rosie was now occupying. Paying the mortgage would have been a struggle, but they would have managed, somehow. But . . . it was too late now. 'Let me finish the washing for you, sweetheart,' he murmured against her neck, 'and you can go to bed. An early night should help.'

Left on his own, he dutifully scrubbed, then rinsed, all the little garments and spread them out on the pulley hanging from the scullery ceiling – the weather was too dodgy in October to chance leaving them outside all night – before tackling the napkins which were soaking in a pail. That was when he felt true sympathy for his wife. Fancy having to do this every day, maybe more than once, he thought, screwing up his nose. Wee David wasn't a year old yet, but he smelt like a blinking adult.

Before going home the following night, he made a detour to see Ivy, to tell her how worried he was about his wife, and as he had hoped she would, his former landlady volunteered to have the 'little dears' for an afternoon every week. 'More than one, if she wants,' Ivy had grinned, 'for I could eat them, they're so adorable.'

'We're not so desperate you need to do that,' Alistair laughed, 'and you'd better not let Gwen know I've been talking to you. She's a bit touchy.'

Ivy gave his rear end a playful pat when he turned to leave. 'I'll be the soul of tact, you know me.'

She did more than have the children for an afternoon a week. Working round to it gradually, she got Gwen to admit how tired she always felt, and how much of a struggle it was to get to Lee Green on her own with an infant, a toddler and a bag bulging with nappies for David and a change of clothes for both in case of 'accidents'. This, Gwen explained tearfully, meant that she could only see her mother on Sundays, when Alistair was with her. Not letting the young woman suspect a thing, nor putting any pressure on her, Ivy arranged to accompany her there every Thursday and also to take the children off her hands for the whole of every Monday to let her get her weekly wash done and ironed, weather permitting.

'And so peace reigns once more in the Ritchie household?' Manny queried, amiably.

'Oh yes,' breathed Alistair. 'Gwen's much brighter, and Ivy's tickled pink at having the brats. It's a shame she never had any of her own, she'd have made a good mother.'

'That so often happens. My Anna was the same . . . also your dear sister-in-law,' Manny added, in case his employee thought he was lingering on his own trouble.

'Dougal's awful disappointed that Marge hasn't fallen yet. He doesn't think she'll ever have any, and Rosie keeps asking when they'll hear the patter of tiny feet, so you can imagine tempers are a bit frayed there. As a matter of fact, he's speaking about joining the TA so he can have some peace. He says they train at weekends and have a week's camp in the summer, and he wants me to join, too, but . . . I can't leave Gwen.'

'No, it is different for you,' Manny agreed. 'He can go off with a free mind, knowing that his wife's mother and sister are next door if anything happens, or if she merely wants company. Still, if you did want to go, I am sure Ivy would be only too happy . . .'

'I couldn't ask her to do any more, she's been so good to us already. I don't suppose she'd mind, but I don't want to take advantage of her.'

'You are right, my boy.' Manny lifted his black homburg and settled it comfortably on his head. 'I may not come back until afternoon sometime,' he said, as he opened the door. 'Billy Ternent has asked me to have a look at some property he is thinking of buying.'

As he made his way to the bus stop, he pondered over what he had been told. He was always glad when Alistair confided in him; it took his mind off the worry which had been growing in his mind of late. No word had appeared in the newspapers, but it had begun to filter through by word of mouth that Adolf Hitler had been clearing the Jews out of Germany since he came to power, and so deep was his fixation against them, apparently, that there was every likelihood of him doing the same in Britain if he ever got the chance.

No! Manny scolded himself, he must stop fretting about something that may never happen, and think of a way to help poor little Gwen. It was only natural, never having been separated from them before, that she was missing her mother and sisters, as Alistair should have realized, but what could be done about it?

David had newly been bathed and changed when he filled his nappy, and Gwen felt quite irritated with him as she stripped him once again. 'You do it on purpose!' she ranted. 'It's the same every blinking day!'

'Blinking day?' queried little Leila, watching the operation with interest.

Her mother dropped the offensive articles into the pail she'd made ready. 'I meant it's a . . . bad day, darling.'

The little girl shook her head. 'See sun! You pwomised.'

'We *will* go out, when I get this brother of yours ready.'

'David bad, Mummy?'

Gwen could feel her throat tightening in self-pity, her eyes prickling. 'He can't help it, though, he's only a baby.' It had been different when Leila was a baby, she thought, miserably. At the least sign of discomfort from her daughter, either Peggy or Marge had hastened to comfort her, and change her if that was what was wrong. She looked at her tiny son now, her heart filling with love instead of the anger she had felt a moment before. Things were getting her down so much that she'd have to be careful not to lose her temper altogether and do him some harm. She'd read of mothers who killed their infants because they were so tired they couldn't cope with them.

She was throwing on her own coat – Leila having been

told to rock the pram if the baby started crying – when the doorbell rang. 'Manny!' she exclaimed anxiously, when she saw who it was. 'Has something happened to Alistair?'

'No, no, I am sorry to have alarmed you. I was on my way to one of the markets when I suddenly felt like coming to see you. But you were going out?'

'I take the children for a walk every morning and do the housework when they're having their afternoon nap, but it doesn't matter. I'm so glad to see you. Won't you come in for a cup of tea?'

'If you do not mind, may I accompany you on your outing? I was not looking forward to trailing round the stalls, but walking with a lovely young woman? That is something I have not done for many a long year.'

A flattered smile stole across Gwen's face. 'I think you would have been a one for the girls when you were young, but I'll be glad of your company.'

As they negotiated their way through the morning shoppers, Manny drew Gwen out to talk about herself, about her life at the hotel, and she described it so well that he could picture the three sisters making beds, helping in the kitchen, waiting at tables with a smile and a few words for each of the businessmen.

'You miss it, don't you?' he murmured.

'I shouldn't, when I'm kept busy with these two, but it's not the same. I think it's the adult company I miss.'

'Especially your mother and sisters, is that not so?'

'Yes,' she admitted, 'it's them I miss most. I miss having them to tell my troubles to, and I get so tired, sometimes, and I've nobody to speak to till Alistair comes home at nights. I do see Ivy Crocker twice a week, but she's more interested in the kids than me.'

During the past fifteen minutes, Manny had been turning an idea over in his mind, a suggestion which would benefit himself as much as Gwen, and her last words gave him the courage to voice it. 'I hope you do not think that what I am about to say is in any way improper, but I would consider it a privilege to be allowed to repeat this morning with you on a weekly basis. I, too, often feel the need of a confidante, someone with whom I can discuss my little worries . . . not that I have many since Alistair took over the running of the shop.'

'I'd love to have you with me once a week, Manny, but are you sure you want to? I hope it isn't because you're sorry for me?'

'No, I want to, I assure you. I am an old man now, and many of the people with whom I come in contact do not have much time for me, but you have been so friendly, I can talk to you and not feel I am being a nuisance.'

'I should hope so!' Gwen said. 'But I've been doing most of the talking today.'

'There will be other days, yes?'

'Yes, of course, and if it happens to be raining on any of the days you come to see me, we can have our chat inside. How does that sound?'

'Ideal, and shall we make it Wednesdays?'

When they returned to the house, he accepted her offer of a cheese sandwich and a cup of tea, and remained with her after the children had been settled upstairs for their nap. 'I suppose Alistair has told you that I used to have a dream . . . ?'

Gwen raised her eyebrows. 'Used to have? Oh, Manny, you haven't given up on having an antique shop, have you?'

He didn't answer for a moment, then said, softly, 'If I tell you, you must promise not to say anything to Alistair. I want it to be a surprise for him.'

'I won't tell him.'

'I am not really fit to be making a daily trek round the

stalls and second-hand shops, and I have also decided that I am too old to start out on a new venture, but I have not forgotten my dream. I have . . .' He stopped to consider the wisdom of going on and came to the conclusion that it was not fair to expect the young woman to keep such momentous information a secret from her husband. 'No, my dear, I shall leave it there. You will both have a pleasant surprise when the time comes.' He was relieved that she did not press him for details, yet he should have known she wouldn't. She was every bit as honourable as Alistair. They were a perfect match.

Gwen did tell her husband that Manny had called, and that he was making it a weekly occurrence, but she did not mention what else he had said, and although Alistair knew why the arrangement had been made, he said nothing about that, either.

For many months to come, therefore, Gwen's weeks were fairly social, what with seeing Ivy for about fifteen minutes every Monday morning and afternoon, when she collected the children for the day and brought them back, and all Thursdays, when they went to Lee Green. Then there were Sundays, when Alistair went with her to see her mother and sisters again as a family.

Wednesdays, of course, were for Manny, who gradually opened out and told her about his wife having to go out cleaning in the early days of their marriage until the pawnshop was making enough for them to live on, about his parents and his grandparents, who had originally come from Poland, about how honoured he felt to be accepted as part of her family, and she, in turn, told him about her father's army career, about her mother being in service at a farm on the outskirts of Aldershot, which is how she had met her husband.

On several occasions, when she was telling Alistair in bed

about her Wednesdays, she remarked that she felt closer to Manny Isaacson than she had ever felt to anyone else.

'Even me?' he asked, a little hurt.

She gave him an extra-special kiss. 'Even you. I love you as a wife's supposed to love her husband, but I love Manny like a favourite uncle.'

And so the Ritchies, the Finnies and the Jenkinses lived their rather ordinary lives oblivious of what was going on in Europe. Only Manny could see the threat of war looming ever and ever nearer, and he kept his fears to himself.

As did too many others.

Chapter 9

His mother's letter devastated Dougal. 'Why didn't she send a telegram?' he wailed to his wife. 'Fancy waiting till a week after the funeral before she tells me.'

Marge laid her hand gently on his bowed head. 'She knew you'd a mortgage to pay, so she probably thought you couldn't afford the fare to Scotland.'

'I'd have managed somehow. Oh, God, I wish she'd told me before . . . I'd have liked to have seen him again before he died.'

'She says people at the funeral told her they thought he'd been looking tired and ill for months, and I think she's blaming herself for not noticing till it was too late.'

'She was aye too damn busy keeping her house so clean you could eat off the floor,' Dougal observed, sharply. 'It would have been the end of the world if anybody had seen a speck of dust on the dresser, and she didn't like when Dad told her there'd be houses when we're all dead and gone.'

He ranted on about his mother's obsession with having everything excessively clean and tidy, how his father had tried to make a 'clootie' rug one winter but his mother had gone mad about the fluff and bits of thread that blew about so he'd had to stop, and Marge let him get his angry frustration off his chest.

His mother's next letter just told him that she was managing fine, the one after that said she had got one of the men to throw out all the rubbish in the outhouses, the next one said she had asked the Salvation Army to collect his father's clothes. Then came the final blow. 'I've sold the farm and everything that goes with it,' she wrote, 'and I'm leaving for America tomorrow to be with Flora.'

'God Almighty!' Dougal exploded, making Marge jump. 'What's wrong with the woman? Tomorrow? It's today she's sailing! Has she taken leave of her senses?'

Marge felt a strong resentment against his mother for not only excluding him from his father's final hours but selling up and going off to live with her daughter in America without as much as a by-your-leave from her son. Marge had always had the suspicion that Meg Finnie was a woman who ruled the roost – though she had been very friendly when they went to Forvit for a week one spring – and this was proof, wasn't it? She might at least have asked Dougal what he thought about her giving up the farm and the house that had been his childhood home, not waited until everything was cut and dried. But knowing her husband as she did, Marge deemed it best not to mention that; it would do more harm than good.

'Your mother's bound to be lonely,' she murmured, tentatively, 'and we're too far away to help if she needs anything, or if anything goes wrong. She'll be better where your sister can keep an eye on her.'

Giving a sigh so prolonged that his wife thought it would never end, Dougal muttered, 'I suppose so. It's just . . . well, she's cut my last link with Forvit, and I wish I'd seen the house just one more time. I'm sure there must be odds and ends of mine still there.'

'They'd just be childish things, though?'

He managed a weak smile. 'Treasures at the time. Ach, don't mind me, Marge, I'm just being sentimental. You're quite right. Mam *will* be better with Flora, and it's her life, after all, though I know I'll never see her again, either.

I'll never be able to afford the fare to America. The east side would be bad enough, but Flora's man's a deputy sheriff in one of the counties in Oregon, that's right over on the west.'

'If she'd been sailing from Southampton, you could have met her at King's Cross and gone down there with her, but Greenock . . . that's not far from Glasgow, is it?'

'Aye, it's on the Clyde. If she hadn't gone at it like there wasn't a minute to lose, I'd have tried to get up there to see her on to the boat and wish her *bon voyage*, but she'll be on the Atlantic by now, telling the captain the stewards aren't keeping the cabins clean. And I bet she'll not be seasick, for whatever kind of food they give her, it wouldn't dare to disagree with her.' Dragging his sleeve across his eyes, he got to his feet. 'If I don't go now, I'll be late for work . . . and don't worry about me. The shock knocked me for six, but I'll get over it.'

That morning, Marge did not follow her routine of clearing up after her husband had gone, but kept sitting at the table thinking how heartless his mother was. It was the only word to describe Meg Finnie, though the woman herself wouldn't think so, and likely neither would Dougal once he simmered down. But, to have been blessed with a son and then shoot off to the other side of the world, actually emigrate, without a thought for him, what else was that but heartless? If she and Dougal ever had a son, she would never let him out of her sight. She would lavish all her love on him . . . till the day she died.

She often dreamed in the night – not sleep-dreaming but wide-awake-dreaming, which was better because she could arrange things to suit herself – of having a little boy of her own, younger than Gwen's David but having the same happy-go-lucky temperament. In her mind, she called him Ritchie, as a compliment to Alistair whose son she was more or less appropriating in her imagination. They would each take after their own father, David was fair like Alistair, and Ritchie would be dark like Dougal. In her wide-awake-dreams David was living next door and the two boys would have fun and adventures together, and sometimes their parents would be up to high doh with worry because they were late in coming home from the Heath, or from school, or wherever they'd gone.

Her heart aching for her pretend son, Marge told herself not to be silly, and got to her feet. It would be six years in September since she and Dougal were married, and there was no likelihood of them having a son now . . . nor a daughter. There was work to be done before she popped next door to see that her mother was OK. It was a bit of a tie-up, really, but she didn't mind. Peggy had been heartbroken when the boy she was in love with dumped her for another girl nearly a year ago, and had moped about the house for weeks with a face as long as a fiddle, so they'd all been glad when she applied for a job with the Civil Service and was taken on as Clerical Assistant. The snag was that Lee Green was such a distance from the City and she hadn't time to come home in the middle of the day, so Marge had volunteered to give their mother something hot and substantial for lunch.

Of course, Rosie still insisted that she could manage to cook something for herself, that she didn't need to be coddled like a child, but she was inclined to do stupid things. Marge had been alarmed one day to find her standing on top of the coal bunker cleaning the kitchenette window. She had used a chair to get up there, but one slip and she would have fallen onto the cement slabs Dougal had laid along the back of the house.

'You could have broken your neck!' Marge had scolded, after helping the almost sixty-year-old down to terra firma. 'You're not as young as you used to be, you know.'

'You're only as old as you feel,' Rosie had grinned, 'and today I feel about twenty.'

Marge had shaken her head helplessly and ushered her inside. 'You could have asked me, if you were so desperate to have it done, or Dougal or Peggy could have done it at night, but no! You're so dashed independent!'

It had worried her, though, and now she always had this fear lurking at the back of her mind that her mother would kill herself with her acrobatics at her age. That was why she didn't like to leave her too long on her own.

In late September of 1938, although trenches had been dug in Hyde Park to erect air-raid shelters, buildings were being sandbagged as a protection against bombs and ARP posts were springing up everywhere, Londoners, like the rest of Great Britain, were going about their business as usual, confident that Chamberlain had smoothed things over. He'd come back from his talk with Hitler in Berlin with a smile on his face, hadn't he? He'd waved a piece of paper and promised everybody there would be peace in our time, so what was there to worry about? Them old farts in Whitehall would put the wind up Wellington himself, if he'd still been alive, with all their doom and gloom.

People like Dougal Finnie, however, who had been in the Territorial Army for some time now, kept their thoughts to themselves. It would only put the fear of death in their women folk to tell them that war was inevitable no matter what the Prime Minister said. They tried to hide their fears, reasoning that it would be a shame to spoil the beautiful weather they were enjoying, though they couldn't understand why the majority couldn't see for themselves what lay just round the corner.

* * *

'What does Dougal think of the situation?' Manny asked Alistair one morning. 'He should know what is going on.'

The younger man screwed up his nose. 'Well, he did say, on the q.t. mind, that they're being geared up for war, and if it does come, they'll be hauled in right away to help the regulars.'

Manny nodded wisely. 'Yes, I am afraid Britain is on an irreversible path. We were lulled into thinking that Hitler would abide by the promises he made, when those in power must know the kind of man he is. Being Chancellor, Fuhrer, has given him a false impression of his own importance, of his own abilities, of his fitness to rule the entire world, and, unfortunately, he does possess the power to sway the German people with his oratory – the ravings of a lunatic, if they could but see it.'

'Of course, being a Jew, he'd be against Hitler,' Alistair observed to Dougal in Lee Green the following Sunday, while they were relaxing in deck chairs in the Finnies' garden with a bottle of beer. Dougal had just come back from his TA training and Alistair had been for a walk over Blackheath with his children, who were now sprawled out in their grandmother's garden next door. 'He believes all the stories going around about what's happening to the Jews in Germany. I think it's a lot of scaremongering, myself. They wouldn't have had the Olympics in Berlin in 1936 if things like that were going on. All the spectators from other countries, never mind the athletes, would have seen if the Jews were being persecuted, wouldn't they? And don't tell me King Edward would have been so easily fooled, him and Mrs Simpson. She'd have noticed something, I bet.'

'People only see what they want to see, and hear what they

want to hear,' Dougal said, darkly. 'That's what's wrong with the world today.'

'So you think it's true? You honestly think there'll be war?'

'No doubt about it, and now's the time to start preparing yourself for it. There's word they're going to supply shelters for people's gardens, so take one if you're offered it.'

'The Jerries'd never bomb London, surely.'

'It's the first place they will bomb. If they manage to knock out the capital, the whole country would be theirs.'

'Has something upset you?' Gwen asked Alistair on their way home, but he couldn't tell her. He didn't want to alarm her unnecessarily, because he didn't honestly think there would ever be another war, no matter what Dougal, or anybody else, said.

Having been seeing Ernie Gammie once a week for around three years, more often when he was on holiday from the Fire Service, Lexie could hardly say she was satisfied with the way the romance was going. He was so . . . gentlemanly, that was the only word to describe him. He still kissed her as though he loved her, but the second a hint of passion crept in, he backed off, and he'd been shillyshallying for far too long. Tonight, however, she meant to ginger him up a bit. She took extra pains with her appearance, brushing her blonde hair until it shone and glinted like gold, and coaxing it into the new pageboy style that seemed to be all the rage, according to the magazines. She smoothed some Pond's Cream over her face and neck, added a touch of rouge to her cheeks and softened it by applying a lavish amount of Phul Nana powder. The last touch was a firm coating of Yvette Tangerine lipstick with a pat of powder over it to keep it on a bit longer. This last was probably a waste of time, she thought, for Ernie would kiss it off in five minutes. She did nothing to her eyes, they were lovely enough as they were . . . so he was always telling her. 'I could get lost in them,' he sometimes murmured, 'so big and so blue.'

Her pulse speeded up at the thought of the next few hours, and also the extra hours she was going to offer him. She could hardly bear to think about what might happen then – the willing sacrifice of her virginity to a man who had once been married and would know everything there was to know about making love. It would make up for all the bad things that had happened, for her father, for Alistair, for her mother.

The little tap at the door made her run to let her soon-to-be lover in and, if she thought his kiss was a little perfunctory, she put it down to his shyness at being asked to spend the evening in her house. If only he knew, she exulted, he would be spending the night there, as well – in her bed!

'Something smells good,' he remarked as he sat down on one of the armchairs.

'Thanks,' she grinned, 'I hope you enjoy it.'

'I'm sure I will.'

She couldn't help feeling that there was a lack of warmth in his manner towards her, but he seemed to be quite impressed with what she served him, nothing fancy but good homely fare, and it wasn't until they had cleared up and were back sitting at the fireside that he said, 'I'm afraid I've something to tell you. I'm being sent on a three-month course, then I'm being transferred to Birmingham.'

'For good?' she gasped. She hadn't expected anything like this.

'I might try for promotion in a few years and be posted somewhere else, but it'll depend on how well I do down there.'

He fell silent, obviously waiting for her to pass some comment, but what was she to say? She wouldn't demean herself by pleading with him not to go. He had never made any commitment to her, the love had probably been in her imagination, and it was his career he was speaking about, after all. She couldn't even ask him if there was any chance that he would come back to her. 'I wish you luck, Ernie,' she finally got out.

A small sigh of relief escaped him. 'Thanks, that means a lot to me. I've really enjoyed our times together, and if I'd been left in Aberdeen . . . who knows? But you're a lovely person, Lexie, you'll find somebody else.'

He didn't even kiss her goodbye when he left, but held out his hand for her to shake, and she went inside without waiting until his car drove off. Damn him! she thought. He had walked out on her! Like her father! Like Alistair! Well, she wouldn't get serious with any other man, even if he swore on a stack of bibles that he loved her.

Something she had once read came to her now. 'Love is to man a thing apart, 'tis woman's whole existence.' She probably hadn't got the words exactly right, but their meaning was as true now as it had been when the poet wrote them.

But she would get over Ernie Gammie! Just as she'd got over everyone else who had betrayed her!

Throughout the winter of 1938–39, more and more rumours circulated of unrest in Europe, newsreels in the cinemas showed Hitler's storm troopers marching into this country and that. And overnight, it seemed, grey bloated fish-shapes appeared in the skies over the large cities – barrage balloons to stop enemy aircraft getting through, and anchored to the ground by long cables – and still the British stoically ignored what they knew in their hearts was almost upon them.

* * *

Lexie Fraser was fed up – the only folk she ever saw were women buying groceries and odd things like shoe polish and laces, and old men collecting their pensions and getting their supply of XXX Bogey Roll for their stinking pipes. Nothing exciting ever happened.

She had expected to see Alistair Ritchie at his sister's wedding in May, but he hadn't come. Of course, Alice had made excuses for him, saying he'd a wife and two kids to support so he couldn't afford the fare, but he could have, if he'd wanted. Not that Alice had been upset about him not showing up; she'd been so soppy about Sam Guthrie, she wouldn't have noticed if there had been nobody there except the two of them. As it was, it had been a really quiet wedding, no big show, a handful of friends, a sandwich tea in the kitchen at Benview after the kirk service, and that was it.

Even the best man, one of Sam's workmates, hadn't been anything special. She'd offered to put him up for the night, and had made him walk to her house to try to sober him a bit, only because he hadn't been fit to drive back to Aberdeen. He'd been at the sorry-for-himself stage, bewailing the fact that no girl ever stuck to him for long, and she'd been sorely tempted to tell him to try washing himself with Lifebuoy to see if that would get rid of his b.o. And so, although Alice and Sam still teased her about her one-night-stand with what's-his-name, she was still a virgin, a finicky virgin who couldn't find a man to make her heart beat like Alistair had once done, and more recently though less strongly, Ernie Gammie.

Although she often told herself she should have nothing to do with men, she still felt a craving for male company, and after she had got over Ernie letting her down, she had begun to go to any dances that were held within ten miles of Forvit – there was always somebody with a car willing to give her a lift. She had hoped to meet a man who would at least take her out occasionally, but of those who *had* made a date with her, two could only speak about football, motor bikes and engines of any kind, and the rest had just one thing on their minds. They all knew that she lived on her own, and at first, she'd been thrilled when one of them tried it on – Pattie Morton from Bankside, for instance. He was really good-looking, and he'd taken her to the first house of the theatre in Aberdeen one Saturday, and when he took her home she had invited him in without thinking. She had expected him to kiss her so she wasn't upset by that, but she had ended up having to fight him off. She'd decided to refuse if he asked her out a second time, but he hadn't.

But Pattie had been a gentleman compared with Ed Ross. *He* had an old BSA motor bike, and she'd been quite thrilled to be sitting on the pillion with the wind whistling in her ears and whipping against her cheeks. It had been quite an exhilarating experience, but then he went and spoiled it by running off the road and into a wood. She'd hardly got herself seated on the ground when he was on top of her, and she'd a devil of a job to stop his hands – and worse – going where they shouldn't.

'No wonder you're still an old maid!' he had shouted at her as he jumped on his bike and roared off, leaving her to walk all the way home, like the ill-mannered lout he was.

So she'd been cautious after that, hadn't let any of them see her home. But some were just as bad inside a cinema or theatre, even at the bus terminus, or wherever they thought they would get away with it . . . but she always managed to stop them. Not a soul asked her out now, once the word had got round.

It did puzzle her sometimes, though. She couldn't understand why she got in such a panic about it, when she wanted to know what it was like, wanted to do it at least once so she would know what other women were speaking about, but the minute she heard the man's breathing quickening, her stomach started to churn with terror and her body went rigid, and if his hand strayed anywhere near the leg of her knickers, she went mad and fought like a tiger.

If only she had somebody to confide in, to help her to get at the root of her problem. Once upon a time, she would have had Alistair Ritchie, not that she could have spoken to him about anything like this, or if Doctor Tom had still been here, he'd have reasoned it out with her. Folk still spoke about how kind he'd been, how he'd listened to everything they had to say.

The shop bell tinkling, Lexie looked up to see Doodie Tough coming in, sidling in would be more like it, she thought, for the woman had a queer way of walking, though there was nothing wrong with her tongue. She could speak till the cows came home and never draw a breath, as the saying went.

'I'm nae needing much the day, Lexie,' Doodie began, 'jist a quarter o' back bacon . . . and cut it thin so it'll be enough for me and Dod and oor Georgie.'

'Right.' Lexie lifted the bacon joint off its shelf, placed it in the slicing machine and reset the thickness gauge before she turned the handle. 'And how are you this morning?' She knew that asking would bring forth a whole catalogue of ailments, but it was out before she thought.

'I'm nae that good the day.' Doodie's face took on a more melancholy expression than normal. 'My varicose veins are gieing me gyp, my corns are yarking like the very devil wi' the damp weather, and I've come oot in a rash.'

'I'm sorry to hear that.' Lexie wrapped the sliced bacon in the greaseproof paper she had laid ready. 'Was it something you ate?'

'If it was, it come oot o' this shop!' Doodie did not dwell

on it, however, and carried on, 'What's mair, I broke ane o' my false teeth last night eating a caramel, and I thocht it was a nut and swallaed it.'

Hard pressed not to laugh, Lexie gave a sympathetic mumble, then said, 'Now, was there anything else, Doodie?'

'A box o' Swan Vestas. Dod likes them best to light his pipe. I tried him wi' a twirl o' paper to use like a taper, you ken, but he wouldna even try it. He's set in his ways, my Dod, and getting worse every day, the thrawn auld bugger.'

She cackled loudly, and knowing that there were few couples in Forvit as close as the Toughs, Lexie laughed along with her while she handed over the matches and counted out the change from the half crown Doodie tendered.

Thankfully, the woman didn't linger, and Lexie was putting the bacon back in place when something niggled at her mind – set off by Doodie Tough's visit, but nothing that she had said today. Lexie had the feeling that it was something she had overheard when she was quite young, something quite important to her now, and she knew she wouldn't get any peace until she did remember.

Chapter 10

The Prime Minister's broadcast was over by the time the Ritchies reached Lee Green on the first Sunday of September, but Alistair had no need to ask the outcome. Peggy looked shocked, Marge was sobbing because Dougal had been mobilized the day before, and Rosie was trying to comfort her. 'I keep telling you, dear, he won't be in any danger. The regulars'll bear the brunt of the fighting, though I can't really see Adolf tangling with the British Army, not when we beat them last time. It'll all be over in a few months.'

Understanding that his mother-in-law was warning him off the subject, Alistair did not voice any opinion, and the rest of the day passed in forced merriment.

Gwen, however, had sensed something in her husband that made her distinctly uneasy, but she waited until they were on their way home before she asked, 'I hope you're not thinking of joining up, Alistair?'

He couldn't meet her eyes. 'Yes I was, if you must know . . . but Manny depends on me, so I'll stay with him till I'm called up.'

Certain that married men with children wouldn't be conscripted, Gwen said no more. Pushing him to give up the idea of going into the forces might have the opposite effect.

War now a reality, the government was underlining its earlier advice that parents in all major cities should evacuate their children to protect them from air raids, and train loads of poor youngsters, with labels on and carrying square gas mask boxes, had already been whisked away from their tearful mothers.

Gwen couldn't bear the thought of six-year-old Leila and David, newly five, being taken away from her, and she certainly wouldn't go with them and leave Alistair on his own. 'I don't know what all the fuss is about, anyway,' she told him.

'They're expecting the Jerries to bomb London,' he explained.

'So they say,' she sneered, 'but Hitler's not that stupid.'

'Dougal said there's nothing surer.'

'And he's an authority on Hitler, is he?'

'Alistair says I'm not facing facts,' she told Manny when they were on their usual Wednesday morning walk, much shorter than it used to be on account of his failing legs, and without Leila and David except in the school holidays, 'but it's an awful decision to have to make – my children, or my husband? What are mothers supposed to do?'

'The government thinks that all those who live in big cities, and are free to do so, should go to some rural area away from the danger,' the old man answered unwillingly, because he didn't want to lose her company, but he considered that it would be best for her. 'It is only sensible, hmm? Getting out before the mayhem starts?'

'You feel sure we'll be bombed?'

'I would bet my life on it.'

He left Gwen feeling that she was between the devil and the deep blue sea. She couldn't trust her darlings to absolute strangers, as so many other mothers had done, and how could she leave Alistair in Bethnal Green where he might be killed? But there was no real fear of bombs! There couldn't be!

That evening saw the first serious quarrel the Ritchies had ever had, short but bitter.

Alistair set it off by saying he was going to write to Alice. 'She's got plenty of room to take you and the kids, so you'd better start packing.'

'I'm not going anywhere!' Gwen declared, eyes dangerously bright.

'Yes, you are! You're taking Leila and David to Forvit, and you're staying there till the war's over!'

'I can't see any need . . . nothing's happening . . .'

'Not yet, but it will, and a mother's first thought should be for her children,' Alistair said, brusquely.

'A wife's place is with her husband,' she snapped.

'This husband can look after himself.'

'This wife happens to *want* to be with her husband and children!'

'Don't be so damned thrawn, woman!'

'You won't change my mind by flinging your Scottish swear words at me!'

Their voices had been rising steadily, and now Alistair threw his arms up as he roared, 'I wasn't swearing! I said you were stubborn! And that's exactly what you are! A bloody stubborn woman, with no thought for anybody but her bloody self!'

'So what's that if it isn't swearing?' Gwen countered, but it was clear that she was on the verge of tears. 'I wasn't thinking of myself. I was thinking of you. I thought you'd want to have your children here where you could protect them.'

'I want them, and you, out of harm's way,' he said, but his voice was less harsh.

'I won't put them away, Alistair, and I can't leave you here on your own. I'd never sleep a wink wondering if you were all right.'

Stumped by her brimming eyes, Alistair caved in, and took her in his arms. 'I'm sorry for shouting at you, my darling.

I know how you must feel, and like you said, nothing's been happening anyway.'

'Nothing's going to happen! No air raids, no bombs! It was just a silly rumour. A lot of those children who were sent away have come back already. People just panicked, that's all it was.'

Not altogether convinced that she was right, Alistair nevertheless stopped arguing.

However hard she had tried, Lexie Fraser could not grasp the elusive shadow which had flashed too quickly through her mind all those months before, so she had been quite glad, in a funny sort of way, when Mr Chamberlain announced that Britain was at war with Germany. Most conversations in the shop were now centred on how Forvit would be affected, a few sons, or brothers, or boyfriends already having volunteered or been called away as Territorials, so she was quite pleased that her last customer one day was Alice Ritchie, Mrs Sam Guthrie now, of course. They had always been good friends, although there was a three-year gap in their ages.

'I'd a letter from Alistair yesterday.' Alice eyed the shopkeeper warily.

Years of practice had enabled Lexie to show no emotion at any mention of his name. 'What's he saying to it, then?' she asked, matter-of-factly.

'He wants Gwen to come up here with the kids till the war's finished, but she won't hear of it. He's scared London'll be bombed and he wants them to be somewhere safe, so I think they'd a big row. It beats me how she can bear to keep her bairns down there when they could be killed, and I could tell Alistair's not happy about it.'

Lexie didn't really feel up to discussing the problems

Alistair Ritchie was having with his wife – she had given up on him years ago – and was relieved when Alice changed the subject. 'I'm a bit worried about Sam,' she confided. 'He's speaking about joining up though I'm trying to talk him out of it.'

'He'll not be happy if you stop him.'

'He could surely wait till the baby's born?' Alice sounded quite tearful.

'You said last week he hadn't touched you since you told him you were expecting, but if he's away for months at a time, think what he'll be like when he's home on leave.'

'Aye,' murmured Alice, thoughtfully, 'there's something in that.' Then she burst out laughing. 'Ach, Lexie Fraser, you're an awful tease, and I still don't want him to go.'

Locking up and going through to the house to make her supper, Lexie mulled over what she had been told. She could understand Alistair's wife not wanting to come away up here, hundreds of miles from her husband, for God knows how long. Any wife would feel the same, and Alistair was being unreasonable to expect it. It was funny the way things turned out, though. At one time, she'd have jumped for joy at the idea that things weren't going smoothly for the Ritchies, that there was every chance of them splitting up, but not any longer. In any case, was there any truth in it?

With absolutely no warning, Lexie's musings were blown apart by what could only be likened to a bolt of lightning, a flash which set free something deep in her memory . . . but just a few words. She had been standing in the shadows just inside the door of the kirk, she could remember that, waiting for her mother to stop speaking to Bella Ritchie and catch up with her, when she'd heard a snippet of a conversation between three women who hadn't noticed her there.

'. . . and they're saying she was taking up wi' him for months afore . . .'

That was all she could remember, but it had definitely been Doodie Tough's sharp voice. The words had meant nothing to her at the time, but they aroused her curiosity now. Who had been taking up with who? For months before what?

Lexie's appetite had vanished and she got no sleep that night. Like all small villages, Forvit had always spawned gossip, true and imagined, and this titbit could have referred to anybody . . . even if they seemed unlikely culprits. The woman had obviously had some standing in the community because Doodie's cronies had been standing with their mouths agape and eyes glittering. Funny how things were coming back to her, though it wasn't them she was interested in. It was who was at the centre of the scandal.

Going over all the women who might have fitted the bill – and bearing in mind that she would have been too young at the time to recognize illicit goings-on as such – Lexie could only come up with three candidates – the minister's wife, the doctor's wife, the wife of the banker in Bankside. Two of them could be crossed out straight away, the first would have been too old, the second too fat even then, but Mrs Kincaid, the banker's wife, was a possibility. She was around fifty now, still quite attractive, dark hair shot with grey, always well-dressed and very friendly, spoke to everyone she met.

Had Mrs Kincaid been the scarlet woman? It didn't seem likely. Her husband was a really handsome man, dark eyes that twinkled at everybody, and a straight almost Roman nose. He was well over six feet tall, still as slim as he was when he was younger, still playing golf. No, Mrs Kincaid could be ruled out, as well.

There was nobody else. Her own mother, being the postmaster's wife, could have been classed as a 'somebody', of course, but she'd never gone out at nights and she would never have had a lover. She had been in poor health for as long as Lexie could remember, which was likely why folk had been so ready to believe ill of her father when he disappeared. She could almost hear them saying that Alec Fraser was a good man, a decent man, but . . . a man who could turn his back on an ailing wife would be capable of anything, even going off with a lassie young enough to be his daughter.

Her stomach giving a jolting heave, Lexie's thoughts wavered. Had it been him and Nancy Lawrie that Doodie had been speaking about? '. . . *she'd been taking up wi' him afore . . .*', but if it was her father and Nancy she'd have said, '. . . *he'd* been taking up wi' *her* afore . . .', for it would have been his name that would have raised people's eyebrows.

Glancing at the little clock at her bedside, Lexie stretched out to flick off the alarm switch. She didn't need it today. She'd have to get up in twenty minutes anyway, and there was no risk of her falling asleep now. Who had the woman been? Young enough to be having an affair, important enough to have made the village tongues wag? Who?

A speck of excitement suddenly took wing inside her, growing in intensity until she felt suffocated by it. Why hadn't she remembered before? The present doctor had come after Tom Birnie went to join his wife in Stirling, which would have been quite late on in 1929, three months at least after her father had gone off – maybe six, because he'd had to get somebody to buy his practice before he could leave.

So! Lexie drew in a long, juddery breath of relief, and let it out slowly. It could be Margaret Birnie! She might have been seeing another man before she left to look after her mother. Doctor Tom was often out all evening, sometimes nearly all night – like he'd been with her mother and her, Lexie recalled – and she'd have had plenty opportunities. She'd been a really pretty woman, they had two cars, and she could easily have driven miles to meet her lover. That was it, thank goodness.

Flinging back the bedclothes, Lexie swung her feet to the floor. Why couldn't she remember what else Doodie had said that long-ago day?

1940–1945

Chapter 11

Never had Marge Finnie sat by her wireless set for so long at a time. It was an effort for her to leave it long enough to prepare the meals she took next door to her mother but could only pick at herself. While Dougal had been home over New Year, he had told her proudly, 'Our mob's going to France as part of the BEF.'

'BEF?' she had asked. 'What's that?'

'British Expeditionary Force,' he had explained.

Out of all the people present at the time, only his young nephew had been impressed. The others had expressed their fears for him, but David, on the Ritchies' usual Sunday visit to Lee Green, had said, 'Gosh, Uncle Dougal, I bet you're excited.'

'I am a bit,' admitted Dougal, adding truthfully, 'but I'm not looking forward to it.'

'Why not? You'll be able to kill as many Jerries as you want, won't you?'

'That's enough, David,' Alistair reprimanded.

Marge had realized that he was trying to prevent the four women – her two sisters, her mother and herself – from realizing that it could also work the other way, but if *she* had tumbled to it, they probably had, too. She had worried herself night and day ever since, making herself ill at the idea of Dougal being wounded or, worse, killed – she could scarcely bear to think about that – but since France was on the brink of falling, a new fear had blasted its way into her mind. The Germans had the BEF in full retreat, according to the reports, and it seemed likely that every last one would be taken prisoner. The announcers, usually so cheerful during their reading of the news, gave no false hope, and neither did the newspapers. It was as if, Marge thought, everyone had given up.

But they couldn't give up! There were thousands of men's lives at stake, French as well as British. Surely there was some way of rescuing them? Couldn't they be lifted away by air? When she had mentioned this to Alistair last Sunday, though, he'd said, softly but firmly, 'Planes would be shot down before they got a chance to land, and in any case, I don't think we've enough aircraft to pick up even half the men involved.'

While she tried to prepare herself for bad news, she couldn't help wondering what her husband might be facing if he had been captured. He wasn't a coward, of course, and no matter what the Germans did to torture him, he wouldn't tell them anything. She wasn't strong like that, unfortunately. She doubted if she'd have the strength to go on with her life if anything happened to him.

If he was spared, she'd never go dancing with Petra again, although she had done nothing wrong. Some of the servicemen were clearly out for all the fun that was going, and anything else on offer, but it was mostly girls who were the predators, Petra being one of the worst. She dressed up to the nines, full war-paint on, and instead of her usual aloofness, she was so animated she wouldn't have been out of place in a Disney cartoon. There was no point in falling out with her for what she had said about Dougal, though; she wasn't worth it.

Marge was angry at herself now for doubting her husband even for one minute. He would *never* play around with other women. She trusted him. She would always trust him . . . for as long as she lived . . . if he came back to her.

Tears were slowly edging down her cheeks when she heard the back door opening and knowing it was her mother, she pulled out her hankie and hastily tried to wipe them away. 'Mum! It's not dinner time yet.'

Rosie, bothered with arthritis now, made her stiff way across the room. She didn't intend to let her daughter swamp herself in misery. 'We won't get any dinner at all if you can't tear yourself away from that thing! Anyway, I came to give you the latest news.'

Ashamed at being caught weeping, Marge said sharply, 'I've heard all the latest news. Why d'you think I'm sitting here?'

'I mean the latest *latest* news,' Rosie said airily, unfazed by her daughter's reception of her. 'Alf was telling me somebody in the grocer's knows somebody who's got a cousin with a boat on the Thames, and *he* told his cousin – the one with the boat told the one Alf knows – there's a whole lot of them there . . .'

'I know! Dougal used to take me to Windsor to see them. But what . . . ?'

'Just listen! They've all been asked to help to get the soldiers off the beaches.'

'But little boats like that could never . . .'

'Well, that's what Alf heard, and he seems to think it could work.'

'Alf's an old woman,' Marge sneered. 'He believes everything anybody tells him.'

'He's been a good neighbour to me,' Rosie pointed out. 'Since your Dougal went away, he's been keeping my grass cut, and he gives Peggy a hand to weed sometimes.'

'I know, but don't you think he's a bit . . . soft? In the head, I mean.'

'He's got all his marbles, and he's not a pansy, though some people think he is. It was his mother's fault he never had a girlfriend, you know – she kept him running after her till the day she died – and he thinks he's too old now. But he can only be . . . what . . . in his late forties?'

'More like his fifties.' Marge couldn't keep her annoyance up any longer. 'Um . . . will I put on the kettle for a cuppa?'

'Yes, love, that'd be nice. And I'll have my dinner here, if that's all right with you? You won't miss anything, I'll listen to the wireless the time you're getting it ready.'

It was several hours before reports came across the airwaves that a great armada of boats of all shapes and sizes had started on the unenviable task of evacuating as many of the troops stranded on the Dunkirk beaches as they could.

'Now do you believe Alf?' Rosie was pleased that her neighbour had been vindicated.

'I'm sorry,' Marge muttered, 'but I've been so worried about Dougal I couldn't think straight, but I feel better now I know he'll be home soon.'

'You don't know for sure that he's at Dunkirk, though?' Rosie felt obliged to remind her daughter of this.

'I feel sure he is, Mum, but I suppose I'll just have to wait and see.' Marge was relieved that her mother left it there. She wasn't sure . . . of anything. For all she knew, Dougal could be lying dead somewhere. She strangled this thought before it suffocated her. He couldn't be dead. She'd have felt it in her bones, in her very heart, whereas all she felt was this uncertainty, as though she'd been caught up in a sort of limbo.

'Your sister-in-law must be very worried about Dougal,' Manny remarked on the second day of the evacuation.

'I thought she might be glad of some extra support, so when Gwen said she was going to see Marge, I told her to stay with her till they found out, one way or the other. David and Leila know to go to Mrs Wright next door when they come home from school. She took them in yesterday.'

'You should have told me, my boy. You could have closed the shop early. And you must go home in time for them coming out of school today, and for as long as dear Gwen is away. You do not want to impose on your neighbour, do you?'

'She doesn't mind. She loves the kids.'

Alistair would have liked to ask Manny if he was well enough. For some time now he had noticed how frail the old man was becoming, how grey and crepey his skin was, but he knew better than say anything. His employer did not take kindly to being reminded of the passage of time, but he shouldn't be living alone at his age. Manny was one of the old school, who considered nothing was wrong with them as long as they could stand on their own two feet. The weakness in his legs had stopped him from going round the markets, but it hadn't stopped him from being in the shop from just after nine each morning, though Alistair had told him he should take things easy.

He'd been wondering if he should sound Gwen about asking Manny to live with them, so that she could keep an eye on him, but he had better wait till this business at Dunkirk was over. He gave a shivering sigh.

Manny looked at him compassionately. 'You are also fearful for Dougal?'

'If anything happens to him,' Alistair muttered, 'it'll be like I've lost part of myself. We've been friends since the day we started school. We did everything together, we came to London together, we shared a bed, even married into the same family. If he doesn't come back, it'll tear the heart out of me – out of all of us.'

Manny nodded his understanding. 'I think you should be there when your children come out of school today. Go home now, pack a few things, and take them to Lee Green. It is better for all of you to be together in this worrying time. If it is bad news, you will help each other through it, show your sister-in-law that she is not alone in her grief. Oh dear, perhaps you think I am morbid, talking like that, but if we prepare ourselves for the worst it helps to ease the pain, and if the worst does not happen, so much the better.'

'You know, Manny, I think I *will* go to Lee Green today, that's if you don't mind?'

'I do not mind. In fact, I feel like going with you.'

'You're welcome to come . . .'

'No, no, my boy. Although I regard myself as one of your family, I am not truly a member. Tell dear Marge that I am praying for Dougal's safety, and do not come back until you know for sure what has happened. I can cope, I am not finished yet.'

By a strange quirk of fate, Leila was alone in Marge's house when the soldier walked in and, in spite of several days' growth of beard and the strain evident in his grey face, she recognized him immediately and flung herself at him. 'Uncle Dougal! It's you!'

Hoisting her up in his aching arms, he gave her a bear hug. 'Aye, my lamb, it's me! Where's everybody?'

'They're all in Grandma's. I didn't like seeing Auntie Marge crying, so I came here to read my comic for a while.'

He set her down gently. 'We can't let your Auntie Marge cry any longer, can we? We'll go and surprise her, eh?' Catching sight of himself in the mirror above the fire, he pulled a face. 'Maybe I'd better wash and shave first, eh?'

The little girl waited, excitement bubbling inside her at the thought of being the first to know he was safe. She would have liked to run and tell the others, but knew that it would spoil his surprise. It had been awful, watching Auntie Marge crying, and Grandma and Mum trying to comfort her though they were nearly in tears, too. She had wondered why they were so sad when they didn't know what was happening. They shouldn't have been so sure Uncle Dougal was dead. If she could remember that bit she'd read somewhere . . . what was it again? Where there's life, there's hope? No, that didn't fit. Where there's hope, there's life. That was it, and she had never lost hope. That was why Uncle Dougal had come home safe.

Grown-ups were funny – not ha-ha funny, just queer funny – and it hadn't been only the women. Dad had been gripping his mouth tightly, and he'd blown his nose a few times before she came out, like he was trying not to cry. She loved Uncle Dougal nearly as much as she loved her Dad, but *she* hadn't cried, though she might have, if he hadn't come back.

The adults proved to be more than funny when she and Uncle Dougal walked into her Grandma's house. Auntie Marge cried louder than ever when she saw her husband, and she didn't stop even though he held her close and patted her back and whispered things in her ear. Grandma was dabbing at her eyes, and Mum was wiping her cheeks. Worst of all, tears were running down her father's face, but he was gripping David's hand to stop him from jumping on Uncle Dougal's back, which he was likely to do, but it wouldn't be fair at this special time.

Leila gave a satisfied sigh. She'd never seen anything so romantic as the way her uncle and aunt were kissing each other now. It was as good as the pictures, better, because she *knew* them, was related to them. Wait till she told her chums at school!

Looking fondly down at her sleeping husband, Marge blessed Alistair Ritchie for his understanding of the situation. 'Come on, troops,' he had laughed to his children about half an hour after Dougal had made his surprise entrance. 'It's time we went home.'

Rosie was horrified at this. 'Wait till Peg gets in from work. She'll make something to eat. Or why don't you have a look in the pantry, Gwen, and see what there is?'

'Only if we let Marge take Dougal next door.' Alistair had stood his ground. 'Can't you see he's dead on his feet with exhaustion?'

'I *am* a bit tired,' Dougal had said, which was when his wife had fully realized the ordeal the evacuation must have been – he never ever admitted to being tired.

As they entered their own house, she had said, 'I'll run a bath, just the regulation five inches, of course.' He followed her upstairs and went into the bedroom to undress, but in the few minutes it had taken her to put in the plug, turn on the taps and fetch a large towel from the airing cupboard, Dougal had fallen asleep on top of the bed-clothes, still wearing the ill-fitting clothes he'd been given to replace his waterlogged uniform when the rescue boat landed at Dover.

That was about all he had told them, really. Maybe he would tell her more tomorrow, or maybe he would never tell her. Maybe he wouldn't want to be reminded of the long hours of waiting until he was picked up from the beach nor of the terrible things he must have seen. He looked so vulnerable lying spread-eagled across the bed that her heart swelled with love, and wishing that he had turned down the blankets before exhaustion overtook him, she covered him up as best she could without disturbing him. She would lie down on the settee in the living room for this one night, because she, too, had a lot of sleep to catch up on.

Bending down, she kissed her husband's cheek, scarcely able to believe that he had come home safely, then tiptoed out. She found an old eiderdown at the back of the cupboard at the top of the stairs – she'd meant to throw it out long ago but was glad now that she hadn't – and rolled it round her before she lay down. All the earlier worry and the later excitement, however, prevented her from falling asleep. It wasn't seven o'clock yet, she saw when she glanced at the clock. No wonder she couldn't drop off.

She hoped that none of her family would come in to see if Dougal was all right. What would they think when they found her in her nightclothes on the settee and she told them her husband was in bed upstairs? After a while, she heard soft voices bidding each other good night, and guessed that Alistair was taking his brood home. She listened in case Peggy might take it into her head to come and see Dougal, since she hadn't seen him yet, but nothing happened, and before long, Marge herself had fallen into a deep sleep.

'Poor devil!' Alistair commented, as they walked down Burnt Ash Road to the railway station. 'He's been through a helluva lot, by the look of him.'

'Language,' cautioned his wife. 'Little pitchers . . .'

'Sorry, dear, but it's awful, isn't it? It makes me want to get in there and fight the bl . . . blinking Jerries.'

Young David proved that little pitchers did indeed have big ears. 'Are they always blinking, Dad? What makes them blink?'

'No, no,' Alistair smiled, 'it's just an expression.'

'What does it mean, then?'

'It means they're bad. The awful Germans, or the nasty Germans. See?'

'Are you really going into the army like Uncle Dougal to fight the blinking Jerries?'

'No, he's not!' declared Gwen firmly. 'He's got a wife and two children to consider, not like Uncle Dougal.'

Seven now, Leila took it upon herself to pour oil on the troubled waters, although she probably didn't know that was what she was doing. 'Auntie Marge was really glad to see him, wasn't she?'

Her mother nodded. She, too, had been impressed, and a trifle jealous if the truth were known, by the tenderness of the kisses they had all witnessed earlier, but David said, scornfully, 'I didn't think soldiers would be as soppy as that.'

'When you fall in love with a girl,' Alistair laughed, 'you'll be just as soppy as him.'

'Why do you never kiss Mum, then? Don't you love her?'

His father's cheeks reddened, but he said, 'I've loved your Mum ever since I met her, but there were times when I didn't show it enough.'

'What times? Why?'

Gwen ruffled his curly head. 'You were one of the reasons, I think, and Leila. I was so busy attending to you two, I didn't have time to show Dad how much I loved him. He must have felt neglected.'

'When I get married,' Leila said, dreamily, 'I'll never neglect my husband. I'll tell him every day, every hour, every minute, how much I love him.'

'I think every minute would be too much of a good thing,' Alistair smiled.

David blew a loud raspberry. 'All this talk of love and kissing! Yeugh! It makes me want to puke.'

'David!' exclaimed his mother. 'I will not have you talking like that! Where did you hear that word, anyway?'

'One of the boys at school says it all the time.'

'If I hear you saying it again, you'll . . . you'll be sorry.'

'Puke, puke, puke,' the boy muttered under his breath, but, although they heard, they decided to ignore it.

As Alistair said, much later, 'Puke's not really so bad, is it? But we'll have to watch him. He picks up every damned thing he hears.'

'Remember that, then.' Gwen's eyes suddenly clouded. 'You're not really thinking of going into the army, are you?'

'Yes, I am. Dunkirk has set the country back. The army needs replacements for the men who were lost.'

'Please, Alistair, don't go. Look at what Marge's had to put up with these last few days. Do you want to put your children and me through the same agonies?'

After a pause, he mumbled, 'If it wasn't for you three, I'd have been off months ago.'

'But you still have us.'

'That won't stop me from being called up, you know. In fact, I'm surprised they haven't done it already. I registered with the over-twenties.'

'You'll soon be twenty-seven. Surely they'll have enough without taking you?'

Her eyes were so distressed that he pulled her into his arms, and, whether it was a result of the eventful day he'd had or not, he found himself wanting her more acutely than he had done for years.

'I bet Dougal and Marge will have been . . .' she whispered afterwards.

'I doubt it.' Alistair ran his fingers down her neck. 'I don't think Dougal's up to it yet, but once he comes to himself properly, then . . . !'

'I wonder if all the worry they've had will make a difference? I know they're both desperate for a baby, and this might have done the trick. What do you think?'

'I've no idea.' Alistair wished that she hadn't brought up this subject. With all the upheaval and uncertainty in the world, he hoped that he hadn't made his wife pregnant a few minutes ago. They had a big enough struggle to make ends meet as it was, what with the rent to pay, and gas and electricity. This old house was a killer in the winter, and coal was getting dearer and dearer as well as scarcer and scarcer. He couldn't expect Manny Isaacson to give him more wages; what the shop was taking in barely covered the old man's expenses as it was.

Afraid that Gwen would expect him to make love to her again, he gave her a quick kiss, said, 'Good night, dear,' and turned away. The only safe method of contraception was to keep well away from your wife in bed.

Chapter 12

The Battle of Britain, as it came to be known, was over at last, the little Hurricanes and Spitfires had pluckily repelled the enemy's attempts to blow our airfields and all our aircraft to smithereens. Yet despite this unexpected and insulting defeat, Hitler was still set on beating the British into submission. The Luftwaffe's heavy bombers were sent in – the Dorniers, the Focke-Wulfs, and thus began the Blitzkrieg.

Civilians now found themselves in the front line. Not only the Home Guard, air-raid wardens, ambulance drivers, firemen, medical staff, munitions workers, but those merely going about their daily business. This was when the true meaning of war was brought home to the man (and woman) in the street. Being the capital, London took the brunt of the raids at first, night after night of bombs screaming down, night after night spent in the large shelters built by the councils, or in Anderson shelters provided for back gardens, or Morrison shelters intended for those confined to the house but who were often too afraid to make use of them in case they were trapped inside like mice.

There were some, of course, who relied instead on their own makeshift boltholes – under the stairs, in a narrow lobby, in the cellar, even just under a table – and those who made a point of 'not giving in to the murdering bastards', who did nothing when the howling of the alert sirens rent the air. As the days passed, and they saw the havoc that was being wrought, the devastation the bombers were wreaking, their bravado was replaced by rationality or, more likely, by the need for self-preservation.

Night after night, Alistair Ritchie had helped his wife to carry the food and blankets she had laid out ready to take with them to the council shelter just along the street, where they and their neighbours tried to take the children's minds off the bombs by playing games with them and singing songs. Neither of these methods were 100% effective, especially when the terrifying sounds of explosions came nearer and louder. At times like these, every single person shook with fear, youngsters sobbing and clutching their mothers, who prayed while they held them that it would end soon.

'I don't know what to do, Manny.' Alistair Ritchie shook his head viciously as if that would dispel the worries he had. 'It looks like Jerry's trying to bomb us into submission now, and Gwen still won't hear of going to Forvit with the kids.' He paused, then went on hesitantly, 'Could you have a word with her, please? She'd listen to you.'

Laying down the pocket watch, an heirloom, which he was repairing as a favour to an elderly neighbour, Manny removed the little magnifying glass from his eye and regarded his manager sadly. 'I am sorry, Alistair, but I could not take that upon myself. It is entirely up to you, but let me warn you, my boy. Women are fickle creatures, and if they feel that they are being forced into something, they will fight against it.' He picked up the magnifying glass, but before fitting it into his eye, he cleared his throat. 'Um . . . I take it that you . . . still love her, hmm? You do not have what they call the seven-year itch?'

'Oh, no! I've never stopped loving her!'

'And I know that she has never stopped loving you. That is good. There must always be love there for a marriage to survive, but you must persuade her to change her mind . . . and soon.' He replaced the glass, retrieved the watch and the subject was closed.

'I hear your Sam's joined the Air Force,' Lexie remarked to her friend.

Alice Guthrie sighed heavily. 'I couldn't talk him out of it this time. He just went to Aberdeen and signed up, and he's got to report at Padgate on Monday. He's just a big bairn really, thinking he'll get to fly an aeroplane some day, though I've kept telling him he hasn't got the brains to be a pilot.'

'He'll be a lot safer on the ground, at any rate. It's a wonder to me your Alistair hasn't joined up. With Dougal Finnie just getting away from Dunkirk by the skin of his teeth, I'd have thought he'd be itching to do his bit and all.'

Alice's shrug was hardly worthy of the name. 'There was no word of it in Gwen's last letter. She says he doesn't want to leave Manny, but no doubt he'll be called up shortly.'

'Lizzie Wilkie was saying the first lot of troops are to be arriving at Ardley before Christmas, so Hogmanay should be a bit brighter than we thought.'

'For you, maybe, not for me. Even if Sam gets home, I'll still be stuck in the house with wee Morag. He's always gone out boozing with his pals about seven o'clock, and he comes home too drunk to remember anything about seeing in the New Year.'

'You'd started on the wrong foot with him,' Lexie laughed. 'You should have let him see on your wedding night it was the end of him being a single man. But that's your own business, and if there's any soldier-boys going about the place, I'll tell you all about it if I manage to click with one.'

'Well, thanks,' Alice said, heavily sarcastic, 'and have

me green with jealousy?' But she was laughing as she left the shop.

Lexie, however, wasn't laughing. Her last chance of, perhaps not going as far as getting a husband, at least getting some fun out of life, lay with the men who would be arriving at Ardley House some time in the near future. Rumour had it that there would be over two hundred, and there certainly had been dozens of large Nissen huts erected in the grounds, so she should have plenty to choose from. And, as Lizzie Wilkie had pointed out, there weren't that many girls left in Forvit now. A lot of the younger ones were in uniform themselves, branching away from their humdrum existences and going out to find adventure for themselves. She had considered following their lead, but it would have meant giving up the shop her father had worked so hard to establish . . .

Her father. He was the centre of so much of her thoughts. She had almost learned to accept that he had run away to be with Nancy Lawrie – not Margaret Birnie, that had been a daft idea – but another, far more distressing explanation had occurred to her the other night and she couldn't get it out of her head.

Maybe Nancy hadn't gone away at all! Maybe Alec Fraser had offered to pay for an abortion, but she had refused and threatened to tell the whole village if he didn't support her and the infant when it was born. Knowing that his life would be in ruins if she did, he might have lashed out in his anger and accidentally knocked her off her feet. She *could* have hit her head on a stone and when he tried to help her up, he had discovered that she was dead. He would have been aghast at what he had done, but his first thought would be to protect himself, to hide the body.

Lexie's troubled mind blotted out the actual disposal and picked up the story where it had crossed Alec's mind that one or more of the other choir members might have known about him and Nancy . . . even about his indiscretion. His overruling instinct then would be to escape, to flee from the aftermath of his crime.

'A penny for them, Lexie. You was miles awa'.'

Startled, she looked up into the inquisitive eyes of Mattie Wilkie and forced a smile. 'Alice Ritchie was saying Sam's joined the Air Force, then we got speaking about the soldiers coming to Ardley, and I was just thinking . . .'

A sly grin spread over the older woman's face. 'Was you hopin' to get a lad? My Lizzie's the same, but she's younger than you. You'd best pull your socks up if you're nae wantin' to be left on the shelf. Now, can I get a quarter o' tea and a half loaf, for I clean run oot and Joe'll be hame for his denner in ten minutes.'

Lexie was thankful that the woman was in a hurry, she usually hung about hoping to have a gossip with the next customer. She had an edge to her tongue though she meant nothing by it, yet she shouldn't have said that about being left on the shelf. She would have to find a lad soon, Lexie told herself, and not be too choosy. What was more, she'd have to put what she'd been thinking about her father completely out of her mind. It was just a lot of nonsense. He'd been a good-living man, and even if he *had* slipped with Nancy Lawrie, he'd have owned up to his responsibility and taken the consequences. In any case, what was the point of dwelling on it? It wouldn't change what had happened.

Alistair kept pressing Gwen to take their children away but, adamant that it would be giving in to the enemy, she still held out against it, until one Sunday morning in January 1941, when they emerged into the open air to find that the house behind theirs had been damaged. The bomb had actually fallen in the roadway, but the blast had practically sheared off the entire side yet left the gable of the next house intact.

Looking out at the pile of rubble and realizing what a narrow escape they'd had themselves, Gwen at last questioned if she had been doing the right thing. Leila and David were pale and haggard, jumping nervously at the slightest noise, and she was to blame by being so stubborn. It wasn't fair to keep them in London when most of their chums had been sent away again. Only a few stragglers were left, those with mothers as stupid as she was.

Not surprisingly, while they were preparing to make their usual Sunday visit to Lee Green, Alistair told her that he'd had enough. 'I'm writing to Alice tonight and that's final! And I don't want any nonsense from you about not going. I want the three of you out of London, and you'll stay away until I say you can come back. Do you understand what I'm saying?'

It was Rosie who wondered, when they told her what they were proposing, if Marge would also be welcome at Forvit. 'Your sister knows her, Alistair, so I'm sure she wouldn't object to taking Dougal's wife along with yours.'

Gwen put her finger on the one flaw in this arrangement. 'Who would look after you, then? Peg's out at work all day, and you can't manage by yourself.'

'If she left things for me to heat up, I'd manage perfectly well,' Rosie declared.

'If we ask Alf,' Peggy put in, colouring a little, 'I'm sure he'd look in now and then. He's got a dicky heart, and he feels bad about not being fit for any of the services or anything. Checking on Mum, he wouldn't feel so useless.'

Gwen did make a tentative effort to get her mother to go to Scotland with them, but Rosie wasn't having that. 'I'm not letting that cocky little German clown put me out of my home. When I leave, it'll be feet first!'

This didn't make her daughters feel any easier. As Gwen said to Alistair later, 'She should have years ahead of her yet, but if she stops in Lee Green . . .' Realizing that this was the argument he had used to her, she said, softly, 'OK, you'd better write to Alice.'

An answer came by return, saying that they were all welcome, for as long as was necessary. 'Sam's been trying to get somewhere for me and Morag to stay,' her letter went on. 'He's stationed at Turnhouse, and I've been worried about leaving Benview empty, but with Gwen and Marge here to look after it, I can go with an easy mind.'

'Alistair's wife and kids are coming here to get away from the raids,' Alice told Lexie when she went to cash her RAF allotment. 'They've hardly been out of the shelter for weeks and weeks, poor souls. He can't give up his job, of course, but Marge, that's Gwen's sister, she's coming with them. Well, I'd better get back, for I've things to get ready and they'll be here tomorrow forenoon.'

Nothing fazed Lexie for the rest of the day, not even the grumpiest of grumpy old folk who came in to collect their pensions and wanted to chat though there was a long queue waiting behind them. She was normally flagging more than an hour before closing time, but this wasn't a normal day, and she locked the shop door jauntily at six o'clock and walked through to the house with a spring in her step.

If Alistair's wife and kids were going to be staying at Benview for any length of time, she thought, as she lit the gas ring under the kettle, he would have to come to visit them at some point. It must be almost nine years since he was married, and the magic was bound to have worn off. It might be worth while to make friends with his bairns. The way to a doting father's heart would surely lie through his children, wouldn't it?

Her mood changed suddenly. What the devil was she thinking of? Alistair Ritchie hadn't figured in her plans for a long time now . . . and there was still the long-awaited arrival of the troops to look forward to.

'It's worked out fine,' Alistair told Manny after seeing his family off at King's Cross. 'Alice is glad they'll be in the house to keep it heated, and it's a big relief to me. Marge has rented out their house, and Rosie says I should give up ours and move in with her, but I don't want to upset Peg. I think there's something between her and Alf Pryor next door, and it'd be a shame if I spoiled it for her. She's never kept a boyfriend long before, and Alf's a really nice bloke though he must be nearly twenty years older than her.'

'If she loves him,' Manny observed, shrewdly, 'twenty years is a mere nothing. But what have you decided, Alistair?'

'I'm going to stay where I am. Lee Green's too far for me to travel every day.'

Manny made no comment, and Alistair wondered if the old man had realized why he hadn't volunteered for the forces as he'd spoken about after Dunkirk. When he'd had time to think, his affection for his employer had been stronger than his wish to have a go at the Germans. He couldn't leave poor Manny in the lurch.

Alice Guthrie was shocked when she beheld the little group trailing off the bus – two women and two children, all looking like . . . oh, she couldn't find words to describe them. Rushing forward, she clasped the boy and girl to her breast. 'You poor wee lambs! Was it a terrible journey?' Letting them go, she took the bags they were carrying and led the way along the rough track to Benview. 'I hope you're not too tired, there's a good bit to walk,' she apologized. 'And I bet you'll all be ready for a cup of tea once we get in?'

Getting no response from any of them, and thinking how sunken their eyes had been and how they'd looked as if they didn't care what happened to them, she came to the conclusion that what they needed most was peace and quiet.

'Come upstairs and I'll show you where you'll be sleeping,' she said when they entered the house. 'I've taken Morag in with me so Leila can have her room. Gwen and Marge, you can have the other double bedroom, if you don't mind sharing, and David's in what we call the boxroom, but I've cleared it out and he should be quite comfy.'

She showed the girl and boy their rooms first, saying, 'Don't worry about anything. Just get undressed and into your beds, and I'll take up a tray with something to eat.'

'No,' Gwen said, wearily, as Alice ushered Marge and her along the landing. 'They won't want anything and neither do we . . . thanks. We had sandwiches with us on the train, and flasks of tea, so we're not hungry.'

After standing for a few minutes watching the two women unpacking some things until they found their nightdresses, Alice said, 'I'll leave you to it, then. The bathroom's next door to you. Sam had it put in over a year ago – another room we never used.'

Before going downstairs, she looked in at Leila and wasn't altogether surprised to find her already asleep as was David, when she peeped round his door. Poor wee devils, she thought, compassionately. It was going to take all four of them a good while to get over their terrible ordeal.

* * *

Even in the shelter with all the noise going on, Alistair slept better that night than he had done for some time, and guessed it was because he didn't have to worry about his family any more, just himself. He emerged into the daylight with a light heart. His house was still standing and there didn't seem to be any damage near them as far as he could see. He boiled the kettle to have a wash, then made himself some tea and toast. The house was so quiet, though. He missed the chatter of his children, his wife's constant urging at them to hurry up and get dressed.

On his way to work, he discovered that the bombers hadn't been all that far away the night before. Many of the buildings he passed had been damaged by blasts that had completely destroyed others, and as he went on, it became more difficult to get through. He was almost sick with apprehension when he neared the end of Manny's street, and his legs faltered when he rounded the corner and saw that the pawnshop was no longer there.

'A direct hit!' he was told by one of the gang of workers trying to clear the area.

'What about the . . . have you found the owner?' Alistair could barely get the words out, he was so upset.

The weary tin-hatted man eyed him sympathetically. 'The old man in the back room? Did you know him? I'm sorry, mate. He's dead, crushed under a pile of rubble. We wouldn't have known to look for him except a woman a few doors along came and told us he slept in there. Her place got a good shaking up, windows all out, doors blown off, yet she was all worried about him. Was he a friend of yours?'

'I worked for him . . . and he was the very best friend I ever had.' Alistair staggered a little now, the shock beginning to tell on him.

'Are you all right, mate?'

'I'm fine. It's just . . . I wasn't expecting this . . . I never thought . . .'

'You'd better get off home, mate. There's nothing you can do here, and there's an awful lot like you this morning, with no work to go to.'

He drew the curtains when he went in – Manny wasn't there, of course, but he wanted to show some respect for the dead man – then sat down by the fire. It wasn't lit, but it seemed the only place to sit. He had to come to terms with what had happened before he could face anybody. Losing his job was a mere fleabite compared to losing Manny. The old man had been part of his life for so long, going on without him was unthinkable.

Alistair huddled into his chair for hours, numb with cold as well as shock, until at last the tears came, the welcome, warm tears which initiated a thawing in his innermost being. And only then, after allowing himself the luxury of rinsing out the awful, painful, gnawing grief – which didn't banish it altogether but made it slightly easier to bear – was he able to consider what he should do. Not that he had to ponder over this for long. Fate had decided for him, hadn't it?

His expression was grim when he went to Lee Green in the late afternoon. 'Oh, my Lord!' Rosie exclaimed, her cheeks blanching when she heard about Manny. 'That poor, dear old man . . . all alone at the end.'

'Aye, Rosie, that's what's eating at me, and all. But I keep telling myself it had been quick and he wouldn't have suffered . . . would he?' His eyes sought her reassurance.

'I shouldn't think so,' she comforted, 'but what are you going to do now? You don't have a job and . . .'

'I've been to the recruiting centre,' he admitted, a little sheepishly, 'and I've signed on for the Artillery. They said it mightn't be long till I'm told where to report, and I'm not allowed to sublet our house, so I'm going to give it up altogether and come here till it's time to go . . . that's if your offer still stands?'

Rosie eyed him sadly. 'You're very welcome, dear, for as long as you want, but are you absolutely sure the army's what you want to do?'

'Absolutely certain! I'd have joined up before, but I didn't want to let Manny down.'

Rosie looked pensive now. 'Do you know if anything was left of Manny's shop, any jewellery or valuables of any kind?'

'Nothing, apparently, and if there had been, somebody would likely have taken them. There's a bit of looting going on, you know.'

She frowned her disapproval of this. 'That's awful! How can people take advantage of other people's misfortunes? What's the world coming to? The Germans trying to blast us all to Kingdom Come, and our bombers doing the same to them. It's the poor civilians that are suffering most.'

'It just came back to me,' Alistair said suddenly, 'when the war started, Manny made me take all his best pieces to the bank for safekeeping.'

'That's a blessing, then, but what will happen to them now? Will the bank claim them now he's dead?'

'I've no idea.'

'I think you should go and ask, Alistair . . . if it's still standing.'

'It's not really any of my business, though. Manny did once speak about a cousin or a second cousin, in Australia . . . somewhere just outside Melbourne, I think he said. It was his only relative, so he'd be the next of kin, wouldn't he?'

'Tell the bank manager about him, and maybe you should see his solicitors, as well. They'll need to know things like that, unless Manny had it in his will. Did he ever say anything about a will?'

'No, never, but he was always so well organized, he must have made one.'

Rosie seemed better pleased. 'Of course he would, but if he didn't put his cousin or whatever's address down, you could save them hunting all over Australia for him by letting them know he lives near Melbourne.'

Alistair thought it highly unlikely that Manny would not have given an address for his heir, but decided to go to see the solicitor the next morning anyway. Apart from pleasing Rosie, it would give him something to do, and they would have to be told that their client was dead.

Chapter 13

To the bank manager – a short, thin balding man with sharp features – Manny Isaacson's death meant just another name to add to the rapidly increasing list of accounts he'd had to close lately, although he did express sorrow that the old man's life had been terminated so suddenly and so violently. 'Mr Isaacson did not leave a great deal,' he went on, after consulting his records

'Not in cash, perhaps,' Alistair agreed, 'but I deposited some jewellery on his behalf at the start of the war for safekeeping.'

The man looked at him apologetically. 'I can not release anything to you without proper authority.'

'I wasn't expecting you to hand anything over to me, but I wondered if he'd deposited his will with you at some time.'

'Ah.' The other man stroked his upper lip reflectively. 'I have been manager of this branch for less than six months, so I am not familiar with transactions made prior to that, but if you care to wait, I can find out.'

Alistair was puzzled by the peculiar, almost accusing, look the man had given him as he passed. Surely he didn't suspect him of trying to steal the jewellery? It was just as well that he *wasn't* the heir. How on earth could anybody get proper written authority from a dead man? He shouldn't have come. He should have gone straight to the solicitor and let him deal with it.

While he waited, with nothing else to occupy it, his mind

went back to Manny, the one and only real friend he'd made in London, apart from his in-laws, and that was different. Of course, there were Ivy and Len Crocker, but that was different, too. In any case, Len had retired some time ago, and they were now living in a small fishing village not far from Newcastle to be near Ivy's sister, who had married a Geordie during the last war. They still kept in touch, of course, sending birthday cards and gifts to his children on their birthdays, though Ivy was godmother only to David. The monthly letters she had sent to Gwen, though, had dwindled down to a hastily written note in a card at Christmas. That was how things went, he mused. Your friends change over the years; they move away and find other friends, and so do you. In any case, he'd never been one for having a lot of friends. Acquaintances, yes, but friends, no. He was slow at getting close to people, a result, probably, of being brought up in a house with no near neighbours.

He wondered now how Gwen and Marge would take to the isolation. He didn't think Gwen would mind. She was quiet, a home body, whereas Marge was . . . well, Marge was just Marge – a goer. She didn't like being stuck in the house. Her next-door neighbour on the other side from Rosie had told him once that he'd seen her going into a dancehall in Lewisham a few times. 'I don't suppose there's anything in it,' he had gone on. 'She likes a laugh does Marge, but I thought I'd better tell you, and I'll leave it up to you if you tell her mother or Dougal.'

He hadn't told anybody. Knowing Marge as he did, he was quite certain that there was nothing in it, that she had just wanted to break the monotony of being alone while Dougal was serving his country. She had been looking for some amusement . . . and she'd get precious little to amuse her in Forvit. It crossed his mind that maybe

Rosie had guessed what had been going on. Had that been why she'd been so adamant that Marge should leave with Gwen and the kids? It would be a shock to his sister-in-law's system, though. She'd never walked farther than she could help, and she'd be stuck in Benview from one week's end to the next, unless she used shanks's pony. No buses ran past Alice's house. The bus from Aberdeen to Strathdon did go through Forvit, but when the Ritchies wanted to go into the city, they'd had to walk, or bike, a full mile of rough track before they came to the turnpike and could get transport, and if they were just going to the village, it was three miles there and three miles back.

He and Alice had walked to school in the early days. He'd forgotten that in his anxiety to get his family away from London. He'd been nearly ten before his father bought bikes for them at a roup, a house clearance, but if they were still in the shed, they'd be rusted out of commission by this time, so Leila and David would have to hoof it. Well, it hadn't done him or Alice any harm, in fact, it had likely kept them in peak condition – neither of them had ever been off school through illness.

'Sorry to have kept you waiting so long, Mr Ritchie.' The manager bustled in again, taking Alistair's mind off the past. 'You were quite right, there was a significant amount of valuable items deposited in our vaults by you on behalf of Mr Isaacson, but I am afraid that I am not, without written authorization, at liberty to . . .'

'I don't want them,' Alistair put in, angry because of the thinly veiled hostility in the man's eyes. 'I had to be sure they were still here, and I also wanted to find out if he had deposited his will with you. You see, I know something of the whereabouts of his next of kin, which I thought would be of use to you, but if you don't have the will . . .' He stood up and said coldly, 'Good day, and I'm sorry to have troubled you.'

The man shot to his feet, all apologies. 'I am sorry, Mr Ritchie, I did not mean to be offensive, but you must understand that I have to be careful.'

'Yes,' Alistair sighed, rather regretting his own attitude, 'I can quite understand that.'

When he went outside, he took a few deep breaths to compose himself. The man had been right. It *was* his duty to protect what had been entrusted to his care, but he could have explained things in a less aggressive manner.

Arriving at the door of Brown, Smith and Baker, Solicitors, Alistair wondered if he should just give up and let things take their own course. It really wasn't up to him, but something was urging him on, almost as if he couldn't let go of Manny until he was sure everything that could be done was being done. Everything? That jolted him. What about the funeral? Somebody would have to arrange it. He opened the street door and went up the narrow stairs to talk to whichever of the Messrs Brown, Smith and Baker had dealt with Manny's affairs.

'I couldn't believe it!' Alistair told Peggy when she came home from work that evening, while Rosie, having already heard the good news, leaned back in her chair to watch her daughter's reaction to it. 'There I was, all set to tell him about Manny's next of kin in Australia, and he held out his hand and congratulated me.'

'I don't understand,' Peggy frowned.

'Manny left everything to me.'

'He couldn't have had much to leave? You've said yourself the shop wasn't doing as well as it used to, which was why he couldn't give you a pay rise, so . . . ?'

Rosie could contain herself no longer. 'He hasn't left much cash, but he'd a whole lot of jewellery deposited in the bank, and it's all Alistair's now.'

Peggy's chin dropped. 'Wow! How much, d'you reckon?'

'I don't know how much is in his bank account, but the jewellery must be worth a good few hundred, from what I remember of the things I put in.'

'You'd no idea he was going to leave it to you?' The question came from Alf Pryor, almost like one of the family now, giving Rosie a hot snack for lunch, and spending all afternoon preparing an evening meal for her and Peggy, who had soon persuaded him to dine with them when she came home from work. Having heard the tale along with Rosie, he'd had time to consider it from all angles.

'Not the faintest!' Alistair assured him.

'However much it is, I'm happy for you!' Alf exclaimed, a grin transforming his usually serious face. 'Will this make you change your mind about going into the army?'

'Oh no. I told Mr Brown I'd volunteered and would have to report soon, and he said I could sign all the necessary papers the first time I'm home on leave.' His eyes clouded. 'The funeral's been arranged – well, not only Manny's. Apparently the borough council takes that in hand for people with nobody to see to things. It'll just be one service . . .'

'Not in a mass grave?' exclaimed Rosie, horrified at the thought of it. 'Manny would hate that.'

'No, no, they get individual graves.'

'But they could be different religions. How do they deal with that?'

'Apparently they provide a vicar, a priest and a rabbi.' Alistair shook his head sadly. 'I wish I could have afforded to give him a proper funeral.'

'You can, though . . . can't you?' demanded Peggy. 'You'll have all the money from the jewellery when you sell it.'

'I did mention that, but Mr Brown thinks it would be best to leave it where it is, to let it appreciate in value. Besides, he's had dealings with Crawford, the bank manager, before and doesn't think much of him. It seems he's a bit sticky at releasing cash, and he'd likely be worse with jewellery. Mr Brown said I should accept that I won't benefit from my windfall, as he called it, for a few months, and he advised me to let the council funeral go ahead, and to be honest, I don't think Manny would have minded. He never liked a fuss.' Alistair looked helplessly round the other three. 'In any case, there's absolutely nothing I can do.'

'You won't need to touch your inheritance till after the war,' Rosie reminded him. 'You'll come back to Civvy Street a rich man.'

'Not exactly rich,' he pointed out, 'but a lot better off than I've ever been. I can still hardly believe it!'

'So you keep saying,' Rosie smiled, 'but there are times when what seems to be the blackest of situations turns out to have a silver lining – or in this case, gold and precious stones. If Manny had meant it to be a surprise, he's certainly succeeded.'

'I wish he'd given me a clue, though. I'd have liked him to know how grateful I am.'

'He'll know,' Rosie murmured, nodding sagely. 'He'd have known before he did it. He knew the kind of man you are, honest and reliable.' She turned to her neighbour now. 'I've been very lucky with my son-in-laws, you know, Alf – two really fine men.'

Alistair's cheeks flamed, and Peggy said, 'Oh, Mum, you've embarrassed him.'

It was she who was embarrassed next. Alf cleared his throat nervously, and said, perhaps more loudly than he meant, 'I agree with you there, Rosie, and I sincerely hope you won't be disappointed in your third . . .' He paused and looked imploringly at the elderly woman, then ended, 'Rosie, I'm asking your permission to marry Peg.'

There were three separate gasps before Peggy flung herself at him. 'Alf! Why didn't you . . . You never asked me. You didn't even give me a hint.'

Over her head, he looked at her mother. 'Rosie?'

'Yes, you have my permission.' She gave a gurgling laugh. 'I've expected this, you know, and I couldn't understand why it was taking you so long.'

'I've been meaning to ask you for . . . oh, years, but I could never get the words out. It was you speaking about your two sons-in-law that gave me the courage.'

She beckoned him over and kissed his cheek. 'I'm even luckier than I thought. I'll soon have three daughters married to three wonderful men.'

After congratulating the happy pair and toasting their future happiness with the sherry Rosie had kept hidden for this very occasion, Alistair said, 'I'd better get going.' He wasn't really in a celebratory mood and he didn't want to put a damper on things.

'You'll have something to eat before you go?'

'No thanks, Rosie. I want to get things organized at home. I'll have to pack all our personal belongings before I can give up the house, and clear out all the useless odds and ends we've collected since we moved in. What about the furniture though, and the rest of the stuff you gave us when we started out?'

Rosie took a moment to think, then said, 'They're yours, so it's up to you, but you'll need them after the war, won't you? Why don't you put them in store somewhere?'

'That'd be a bit expensive, though? The war could go on for years yet.'

Alf cleared his throat. 'If you don't think I'm being out

of order, you could move them into my garage. If there isn't room for everything, my cousin in Romford also has a garage standing empty. He gave up his car a few months ago and is thinking of renting it out. It wouldn't be nearly so expensive as paying for a proper store.'

'The very thing!' exclaimed Peggy.

'I can give you a hand to pack everything,' Alf offered. 'I can come over any day – not tonight, of course.'

Quite overcome by everything that was happening, Alistair was forced to swallow before he said, shakily, 'Thanks, Alf, I'll let you know. I'll have to get some tea chests or boxes of some kind first.'

On his way home, he concentrated his thoughts on Peggy and her future husband. They were a well-matched couple, both quiet and soberly dressed, and the age difference scarcely showed; despite his wiry hair being streaked with grey, Alf's face was unlined, his blue eyes bright and clear, his back straight for all he was six feet tall. He had an air of eternal youth about him, and Peggy had always looked older than her years, not going in for much make-up or fancy hairstyles. Of course, Alf wasn't as fit as he appeared to be, but, as Peggy often said, as long as he took things easy, he shouldn't do himself any harm.

When he went into his own home again, Alistair's spirits dropped. 'Home sweet home and the fire black out,' as Len Crocker had said on the day he and Dougal arrived in London. But that had been a joke. This was reality. There was no cheer in any of the rooms as he wandered through them, and he decided he'd be as well going to bed. He would make a cup of tea, then he'd fill a hot water bottle, and then oblivion . . . hopefully.

He filled the kettle, lit the gas ring then sat down at the kitchen table. And now, with nothing else to take up his attention, his thoughts turned to Manny again. Manny, his employer, his friend, his confidante, his mentor. But Manny had been more than all of those. He'd been like a father. In fact, Alistair decided, he'd been much closer to Manny than he'd ever been to his real father. There had been a bond between them, a steel-cabled bond which could never be broken, not even by German bombs.

How patiently he'd explained the business of pawnbroking to his raw helper, how well he'd schooled his apprentice on human nature, how much interest he'd shown in all the teenage boy had to say, sorting out his trivial troubles, never telling him what to do but guiding him towards the right solutions. Later, when he discussed world events, he hadn't shoved his opinions down an impressionable young man's throat, but had deftly let him come to his own conclusions and shown no disappointment if they were not in agreement with his own.

But Manny had also done what he could to help him materially. He had made it possible for both him and Dougal to give their future wives decent engagement rings. He had given Leila and David valuable christening gifts, gifts they would treasure for ever. He had been like one of the family, yet he never took advantage of it. He had never wanted to intrude, no matter how fervently Gwen or Rosie assured him that they would never look on him as an intruder. It seemed that he preferred his own company out of business hours – no, that wasn't right. It wasn't preference, it was reserve, an inborn reserve, that held him back from mixing freely with other people. That was why he'd been on his own when . . . his life came to such an abrupt end.

This last thought was too much for Alistair. Laying his head on his arms on the table, he let the tears flood from him, tears that held guilt that he hadn't forced the old man to come and live with them, gratitude for all he had done for the Ritchies, but more than anything, deep sorrow at his passing. After God made Emanuel David Isaacson, He had broken the mould. It was an old saying, a trite saying, but how true in Manny's case.

The piercing whistle of the boiling kettle broke into his troubled thoughts, and mopping his tears with a somewhat damp handkerchief, Alistair got to his feet, filled his hot water bottle and went to bed without bothering with tea. Two hours later, he was roused from a deep sleep by the banshee-howling of the sirens, but he didn't move. If the Jerries wanted to kill him, let them. He was far too tired to care.

Alice Guthrie looked up in alarm at her sister-in-law's loud gasp. 'What's wrong? Has your house been damaged?' She knew nothing could have happened to Alistair, because it was his writing on the envelope.

'No, it's Manny. He's been killed.'

'What?' cried both Alice and Marge.

They were still sitting at the kitchen table. The children had gone off to school on the old bicycles Alice had managed to summon up from families in the village, and all three women had been reading the letters they had just received from their husbands. 'His shop got a direct hit,' Gwen went on with a catch in her voice.

'We'll have to go down for the funeral,' Marge declared.

'Yes, you can leave the kids with me,' offered Alice.

There was a moment's silence as Gwen read more of the letter. 'It's too late. The funeral's past.'

'Why didn't Alistair tell us sooner? Why on earth did he wait so long?'

'He says he was too upset, and he didn't want us to go charging down there.'

'Just as well,' Marge muttered. 'We couldn't really have afforded the fares.'

Gwen's hand shot out suddenly to stop further remarks as she came to another item of news. 'Listen to this.'

In a few moments her listeners were demanding to see the letter for themselves and scanning the neat writing while they each held a side of the pages. 'My God!' exclaimed Marge at last. 'You lucky blighters!'

'He does say they won't get any of it till after the war,' Alice pointed out. 'Still, it must be nice to know there's a nest egg waiting at the end of the tunnel.'

'I don't know what to think,' wailed Gwen. 'I can hardly believe it, and will you please give me my letter back? I haven't finished reading it.'

Her head bent over it again, and Marge said, accusingly, to Alice, 'I can't understand your brother. He's been writing every day and this happened nearly a week ago and he never mentioned it.'

'Like he said, he didn't want you to go charging down there.'

'But he must have known we'd have wanted to go?'

'He hadn't wanted Gwen to see how upset he was.'

Marge nodded now. 'That's more like it. He must be absolutely devastated – he loved that old man . . . we all did.' Both women jumped as Gwen let out another wail.

'Oh, no! I should have known he'd do that! But why couldn't he have waited?'

'What's wrong now?' Marge sounded testy.

'The day Manny was killed, Alistair volunteered for the army.'

'You knew it was only because of Manny he didn't go before.'

'Yes, but . . . oh, Marge! He should have told me as soon as . . .'

Marge shook her head sadly. 'Think how he must have felt, Gwennie – as if *his* life had come to an end, as well . . . his life as he'd known it, I mean. No Manny, no job . . .'

'No wife and kids, either,' Gwen said, bitterly, 'but he didn't care about us, did he?'

'Of course he did! He sent you away from London because he loved you and didn't want anything to happen to any of you.'

Alice, keeping out of it until now, said, rather sharply, 'You should be proud of him, Gwen. At least he didn't go to pieces at what had happened. He took a decision to do what he could to pay the Germans back for . . .'

'Yes, that's what it had been.' Gwen sounded quite relieved. 'It was a shock, that's all, after reading about Manny . . .'

'Not forgetting the windfall,' Marge reminded her. 'Are you sure he didn't have any more surprises up his sleeve?'

Her sister looked down at the letter again. 'No, he just says how pleased he was at Peg and Alf getting engaged, and we already knew that.'

They had been told in a letter from Peggy five days earlier, which had been the subject for much discussion at the time.

'I'm glad I had time to get over that,' Gwen said now. 'I had enough to take in today. Poor Manny! He used to come to see me once a week before his legs gave up.' She paused, her brows coming down in puzzlement. 'You know, I think he did try to give me a hint once that he was leaving everything to Alistair, but he didn't come right out with it and it didn't dawn on me what he was meaning.' Her face clearing, she went on, 'Alistair must have been heartbroken. He worshipped that old man, and he always said he'd have joined up long ago if it hadn't been for him. Yes, I can understand now why his first thought was to have a go at the Germans.'

She paused, then smiled. 'Anything interesting in any of your letters, girls?'

Marge shrugged. 'Nothing much in Dougal's, just how much he's missing me. He's bored stiff in Wales, and wishing he could get back into the fray, but I'm just thankful he's in a place where he's safe.' She turned to Alice. 'What's Sam saying?'

'I was waiting to tell you. He's been told he'll be at Turnhouse for the foreseeable future, so he's rented what had once been a farm worker's cottage on the outskirts of Edinburgh, not far from the drome. He's expecting us down the day after tomorrow, so after we go, you two can have a bedroom each, and . . .'

'That means . . .' Marge hesitated, then grinned wickedly. 'You know what I mean. Good show!'

'Did I hear you saying we could have a bedroom each?' Gwen inquired, returning her letter to its envelope. 'That's good. Alistair says he might manage a visit before he has to report at Catterick, and I was wondering where he would sleep.'

When the children came home, Gwen told them first, quietly and patiently, about Manny, and then, to save them dwelling on it too much, she gave them the good news. 'Daddy might be coming to see us soon, before he goes into the army.'

'Oh, great!' shouted David. 'I can't wait to see him in his uniform.'

'He won't be in uniform, not yet. Next time he comes, though.'

It was Marge who noticed the boy's hand slipping into his pocket occasionally, then transferring something to his mouth. 'What's that you're eating?' she demanded.

'Some sweets we got from the shop lady.'

'You shouldn't have been in the shop!' Gwen snapped.

'We weren't.' David was at his most indignant. 'She came out and gave them to us – a bag each. She said she used to know our Dad.'

Alice laughed. 'That's Lexie Fraser. She was . . . um . . . at school with your Dad and your Uncle Dougal.'

'You mustn't take sweets from her again, though,' Gwen warned. 'They're rationed.'

'She said she never eats her ration,' Leila defended her brother. 'She said she knew Dad really well when they were young.'

'And she winked,' David added.

Once again, it was Marge who picked up the underlying meaning to the seemingly open gift to two children, but she said nothing until she and Gwen were in bed. 'What did you make of that shop person?'

'Giving them sweets? It was good of her, but she shouldn't, they might come to expect it, and it's not good for their teeth.'

'That's not what I meant. David said she winked when she said she knew Alistair really well when they were young. She could have been a girlfriend.'

'She was. He did tell me, and it was long before he met me. Anyway, she could have been winking about the sweets. Maybe they weren't off her ration. Maybe she just helped herself from the jars, or boxes, or whatever.'

'I'd watch her, if I was you.'

'Don't be silly. She knew who they were and she was just being friendly with them.'

'Well, don't say I didn't warn you.'

Alice packed two suitcases and an old valise with her own and her small daughter's clothes. 'Sam says we don't need anything else,' she told Gwen and Marge while she waited –

the doctor had promised to take her to the railway station in Aberdeen. 'The house is fully furnished, even chamber pots under the beds. Just as well, for the lavatory's outside.' Giggling, she added, 'It'll be back to using a chanty in the middle of the night, or getting my bum frozen in a privy. I thought I'd seen the last of that.'

'Never mind,' consoled Marge, grinning, 'Sam'll soon heat it up again.'

Gwen ignored her sister's ribaldry. 'Are you sure you'll manage all that, Alice?'

'Sam's going to meet us at Waverley Station. Their camp isn't all that far out of Edinburgh. Here's the doctor, thank goodness. I was worried that he'd been called out and couldn't take us.'

A quick flurry of good wishes and they were gone.

'And that's us left on our own,' Marge declared, sitting down with a bump. 'We don't know a soul, we can't speak the lingo if the postman's anything to go by. I can hardly understand a word he says.'

Alistair arrived the next morning, and having travelled overnight after two days of intensive clearing out his rented house, he did not look at his best, but it didn't matter to Gwen who rushed at him as if she hadn't seen him for years not just two weeks.

'You won't want me hanging around,' announced Marge, 'so I think I'll get out Alice's bike and take a trip to the village shop. I'll get a loaf of bread, shall I, and we'll need some butter, so I'll need the ration books.'

Gwen made a face. 'It's a good thing you remembered, I'd have forgotten, but get some bacon as well, if you can.'

'Sorry, Marge,' laughed Alistair. 'I haven't had time to speak to you yet.'

'No, you've been too busy kissing your wife, but it's OK. I can take a hint.'

She hadn't been on a bicycle since she was a little girl living in army quarters in Aldershot, and she was quite wobbly until she got the hang of it again and set off along the track. Never having cycled more than the length of a short street before, she was amazed at how far a mile seemed to be . . . one rough, rutted mile before she reached the road, with another two miles to go.

She took more notice of her surroundings now than she had done when she was here with Dougal a few months after they were married. She had thought it was hardly fit to be called a village then, but she had supposed that there must be another few streets tucked in behind the houses fronting on to the main road. There didn't seem to be any hidden streets or lanes, nothing. Passing two low cottages on her left, with gardens given over to vegetables as at Benview, she was surprised that there was only a field of turnips or something to her right. After the second little dwelling, there was the opening which Dougal had told her led through to the Frasers' house, only Lexie would live there now, of course, and then the shop itself.

Curious about other habitation and/or amenities, she cycled on, past about six houses of varying styles and sizes and in different degrees of repair, but each with its fenced garden. Then came a much bigger house, with correspondingly bigger garden. Then she came to the Royal Hotel, where according to Dougal, all the local men took refuge from their wives when they were on the warpath. She had asked him to take her in, but he had explained that no 'nice' women went drinking in Forvit. It wouldn't worry her, Marge decided. She liked a drop of sherry now and then, but wouldn't be too upset if she never saw the stuff.

The next house had a Great Dane in residence, barking at

her until she was clear of his 'space'. Then she came to the church, not very imposing, but big enough, she supposed, for all the congregation it could have, with its graveyard at one side and the vicarage – or whatever the Scots called it – at the other. There was a long gap now, suggesting that two, or perhaps three, houses had been knocked down to make way for more modern housing, which would be a pity. The appeal of Forvit lay in its quaint old cottages and lack of any kind of symmetry.

And that was the end of it, a bridge over what was little more than a stream, and moorland from then on. In fact, the village could be described as an oasis set in the midst of miles of heath. Dismounting, she turned her cycle round and started back.

The last house on that side – the first coming this way – was a more up-to-date, three-storeyed building with a long walled garden. A brass plaque on the gate said, Dr Christopher Geddes, Surgery Hours 3–4, 6–7. Well, Marge thought, she knew where to find the doctor if any of them were ill.

Next came the little school, with its tarred playground at the side farthest from the doctor, followed by the Jubilee Hall, with 1897 engraved in the lintel stone, which, of course, was the date of Queen Victoria's jubilee year.

Proud of remembering this, and having come to the field of turnips once more, she came off the bicycle and wheeled it across the street, glad to have a break. Her legs were aching, her rear end was practically numb and she was frozen to the marrow . . . and she still had three miles to go before she reached 'home'.

She was glad to see two women in the shop. It gave her a chance to stand at the side of the open door for a few moments and have a good look at Lexie Fraser. She was actually quite a pretty woman, with rosy cheeks and hair that was as fair as Gwen's, eyes a lighter shade of blue, and roughly the same height. Marge could more or less understand what she was saying, but the other two women were speaking in a kind of rapid-fire gibberish. Marge did manage to make out a few words here and there, but it wasn't until Alice's name was mentioned that she took an interest and concentrated as hard as she could.

'Did you ken Alice Ritchie's awa' to Edinburgh to be wi' Sam?' the waiting customer observed. 'The doctor was to be takin' her an' Morag to Aberdeen.'

'Alistair's wife an' her sister'll be left to look after the place,' commented the one being served. 'Have you come across ony o' them yet, Lexie?'

'I've spoken to the bairns, Doodie, nice wee souls they are. The girl's real shy, but the boy's more friendly.'

'Weel, we're nae wantin' their kind here. Up fae London and likely lookin' doon their noses at us. What do you say, Aggie?'

Her friend nodded. 'No, Doodie, we'd enough o' English folk when yon minister and his wife was here . . . I canna mind his name, but you'd have thocht he was God himsel', the wey he swaggered aboot, and as for his wife and her short skirties . . . she was a stuck-up besom.'

'They werena Cockneys, o' coorse,' Doodie pointed out. 'It was . . . Liverpool they belonged, and what a queer wey they spoke. Thank goodness he only bade five month.'

Aggie looked archly at Lexie now. 'You an' Alistair was affa close at one time, wasn't you? We a' thocht you an' him would get wed some day.'

Lexie's face darkened. 'And so we would, if Dougal Finnie hadn't dragged him away down to London with him.'

Marge's involuntary gasp at this made them aware of her presence, so she walked inside. Lexie obviously recognized her as Dougal's wife, but just as obviously had decided to brazen it out. 'I'll be with you in a jiffy, Mrs . . . ?'

'Mrs Finnie,' Marge said icily. 'Mrs Dougal Finnie.'

The other two women whipped round, their faces colouring, then turned back to Lexie, who said, smoothly, 'That'll be four and sevenpence, Doodie, if you please.'

Doodie counted the money out on to the counter, four shillings, a sixpenny bit and a penny, then stood aside to let Aggie be served. The tension in the shop was almost tangible, and nothing more was said, so when the second transaction was over, the two women left the shop.

'I'm sorry about that, Mrs Finnie,' Lexie said then, 'but I didn't notice you there and in any case I didn't know who you were. Besides, I was only speaking the truth. Alistair wouldn't have gone to London if it hadn't been for Dougal. You see, we were . . .' She gave her head a slight shake. 'But it's best to let bygones be bygones, isn't it? What can I get for you?'

The bread, butter and bacon paid for, the ration books duly marked, Lexie said, 'I don't think you should say anything to Alistair's wife. It was over between us long ago and there's no sense in upsetting her, is there?'

'There's nothing to tell anyway . . . is there?'

Lexie's red cheeks took on a slightly deeper hue. 'If you're asking if Alistair and me . . . were lovers, the answer's no.'

'He arrived just before I came out.' Marge watched for the reaction.

'Alistair's back?' Lexie gasped, her face aflame now.

'He'll only be here for a few days, so he wasn't wasting any time when I came out. I could see they weren't wanting me there.'

Marge hoped that this would stop the woman from trying to see him, but as she cycled back, she couldn't help feeling sorry for her.

'You don't know how much I've missed you, Gwen.'

'I missed you, too, darling, but it must have been worse for you, losing Manny . . .'

They were snuggled together on the old sofa Alistair remembered being told to keep his feet off when he was a child. He wanted to make love to her, but after almost ten years of marriage, it didn't seem proper to be so lustful, especially here . . . in the middle of the day.

'Yes, it was a terrible shock.' He was glad she had given him a lead into what he'd been turning over in his mind since the funeral. 'I'm damned glad you and the kids are away from it, so I can have an easy mind when I'm away. Better still, Mr Brown, that's Manny's solicitor, he's arranging for Crawford at the bank to sell one or two of the pieces of jewellery if he can, and add it to the account they opened for us with the two hundred Manny left. That'll let you draw a few pounds every week to help out, for the allowance you'll get from the army won't be very much.'

'I know how much Marge gets,' Gwen put in, 'and we'll easily manage between the two of us. I'm used to having to be careful with my spending.'

'Yes, but you can't expect Marge to pay half the expenses here when you've the two kids to feed as well. Anyway, it's done now and you don't have to touch it if you don't need to. It can lie in the bank till the war's over – God knows how long that'll be. Oh, I nearly forgot. Mr Brown drew up a proper will for me, so if anything happens to me, everything'll come to you.'

'Don't say things like that, darling. Nothing's going to happen to you!'

'We have to face facts, dear, and it's best to be prepared.' He stopped momentarily then rushed on, 'But I'll tell you this, if I do get killed, I'll murder the Jerry that did it.'

His grin was not enough to make his wife take this in the

light-hearted way it was meant. 'Don't be morbid, Alistair Ritchie!' she cried, tears gathering in her eyes. 'You have to make your mind up you won't be killed.'

'Oh, my sweet, I'm sorry for upsetting you. I was only joking, and it's time we got on to something else. Have you been to the village yet?'

'Not yet. Alice has done all the shopping since we came, but Marge and I will have to take turns now she's away, I suppose. She said we could use her bike, though I don't know when I last rode one.'

'It's something you never forget,' her husband consoled.

'Oh, I nearly forgot. Leila and David came home with sweets the other day. He said the shop lady gave them to him. She said she was an old friend of yours.'

'That's Lexie Fraser. I told you – she was at school with Dougal and me.'

'Nothing else?'

'What d'you . . .' The answer dawning, he chuckled loudly. 'Oh, I knocked around with her for a while, two fifteen-sixteen-year-olds playing at being grown up, you know.'

'Just playing at it? You weren't . . . you didn't . . . ?'

'We stopped at kissing, if that's what you mean. Just kids kissing, nothing in it.'

'You're sure that was all?'

'Look, Gwen, darling, I've only ever loved one girl in my whole life and that's you. I've never thought twice about any other girl, and I never will. You're my whole life, Gwendoline Ritchie, you and the kids.'

He pulled her to him and their kisses might have made him forget his reluctance to do anything on his mother's old sofa if Marge hadn't walked in.

'Oh, shit!' she laughed. 'I've come back too soon, have I? Couldn't you two have waited till bedtime?'

Flustered, Gwen sprang to her feet and smoothed her

clothes. 'Don't be silly, Marge. We haven't seen each other for weeks and we were . . . talking things over, that's all.'

'I believe you, thousands wouldn't.' Marge set the shopping bag down on the well-scrubbed table in the middle of the kitchen to unpack it. 'You know, I'm getting quite an expert on the bike again, if only my bum gets used to it.' Rubbing her rump wryly, she began to put away her purchases.

'Was it Lexie Fraser who served you?' Gwen tried to sound nonchalant, but she was desperate to hear something about this girl, woman now, who had once been part of Alistair's life.

'Yes, she was serving two middle-aged harpies when I went in, Aggie and Doodie, but she knew who I was. It wouldn't be difficult. We must be the only two strangers within miles of the place, and she had likely seen me when I was here with Dougal.'

'That would have been Aggie Mearns and Doodie Tough,' Alistair observed, his memory having successfully put faces to the familiar names. He glanced at the clock. 'Can I use that kettle to wash and shave, or was it for making tea?'

Both women burst out laughing at this. 'There's a bathroom upstairs,' his wife told him, 'with hot and cold running water. Alice's Sam had it put in.'

Alistair pulled a face. 'Shows how long it is since I've been here. OK, won't be long, but I have to get this stubble off before my wife complains of my sandpaper chin.'

When he went out, Marge eyed Gwen affectionately. 'He looks better than I thought he would, what with Manny's death, and going in the army. How does he feel about that, has he said?'

'I think he's quite looking forward to it.'

'No regrets? After all, he volunteered as a reflex action after Manny . . .'

'He wants to do his bit, for Manny's sake.'

'Well, I hope this damned war doesn't last long.' Marge pulled a face. 'The locals don't want to be friendly, they're anti-all-English.'

'Surely not.' Gwen was shocked at this. 'You'd been imagining things.'

'That's what they were saying, anyway, before they realized who I was, but I suppose we won't come much in contact with them, so it won't bother us.'

'Should we invite Lexie to come and see Alistair? They *are* old friends.'

'He'll be gone the day after tomorrow, and I'd have thought you'd want him all to yourself . . . no old ladyloves butting in.' Marge wasn't meaning to instil suspicion in her sister's mind. She was just being careful.

Chapter 14

The first contingent of the Black Watch had not arrived at Ardley House until the 26 April, and for two full weeks not even one private had made an appearance in either Forvit or Bankside, and the female populations of both were beginning to wonder if their dreams of romance were to come to nothing. By the end of the third week, however, most of the young soldiers had made contact with one or more of the girls in all the villages within a ten-mile radius of their base, scouting around in jeeps and trucks, on motor cycles, even riding bicycles. Lexie Fraser, being in the shop-cum-post office, saw more of them than anyone else, but sadly found that the majority of them were much too young for her – or, to be more precise, *she* was much too old for *them*.

But salvation was at hand. Some of the local farmers decided to do their bit for the war effort by funding a 'get-together' to welcome the newcomers; what could be more patriotic than providing amusement for the fighting men? The Jubilee Hall in Forvit – built by the laird of the time to celebrate sixty years of Queen Victoria's reign – was filled to capacity during the entire evening.

The Royal Hotel had supplied the drinks, free for the first hour and half-price from then on, which resulted in such shenanigans as made the owners regret their generosity and vow never to repeat it. Both youths and girls being determined to find a suitable partner, there were several Paul Joneses played, and the bus the army laid on didn't come to take the boys back to camp until two a.m. This official introduction of soldiers to locals was a great success, at least one instance of true love being initiated, but mostly just brief encounters. Each side would need to get to know the other better before any commitments were made, temporary or otherwise.

Lexie Fraser had played the field of the NCOs, nearer her age, but when the dance ended, was no nearer to finding a life partner than when it began, but she had thoroughly enjoyed every minute.

'Wasn't it great?' she asked Lizzie Wilkie the next day. 'I really enjoyed myself.'

'Aye, you made a right exhibition o' yourself,' Lizzie said, caustically, 'but I suppose you was desperate. The men round here havena had much time for you lately.'

Ignoring the slur, Lexie gave a carefree laugh. 'You're just jealous, and you needn't worry. It looks like I was cut out to be an old maid, but, I tell you this, Lizzie, I'm going to get as much pleasure out of life as I can before I settle down with a cat at my feet and a bag of knitting on my lap.'

The other woman looked somewhat ashamed. 'Ach, Lexie, I didna mean what I said. You're right, I was jealous, but I'd like to see you finding somebody.'

'I'm not bothered, honestly.' She looked up as the shop bell tinkled and addressed her next words to the new customer. 'None of the wives round here are really happy, isn't that right, Gladys? Every one of you's forever complaining about your man.'

'That's different,' Gladys said, indignantly. 'We complain about them, but it doesn't mean we're nae happy wi' them. They can still make us . . . forget the bad things they get up to. Tak' my Chae now.'

'No, thank you very much,' Lexie giggled, while Lizzie spluttered with laughter.

'You can laugh a' you like,' Gladys declared firmly, not in the least put out, 'but even though he comes rolling in fu' on Saturday nichts, he still . . . he can . . .' She broke off, her cheeks pink. 'No, no, you single lassies dinna understand, but I wouldna change him, supposing the maist handsome man in the world walked in right this minute and offered me a thousand pounds to share his bed.'

'Fat chance of that,' Lexie muttered, doing her best to keep a straight face.

'Aye, well, you're right there, but you ken what I mean. I took my Chae for better or worse on oor wedding day, and I'm quite happy to thole the worse, for the better couldna be better, if you get my meaning?' She gave a lewd wink. 'Now if you're nae in a hurry, Lizzie, would you let Lexie serve me first? I just want a bit o' haddock for the supper. Is that fresh?' She pointed at a shimmering enamel tray under the glass counter.

'Fresh in from Peterhead this morning,' Lexie assured her.

'Gi'e me two, then, that biggest ane for Chae, and a littler ane for me.' While the fish were being wrapped, she fumbled in her purse, then laid down the exact money and left with a cheery, 'Ta-ta, then.'

Waiting until she went past the window, the two younger women gave vent to their laughter at last, holding on to the counter until they simmered down. 'Oh, my God,' Lizzie gasped, holding her aching sides. '"Tak' my Chae," she said, and I near fell ower when you said, "No, thank you very much." I dinna ken how you managed. Her Chae's got a big fat boozer's nose, and his face is mottled-purple, and his eyes look two ways for Sunday. It would turn my stomach if I found him lying in the bed aside me.'

'It's his great beer belly that sickens me,' Lexie gurgled, 'hanging over his breeks like that. And Gladys isn't what you'd call slim, either, is she? I wonder how they manage to get near enough to . . . ? Their two bellies would be a big obstacle.' They looked at each other and dissolved into another fit of uncontrollable raucous laughter.

After a few moments, Lizzie managed to get out, 'I suppose his bandy legs help them to get closer. They're that bowed Sandy Coull's auld sow could run under them.'

It was perhaps fortunate for them that another customer walked in at that point, a passing motorist who, being an absolute stranger, had an instant sobering effect on them. Lizzie paid for the items Lexie had already set out for her, packed them in her shopping bag and walked out with a surprisingly dignified gait.

The monotony was getting to Marjory Finnie.

'I'm sick of this,' she moaned one morning after the children had set off for school. 'We've been up in this Godforsaken hole for months now, cut off from everything and everybody, and there's nothing to do except work in the blasted garden. I didn't mind having to do our wee patch at home after Dougal went away, but I never thought I'd have to tackle anything like this – it's like a bally field. Just look at my hands.' She held out the offending parts of her anatomy to let her sister see the reddened, chafed palms and callused fingers.

'Mine are the same,' Gwen told her, 'but think of the perks. We never have to buy any vegetables, all we have to do is pull them or dig them up when we need them.'

'I wish they got up by themselves,' Marge said ruefully. 'All this pulling and digging, and weeding and raking, I'd be as well in the Land Army, and I'd get paid for it.'

'You wouldn't pass the medical with your bad ear, and your asthma.'

'I haven't had one bout of asthma since I came up here – fresh country air's good for chest troubles – and being a wee bit deaf in one ear wouldn't be a handicap in the Land Army, now would it?'

'You can't go into the Land Army, Marge. I couldn't bear it here on my own.'

'It's not all sweetness and light under your bushel, then? You're as homesick as me.'

'Not really. It's just that . . . oh, I don't know. Alice is expecting us to keep her garden going the way she had it, and I haven't a clue how to plant things for next year.'

Marge's face became a study in horror. 'We won't still be here next year . . . will we?'

'I hope not, but Alistair says I've to keep the kids here till the war's over.'

'It's all right for him. It's where he was brought up, and I suppose he sees it through rose-coloured specs, but we've been accustomed to the stir of London, going round the markets on our days off, or off up west to window-shop. This isn't even a dead-and-alive hole . . . it's just dead. Only one street, one shop, if it can be classed as a shop, one church, one doctor according to what Alice said . . .'

'But it's much better for the children,' Gwen pointed out. 'They look much healthier already with all the good, fresh air and all the open space around us, nothing to see from our windows except hills . . .'

'That's what I'm complaining about,' Marge sighed. 'The Back of Bally Beyond, that's where we are, and I'm sick of it. Dougal wouldn't know if I went home . . . not until he has his next leave.'

'You can't leave me here on my own!' Gwen burst out. 'Please, Marge, don't go! I couldn't cope with looking after this place by myself! I wouldn't know where to start.'

'I was only joking, Gwennie.' Marge's smile, however,

was perhaps a little forced. 'Dougal would have a fit if I went back to Lee Green. But about this blasted garden . . . I suppose we could ask somebody? The postman seems quite nice.'

'What about asking Lexie Fraser in the shop if she knows of a young lad who might come and give us a hand? Do the heavy work.'

'I'm not asking her, Gwen – I just can't take to her. You'll have to do it.'

'You know I don't like asking people for anything . . . but all right. I'll ask her next week when it's my turn to do the shopping. Now, if you fetch the pail, I'll dig up the potatoes this time, to save your precious hands.'

They worked in silence, until the ringing of a bicycle bell made them straighten up. 'You're busy, I see,' observed the postman, a small wiry man, always cheery and ever ready for a chat, though the two Englishwomen hadn't jumped to his bait yet. 'A letter for you, Mrs Ritchie, but nothing for you today, Mrs Finnie, I'm afraid.'

As Gwen tore open the envelope, he remarked to Marge, 'I'm nae one to interfere, but tell your sister she'd be better to use a graip to lift the tatties, nae a spade.'

'A grape?' gasped Marge. 'What use would a grape be? And where would we get any up here?'

His rather sharp features were transformed by a wide smile at this. 'Nae a G-R-A-P-E, a G-R- . . . Ach, I'm nae sure how you spell it, G-R-A-I-P I suppose, and you'll mebbe ken it as a fork. That's what she should be usin'.'

The perplexity in Marge's eyes deepened. 'But a fork wouldn't make any impression on this earth, Mr . . . um . . . ? It's as heavy as blooming lead.'

He threw back his head and roared with laughter now. 'The name's Sandy Mearns, an' it's well seen you're nae a country lassie. A garden fork, that's what you need for this job, so you can dunt aff the earth afore you put the tatties in your bucket.'

'Dunt aff?' Marge looked more bewildered than ever.

'Eh . . .' The man searched for words she would understand. 'Knock off, before you put them in your pail. I'll show you.' Opening the gate he was leaning on, he walked up the path and round the corner of the house, to return in a few moments carrying the implement he was recommending, clearly having known which of the three outhouses held the garden tools. 'Watch, noo!' he ordered, sticking the fork into the ground behind and under the withered leaves of one of the plants, giving it two hefty thumps with the sole of his right boot, then levering it up again.

'This is the wey, look. Shoogle it aboot a bit, then gi'e't a dunt against your knee.' The bang on his knee dislodged most of the soil clinging to the potatoes, and as he transferred the vegetables to the pail, he said, triumphantly, 'D'ye see? It's nae near so hard work.' He handed the fork to Marge. 'You tak' the next shaw, noo.'

Her effort didn't produce as many potatoes as Sandy's, but she was quite pleased with what went into the pail. 'It's easy when you know how,' she exulted.

'Aye,' he grinned, 'I tell't you.' First giving his grimy hands a wipe down his trousers, he removed his cheesecutter and ran his fingers through his thinning mousy hair. Then he took the palm of his hand across his damp brow before putting the hat back on. 'I'd best be goin', though, or folk'll think there's nae post the day.'

Marge wondered how to show her gratitude. She had the distinct feeling that he'd be offended if she offered him money, and settled for asking if he would like a cup of tea.

'Thanks, Mrs Finnie, but I'm late as it is. Anither time, mebbe.'

'Right, well, thank you very much, Mr Mearns.'

'Sandy, for ony sake, an' it was nae bother. Cheeribye, noo, and I'm sure you'll get your man's letter the morn.'

'What was all that about?' asked Gwen, some minutes after the man had cycled off.

'Sandy was showing me the proper way to lift the spuds. Watch.'

Gwen was astonished at the way her sister unearthed another lot of potatoes, but only said, 'Sandy? For goodness' sake, Marge! You didn't ask his name, did you?'

'No, he told me.'

'You should have asked if he knew anybody who'd give us an hour or two's help now and again. That would have been more to the point.'

'I clean forgot, Gwen, I was so interested in what he was doing. But we can ask him tomorrow, or next time he comes. What's Alistair saying?'

'He says they've been kept at it, marching, drill, all sorts of things, but . . . the good news is, he has a few days leave after this initial training's finished, before he's posted. He'll be here next Friday.'

'I hope I get a letter from Dougal tomorrow. Wouldn't it be great if they could be here together?'

Alistair was amazed at how well the large garden was looking, almost as good as when his father had tended it, and deeply impressed by the potato pit installed by Barry Mearns – Sandy's thirteen-year-old son – but, on only his second day home, he said, 'If you don't mind, Gwen, I'll take Alice's bike and have a wee scoot round to see some of my old pals.'

'I don't mind,' she assured him. She couldn't get over how handsome he looked in uniform, and David had been ecstatic at having a Dad in the services.

'He might go to that Lexie person,' Marge remarked when Alistair had gone.

Gwen smiled happily. 'I hope he does. It'll be nice for him to see her again.'

After discovering that all his school friends had been called up or had gone into the forces voluntarily like himself, Alistair wished that he had spent his precious time with his wife. As he passed the shop on his way home, however, it crossed his mind that at least he could have a few words with Lexie. They'd been quite close at one time – too close for his own comfort on the day of his mother's funeral – and she couldn't still be angry at him for going to London.

Her face lit up with pleasure when he walked into the shop. 'Alistair! I didn't know you'd come home.'

So long used to Gwen's soft tones, he felt a brief stab of irritation at Lexie's rough country voice. She hadn't changed much physically, either – waist still as small, bust still as rounded. She wasn't so refined-looking as his wife, but prettier than he remembered. 'You're looking well,' he smiled, trying to rid his mind of what he had almost done the last time he was with her.

'You, and all.' She glanced at the large clock on the wall. 'It still wants five minutes to dinner time, but ach . . . nobody'll be in now, so I may as well shut.' She came round the counter, brushing past him as she went to lock the door. 'Come through to the house so we can speak without being interrupted.'

He followed her through. He wanted to hear all the gossip of the village and Lexie didn't disappoint him. She told him that Gerry Lovie had run away with Dod Prosser's wife about five years ago, 'Then Dod upped and off himself, God knows where to.'

'I was hoping to see Gerry Lovie,' Alistair said, sadly, 'and I did think it was funny his mother saying she didn't know where he was, but that explains it.'

'And remember Bunty Simmers? Well, her father threw her out for not telling him who put her in the family way. Jake Simmers was aye a narrow-minded, cantankerous brute, but his wife hasn't spoken to him since, and nobody's ever heard tell of Bunty.'

She went over as much as she could recall of the events that had enlivened the small community over the years; humorous, like the time Willie Kemp had been so drunk he'd fallen off his bike on his way home from the pub and landed in a bed of nettles; sad, like when Maggie Durward, Johnny Greig's wife, died in childbirth at the age of twenty-four; tragic, as when Freddy Findlay's four-year-old daughter fell in the mill race and drowned before anybody could get her out.

Alistair listened avidly, dredging his memory to put faces to the names, seeing the people concerned as they were when he had known them. Time flew past, but neither of them noticed until a loud rattling of the shop door handle shocked them out of the past.

'Oh God!' Alistair exclaimed, looking at his watch and jumping to his feet. 'I've been here over an hour and a half. Gwen'll be wondering where I am.'

Lexie got off her seat reluctantly. 'I should have opened half an hour ago, but that's the first person that's needed in. So . . . what the hell?'

He waited for her to go into the shop area first, and as she passed him, she said, 'If you don't want to be seen, you can wait there till whoever it is has gone away.'

'No, it doesn't matter. I left Alice's bike outside.'

Following her through, he waited until she unlocked the shop door and walked past the astonished customer with a smiling, 'Aye, aye, Gladdy.'

Jumping on the bicycle, he hoped that he hadn't laid the grounds for talk, it would be embarrassing for Lexie, but she could fend for herself, and they hadn't done anything wrong, anyway. His conscience was quite clear.

'Where on earth have you been?' Gwen greeted him, when he entered the house. 'We've had our dinner and yours is in the oven, but it'll be all dried out by this time.'

'I don't mind, I can eat anything after the muck we got in the mess. I'm sorry I'm late, though. I was all over the place trying to get hold of some of my old mates, but they're all away, so I went to the shop as a last resort, and . . . well, Lexie was giving me all the gossip, what's been happening since I left.'

'I could do with a friend,' Gwen sighed. 'I feel isolated, so far from the village.'

Marge nodded her agreement to this. 'Why don't we go home, Gwennie? Back to Mum and Peg . . . we could be there for the wedding.'

'No!' Alistair said, firmly. 'You can go back if you want, but my wife and kids are staying right here. God Almighty, have you forgotten what it's like in London?'

The children took possession of their father when they came home, and both Gwen and Marge were glad when he offered to take them out of the way for a while. He took the short cut through the wood to the tower, joining the path from the main road about three quarters of the way up the hill, and while they walked, he exaggerated some of his experiences in the Artillery for the benefit of his son, who hung on to every word. Leila was content to listen, though she kept a firm grasp of her father's hand.

When they reached the top, he made them look around them while he explained the various landmarks and named the mountains in the distance, Ben this and Ben that. 'So that's why the house is called Benview,' David exclaimed, delighted at having made the connection. Then the two youngsters ran to have a closer inspection of the old ruin, and Alistair sat down, his mind turning to another time he'd been there – the night before he sailed to London, the night he had finished with Lexie. It struck him now how brutal he'd been, snapping their relationship as if it was nothing stronger than a matchstick. She'd been much more vulnerable at the time than a normal sixteen-year-old because of her father deserting her, and there was no doubt that he'd wounded her badly, for she had never taken a husband. Poor Lexie. She wasn't so pushy now, and he'd honestly enjoyed their talk. She had brought his youth back to him so vividly . . .

'Dad! What d'you call this?' David was holding a fluttering insect between his fingers. 'I say it's a daddy-longlegs and Leila says her teacher says they're called crane flies, or something like that.'

Alistair couldn't help laughing at the boy's earnestness. 'Well, son, we called that a daddy-longlegs when I was a boy, too, but maybe crane fly's its real name.'

'Miss Rettie says it is,' Leila said quietly, 'and she's always right.'

'OK, then, crane fly it must be,' her father chuckled.

'But me and Dad's still going to call them daddy-longlegses,' David insisted.

'Let it go now, son. We'd better get back before Mum and Auntie Marge send out a search party for us. I'll be in the bad books if I'm late again.'

'Who keeps the bad books?' David wanted know.

After making love to his wife for the first time in months, Dougal was in a state of happy contentment, smoking a cigarette to let a decent time pass before reaching for her again, when she upset his euphoria by whispering, 'I'm thinking of going home, Dougal.'

Irritated that her mind was on other things, he blew a smoke ring at the ceiling before snapping, 'Home? Back to Lee Green? Don't be daft, woman! They're still being bombed. Not every night, maybe, but too damned often. What brought this on? Have you and Gwen had a row?'

'Of course not! I'm bored out of my mind here, that's what. Nobody to speak to, no cinemas, no dance halls, nothing to do at nights except listen to the wireless . . .'

'At least you don't get any air raids,' Dougal growled. 'You're not going back, Marge, and that's final. I'd be out of my mind worrying about you.'

'Would you? Honestly? Oh, Dougal, so you still love me?'

'I'll never stop loving you, my darling.' His face showed his surprise that she had ever doubted it. 'You mean everything to me, always will, you should know that.'

'I know I've been silly, but I don't think I'd actually have left Gwen here on her own with the kids. It was just . . . oh, Dougal, I miss you so much, and I'll never stop loving you, either.'

Dougal ground out the stub in the ashtray. 'Thank God for that! When I was away from you, I did sometimes wonder.'

She felt like teasing him a little. 'There are some troops stationed not far away, apparently, but I've only ever seen one or two of them in the village when I'm shopping.' She kissed away his frown, and lay back again, adding, 'I'm not interested in anybody else, darling, and never will be. Don't ever forget that!'

'I'll try, Marge. I know you'd never cheat on me. It's just being so far away . . .'

'I wish you could have been here to see Alistair. Fancy missing him by one week.'

'Aye, I'd have liked to see him. But that's war! Come here, wench!'

She turned towards him eagerly. Ever since she had got his letter saying that he'd be home on Saturday, she, too, had been happily anticipating their first night together.

On Sunday, it was David who suggested that they all take a walk to the tower. 'Dad took me and Leila up there when we came home from school one day, remember, Mum?'

Gwen nodded, but made sure that she kept the children in front with her, to leave Marge with her husband.

It was a sunny day, warm for the end of October if rather windy, and David darted hither and thither looking for wild flowers or interesting insects, while eight-year-old Leila walked sedately by her mother's side, chattering about things that had happened at school.

Ambling some distance behind them, Marge broke a silence by saying, 'Is something bothering you, Dougal? You've hardly said a word since we came out.'

'I was thinking,' he said, slowly, quietly. 'It's watching young David, I suppose, but I can't help wishing . . . oh, Marge, I wish we could have made a son . . . or a daughter.'

Her heart swelled with a painful love. 'I know how you feel,' she murmured. 'I've felt exactly the same ever since Leila was born, and it's been worse since we came to Forvit and I see the two of them every day.'

Dougal brightened as something occurred to him. 'Maybe being in Forvit's the answer. A change of location could do the trick. Maybe I hit the bullseye last night? What d'you think?'

She blushed. 'Possibly, my dearest. You tried hard enough.'

Their laughter made Gwen turn round. 'Aren't you two going to share the joke?'

'Maybe . . . in a couple of months,' Marge grinned.

Chapter 15

Even after months of longing to be with his wife, Dougal, like Alistair, was drawn to seeking out his old pals to talk over old times, and, like Alistair, found that they were all in the forces or had moved away from Forvit altogether. Unlike Alistair, however, he had made his search in the evening, and he was taken into most of the houses he called at to have a 'news' with his school friend's father.

Along with the chat, of course, he was offered a dram for good luck, or, from those who had long since run out of whisky and been unable to restock, a glass of port or even home-made rhubarb wine. He should have known the effect this mixing of drinks would have, but it wasn't until he came out into the fresh air after his sixth call, Sandy Mearns's house, that it hit him. His legs and feet had wills of their own, each going in a different direction, his eyes couldn't focus properly and somebody had set up a smiddy inside his head – the hammer hitting the anvil, clang, clang, clang, and no sign of it stopping. It wouldn't have been so bad if it had been a regular beat, and it was driving him out of his mind as he wove his way along the centre of the road.

Out of a conglomeration of confused thoughts, one kept coming to the surface – Marge would go absolutely mad if she saw him like this. In an effort to clear his head, he sat down on the cobbled pavement, wondering, as he did so, if he would be able to get up again, but telling himself he could worry about that when the time came. He had been sitting, back against a wall, for some time when the church clock began to strike, and even in his inebriated state, he knew he'd have to count the strokes.

Nine! That wasn't so late . . . unless he'd missed one. But he couldn't go home until he'd sobered up a bit, and sitting here wouldn't help. He'd have to try to stand up. The hotel bar closed at half past and he didn't want every man in the place laughing at him.

Stretching his arm out behind him, he tried to brace himself against the wall, but it was hopeless, so he slid his hand along until he found something for his fingers to grip. After several attempts, he found himself leaning on a long window-sill with his nose against the glass . . . looking into the shop. Lexie Fraser! She'd give him something to clear his head! Why hadn't he thought of her before?

Having wit enough to know the shop would be shut, he managed to get himself round to the house without serious mishap – his knuckles got skinned against the wall, but that was nothing. Pulling himself as erect as he could, he gave three loud raps on the door.

It was opened within seconds, and Lexie snapped, 'Dougal Finnie! What brings you knocking at my door at this time of night? The shop's closed and I'm not opening . . .'

'I wanted a wee word with you, Lexie . . . in private.'

'And what's so private you couldn't say it in the shop tomorrow?'

Although irritated by her sarcasm, he said, humbly, 'Can I come in . . . pleazhe?'

'I never thought I'd hear *you* pleading to get into my house.'

'Shtop your daft nonshenshe!' he slurred, pushing past her.

She closed the door with exaggerated care, then followed

him inside, and stood in the middle of the kitchen floor with arms folded across her bosom. 'What a state you're in! Has your wife thrown you out?'

He looked ashamed now. 'She will, if I go home like this.'

'Oh, you want something to sober you up, is that it?'

'If you wouldn't mind, Lexie.'

Her voice softened at his hangdog expression. 'Right then. A strong cup of tea with no sugar or milk, that should do the trick. If it doesn't, we'll try a few more.'

He was on the third cup of revolting tarry liquid before he felt his head clearing, but his stomach had started to revolt.

'If you want to be sick,' Lexie said, seeing his face change colour, 'the lavatory's through there.'

Having got rid of everything he had eaten and drunk that day, he washed his face and hands, shuddering at the sight of himself in the mirror, and wondering what his hostess would say to him now. She'd laugh her head off, more than likely, because he'd never been very friendly towards her when they were young.

Lexie didn't laugh, however. She eyed him with some concern. 'I hope nothing's wrong, Dougal, to make you get as drunk as that?'

'Nothing's wrong,' he muttered, 'I've just been a silly fool.'

He told her what had happened, then added, 'I should have realized . . .'

'It's easy to say that afterwards,' she said, softly, 'but not when you're enjoying the company. Anyway, you'll know not to do that again.'

'I'll never do it again, that's one thing sure, and . . . thank you, Lexie, for helping me. Marge wouldn't have been pleased if she'd seen me like that.'

'I like your wife,' she smiled. 'I don't know her very well, of course, but I've got the feeling she doesn't like me very much.'

'Marge isn't like that . . .' he began, and then he remembered. 'She knows Alistair used to go with you, and she's scared you'll try to get him back.'

Lexie looked down at the fire, still with a little glow in it. 'I'll be honest with you, Dougal. At one time, I'd my mind set on getting him back, even when I knew he had a wife and two kids, but that was before I met them.' She lifted her eyes to meet his. 'I couldn't take him away from them now, suppose he wanted me to, which is the last thing he'd want. So tell your Marge, and her sister, to stop worrying. I still look on him as an old friend, but that's all.'

'You've never married, though.'

'I've never met a man I want to marry.'

'You will, one day. You're only twenty-seven. Time yet to find a husband.'

She stifled a yawn and laughed. 'I need my beauty sleep, though. I've to get up for the papers in the morning.'

He jumped to his feet, astonished to find that the sick, dizzy feeling had abated. 'I'm sorry, Lexie. I never thought . . . I shouldn't have bothered you.'

'I was glad to help, but don't get drunk again. Think of your wife.'

Continuing on his way home with a quicker and steadier step, Dougal couldn't help admiring her. She'd had her share of troubles, she'd been left to run that shop and post office single-handed, and, reading between the lines, Alistair hadn't been the only man to let her down, yet the years had definitely matured her outlook on life.

He was a bit rattled to find the ground floor of Benview in darkness when he arrived back, and Marge pounced as soon as he went up to their room. 'Where have you been,

Dougal? You said you were only going to see a few old pals, so I expected you back about half past eight, and it's after half past ten.'

Deciding that honesty was the best policy, he told her everything, but when he had finished, Marge regarded him icily. 'You're disgusting, and Lexie wound *you* round her little finger like she did with Alistair.'

'She got me more or less sober. Marge, you've got her all wrong. She's changed! She doesn't want Alistair back. If you'd been there, you'd know she really meant it.'

'Well, thank heaven for that. Are you coming to bed or not?'

He undressed as quickly as he could, but he was relieved when his wife just kissed him goodnight and turned her back. His constitution wasn't up to what he'd been doing for the past few nights.

At the beginning of December 1941, Marge spotted a poster in the shop and stopped on her way out to see what it said. 'What's a Hogmanay Do?' she asked in a minute.

'It's being put on by the men at Ardley,' Lexie told her. 'They'd one at Hallowe'en. A wee concert first, singing and would-be comedians and magicians and turns like that, all soldiers of course, and even if they weren't professionals, some of them were really good. Then, about nine o'clock, they treated all us civilians to a slap-up meal better than any of us had seen for a long, long time, and then the fun began.'

Marge was intrigued. She hadn't known that any kind of entertainment was ever on offer in this backwater of a place, but she did wonder what these country people classed as fun. 'What happened?'

'The dancing started! And the drinking, of course.' Lexie

regarded her with open curiosity now. 'Would you and your sister like to come? You'll have to put your names down for the bus. It picks up the Forvit folk outside the shop at half seven.'

Marge pulled a face. 'I'd love to come. I'm desperate for something to brighten my life, but I know for a fact that Gwen won't even consider it.'

'If she's worried about leaving the bairns, I'm sure I could . . .'

No longer harbouring any suspicions about the shopkeeper, Marge said, 'I'll tell her, but I still don't think she'll come. She's always been a home bird, not like me. I hate being stuck in the house night after night listening to the wireless with the wind howling down the chimney and my legs getting mottled with the fire.'

Lexie reached under the counter and produced a sheet of paper with quite a number of names on it already. 'I tell you what. I'll put you both down, just in case.'

Watching Marge's retreating back, Lexie couldn't get over the difference in the two sisters. Marge was such a friendly person and seemed to be full of fun, and Gwen was so quiet, so reserved. It was just as well they married the men they did. Dougal had always been go-ahead, the same type as Marge, and Alistair had always stayed in his shadow, much more quiet, more serious about everything. She was glad he'd found the right girl.

The entrance of a customer made Lexie look up with a welcoming smile, although Doodie Tough wasn't exactly one of her favourites, poking her long nose in where it wasn't wanted and spreading her gossip to the four winds. 'That was Dougal Finnie's wife, wasn't it?' Doodie asked.

Not wanting to encourage her, Lexie ignored the question. 'What can I do for you today, then, Doodie?'

'Is that the list for the bus at Hogmanay?' The woman swivelled the paper round so that she could read it. 'Oh, well, would you look at that?' she exclaimed, as Mattie Wilkie came in. 'The twa Cockneys are to be honourin' us wi' their presence at the Do. I just canna tak' to them, me.'

'Me either,' nodded her friend. 'There's something about them, you ken, like they look doon on us country fowk.'

Lexie tried to stop them. 'What was it you wanted, Doodie?'

'A plain loaf, a pound o' rice, a bag o' sugar, and . . .' She broke off and delved into her shopping bag. 'See, I've wrote it doon.' She handed over a crumpled piece of paper and turned to her companion again. 'It's the posh wey they spik that annoys me – puttin' it on, of coorse, makin' oot they're better than us, though I can mind on Alistair Ritchie when he hadna a backside to his breeks.'

'Na, na, Doodie,' Mattie protested, 'Bella Ritchie wouldna have let him go aboot wi' his bare erse showin'. She'd have putten in a patch.'

'You ken fine what I meant!' Doodie did not like to be corrected. 'Will you be at the Do, Lexie?' she enquired now.

'I hope so. If it's anything like the last one, it should be a big success.'

'My Lizzie canna spik aboot naething else. If she doesna get a lad this time, she'll be right disappointed.'

'I thocht she got a lad last time,' Doodie put in. 'I mind on seein' her wi' a lang streak o' misery . . .'

Mattie managed a wan smile. 'Oh, him? He . . . tried it on wi' her, but she tell't him to get lost.'

'A lot o' the sodjers was like that, though,' Doodie remarked. 'You ken Mina Robbie at Milton o' Crombie? Well, her lassie's expectin', an' her father'll kill her when he finds oot.'

Mattie's eyes had clouded. 'There was a lot o' that went on in the last war, as weel. A gey puckle bairns come into the world withoot a father, poor things.'

'That'll be one pound, seven shillings and thruppence, Doodie!' Lexie said loudly, thumping a box of yellow soap, the last item, down on the counter.

'As much as that? Wait or I get my purse oot.' Her eyes were glittering with what could only be triumph as she tendered a pound note and a ten shilling note.

While Lexie counted out the change, she recalled having heard somewhere that Ricky, Mattie's twenty-five-year-old son, had been illegitimate. He had been born in 1916, then, so the father could have been a serviceman. But it was nobody else's business, she thought, turning to Mattie, who only wanted a *Press and Journal*. 'Jock likes to read it when he's takin' his denner,' she explained.

Lexie heaved a sigh of relief when the two women went out, tearing some other poor soul to pieces, probably. This was the one thing she didn't like about village life; there were always people ready to think the worst of everybody else. Not that she would care what any of them said about her, but she should maybe warn the two Londoners not to give the likes of Doodie Tough any chance to spread scandal about them.

Gwen wasn't sure about Marge going to the Hogmanay Do. 'What will people say?'

Her sister tossed her dark curly head. 'They can say anything they bally well want, but I'm not backing out now. It's only a concert, a meal and maybe an hour of dancing, for heaven's sake, and you know I'm bored stiff here. You can come and watch I don't step out of line. Lexie Fraser offered to sit with Leila and David to let us both go.'

Gwen shook her head. 'I never cared much for dancing, nor for meeting new people. Besides, we're both married women.'

'What's that got to do with it? It's not an orgy, just an evening's innocent fun.'

'But you said last night there'll be drinking as well as dancing,' Gwen reminded her. 'That's a lethal combination.'

'I won't be drinking much.'

'The men will, though, and a drunk man can overpower any woman. No, Marge, I don't think you should go, either.'

Marge looked at her sister now with a touch of anger in her eyes. 'I know you don't want to go, and you're older than me, but you can't boss me around like you did when we were kids. I'm going whatever you say.' Her expression softened. 'I don't mean to be nasty, but I've been pining for something to brighten my life, and this Do's just what I need. It'll set me up for months.'

Gwen gave a resigned sigh. 'How far's this Ardley Camp, anyway?'

'About ten miles, Lexie said.'

'For heaven's sake! How are you going to get there? You're not thinking of cycling as far as that, are you?'

'God no! I'd have corns on my bum for weeks if I did. They're laying on a bus, pick up point outside the shop. I'll leave the bike there, and I'll only take one drink so I'll be all right for coming home. Say it's OK . . . please, Gwennie?'

'I suppose . . . oh, just don't forget you've got a husband.'

Marge's spirits were effervescent now. 'It'll be great to get the feel of a dance floor beneath my feet again, and a man's arm round my waist.'

'But . . .' Gwen began, but her sister's ecstatic, yet determined, face stopped her from going on. Marge clearly didn't mean to let this opportunity slip through her fingers.

'Nobody's got coupons to buy anything new,' Lexie had told Marge when she asked what she should wear to the Do. 'Just a smart summer frock.'

'I've put on a bit of weight since we came up here,' Marge moaned to her sister on New Year's Eve, when she was putting the finishing touches to her make-up. 'I've had to wear this old dirndl dress, it's the only one I feel comfortable in.'

'You look nice, Auntie Marge.' Leila had been watching all the proceedings with interest. 'I wish I was old enough to go dancing.'

'Another few years and you will be. Gwen, are you sure this hairstyle suits me?' Marge poked her finger into the upswept roll of hair at her temple.

'Stop fussing,' Gwen ordered. 'It's perfect.'

David, who had been looking on with a jaundiced expression, suddenly observed, 'What a bloody fuss for a nicht oot!'

Gwen turned on him angrily. 'David! Who did you hear saying that word?'

He knew immediately which word she meant. 'The loons at school say it.'

She decided to let it go meantime and have a quiet word with him tomorrow about swearing and using the rough Scottish words he heard in the playground. Her mind was too taken up tonight with worrying about what the evening ahead held for her younger sister. Could Marge be trusted to behave like a married woman?

'Be careful now,' she warned, when they all went outside to see Marge off. 'Don't drink too much, and don't give any of the men any encouragement.'

'No, Miss.' Marge grinned cheekily as she tucked the skirt of her tweed coat – which she hadn't wanted to wear but had been too cold not to – round her knees to keep it clear of the oily chain. Then she flung up her left hand in a wave and laughed, 'Now, as I take off on my trusty steed . . .' She burst into song. 'Goodbye, Goodbye, I wish you all a last goodbye.'

It was a song they loved to hear on the wireless, but Gwen said, sharply, 'Don't say that, even in fun. You never know what could happen.'

With the light streaming out through the open door, they watched her until she disappeared round the bend in the track, her flowered headsquare flapping, then Leila took her mother's hand and drew her inside. 'Don't worry about Auntie Marge, Mum. She can look after herself.'

It was wearing on for three o'clock in the morning, however, before the wanderer returned, by which time Gwen was imagining all sorts of things – her sister running off with a man she had fallen instantly in love with, or so drunk that she was lying in a ditch somewhere between the village and Benview, or worse still, the bus skidding on the icy road and all the passengers either dead or seriously injured. She had got herself in such a state that she couldn't stay in bed, and was sitting in the kitchen by the dying fire when Marge came bouncing in.

'Where have you been?' Gwen burst out, anger taking over from anxiety. 'I've been out of my mind with worry.'

'Oh, Lord, Gwen, I'm sorry! Nobody told me it would go on till two, and I'd to wait for the camp bus to take us back. Actually, I landed quite lucky, because when Ken, the driver, saw me getting my bike from the side of the shop, he came off the bus and said, "Hop back in and I'll lift that thing aboard. There's no sense in you having to cycle when I can drop you right at your door." Of course, he couldn't take a bus up the track, so he didn't manage to take me right home, but it was a big help, just the same.'

'He wasn't . . . he didn't . . . ?' Gwen couldn't quite put her fear into words.

'No, he didn't,' Marge laughed. 'He was too busy telling me about his wife and his two kids. Ho, hum!' She rolled her eyes expressively, then carried on, 'It was lovely, though, Gwennie. I really enjoyed myself. The concert wasn't as bad as I expected, the meal was pretty good, and I never missed a dance. Oh, and I only had one port and lemon to start me off, and a few glasses of pop. Iron-Brew they called it, quite nice.'

'I made a fresh pot of tea a minute ago. D'you want a cup?'

'If you like. But d'you know what I found out? Going there on the bus, I was sitting beside one of the girls – most of them were much younger than me – and she said there's going to be a dance laid on once a month in the church hall for servicemen. It's the first I heard of it, so that's something to look forward to.'

Marge broke off long enough to accept the cup she was handed and to take one quick mouthful before she was off again, but her sister was so tired that she hardly took in the descriptions of the piper who played in the New Year, of the Highland Fling two of the squaddies had danced, of the singer who had been with a touring band before he was called up and the applause for whose rendering of 'We'll Meet Again' had almost brought the roof down. 'And at the finish,' Marge went on, 'the padre stood up and said a prayer for all the loved ones who were absent, and all who were missing them. It was so moving, Gwennie, there was hardly a dry eye to be seen, and it made people more aware of what they were doing. I think even those who had intended having a little fling before they went home, or had planned an illicit assignation, thought better of it. So you see, there was absolutely nothing for you to worry about.'

Not a thing, her sister silently agreed, except what might develop at the monthly dances in the church hall. Regular doses of temptation could prove too much for Marge. She got to her feet wearily. 'I don't know about you, but if I don't get some sleep, I'll be like a walking zombie tomorrow.'

Chapter 16

Nearing the end of March 1942, with Marge at her third dance in the church hall and the children asleep upstairs, Gwen Ritchie made a pot of tea and had just sat down to write to her husband when someone knocked at the door. With no near neighbours, this was so unusual that she wondered whether she should answer it or not, but whoever was out there would only have to turn the knob to get in, because she never locked up until her sister came home. Besides, she told herself sternly as she went to obey the summons, this place wasn't like London. There were no burglars or bad people in Forvit.

She was a little disconcerted to find a rather tall soldier on the doorstep. 'Sorry to bother you at this time of night,' he said apologetically, 'but I need some water.'

'Water?' she echoed, hoping that he wasn't ill . . . but he looked the picture of health.

'The old bus is blowing off steam,' he told her. 'Somebody must have forgotten to check the radiator and it's overheating.'

An icy hand clutched at her stomach. There was no sign of any vehicle for as far as she could see, but of course, the track was too narrow for a bus, if that really was what he was driving. 'How . . . how did you know there was a house up here?'

'Well, I gave a young lady a lift home on New Year's morning, and when she told me where to drop her off, she said she and her sister were living up the track in a house called Benview.'

Light dawned. 'Oh yes. I remember Marge telling me she'd got a lift with her bike. It was very kind of you.'

'I'm afraid I'm here to reap the benefit of my good deed.'

His engaging grin convinced her that there was nothing sinister on his mind, no evil intentions. 'What . . . um . . . ?'

'A jug of water's all I need . . . a big jug.'

'You'd better come in till I see what we've got. You'll have a cup of tea?'

'Thanks.' He sat down at the table and laid his forage cap on the floor beside him. 'As I recall,' he began, watching her fill the second cup which had been set out, 'your sister said you were evacuees from London.'

'Well, our husbands insisted that we take the kids away from the bombing.'

'How many kids do you have between you?' he asked, conversationally, curling his hands round the large cup she handed him.

'Marge has nearly given up hope of having any, but I've got two, a girl and a boy.'

'That's a coincidence,' he smiled, 'I've got a girl and a boy, as well. Pam'll be nine in five weeks, and David's ten past.'

'Gosh, that's another coincidence. My son's David, too, but they're the other way round – he'll be eight in August, and Leila's nine in May.'

'Well, I'll be damned. Oh, I beg your pardon, Mrs . . . em . . . Ken Partridge, by the way. At your service.' He gave her a smart salute.

'Gwen Ritchie.' Her face had coloured at talking so freely to a man she had just met, but he didn't feel like a stranger, somehow. 'My husband's in the Artillery.'

'I'm Ordnance Corps attached to the Black Watch.' His smile broadened. 'So now we're old friends, but I'll be in trouble if I'm late. I've to take the boys back to camp, and some of them get a bit rowdy if they're kept waiting.'

'Don't forget the water,' she giggled, jumping to her feet and opening the door of the cupboard at the side of the fireplace. 'Will this old jug hold enough?'

'That's perfect, but let me fill it.' While they waited for the water level to rise to the brim of the ewer, he said, 'Will it be OK if I bring this back another time? It'll take me a while – it's quite a walk from the main road, isn't it?'

'A mile.' Gwen would have offered to walk with him and take the jug back herself, but she wasn't exactly dressed for a late-night hike. It crossed her mind, as she closed the door behind him, that it would be quite nice to see him again, but the thought made her feel guilty. She was a happily married woman, why on earth should she want to see Ken Partridge again?

Giving this due consideration, she decided that it wasn't for his good looks, anyway, though his cheeky grin was what had made her feel at ease with him. Nor was it the colour of his hair, for she had never liked red-headed men, she didn't know why, and his was the brightest ginger she'd ever seen. His eyes had been really nice, though – an unusual green, but soft and kind with an attractive twinkle – she'd felt like a young girl every time he looked directly at her. Not that she had fallen for him, nothing like that; maybe it was because he seemed a kind of kindred spirit, yet she'd only known him for, at the most, twenty minutes.

Before sitting down again, she took a good look at herself in the overmantel mirror, and was sure she could make out a glint of silver in her hair, not so blonde as it had once been, and her skin was rougher, with working outside so much. For all that, she looked fit and healthy. The open air life was doing her good. It hadn't done much good for her hands, though, she thought, studying them ruefully. Her nails were broken, her fingers and palms always ingrained with dirt, no matter how much she scrubbed them and smothered them in cold cream at nights. Still, she consoled herself, sitting down at the table again, at least the children were safe from air raids up here.

Her mother's letters didn't tell them much – she just said 'our friends still pay us calls', which obviously meant they were still being bombed – but Peggy wrote, in her less frequent scrawls, that some weeks they were in the shelter for nights on end, and hardly any houses in their street had escaped having windows blown out . . . or in.

> There's been a few incendiaries, but we've escaped so far. Alf and I both signed up as fire watchers – not for the same nights, of course, because of Mum – so I'm on duty every fifth night with old Mr Hornby from No. 16, patrolling our little patch and making sure we don't miss any of the blasted things, though God knows what good I could do with only a 70-year-old dodderer to help me. But I'm being unkind. Cyril Hornby's dedicated to the job, pail and stirrup pump always at the ready. He sends regards to Marge and you.
>
> By the way, you might be interested to know that I've persuaded Alf not to wait until the war's over before we get married, (he might be past it by then, ha ha!).

'She's come out of her shell lately,' Marge had commented. 'She wouldn't have said anything like that before. Thirtieth April at Caxton Hall, no big fuss.' She sniffed. 'I wish we could see her, though.'

Remembering, Gwen heaved a prolonged sigh. Peggy had also told them not to feel bad about not being there, she knew they'd be thinking of her. She had no idea how they felt – their baby sister . . .

She sat up abruptly. For heaven's sake, she was getting as maudlin as if she'd been drinking! She'd have to pull herself together and finish writing to Alistair. Thank goodness she had something different to tell him tonight. Lifting the Swan fountain pen he had given her for Christmas some years before, she described the short interlude with Ken Partridge in as interesting a way as she could, telling all the facts yet studiously avoiding anything that might hint at how relaxed she had felt in his company. She didn't want to make her husband jealous of a man she may only see once more, and that only if he kept his promise to return the chipped willow-patterned ewer.

At five to twelve, she boiled the kettle for Marge coming in. The dances in the church hall did not go on until all hours like the Hogmanay Do at Ardley Camp. The Rev. James Lennox made sure that everyone had left the hall by 11.30, so that his beadle could sweep the floor and lock up while it was still Saturday, and so that he, himself, could be in bed at a decent time of night. Even in his student days, he had never been one to burn the midnight oil.

As she always did, Marge came bouncing in, stopping in her tracks when Gwen observed, with a touch of mischief in her eyes, 'I'd a visitor while you were out.'

'A visitor? At night?' Marge was astounded. 'Who was it? It wasn't a man, surely, and you here on your own? Or were the kids still up?'

'Give me a chance to tell you. It was Ken Partridge from the camp – the one who gave you a lift on New Year's morning, remember? All he wanted was a jug of water for the bus, and the kids were in bed asleep, and . . .'

'You didn't take him in, did you?'

'Of course I did. I gave him a cup of tea, as well, and he's coming back . . .'

'Oh, Gwen, no!' Marge wailed. 'After all the times you've lectured me about giving men the wrong idea, you invite back a . . .'

'I didn't invite him, he has to return the jug.' She explained the circumstances in as much detail as she could.

'Yes, yes, I understand,' Marge said, impatiently. 'From what I remember of him, he's quite a nice chap, really – missing his wife and kids something awful, and a bus would be far too wide to come up the track. I suppose he was on the level.'

'Of course he was! Why on earth should he walk all the way up here if he didn't have to?' Gwen paused, her eyes clouding. 'Unless it was you he wanted to see, and the water was just an excuse.'

'No, I don't think so. I'd say he was one hundred per cent genuine, but for goodness' sake, don't let any other strange men in. The village women would love to get their teeth into some juicy gossip about us, and if any of the men, soldiers or not, overheard them saying you were on your own here on the nights there's a dance in the church hall . . .'

'You're letting your imagination run away with you,' Gwen smiled. 'Now, drink that tea before it gets cold, and let's get to bed.'

Another horrifying thought had struck her sister, however. 'You weren't dressed like that when Ken Thingummy was here, were you?'

Looking down at Alistair's old flannel dressing gown, which she'd taken to using because it was so cold in Forvit in the winter nights, Gwen couldn't help laughing. 'Yes, I was, but I hadn't put my curlers in nor put on my cold cream, thank heaven, otherwise he'd have run a mile when I opened the door.'

Both young women doubled up with laughter at the thought of this, but later, before she fell asleep, it occurred to Gwen that Ken was a married man and would probably be used to seeing his wife similarly adorned . . . unless her hair was naturally curly and her skin smoothly perfect, and she wore a flimsy negligee instead of a man's thick robe.

Quite late on Monday afternoon, when Gwen was inside because it was her turn to make the tea, Marge heard a vehicle coming up the track, and straightened up from weeding the winter cabbage patch. It was a few moments later before the jeep came into view, negotiating the stony surface slowly and carefully. 'Hi, there!' she greeted the tall sergeant who got out. 'So it *was* you?'

'It was me,' he laughed, 'and I've brought back the jug your sister so kindly lent me. Is she anywhere about? I'd like to thank her.'

'Inside,' Marge said, laying down the hoe and leading the way.

It was she who offered him a cup of tea, she who hogged the conversation, but quite often, Ken turned to include Gwen. He seemed to be enjoying himself, and looked up with a start and glanced at his watch when David burst in, Leila a little way behind him.

'Good grief! Look at the time! I've been here for over an hour.'

Nevertheless, he took time to introduce himself to the boy and girl before he made his way to the door, saying, as Marge saw him out, 'Good company doesn't half make the time fly past.'

She didn't stop to think. 'Well, look, Ken, you're welcome here any time. We'd be glad of some more of your good company.'

'Are you sure I won't be intruding on your privacy?'

'I'm sick to the back teeth of privacy,' she grinned.

David, who had also taken it upon himself to see this very first visitor off the premises, now put in his tuppenceworth. 'Auntie Marge, why can't he come to tea on Saturday, when me and Leila don't have school?'

'That's a good idea,' she smiled, thinking that the boy needed a man around, even for an occasional afternoon. 'That's if you can manage?' she added, turning to the sergeant.

'Yes, I'm not on duty this Saturday . . . unless I'm on jankers for being late today.' Grinning, he turned to David again. 'Would you like a run in my jeep? Just a bit down the track.'

'Wouldn't I just?' The boy climbed aboard eagerly, and waved to his aunt as the vehicle rattled off.

She returned to the kitchen. 'I suppose you heard all that?'

Gwen nodded wryly. 'I certainly did, and you're the one who told me to be careful . . .'

'Sshh!' warned her sister. 'Walls have ears, remember.'

Leila gave a most unfeminine snort. 'I know you mean me, but why are you telling Mum to be careful? Ken's a very nice man.'

'I was only joking,' Marge assured her.

After that first Saturday, when the two women joined and enjoyed the game of rounders in the afternoon, and sat with their new friend listening companionably to the wireless after the children were in bed, Ken Partridge became a regular visitor, but never again while Gwen was on her own. He gave most of his attention to David, showing him how to dribble a football, how to hold a cricket bat (a flat piece of wood) and judge the speed of an oncoming sponge ball – all the knowledge a father might pass on to his son, Gwen thought one day, but unfortunately Alistair had been in the army before the boy was old enough to take any interest in these skills.

When Ken learned that Alistair was arriving home on leave on the last Monday in May, he said, 'I'd better stay away till he's gone back.'

This put Gwen's mind at ease. She hadn't mentioned in any of her letters that Ken was visiting regularly, though she couldn't say why. There was nothing going on that her husband shouldn't know about.

Marge, however, said, 'There's no need. I'm sure Alistair would like to meet you.'

'I'd better not. I know how I'd feel if my wife produced a man who'd been visiting her while I wasn't there. I go on leave myself in the middle of June, so it'll be four weeks before I see you all again.'

After he left, on one of the bicycles made available at Ardley, Marge gave her sister an enquiring look. 'Haven't you told Alistair about Ken coming here?'

'I just told him about the first time,' Gwen said, a little on the defensive. 'It didn't seem fair . . . when he's so far away . . . I thought he might feel jealous, though nothing's going on – how could it, with you and the kids always here, too?'

'You'll have to gag your David, then. He's got a mouth like the Dartford tunnel.'

A horrified expression crossed Gwen's face. 'I hadn't thought of that.'

After a moment's concentrated thought, Marge burst out, 'I've got it! We could tell him it's against army rules for any soldier to visit another soldier's home.'

'But that would be a downright lie!'

'Lying's not a criminal offence, and it's either that or tell

Alistair the truth. David won't question it, not if I say it's a grown-up secret and he'll have to keep his mouth shut so Ken won't get into trouble.'

'What about Leila?'

'I think she'll fall for it, too, and nobody else knows Ken comes here. I've never said a word to a soul in the village, have you?'

'No, it was nobody's business.' Gwen eyed her sister as if begging for assurance. 'Do you really think it'll work?'

'I can't see why not.'

On his first night home, Alistair had done so much travelling and hanging around railway stations over the previous twenty-four hours that he tumbled into bed and was asleep in a few seconds, and Gwen, curlers in and skin shining from the cold cream she had rubbed in and wiped off, felt her heart turn over at how vulnerable he looked. She loved him so deeply it hurt. They'd all been in the house when he arrived, and he had only kissed her once before David and Leila clamoured for his attention, and the moment had passed, the moment he should have taken her in his arms and shown her how much he'd missed her.

Of course, it was natural that he wanted to hug his children, and he'd said he had fourteen days' leave altogether, but the army didn't allow for the time it would take to travel from the south of England and back. That meant she would only have him for twelve days . . . maybe just eleven nights, and he was sleeping through one of them.

Awake first in the morning, Alistair felt ashamed that he'd been too tired the night before to make love to his wife, but surely she would understand? Something else was niggling at the back of his mind, though, if only he could remember what it was. It had nothing to do with Gwen, nor Marge . . . nor Leila, even if she *had* been a bit reserved with him.

That left David, who had definitely been different towards him after the initial joyful welcome. Of course, it was months since they'd seen each other – when he'd been David's age, the two months between his birthday and Christmas had seemed like a year – but it wasn't just that. There was an excitement, a nervousness, about him. Had he done something really bad and his father was being left to administer the punishment?

Feeling Gwen stirring now, Alistair leaned across to kiss her, then everything else was blotted from his mind as he made up for lost time. It was wearing on for an hour later, and thankfully they were lying peacefully, when the bedroom door crashed back against the wardrobe and David leapt in.

'Dad, Auntie Marge says to ask if you're needing the bathroom before me and Leila go in to wash?'

'Maybe I'd better.'

Gwen sat up. 'I'll go after you, then, because they take ages.'

'And Auntie Marge says your breakfast's ready and just go down in your jim-jams.'

Her face reddening, his mother said, 'Off you go, my lad, and make sure you brush your shoes before you go to school.'

Listening to him running down the stairs, Alistair burst out laughing. 'Go down in our jim-jams,' he spluttered. 'Just as well she didn't say to come as we are.'

Swinging his feet to the floor, he went over to the chair by the window to get his underpants and trousers, his naked body more muscular than it used to be, his stomach muscles taut from the discipline of drills and marches.

David and Leila off to school, Gwen upstairs in the

bathroom, Alistair took the chance to have a private word with his sister-in-law. He hadn't said anything to his wife, in case he was being oversensitive because of what he would have to tell her soon. 'Is David in trouble of any kind, Marge?'

'Not that I know of. What made you think that?'

'It's . . . I dunno, the way he looks at me, I suppose, as though he was expecting me to get on to him for something.'

Marge gave a low chuckle. 'Somebody's always having to get on to him for something, at home and at school, but I'm sure his conscience is clear just now. He's growing older, maybe that's what it is? Maybe he wants you to show him how to do things, like . . . um, like other fathers show their sons.'

Alistair didn't notice her slight hesitation to cover the gaffe she had been on the point of making. 'That'll be it,' he smiled. 'Well, I'll kick a ball around with him for a while when he comes home, how would that do? And I could take him to the burn where Dougal and me used to guddle for fish.' Noticing her puzzled expression, he laughed loudly. 'It means catching them with our hands.'

'Great!' she enthused. 'That's the kind of thing he'll enjoy.'

'How are you and Gwen coping here?' he asked now.

'Like old stagers,' she smiled. 'I was bored stiff before the dances started, but one evening's dancing sees me through the four weeks till the next one.'

Alistair frowned. 'Dances?'

'The vicar or whatever they call him puts on a dance once a month for the men at the camp, and he gets a three-piece band from Aberdeen to play. They're quite good, the band and the dances, though everything stops at half past eleven.'

'You mean you go every month? What about Gwen?'

'She doesn't want to go, you know how she is, but she doesn't mind me going.'

'Does Dougal know? I wouldn't be happy about it if you were my wife.'

'I've told him. All the boys know I'm married and out of bounds, so we just have a few laughs. Besides, with a dozen pairs of beady eyes watching my every move, I wouldn't dare to misbehave even if I wanted to, which I swear I don't.'

'What about Gwen? Does she not mind being left here on her own?'

'It's only once a month, Alistair, for goodness' sake, and you know she's a home bird. She wasn't happy to start with, but only because she was afraid I'd meet somebody. She keeps an eye on me, though she knows I'm a one-man girl, like her. I would never want anybody but Dougal, my big Scottish he-man.'

Alistair's leave flashed past. He was glad that he had taken Marge's advice, for he *had* got to know his son better, showing him all the old haunts he had frequented when he himself was a boy, spending maybe half an hour before teatime every day fooling around together with a football, hunkering down with him at the back door to play marbles. Yet he hadn't neglected his wife and daughter. On the Saturday, he had taken them on the bus into Aberdeen and while Gwen was contentedly looking round the stores in Union Street, he had taken the children to the beach by tramcar, a first for them in both cases.

On the Sunday, they'd had a picnic at the tower, and while he and the two women had lain on the grass lapping up the sunshine, Leila had tried to find as many different kinds of wild flowers as she could, and David searched for insects. Watching them as they darted hither and thither brought a lump to Alistair's throat. He was a lucky man, a truly lucky man, with a beautiful wife who loved him as much as he loved her, and the two bonniest bairns in the world. If only he could be here with them all the time!

On his last evening, Gwen persuaded him to cycle to the village. 'You might see some of your old friends in the hotel bar,' she added, not really wanting him to spend precious time away from her, but trying to let him rekindle old acquaintances and give him something else to remember when he went back.

He had intended to stop at the shop for cigarettes but the shutter was up and he carried on to the hotel. He was out of luck there too, the supplies having run out the day before. It was Dod Tough – husband of Doodie and regarded by her cronies as henpecked, but a force to be reckoned with in discussions and arguments in the bar – who came to his rescue. 'Lexie aye keeps a puckle packets under the coonter for special customers, and you and her being . . . eh, good *friends*, heh, heh . . .' He gave a loud snigger. 'Go roond the back and knock on the hoose window.'

Ignoring the knowing glances and winks being exchanged by the other men, Alistair said, 'I need fags if I'm to be sitting here drinking for a couple of hours.'

Lexie didn't seem surprised to see him as she ushered him inside. 'I heard you were home.'

'I leave tomorrow.' He shook his head as she gestured towards the sofa. 'No, Lexie, if I don't get back to the bar, they'll think . . .'

She regarded him clinically. 'You wouldn't have worried at one time.'

Embarrassed, and more than a little apprehensive, he was unsure what to say. 'At one time maybe, Lexie, but a lot of water's passed under the bridge . . .'

She gave a reassuring laugh. 'And you've got a wife and two fine bairns. You needn't look so worried, Alistair. I'm not going to jump on you.'

'I never thought . . .'

'No? Look, I admit I was hurt when you went off to London and left me, and I did hanker after you for years, but I got over you.'

'You never married, though?'

'Not yet, but I'm still looking.' She gave him a playful punch on the arm. 'There's plenty of men around Forvit now, you know, and dances every . . .'

'Every month, Marje told me.' After a moment's hesitation, he asked, 'Is there any . . . gossip about Marge?'

'Show me one girl in Forvit there's no gossip about . . .' She shook her head, giggling. 'You must remember what Doodie Tough and her lot are like? If we as much as smile at one of the Ardley boys, we're making up to them. But you can tell Dougal he's got nothing to worry about with Marge. She tells each and every one of them she's a married woman and they respect her for it, and they still have a good time and so does she. Now, you'd better come through to the shop and I'll miraculously produce a packet of Capstan out of the air for you – that's all I've got, and I've to keep them hidden.'

He followed her through, insisted that she take the money for the cigarettes she gave him. 'Thanks, Lexie . . . for everything. You're a good friend.' After a slight hesitation, he added, 'I won't be seeing you for a while, we're being sent overseas when I go back. I'm going to tell Gwen tonight.'

'You haven't told her yet?'

'I didn't want to spoil our time together, but tonight's my last night.'

'You'd better make the most of it, then. Well, cheerio, Alistair, and good luck!'

He put both hands round the one she held out and clasped it tightly for a moment. 'Thanks, I'll need it.'

He did not see the wistful look she gave him as he made his way out, and walked into the bar to the accompaniment of loud cheers. Dod Tough leaned across to him when he sat down. 'I didna think you'd get awa' withoot . . . you ken?'

Alistair's laugh was guilt-free. 'Lexie and I have never been more than friends. No matter what anybody thinks.'

'Good enough friends for her to gi'e you a packet o' Capstan, I see.'

Alistair let that pass, he had done nothing that needed justifying, and his companions returned to their previous topics – the weather, the price of beer and cigarettes when they could get them, the progress or otherwise on all the war fronts. He put forward his opinions when they were asked for, but he backed out of commenting on the war. 'Don't ask me. The rank and file are the last to hear what's going on.'

'That's right enough,' agreed Bill Mennie, sitting in a corner with a man Alistair recognized but couldn't name. 'It was the same last time. Them at the top made the decisions, never mind if it was dangerous for the poor bloody infantry. We were . . . expendable, that's the word. We're the ones that had to go over the top though we knew Fritz was waiting for us, and we got mowed down like . . . rats in a trap.'

'. . . like rats in a trap,' echoed his companion.

Dod Tough clicked his tongue. 'Dinna heed them, lad. They mak' oot they saw a lot of action, but they werena five minutes ower there when the Armistice was signed.'

Alistair laughed along with the others, then said, 'I hope it's the same for me. We're being sent overseas – I don't know where.'

He should have known better. He was now plied with drinks to wish him well, and he felt increasingly uneasy – not for his own safety, but because he still had to tell Gwen. After an hour, his head beginning to swim, he took his leave of the group of men and cycled back to Benview.

'You haven't been long,' Gwen greeted him. 'Didn't you see anyone you knew?'

'I knew most of them, but none of my old pals were there.' He took out his cigarettes, and fished for the lighter he'd made from a bullet shell. 'They didn't have any fags left in the bar, though, and I'd to knock at Lexie Fraser's house door to get some.' He could sense a change in the air at this, and he wondered why everybody, even his own wife and her sister, took it for granted that there was still something between him and Lexie. The drink he had consumed was enough to fan his pique into anger. 'Well, I see I've been convicted, judged and tried, so I won't bother denying it. Think what you bloody well like, I'm off to bed!'

He stamped upstairs, threw off his clothes and was asleep in minutes . . .

Gwen looked imploringly at her sister. 'D'you think he was with her all the time?'

Marge screwed her mouth to one side. 'Um, no, I shouldn't think so. He's had a few too many by the look of him, so maybe he doesn't like being questioned.'

'But if he's nothing to hide . . .'

Marge regretted ever having voiced her own suspicions. 'He'll feel guilty for drinking so much. He'll probably tell you in the morning, but if he doesn't, just let it drop.'

Even after resolving to take Marge's advice and not question her husband, the first thing Gwen did when he opened his eyes the following day was ask, 'Were you with Lexie Fraser all the time you were out last night?'

'Oh, Gwen,' he groaned, gathering her into his arms, 'my darling, darling Gwennie, I was only with her for . . . not much more than five minutes. Look, I'll be perfectly honest with you. I've known her all my life, I like her quite a lot, but I do – not – love her! I wouldn't have seen her at all if I hadn't needed fags.'

They were just reaching the point when passion would no longer be denied, when their son barged in. 'Oh!' he exclaimed in disgust. 'Do you two never get tired kissing?'

Trying to control his laboured breathing, Alistair managed to laugh, 'No, and we never will.'

'Well, you'd better stop now, for Auntie Marge says you'll need all your time if you don't come down for breakfast right now.'

There was something of a scramble until they were all seated round the table having breakfast. 'How long will it be before your next leave?' David asked, his mouth full of toast.

A silence fell now, an electrifying silence during which even David didn't speak, then Alistair laid his hand over his wife's. 'I'm sorry, darling,' he murmured, looking deep into her eyes, 'I shouldn't have left this till the last minute, I meant to tell you last night, but . . . things happened. I've been on embarkation leave, we're being sent overseas when I go back, so it could be long enough before I get home again.'

It was left to Marge to dam the hole in the dyke. 'They'll be needing reinforcements somewhere,' she told David, 'and your Dad has to go where he's told.'

'Where, Dad?' the words were croaked, as the boy took his cuff across his eyes.

'I don't know yet, son. It could be anywhere – Far East, Middle East . . .'

'Near East?' Marge was trying to make a joke.

'Anywhere.' Alistair got to his feet and pulled Gwen off her chair, too. 'Give me a hand to fasten my bags.' He took time to hug his son and daughter before he turned away with moist eyes, and Marge cleared the obstruction in her throat in order to reassure the children. 'He'll be fine, don't worry, my pets.

He won't have to fight Germans wherever he's going, that's good, isn't it?'

She managed to shoo them off to school – David crowing 'Wait till the boys at school hear my Dad's going overseas!' – and sat down with another cup of tea. Only a few minutes later, Alistair and his wife came downstairs, Gwen's eyes red from weeping.

'I hope you're pleased at what you've done, Alistair Ritchie!' Marge couldn't help herself. 'Fancy waiting till the very last minute before you told your wife and kids you're on embarkation leave. Can't you see how hurt she is?'

Gwen shook her head. 'I'm all right, Marge. He's explained why he didn't tell me before, and it was my own fault that he didn't say anything last night.' She slid her arm through her husband's. 'I'll walk to the road with you, Alistair.'

'You'll have to put a step in, then.' Marge stood up and kissed her brother-in-law's cheek. 'I'm sorry, Alistair, I'd no right to say . . .'

'You have every right, Marge, and I'll regret being so stupid to my dying . . .'

'No!' Gwen burst out. 'There's no need for regrets. We had a wonderful time while you've been home. Don't let's spoil it now.'

'Well, 'bye, Alistair,' Marge murmured, 'and God bless.'

When Gwen returned, her face ravaged by tears, Marge said, sympathetically, 'I know how you must be feeling. I'd never speak to Dougal again if he did that to me.'

'I was the one who made him go out last night,' Gwen reminded her, 'and I shouldn't have said anything when he came home. It was asking for trouble when I could see he'd had too much to drink.'

'I suppose he told his friends he was being sent overseas,'

Marge offered, 'and they'd been dishing out the booze to him.'

Gwen nodded. 'Yes, that's what he said.' Squaring her shoulders, she added, 'He told Lexie, too.'

'Before he told you?' Marge was outraged.

'He said it didn't matter to him. I mean, he wasn't worried about telling her. She was just a friend, like the men in the bar, but I'm his wife, and he didn't want to spoil our time together. There's nothing between them, Marge, it's just me he loves.'

'Of course it is.'

Not quite believing her own assurance, Marge wasn't surprised at Lexie's first remark when she went to the shop that afternoon. 'Did Alistair get away all right this morning?' Receiving only a slight nod in answer, she went on, 'He wasn't looking forward to telling his wife, you know. I nearly said he wasn't being fair to her, but it wasn't really any of my business.'

'No,' agreed Marge, tersely, 'it's not any of your business.'

'Listen, Mrs Finnie, you know Alistair and me were . . . well, I looked on him as my boyfriend but he didn't feel the same way about me. So if you and your sister think there's still a spark of something between us, there never was . . . not on his side anyway.' She smiled brightly. 'And only friendship on my side now, as well.'

There was something about the woman that got through to Marge at this point. She had heard the gossip about her looking for a lad at the dances, although she didn't seem to have succeeded, but she was positive that it wasn't because of Alistair. Whatever Lexie had felt for him at one time, and perhaps for years after he left Forvit, there was only friendship now, perhaps slightly more . . . affection? Certainly not love.

Marge related the conversation and her conclusion to

Gwen when she returned to Benview, and her sister's spirits were raised even more when she received Alistair's letter two days later, penned as soon as he returned to his base.

My Darling Gwen,

I had to write to let you know how deeply I regret drinking so much on my last night at home, and how ashamed I am for not telling you as soon as I arrived that it was embarkation leave. I could see how hurt you were that I had told Lexie first. I did try to explain how I felt about her, but I don't think you believed me.

My dearest darling, you have no need to feel jealous of her. We grew up together, we had some good times together, but only as pals, nothing more than that. We are adults now, of course, but still friends, close friends, but I treat her the same as I treat the men I've known all my life. I hope you understand.

Thank you for the other nights we spent together, at least I have all those lovely memories to take out and relive when I feel down. You mean everything to me, my darling, and I bless the day Dougal decided to marry Marge, otherwise I might never have met you. By the way, give her my regards.

We are being issued with light kit, and the rumour is it's North Africa, but keep your chin up. Wherever I'm sent, I promise to come home to you. All my love, my dearest, and kiss the kids for me every night, so they won't forget me.

Your ever loving husband,
Alistair. XXX

Gwen handed the epistle to Marge, who gave it a cursory read then said, 'Well, I think you can take it that he loves you.' She regarded her sister with twinkling eyes. 'How was it between you two the rest of the time he was here?'

'Perfect,' Gwen sighed, 'but I wonder if we should . . .'

'If you're going to say we should stop inviting Ken when he gets back, put it out of your mind. He's as straight as that broom handle and he's got no designs on either of us. Being part of our family reminds him of his own, I suppose, and we can't deny him that. Maybe we should have told Alistair about him while he was at home, but there's no sense telling him now, not when he'll soon be in the heart of the fighting. It would just worry him. You know, my Dougal's been saying in his letters for ages that he's fed up still being on this side of the Channel. I ask you! After what he went through at Dunkirk! Funny creatures, men, aren't they?'

On Saturday morning, David asked when Ken would come to see them again. 'They haven't found out he was coming here before, have they, and punished him for it?'

It took both his mother and his aunt a second or two to realize what he meant, then Marge said, 'No, no, nobody found out. He's on leave, like your Dad was, and he's gone home to see his own family.'

'I love my Dad,' David stated, with a touch of embarrassment, 'but I miss Uncle Ken, and all. We can speak about him now, can't we?'

'Not to anybody outside this house,' Marge cautioned. 'You never know, one of your school friends might tell his mother, and she'd tell somebody else, and it could easily get back to Ardley.'

'OK!' David gave an exaggerated salute before picking up

the bag containing his football strip. 'I'll keep my mouth buttoned up, and so'll Leila. You can depend on us. You coming, then, Lei?'

His mother and aunt couldn't help laughing when the two children went out. David's words and actions came as a result of reading the *Wizard* and the other comic strip magazines for boys which he and his chums circulated amongst them. 'I hope we're not being stupid,' observed Gwen in a moment. 'Encouraging them to tell lies.'

Marge cocked one eyebrow. 'It's not lies, just . . . well, a way of saving trouble, really, though we're not doing anything wrong. You're not thinking of being unfaithful to Alistair are you?'

'I should think not!' Gwen was horrified at the very idea.

'If you ever do, let me know,' laughed Marge, 'so I can be on the lookout for someone, too. I don't want to miss out on any fun.'

Chapter 17

'I hope Uncle Ken remembered to buy me a cricket bat.'

Gwen shook her head reprovingly at her son. 'He gives you far too much, Leila too, and don't ask him about it. It's not manners to ask for presents.'

'I didn't ask,' David protested, bright blue eyes flashing indignantly. 'It was him promised to get one so he could teach me how to play proper cricket.'

'If he promised, he'll likely have it, but if he's forgotten, don't get in a paddy.'

The boy looked hurt now. 'I never get in a paddy . . . only when Leila makes fun of me, her and her chums. That Kirsty Droopy-Drawers . . .'

'That's enough, David! Her name's Kirsty Kelman, and it's no wonder the girls tease you if that's the kind of things you say about them.' Becoming aware that her sister was chuckling in the background, she snapped, 'It's not funny, Marge! He's getting worse and he'll have to learn some manners, else people will think I can't control my children.'

'Calm down, Gwennie, he's just a kid, but . . .' Marge gave her nephew a poke in the ribs, '. . . you *will* have to learn how to behave, David. You don't want to make your Dad ashamed of you, do you? He wants to come home to a boy people respect.'

His head drooped. 'I'm sorry, and I won't say anything to Uncle Ken if he hasn't got a bat . . . but Auntie Marge, is it OK if I ask him when we'll be playing cricket?'

She had to turn her head away to hide a smile, but Gwen heaved a lengthy sigh of exasperation, 'David Ritchie! Don't you dare mention cricket!'

Keeping her face straight with something of a struggle, Marge coaxed, 'Why don't you come outside, my boy, and help me tidy up the tool shed. It'll be something for you to do till Uncle Ken comes, and keep you out of your Mum's way.'

'This isn't his weekend on duty, is it? I don't like the Saturdays he can't come.'

David was still chattering when the back door closed behind them, leaving Gwen wondering what would happen when Ken Partridge was posted away from Ardley Camp, as was bound to happen sooner or later. He had been spending three Saturdays out of every four with them for almost a year now, and she had an uneasy feeling that David had begun to regard him as a father-figure. It wasn't surprising, really, when his real father wasn't there to guide him through his formative years. And Ken was so good with him and Leila, giving them the affection and attention he should be giving his own children. It was a terrible world, she reflected morosely, when families were kept apart like this.

She dabbed away an unwelcome tear that had edged out. She mustn't let herself wallow in misery, even though her sadness wasn't just for her own family and Ken's, it was for families everywhere. There must be hundreds, thousands, of wives praying every night for the safe return of their husbands, quaking every time someone came to the door in case it was a telegraph boy bearing the news they dreaded.

'Are you all right, Mum?'

Her daughter's concerned voice shook Gwen out of her reverie. 'Yes, dear, I'm fine. I was just feeling a bit sad, missing your Dad.'

'I miss Dad, too, but Uncle Ken won't be long now and

he'll cheer us all up . . .' Leila paused thoughtfully, then went on, '. . . though he must be missing his wife and children, too. Hardly any of my friends at school have Dads at home. Most of them are in the army, and there's a few in the RAF, but there's only one in the Navy. Why's that?'

'Probably because Forvit is nowhere near the sea. The men haven't got the sea in their blood like people from towns and villages on the coast.'

'It must be ever so dangerous on the sea, and up in the air,' Leila observed. 'I'm glad my Dad's a soldier on dry land.'

Gwen was only glad the girl hadn't realized that her father was in just as much danger on land as in the sky or on the waves. She was better not having that worry.

The shrilling of a bicycle bell made Leila jump up in excitement. 'That'll be Uncle Ken,' she cried, rushing to the door.

Gwen's heart contracted when she saw how the man scooped her daughter up in his arms. He was always so attentive to the children, showing more affection than Alistair, a reserved Scotsman, had ever done, yet she wished that it was he who had just come in.

'How are things, Gwen, girl?' Ken was standing looking down at her anxiously.

'Fine.' Even to herself her reply sounded listlessly insincere, and she tried to correct the impression she must be giving. 'I *am* fine. Just a bit down, thinking of Alistair.'

'Have you heard from him lately?'

'It's been nearly five weeks.'

'Given the state of the army postal service,' he smiled, 'that's not too bad. You'll get a whole bunch at once, no doubt.'

The door banged open as David burst in. 'I knew you were here, Uncle Ken! I saw your bike outside.'

'Did you take a good look at it?'

'No. Why? Should I have?'

'It might be a good idea.'

David whipped round and scampered out, almost knocking Marge off her feet as she came in. 'Where's the fire?' she gasped, but he didn't hear.

In less than a minute, he was back, grinning from ear to ear and brandishing a shiny cricket bat and a set of stumps. 'You did remember!' he crowed.

'Manners,' Gwen prompted.

'Thanks, Uncle Ken, thank you, thank you, thank you. I knew you wouldn't forget.'

With David on heckle pins at his side, Ken took time to drink the cup of tea he'd been given before he got to his feet. 'Well, I guess now's as good a time as any, David. Have you got a cricket ball to practise with?'

'Won't the sponge ball do?'

Ken put his hand in his trouser pocket and drew out a brand new cricket ball. 'I think we should keep this for a while yet, though. It's a bit too hard, and we don't want you breaking any windows. We'd better use the sponge ball till you've had some practice.' He still didn't move, however, but extricated a small package from his other pocket and handed it to the girl with a flourish usually executed by conjurers. 'Can't give to one and not the other, can I, Leila?'

'You shouldn't give either of them anything,' Gwen admonished him.

'I want to,' he said, simply, thus putting an end to her protestations.

'Oh, gosh, Uncle Ken!' Leila held up a little brooch in the shape of her name for them all to see. 'It's lovely! Thank you ever so, ever so much.'

'It's made of gold wire, and the boys are all making them for their daughters.' Gwen's frown made him smile broadly.

'I made one for my own daughter first, then I thought Leila might like one, too.'

'It's very kind of you.'

His ruddy face even redder than usual, he cleared his throat. 'Right, then! Who wants to come and field for us?'

They all trooped out, Leila proudly sporting her 'identity' brooch, and each one participated in the fun game until Gwen said she should go in to organize tea, and Marge and Leila offered to help. So now Ken was free to give young David some lessons on holding the bat, how to stand properly, how to keep his eye on the ball – the serious business of coaching. He called a halt when the picnic meal was carried out by the 'three ladies' as he called them, making Leila straighten her back proudly and Gwen glance at him in gratitude. It was a beautiful day, exceptionally warm even for September, so they lingered over their makeshift meal, taken on the 'drying-green', the only spot in the whole garden not given over to growing vegetables.

Looking around him with satisfaction, Ken suddenly said, 'Fetch the camera, David. I'd like to have some reminders of this day.'

The boy dashed off and returned with the box Brownie Ken had given him a few weeks earlier. 'It's showing eight,' he said, seriously, 'so that means there's still four left to take.'

Ken unwound his long legs and rose to his feet. 'Sit down so I can get you all in.' He waited until they arranged themselves as Marge considered best, then pressed the catch. 'You all look too posed,' he laughed. 'Can't you pretend to be doing something, so it'll look more natural?'

David flung his arm round his sister's neck as if he were about to strangle her, and Marge lolled drunkenly against Gwen. 'How's that?' she asked, grinning.

'That's better.' Ken took another snap, then handed the

camera to her. 'Take one of me and the kids. I'd like to have a keepsake of them.'

'There's still one left,' she smiled, after taking him capering with the two children.

David ran over. 'Let me take the last one, Auntie Marge. Uncle Ken, get in the middle between her and Mum. No, that looks too stiff . . .'

Ken obliged by putting his arms round the women, and David pressed the button while his mother and aunt were still laughing. 'That should be a good one,' he crowed.

'I'd better go inside the shed to take the film out.' Ken held out his hand for the camera. 'The photos'll be spoiled if any light gets in.'

David went with him. 'I want to see how to take the spool out,' he told his mother, who had frowned at him for dogging the man's footsteps.

A few minutes later, when they rejoined the others, Ken said, 'I'm being sent to London on a two-week course next Thursday, so I'll get it developed and printed there. In fact, I'll get two sets, one for myself as well, but you'll have to wait till I get back, David, before you can see them, I'm afraid.'

David looked crestfallen. 'That'll be three weeks, won't it?'

'It'll soon pass, and anyway, you'll have your Uncle Dougal for most of the time.'

'I'd nearly forgot about that.' The boy perked up again. 'Can we have another game now? Mum will want to clear up, so Leila and Auntie Marge can . . .'

'Hold your horses, David, my lad.' Marge got stiffly to her feet. 'I'm not doing any more running after that ball. I'm going to help your Mum.'

They all shared in the clearing up, then the two ladies were left in the kitchen to do the washing-up while the other three went back outside. After a few moments of silence, Marge said, reflectively, 'It's funny Ken having to go on a course just now, isn't it?'

Gwen looked up in puzzlement. 'What d'you mean?'

'I think he's volunteered to go. It's a year and a half since he first came here, and he always stays away when Dougal's on leave. Always some excuse.'

'But he can't plan things like that. He's got to go where he's told . . . when he's told. Anyway, I never asked him not to come while Dougal was here.'

'Neither did I,' Marge said, sharply. 'I'd have been quite happy for them to meet. I'm sure they'd like each other . . . Alistair, too.'

'I wish he would write more often.'

'He's fighting a war, remember, not having a holiday by the Mediterranean. He hasn't got time to write to you every other day.'

'I know that, but . . .' Gwen tailed off, forlornly.

'Getting back to Ken, I don't understand why you want him kept secret. He's only a friend, after all, and he's been jolly good with the kids.'

Not quite sure why herself, Gwen floundered a little before saying, 'I've the feeling Alistair would be hurt if he knew . . . because he can't be here to give them presents or play games with them. It's almost as if they look on Ken as their father, and that's . . .'

'Yes, but when Ken's posted away, they'll soon forget him and look forward to their real Dad coming home . . .'

Another few moments elapsed before Gwen murmured, 'I don't know how David's going to take it when Ken does have to leave Ardley. He dotes on him.'

'He'll cope. He was all right when Alistair went away, wasn't he? Now, can I go, or are you going to make me wait half an hour before you hand over that plate you're trying to scrub the pattern off?'

The last plate duly dried, everything tidied away, the sisters went to join the others, who, exhausted now, were sprawled out on the grass. The women sat down beside them, letting the newly-sprung cool breeze help them to recover from their exertions and ruffled emotions.

At nine o'clock, the usual hour for the children's bedtime on Saturdays, Marge said, 'I'll see these two settled, Gwen, then I think I'll go to bed myself. I've got a blinder of a headache with sitting in the sun too long, but it's too good a night to be cooped up inside. Why don't you two go for a walk?'

Ken beamed at her. 'I'd love to. What about it, Gwen?'

She cast a glance of appeal at her sister, who interpreted it correctly and gave her the push she needed. 'Go on, Gwennie, it'll do you good and nobody'll see you.'

'Even suppose someone did see us,' Ken remarked as they strolled up the track a few minutes later, 'we're doing nothing wrong, are we?'

'We know that,' she murmured, 'but other people wouldn't.'

'Forget about other people. Why can't you just relax and enjoy the walk? I've always felt easy in your company, though I know you took quite a while to feel completely at ease with me. I can assure you I've no intention of doing anything out of place, I respect you far too much, and I know you miss Alistair as much as I miss Rhoda. A man and a woman *can* have a close platonic relationship, Gwen. They can feel affection, even love in a kind of way, without anything . . . physical, if you get my meaning.'

She got his meaning, and the thought of what *could* happen made her nervous, but Ken was a decent man, and Marge must trust him, otherwise she wouldn't have suggested them taking this walk. Besides, Alistair couldn't object if he knew how innocent it was.

Because it wasn't too far, they made for the tower, and

while they stood looking down on the panorama spread out below them, and across at the snow-capped mountains in the distance, she thought of all the men and girls who must have stood there over the years, had perhaps consummated their love there, and gave an involuntary shiver.

'You're cold!' Ken exclaimed, removing his battledress blouse and wrapping it round her. 'We'd better put a step in going back. I don't want you ending up with pneumonia.'

'I'm not cold,' she protested. 'I was thinking of all the people who had stood here – since the tower was first built, and it gave me a queer feeling.'

His arm was still round her waist when they returned to the house, and she was quite relieved that Marge had gone to bed and didn't see. 'I'll make a pot of tea,' she said, her voice low and breathy.

'No, I'd better go.'

She didn't want to let him go just yet. 'It won't take long.' She lifted the kettle and held it under the tap.

'I'd better go. Believe me, Gwen, it *is* better.' He retrieved his jacket and put it on, then said, 'Good night, I've really enjoyed my day . . . as usual. I won't see you next week or the week after, of course, but I should manage the week after that . . . with any luck.'

He was gone before she could set the kettle down, and the rattle of the old bike told her that he hadn't waited for her to see him off. She lit the gas ring and sat down to think over what he had said. They did have a close relationship, she did feel affection for him, but not love. Not any kind of love – well, maybe just a touch. Why did he have to be so nice? Why did Marge have to pair them off? Why was she trembling at the memory of his arm around her?

The hiss of water on the gas flame made her jump up. When the tea was infused, she poured out two cups, one for herself and one for Marge. Her sister would likely wonder why Ken hadn't stayed for a cup, too, so she'd have to think of a reason to explain it.

Marge's light was still on, so she went straight in. 'How's your head now?'

'A bit better. I took a couple of aspirins and I dozed off for a while. Did you and Ken go up to the tower?'

'Mmm. It was lovely up there, so clear we could see for miles.'

'Um . . . he didn't stay very long when you came back?'

'No, he thought I'd caught a cold, because I was shivering. It was only somebody walking over my grave, but . . . he insisted on giving me his jacket.'

'You look kind of guilty, Gwennie, so you'd better tell me. Did he try anything?'

'No, he didn't!' Gwen was truly indignant.

'He didn't even kiss you?'

'No, he didn't.'

'Did you wish he had?'

'No, I didn't.'

Marge's eye hardened. 'Change the record, Gwen. I can read you like a book.'

'Well, you're wrong tonight. Nothing happened, and I wasn't sorry. Ken said ours was a platonic relationship, and that's how we both want it.'

'I'm glad to hear it. I did wonder, after I sent you out with him, if I was stirring up a hornets' nest, so I'm pleased you're both so adult and sensible about it.'

'Well, we're both married and love our . . .'

'Spouses, that's the word. Now you'll maybe understand how I feel when I'm out dancing. It's nice to be in a man's company again, especially when there's no chemistry to foul things up. I won't feel so bad now about leaving you on your own. And that's another thing. Would Ken have volunteered to be the permanent bus driver taking the soldiers to Forvit?

He always makes a point of staying in the hall all the time, nowadays, but he never asks any girl up to dance . . . not even me.'

In her own bed, Gwen turned Marge's last remark over in her mind. Ken probably *had* volunteered to ferry his friends from the camp to the village and back, and had remained in the hall to save even her sister getting any wrong ideas about her.

Because the monthly dance fell on Dougal's second night home, Marge said she couldn't desert him, but he pulled a face. 'I don't want you giving up your night out . . . d'you think any of the boys would mind if I went with you?'

'I don't see why they should. You're in the forces, the same as them.'

The minister was delighted to make Dougal's acquaintance and, after his usual few words of welcome to the 'boys from Ardley', he made a point of introducing 'Marjory's husband'. There were shouts of 'Good old Marge!' and 'Good luck, mate!', and even one cheeky 'He's why we only get to dance with her,' at which she beamed happily.

At that moment, the band struck up, and a laughing Dougal swung her into their first lap of the church hall to the strains of 'You Are My Sunshine', played with gusto on sax, piano and drums by three ex-members of a quite well-known dance band.

Dougal forgot everything and everyone else in the pleasure of holding his wife in his arms, their bodies moving in unison to the pulsating rhythm. 'You'll never know, dear, how much I love you,' he sang softly into her ear.

'Oh, Dougal,' Marge sighed, her heart performing all kinds of somersaults, 'I didn't know you were such a good dancer.'

'We never went dancing, did we? Some of the other girls I took out were dancing mad, so I went with them, and I used to go to all the dances round here before I went to London.'

'Sowing your wild oats?' she teased.

He chuckled at this. 'What we thought was wild oats at the time, I wasn't long sixteen when I left, remember. I looked on myself as a proper Romeo, you know, and if a girl let me kiss her when I saw her home, I thought I was the bee's knees.'

'Did you never . . . ?'

'I used to boast to Alistair I'd gone all the way, he was a lot quieter than me, but it wasn't true. Oh, I admit I made some feeble attempts, but I'd have dropped flat on my face with shock if any of them had let me.'

The quickstep ended with a flourish and was followed by a modern waltz, then a Paul Jones, where, miraculously, they ended up with each other every time the music changed. After the energy expended in most of this, they were glad of the dreamy slow foxtrot to which Dougal substituted the words 'A Nightingale Sang in Russell Square' instead of the proper Berkeley Square, but he broke off when he realized that his wife's eyes had filled with tears. 'I'm sorry, Marge, have I made you homesick?' he asked, anxiously.

'No, it's not that.' She dragged the back of her hand across her cheekbone. 'It's just . . . that Russell Square reminded me of Guilford Street, and the hotel . . . and Dad.'

'I didn't think – I could bite my tongue out. Will you be all right?'

'I *am* all right. I was being silly.'

Next, they were told to form into lines for the Lambeth Walk, which was all she needed to banish the nostalgia, and she joined in the fun right to the final 'Oy!' Spirits were high as the band took a well-deserved break, and the ladies of the Women's Guild took up their positions on the small stage round the tables which held huge tea urns and dozens of plates of scones and pancakes, baked by the ladies themselves. The minister now said a brief grace which doubled as a prayer for absent friends, adding after the Amen, 'Pray silence for the vice-president of the Women's Guild, Mrs Georgina Tough.'

Dougal couldn't trust himself to look at Marge as Doodie stepped forward. 'I just want to say,' she began, in her best speechifying-English, 'how sorry we are that our president is nae able to be here the night, and I think I spikk for yous all when I say we hope her operation's a great success.' She looked round the assembly and then observed, to the minister's very obvious embarrassment, 'Piles is nae a fine thing to ha'e – I ken that, for my Dod's suffered wi' them for years – and I'd be obliged, Mr Lennox, if you'll pass on oor best wishes to your lady wife. Now, that's me finished, so jist come up and help yoursel's! There's plenty, and you can come back for seconds if you want. Like my aul' Granny used to say, "Stick in till you stick oot."' With a toothy smile, she returned to her station, ready for the rush.

Surprisingly, the dancers made their way on to the stage in an orderly line, which resulted in a smooth operation where everyone was served in no time at all. Dougal was astonished by the amount on offer, but didn't heap his plate like most of the other men. 'These pancakes are out of this world,' he enthused when he and Marge were seated. 'How do they do it when everything's rationed?'

'All the women chip in a little something,' she smiled. 'Flour, sugar, eggs . . .'

'Dried eggs? I heard they were awful.'

'A lot of wives here keep hens, so we hardly ever have to use the dried stuff, though it's not too bad when it's reconstituted . . . not good, but bearable. And Lexie's quite good at giving the committee a bit of Stork margarine, or Echo, no butter, of course.'

'Does she ever attend these dances?'

'Not every one, and she's not here tonight. She'd a bad cold on Thursday when I saw her, so she probably didn't feel up to it.'

Dougal eyed his wife reflectively. 'I don't suppose you and Gwen ever made friends with her?'

Marge lifted her shoulders in a small shrug. 'Not friends as such. We talk to her in the shop, that's all. I've never really taken to her, you know.'

'If that's because of Alistair, I'm nearly sure she gave up on him long ago.'

Their little tête-à-tête was interrupted by a roll on the drums, and the first few bars of 'Jealousy' on the saxophone. A tall captain appeared in front of them now. 'I hope I'm not intruding,' he began, 'but I really must have this tango with Marge. She's the only one in the place who can do it properly. I hope you don't mind . . . Dougal?'

Marge jumped to her feet. 'Of course he doesn't mind.'

As Dougal watched them, he thought what a stunning couple they made, their steps gracefully synchronized, as if they'd been partners for years. He felt slightly jealous, only very slightly, he told himself, but was it any wonder? Not only an officer, this man was devilishly good-looking – tightly-curled blonde hair, piercing blue eyes, dimpled cheeks – and Marge was laughing as she looked up at him.

When the tango ended, she pulled the captain back to be introduced properly. 'Dougal, this is Percival Lamont. Percy, this is my beloved husband.'

The attractive smile widened. 'I'm very pleased to make your acquaintance, Dougal.'

The lilting Highland accent would be another point in his favour with the women, Dougal thought, but he shook the man's hand as warmly as he could. 'Pleased to meet *you*, Captain.'

'We don't bother with rank at these dos. But I must tell you how much I envy you, Dougal, having this lovely lady for your wife, a faithful wife, at that. There are very few of them around now.'

Blushing faintly, Marge giggled, 'Get on with you, Percy. You could charm the birds off the trees if you tried.'

'But not you, I fear.' He winked at Dougal to show that he was only fooling. 'Now Dougal, I must spread myself around – I wonder who will be the next lucky lady?'

He turned away and headed for a small brunette at the other side of the hall as the band struck up a slow foxtrot, and Marge said, 'Don't mind Percy, Dougal. He's an awful tease, but it's all in fun. He's very happily married, his wife had a baby a couple of months ago, and for all his flirting, he wouldn't do anything to hurt her.'

Her husband led her on to the floor. 'I just wish he wasn't so handsome . . . like a blinking film star.'

'I like my men rugged,' she said, softly, 'with dark hair and called Dougal, not a cissy name like Percival.'

The rugged, dark-haired man called Dougal tightened his hold on her. 'I love you, Marjory Finnie,' he whispered in her ear, 'and I'm glad I came with you tonight.' She looked so lovely, so happy, that he couldn't resist kissing her. It didn't go unnoticed, however, and they jumped apart as various teasing comments were made, but, because of the minister's presence, nothing out of place.

'We'll have to excuse them – they haven't seen each other for months.'

'Couldn't you two wait till you went home?'

'I hope my old lady kisses me like that when I'm on leave.'

And so on, the Reverend James Lennox's face never changing its affable expression, although he did unbend a little when the other dancers moved away and left Marge and her husband on their own. 'Oh, God,' Dougal muttered, 'I don't like everybody watching every move I make.'

'It's a compliment,' she giggled, 'so let's show 'em!'

Their intricate scissors-steps to 'I'd Like to Get You on a Slow Boat to China' drew frenzied applause from the onlookers, but Dougal was glad when they could return to their seats. 'I felt awful,' he groaned, while they watched the more energetic Eightsome Reel which followed, 'like a goldfish in a bowl.'

'Tell the truth now,' Marge chuckled, 'you really liked being the centre of all eyes, didn't you?'

'Aye, I suppose so. I always did like to show off.'

At the end of the evening, several of the men shouted goodnight to them as they made their way outside, one even saying to Marge, 'Have you got your bike tonight?'

She hadn't, there was only one adult bicycle at Benview, Alice's old rattler, and the thought of having to walk three miles home after dancing all evening was not a pleasant one. The bus was waiting outside to take the soldiers back to Ardley, but the driver – not Ken, Marge was glad to see – came up to her and said, 'It's back along there, isn't it? Hop in, it's not taking me much out of the way.'

As they plodded up the track some minutes later, Dougal observed, with deep feeling, 'Thank goodness we got a lift a bit of the way. My legs feel like telephone poles with dancing so much, but I really enjoyed myself.'

'That's good, 'cos so did I.'

He waited until they were in bed, until he had demonstrated how much he loved her, before he gave her the bad news. 'This is embarkation leave, I'm afraid, darling, and the word is it's the Far East, so God knows how long it'll be before I get home again.'

Marge frowned. 'I know you've been dying to get back into

it, but you did your bit in 1940, more than your bit. Why can't you be satisfied with that?'

'I wasn't the only one, and we were just doing what we were trained for.'

'When I remember how you were when you got back from Dunkirk . . .' She broke off, her eyes softening. 'I know you've got to obey orders, but you're not really sorry to go, are you?'

'I'm not sorry in one way, but I hate the idea of being away from you for . . . well, it's indefinitely, isn't it?'

'I'll survive, my darling, but I'll never stop thinking about you, and praying for you.'

He drew in a long contented breath and let it out slowly. 'Marge, I'm really glad I went to that dance with you tonight. I've always known you liked to enjoy yourself, and no matter how often you said in your letters I could trust you, I couldn't help wondering. But what those men said about you . . . it made me realize what a jewel you are. I love you so much, Marge Finnie, I'd bloody die for you if I had to.'

Her eyes flashed in alarm. 'No, Dougal, don't say that! Please don't say that!'

He held her trembling body in his arms, as she sobbed out her fear for him, the fear that she had planned to hide if this moment ever came, but couldn't when it had actually arrived, and when she pulled herself together at last, he made love to her again.

'I know you'll worry about me,' he said afterwards, 'but there's no need. I'll be back. I swear to you I'll come back. Don't ever forget that, my darling.'

Marge's heartache was almost unbearable, yet she was glad that Dougal hadn't waited until the last minute before telling her his news, like Alistair had done. At least *she* could make the most of the ten nights she had left to enjoy her husband, but even when Gwen took her children to Aberdeen to let them be alone on his last Saturday, it didn't seem long enough.

When Ken Partridge put in his next apperance, the first thing he did was to hand David a slim wallet of photographs. 'They're all quite good,' he observed, smiling at the boy's haste to take them out and look.

'So they are!' David exulted. 'Look, Mum, and Uncle Ken only took three. I took the rest myself.'

The snapshots duly inspected by Gwen, Marge and Leila, and praise given where it was due, David wanted to play cricket again, so they all trooped outside to get some exercise and then soak in some sunshine while they recovered. Both Gwen and Marge had a feeling that Ken was holding something back, but neither of them said anything. If he had something to tell them, it was up to him to choose his moment.

They had another picnic tea, but as soon as a move was made to gather the dirty dishes, Ken said, 'Leave them for now. I'm not going to make a speech, exactly, but there's a few things I'd like to say before I leave Forvit.' He held up his hand to stop any comments on this, and continued, 'First, I want to thank you two ladies for the pleasure you've given me over the past eighteen months. You always made me feel I was part of your family, and as for you two . . .' he ruffled David's hair with one hand and touched Leila's cheek with the other, '. . . well, it was like being with my own kids.'

David knuckled his eyes. 'You're not going away, are you, Uncle Ken?'

'I'm afraid I have to. We're being posted down south somewhere.'

'But you'll come back to see us?'

'I don't think we'll ever be sent back to Forvit.'

'Will you write to us?'

Ken glanced hopelessly at Gwen, then clasped the two children closely for a second. 'No, I don't think that's . . .'

'No, of course, you're not supposed to be friends with another soldier's family, are you?' David still believed the tale Marge had once spun him, but Ken was too involved in making sure he expressed his sentiments clearly to notice.

'I'll never forget you, though . . . any of you.' The man's voice was strained now, and he said nothing more until he composed himself. 'What about a last shot at cricket, David? You learned pretty quick, you know, so maybe, if we promise to be careful, your Mum'll let us use the proper ball?'

It was Marge who jumped in. 'Fifteen minutes, then, to let us get the dishes done, then it's off to bed with you.'

When Gwen finally managed to haul her son upstairs, still begging to stay up a bit later since it was the last time he would see Uncle Ken, Marge took advantage of her brief absence. 'I'm going to tell Gwen I've got another headache,' she told Ken, 'so would you be a dear and take her out for a while? She won't admit it, but she's really worried about Alistair, and she must miss a man's company.'

'It'll be my pleasure, Marge, but are you sure you'll be all right?'

'There's nothing wrong with me, but don't let on to Gwen. Ssh, here she comes.' She raised her voice now and went on, 'Well, I suppose it's goodbye, Ken, so all the best, and take care of yourself.'

'You're not leaving already?' Gwen asked, anxiously.

'No, he's not, but I've got another of my headaches so I'll leave you to entertain him. Good night, Ken dear, and God bless.'

'I'm sorry,' Gwen murmured, uncomfortably, when her sister closed the door, 'she could surely have managed to stay with us till . . .'

'It's all right, it gives me a chance to let me have one last stroll with you.'

'Oh, Ken, I don't know if I should . . .'

'Please, Gwen?'

The entreaty in his eyes was too much for her. 'All right, but just for a little while.'

They walked up the hill again, making light conversation and scrupulously keeping their bodies from touching, but when Gwen stumbled over a bigger-than-normal stone and Ken's arm shot round her waist to steady her, she didn't object. Nor did she protest when he tucked her arm through his instead, and this is how they carried on walking.

'You *will* hear from Alistair,' Ken assured her. 'I'm sure you will.'

'I wish I could be so sure.' Feeling a wave of sadness wash over her, she wished that he hadn't mentioned her husband. It was bad enough that she was about to lose *him*.

As if he knew what was going through her mind, Ken said, softly, 'This is the last time we'll be together.'

She could think of nothing to say. She had known it would come some day and had thought she would be able to wish him luck as she waved him goodbye, as Gracie Fields sang, but she couldn't get it out. She had even planned to ask for his home address, so that she could write to his wife and tell her how good he had been to Leila and David, but perhaps that wouldn't have been such a good idea. In any case, she was struck dumb, unable to wish him well, unable to tell him how much she would miss him.

'Are you OK, Gwen? You're not upset because I'm going away, are you?'

'Yes,' she managed to croak, 'I *am* upset . . .'

Tears welling up, she turned blindly to him and he took her in his arms. 'Oh, God,' he moaned, 'are you crying for me, Gwen? I didn't dream you felt . . . I've steeled myself for months not to let myself get too fond of you.' His murmured words of affection became words of love, of passion, and before they knew it, they were lying on the heathery scrub kissing as if there would be no tomorrow. And neither there would . . . for them.

'Come here, Floss.' Lexie had thought the collie would be all right off the leash, but she was determined to get into a rabbit hole, burrowing away as if her life depended on it, but she did stand, a little impatiently, as the lead was fixed to her collar again.

Lexie had never cared much for dogs, but when old Mary Johnston had asked her to look after Floss while she was in hospital having her varicose veins stripped, she hadn't liked to refuse. The poor woman hadn't long lost her husband, and having always kept herself to herself, she had few friends. Still, walking the collie took a person out, Lexie had told herself, and set out for the tower without thinking. It was the only walk she had ever taken when she was younger, and it aroused memories of happy times with Alistair. But she shouldn't dwell on that; it was long behind her.

She had to pull the dog back suddenly, for she was straining to bound towards a couple lying at the foot of the tower. Lexie didn't consider herself a romantic, but it seemed a shame to disturb the young lovers, though she would have liked to know who the girl was. The snag was, she couldn't see their heads, and she could hardly walk right up to them to find out. Just before she turned to walk back, however, a low voice made her strain to hear what was being said. 'Oh, Lord, I'm sorry!' That was all. It was an Englishman, but a lot of the lads at Ardley were from somewhere in England. 'I didn't set out tonight to do that. I'm truly sorry.'

'It was as much my fault as yours.'

Lexie drew in her breath. She'd know *that* voice anywhere. Alistair Ritchie's wife! Up at the tower, making love with a soldier!

'It just happened because you're going away.'

'That's no excuse. Can you ever forgive me?'

'There's nothing to forgive. We'd better go back now. It must be late.'

Lexie didn't wait to be caught eavesdropping. Stepping off the stony path, she padded as swiftly and silently as she could until she reached the trees and was sure she wouldn't be seen. Making her way obliquely towards the road, she could hardly believe what she had seen and heard. Gwen Ritchie with a soldier? It was manna from heaven!

It didn't matter that she'd have to wait till Alistair came back from overseas. What she had to tell him would blast his marriage apart. To be absolutely sure, she would say she had seen the couple making love. It was only half a lie, for that *was* what they must have been doing. Why else would the man have been pleading for forgiveness? Not for just a few kisses.

Lexie breathed a long, contented sigh. Everything comes to he – she – who waits. God bless old Mary Johnston's varicose veins! God bless the dear old soul for having a dog that needed to be walked at nights! God bless everything and everybody, especially Lexie Fraser!

Chapter 18

It was on the Wednesday of the following week that Sandy Mearns said, as he handed a buff envelope to Gwen, 'Is your sister in? If she's nae, you'd best wait till she comes back afore you open that.'

It took a moment for the meaning of his remark to penetrate, then she muttered, her voice quivering a little, 'It's OK. She's in the kitchen.'

When she went inside, Marge said, 'Is something up? You look kind of . . . funny.'

'The postman thinks it's bad news.' Gwen was fumbling at the flap of the envelope.

Understanding now, Marge said, softly, 'D'you want me to open it?'

'No, I want to do it myself.'

Marge didn't have long to wait to satisfy her curiosity. 'Oh, no!' she exclaimed, when her sister passed the single sheet over without a word. 'But . . . it's not as bad as it could . . . it just says he's missing. That means they must think he's OK. If they didn't, they'd have said "Missing, believed . . . killed."'

'I knew something was wrong! I just knew it!'

'Don't give up hope, Gwennie. I've read of some men going missing for weeks, months sometimes, and then they turn up again – maybe lost their memory, or been wounded and taken in and cared for by some family, or . . . oh, there's lots of reasons.'

'But there's always some who don't turn up,' Gwen pointed out, her voice flat.

Forced to concede that this, too, was true, Marge happened to glance out of the window. 'Sandy's still fussing about at his bike. He'll be waiting to hear what was in the letter. I'll go and tell him.'

When she came in again, she said, 'He's a nice old stick. He said to tell you he'll be praying for your husband's safe return. Wasn't that thoughtful of him?' She paused, then asked, 'Are you going to tell Leila and David?'

'I don't know, I don't want to upset them. The thing is, if it gets round the village, one of their friends at school might tell them.'

Marge's nose crinkled. 'I asked Sandy not to tell anybody.'

'He's bound to tell his wife, and Mrs Mearns is a real gossip. I know, I've heard her in the shop.'

Marge couldn't hold back a slight smile. 'He knows that. He said, "I'll nae tell a soul, lass, specially nae my Aggie." But I suppose it would be best not to tell the kids – not till . . . we hear something definite.'

And so, every morning around nine fifteen, whether he had a delivery to make or not, Sandy Mearns was to be found in the kitchen at Benview, making droll comments in the hope of cheering up the 'poor English lassie'. Marge would laugh hilariously for a moment at something she thought was comical, then quieten down when she noticed that Gwen, the true object of his wit, was scarcely smiling.

It was quite an effort for the two young women to keep up an appearance of normality in front of the children, whose first question when they came in from school was always, 'Is there a letter from Dad?', but Marge managed to paper over any cracks in her sister's manner that might have caused them to fret.

It was an afternoon almost six weeks later – with Gwen's limbs becoming more and more leaden, her face more and more peaky, her temper shorter than even the more volatile Marge's had ever been – before the telegram came, the telegram which Gwen was powerless to bring herself to open, but Marge seized as soon as the door was shut on the telegraph boy.

'He's all right, Gwennie!' she screamed, in a second. 'He's been taken prisoner.' She grabbed her sister's arms and pulled her to her feet to waltz her round the room.

But Gwen was not yet in a dancing mood. 'I want to read it for myself,' she protested, picking up the scrap of paper with the information pasted on in narrow, typed strips. 'I don't know what to think,' she sighed after a while. 'I know it means he's alive, but aren't prisoners sometimes badly treated?'

Tutting at this, Marge said, perhaps more snappily than she meant, 'Stop going on, Gwen, for goodness' sake! At least you know he's alive, and he'll be safer in a prison camp than anywhere else, won't he?'

'I suppose so.' She sat pensively for a few moments, then burst out, 'Yes, I'm being silly. Of course I'm glad he's a prisoner, and now all we have to worry about is Dougal's safety.'

'It's hellish, isn't it?' Marge commented, bitterly. 'I'd feel much better if I could be doing something, instead of being stuck up here at the back of bally beyond.'

'You're not thinking of going back to London?' Gwen asked, looking worried.

'No . . . no, I'm not. I promised Alistair I'd never leave you here on your own.'

The children came home at the usual time, David bursting in like a wild animal to let them know what he had been told.

'They're all saying our Dad's been taken a prisoner. It's not true, is it?'

Marge jumped in. 'Yes, isn't it good news? We just heard this morning, how did your pals hear?'

'Petey Rae said Dad's name was on the list of prisoners Lord Haw-Haw read out last night on the wireless. His Mum listens every night, and she said she was sure it was the same Alistair Ritchie she was at school with.'

He lapsed into silence now, making Marge realize that he, like his mother, was not sure whether to regard this as good or bad news. 'He's out of the fighting now, that's the main thing, David, and there are rules laid down about how prisoners of war should be treated. He'll be all right, dear.'

In the background as usual, Leila made a sudden mewing noise, and flung herself at her mother. 'I knew something was wrong,' she sobbed. 'Dad hasn't written to us for weeks and weeks and weeks, and I thought he . . . I thought he'd been killed.'

Watching Gwen comforting her daughter, Marge marvelled at how quickly a mother could summon up such strength. Having her children to consider would help to take her mind off herself.

Sandy Mearns's smile was a little wry the next morning. 'The news is out, Mrs Ritchie, and it wasna my doing. It seems . . .'

She smiled to put him at ease. 'We know. Somebody listened to Haw Haw.'

'That bloody traitor!' His hand jumped to his mouth. 'Ach, I'm sorry, ladies, but if I got my hands on him, I'd . . . damn well throttle him. But at least you ken your man's safe, Mrs Ritchie. It must have been real hard on you when you was tell't he was missing.'

'It wasn't easy,' she agreed – a vast understatement if ever there was one.

* * *

Another few weeks passed before a guilty Gwen suspected that she might have more to worry about than her husband's and her brother-in-law's wellbeing. The first time she missed, she had put it down to the ordeal of waiting to hear about Alistair, but this second time, well, there was no excuse. Feeling that she couldn't confide in anyone, not even her sister, she became withdrawn and tearful.

'Luv-a-duck, Gwen!' Marge exclaimed when the children left for school one morning another month later, after a somewhat fraught breakfast. 'You've been snapping their heads off since they got up. What's wrong? It's not as if you got out of bed the wrong side today, it's been going on for weeks.'

That was enough. Gwen burst into a torrent of tears.

'Oh, come on, now. I know you've only had one little card from Alistair since he was taken prisoner, but surely . . .'

'I'm . . . pregnant.' The whispered words were almost lost in the weeping.

Marge's head jerked up as her eyebrows shot down. 'You're what? You can't be! It's months since Alist . . .' She broke off, comprehension hitting her like a punch in the face. 'Oh no, Gwen, tell me you didn't . . . ?' Her sister's bent head, bobbing in time with her sobs, told her all she needed to know. 'Dear God! I trusted Ken! I never dreamt he'd take advantage of you! Did he rape you?'

Getting no answer, she continued, 'Obviously not! So you let him! How could you?'

Gwen looked up, her eyes dark with shame. 'I . . . I can't . . . it was . . . his last . . . night, and he was missing his wife, and I was missing Alistair, and we were . . . it just happened.'

'But servicemen are issued with thingummies. Why didn't he use one?'

Her sister shook her head. 'It wasn't planned . . . it happened so quickly . . .'

'But you must have known the risk? Good Lord, you're not a child!'

Gwen dissolved into a fresh bout of weeping, and Marge shook her head hopelessly. 'So what are you going to do?'

'I don't know. I . . . can't think. Alistair'll kill me when he finds out.'

Marge pulled a face. 'He's not that type, but he's bound to . . . oh, what a thing for a man to come home to. His wife with another man's child.'

'Stop it, Marge! I feel bad enough without you making it worse.'

There was an uneasy silence, broken only by Gwen's hiccuping sniffs, until Marge said, 'Have you tried to get rid of it?'

'I'm too scared. I've heard it's dangerous, and anyway, I don't know what to do.'

'Poking things up's dangerous, but there are other ways. Drinking gin's supposed to do the trick. Or a good dose of castor oil or liquid paraffin, so I've heard.'

'I . . . don't think . . .'

'It would be difficult to get any of that, in any case. We'd have to go to the pub for gin, which would start tongues wagging, and if you ask in the shop for castor oil or liquid paraffin it'd be a dead giveaway.'

'Oh, Marge! What am I going to do?'

'It'll be OK, Gwennie. I'll think of something, but I need absolute peace for my little grey cells to work, as 'Ercule Parrot says, so I'll make a start on tidying up David's room for you. He leaves it like a pigsty. Just give me a shout when it's dinner time.' An idea had already occurred to Marge, but it would have to be well planned, every wrinkle ironed out, before she mentioned it to her sister. Gwen had a more analytical mind than she had, and would be sure to pinpoint snags if there were any to be found.

While she gathered up the clothes David had dropped on the floor the night before, and arranged things so that drawers would shut, she looked at her idea from every angle, explored every avenue where there could be a trap for the unwary, and eventually decided that it was quite feasible . . . if they were careful. The main problem, of course, was Gwen herself. Would she agree, or would she think that her sister was taking advantage of her plight? In fact, Marge mused, was that what she really *was* doing? Her solution would benefit herself as much as . . . no, more, a thousand times more, than Gwen. But it was the only way.

When she was called downstairs, she burst into the kitchen and sat down at the table with a thump. 'I've got it! I've got it!'

Gwen regarded her miserably. 'Not one of your silly ideas, please. I've done some thinking, too, and I've come to the conclusion that I'll just have to face up to it, but I won't tell Mum till it's all over. She'll be so disappointed in me.'

Marge said nothing until she had forced down a few mouthfuls of the detested, not rationed, corned mutton. 'My idea isn't silly, Gwen, and you won't have to tell anybody anything. Not Mum, not Peg, not Alistair when he comes home, not a soul.'

Her sister's face blanched. 'You're not going to tell me to get an abortion? I couldn't do that, Marge, not even if you found a woman who's done dozens.'

'You know this? You're a blinking pessimist, Gwen Ritchie! Maybe you can't see a way out of the mess, but never fear! Marge is here!'

'Stop fooling! I'm not in the mood.'

'I'm not fooling, believe me! Just listen.'

Over the next twenty minutes, Marge laid out her plan and satisfactorily, she hoped, fielded off each attempt to pick holes in it. 'It's foolproof!' she crowed at last. 'I've thought of everything, and though we wouldn't get away with it in London, it'll be a cinch here. Nobody near us . . .' she broke into song, '. . . to see us or hear us. Gwennie, it's perfect, so why can't you look happier about it? I've nearly worn my brain to the bone for you, and I get no thanks for it.'

'I *am* grateful, Marge, but d'you honestly think . . . ?'

'I don't think, I know. We'll have to take things stage by stage, of course, so we don't raise any suspicions, but I'm a good actress and I'll carry it off.'

'I don't doubt that,' Gwen muttered, 'it's me I'm worried about. I can't tell lies, you know that. I get all guilty and flustered, and people know . . .'

'You won't have to tell lies, just go along with the lies I tell. I'm going to leave it for now, and we'll discuss it again tomorrow. That'll give you all night to think it over and to . . . realize it *will* work. In the meantime, don't let Leila and David see there's anything up. We don't want them upset, as well.'

For the rest of the day, Gwen went about her usual chores silently, only opening up when her children came home from school and apologizing for being so bad-tempered in the morning.

David nodded vigorously. 'Bad-tempered? I'll say! I was scared to open my mouth in case you jumped down my throat.'

Marge jollied them along. 'It'll maybe teach you to keep your mouth shut, then,' she chuckled. 'You should know by this time it's not sensible to argue with anybody who's in a bad humour. Your mum and me keep well away from you when you're in a paddy.'

'I only get in paddies 'cos it's always me you and Mum pick on.'

'Because you're the only one who needs to be picked on.'

David saw the truth of this and grinned mischievously.

'We calling pax now, are we?'

Marge pretended to punch his arm. 'Till the next time.'

Gwen gave Marge's plan a great deal of consideration that night. At first, it had sounded so outrageous that she'd been sure it couldn't possibly work, that it was just another of her sister's harebrained schemes, but the more she mulled it over, the more she came to think that it might work, with any luck. The one big snag as far as she could see was that, although it would be Marge who was supposed to be expecting, *she'd* be the one growing fat. But Marge had thought of that, too, positive they could overcome even that hurdle.

Having their usual, most appreciated, cup of tea after the children went off to school next morning, Gwen broached the subject first. 'I've decided to play along.'

Marge clapped her hands. 'Thank God for that! I don't know what we'd have done if you hadn't. Now, the first thing to do is for me to tell people you're not very well. I'll do all the shopping from now on, and as you get bigger, you'll have to keep out of the postman's sight, and young Barry's. They're the only ones who come here. And you'll have to keep me right on how fat I'm supposed to be at the different stages.' She beamed expansively. 'You know something, Gwennie? I'm looking forward to this. It's a real challenge to my ingenuity.'

'There's just one thing we've never mentioned,' Gwen said, cautiously. 'When we go back to London, who takes the baby?'

Marge looked a little uneasy. 'If you don't want Mum and Alistair to know . . .' She came to an abrupt decision herself and took the bull by the horns. 'It'll be best all round, Gwennie. Dougal went back off his last leave just a week . . . no, two weeks before you and Ken . . . He'll be jumping his own height thinking he actually hit the jackpot after all these years, so there'll be no doubts in his mind that he's the father.'

Eager to make a start to the long series of deceptions she was instigating, Marge cycled to the village that morning to cash her army allowance. 'Is it possible for me to collect Gwen's as well?' she asked Lexie.

'Is she not feeling well?'

'She's got a blinder of a headache, and I told her to go back to bed. Migraine, likely.'

'Tell her I hope she gets over it soon, and . . . well, I suppose it'll be all right.'

While she served her customer with the groceries she needed, Lexie said, a little slyly, Marge thought, 'I thought I saw her with a soldier up at the tower, one night a few months ago. About half past nine, it would have been.'

'It couldn't have been Gwen!' Marge stated firmly. 'She never goes out at nights, just with me and the kids, and they're in bed by nine.'

'I must've made a mistake then.'

Cycling back to the cottage, Marge decided not to tell Gwen about it. She'd only get more worried, and the success of the whole thing depended on them both staying calm. In any case, Lexie Fraser hadn't seemed sure it was Gwen. She'd probably said it for effect more than anything, maybe she'd been there with a soldier herself, and had wanted her, Marge, to ask what she'd been doing at the tower at half past nine at night. She'd been wanting to prove *she* had a man friend. That was all.

Lexie smiled craftily to herself when Marge went out. Did that Cockney think she'd come up the Don in a banana boat? Maybe – a weak maybe – it was just a coincidence that Alistair's wife was feeling off colour, but more likely it was because her lover-boy had put her up the spout. Judging by the time that had gone past, she would be due to feel sick and that kind of thing. It all fitted in, and the situation should be monitored as closely as possible. If she *was* expecting, Gwen Ritchie hadn't a hope of hiding it.

In London, maybe, but not in Forvit. Not a hope! Definitely not!

Chapter 19

Marge was greatly relieved that Lexie Fraser, usually sub-covertly inquisitive about all her customers' lives, especially Alistair's wife's, had never commented on how pale and haggard Gwen was beginning to look. In fact, the shopkeeper seemed quite surprised when Marge said that her sister was going to see a specialist the following week. 'It's a woman's problem, you see, and she was too embarrassed to go to the doctor here, so I took her to a lady doctor in Aberdeen a few weeks ago. *She* made all the arrangements.'

Lexie just nodded half-heartedly and said, 'So she would. Now, that's one pound, sixteen and four pence, please, Mrs Finnie.'

Marge picked out the correct amount from the money she had just received as her army allowance, and as she packed her purchases into the shopping bag, she wondered what God-sent problem was keeping Lexie so preoccupied. The thing was, she thought, while she cycled back to the cottage, it might not last long, and it was better to face all possible snags before they arose. That was why she had given the first hint of something brewing . . . but leading the shopkeeper, naturally, in the wrong direction.

'You'd better not go to the shop again,' she told her sister when she went in. 'I've told Lexie you're going to see a specialist next week, and even if I'm not sure if she took it in, it's better that you stop going to the village till after . . .'

Gwen looked up sadly from preparing the vegetables. 'But

if you're going to pretend it's you who's having the baby, you can't go either. She'll see you're not expecting.'

'It's going to be OK. I'll stick a cushion up my jumper . . .'

'But you'll need two cushions when it comes nearer the time, and you won't have any clothes to fit over that.'

'I think I will. D'you remember, before Alice left, she said she'd never thrown out any of her mother's clothes? She said they were in an old trunk in the attic, and Mrs Ritchie was quite stout, remember? I'll go up this afternoon and sort something out. It'll work, Gwennie, I promise it will.'

'Oh, Marge, I don't know what I'd do without you.'

Marge pulled a face. 'You wouldn't be in this mess, for a start. You'd never have gone out with Ken Partridge if I hadn't made you.'

That afternoon, while Marge was up in the attic, Gwen went into her son's room to look at the photographs again. David had got some nice snaps of the tower, of the house, of some of his chums, but those taken at Benview were really good. Of course, Ken had taken two and Marge had taken one, but the one David had taken was by far the best – Ken standing between her and her sister with his arms round their shoulders. David had told them not to be so serious, she recalled, so Marge, grinning up at Ken, had passed some silly remark, he was smiling broadly at her, and she, herself, was laughing.

Gwen studied this print for several seconds, waiting to see if what she'd felt for the man on that last night would return, the powerful emotion that had led to her present predicament, but there was nothing. She still felt an affection for him, missed him coming to the cottage, but that was all. Her heart hadn't speeded up in the slightest. It was Alistair she loved, and God knows what he would think of her if he ever found out what she had done.

She returned the slim wallet to the shelf when she heard

her sister creaking down the rickety ladder. 'Did you find anything?'

'A few skirts and some knitted jumpers and cardigans, and a coat, so we're OK. It's a good thing we went to Aberdeen last Thursday. If Lexie does start asking questions about us, she'll find out *that* was true, though she'd have a fit if she knew it was for a maternity skirt for you. We'll have to go again next week to keep to my story, but we can buy some baby things. Nobody'll think it's queer that you couldn't ask the local doc about your "problem". They all know how shy and easily embarrassed you are.'

Gwen sat down with a thump when they returned to the kitchen. 'You said I wouldn't have to tell any lies, but I've still got to go along with this awful deception.'

'If you don't,' Marge snapped, in exasperation, 'you'll lose Alistair. So what would you rather do? End your marriage, or listen to me tell a few whoppers?'

'Don't try to make me laugh. I never felt less like laughing in my whole life.'

Gwen could see that Marge was enjoying the masquerade. She came down to breakfast every day already padded in case the postman came, and if he did, she took him in for his usual 'cuppa' as bold as brass. Real pregnant women tried to hide their condition, not flaunt it in front of people like she was doing. Being Marge, of course, she could get away with it, Gwen mused, a trifle enviously, whereas she was so scared in case Sandy Mearns suspected anything that she wrapped herself in a blanket before he was due, and sat in an armchair until he left. As if that wasn't bad enough, she was worrying more and more about what had still to come.

'I can't leave it too long before I go . . .' she began one day. 'Travelling so far wouldn't be good for the baby.'

Marge wrinkled her nose. 'Safe up to the end of your eighth month, I'd say.'

A little put out, Gwen said sourly, 'What do you know about it? You've never had any.' The minute the words were out, she regretted them. 'I'm sorry, Marge, but I'd like to make up my own mind sometimes.'

'Go when you like!' Marge retorted, 'I thought . . . if you're away too long, the kids'll wonder what's up.'

'OK, I'll wait a month, though Ivy said to go any time I wanted.'

Ivy Crocker had been another of Marge's brainwaves. 'You don't want to let Mum and Peg know,' she had observed, 'and it's safer not to ask Alice. Ivy was the only other person I could think of, and she'll likely be glad of some company for a while. She's had a pretty rough time this last year, what with her sister dying and then Len, so she'll likely be glad of some company for a while. Besides, she's not the kind to condemn you.'

For the next two weeks, the pseudo-pregnant Marge cycled into the village to collect their army allowances, and to stock up with groceries for the week, answering, when anyone hinted that she shouldn't be on a bike and her so far on, 'It's good exercise for me, and I'm as fit as a fiddle . . . a dashed big fiddle, but still fit. It's Gwen who's . . . she's to go to London to see some kind of specialist. She's just waiting to be told the date.'

At last, noticing one day how awkwardly Gwen was walking, Marge decided it was time to implement the next stage of her plan, and asked Lexie if it was all right if David and Leila handed in a shopping list on their way to school each Monday, and collected the items on their way home. 'Gwen's annoyed at me for carrying on biking so long,' she explained, 'and she's not fit for it . . . she's got some woman's trouble, you see. Her hospital appointment's on the second of May, so that's less than a week to go, thank goodness. I just hope the London surgeons can cure what's wrong with her.'

Lexie appended the official Post Office rubber stamp to the two allotment books, and said, 'If you sign your book every week, I can let the bairns have the cash, as well. It's against the rules, but . . . under the circumstances . . .'

'Thanks, that's ever so kind of you,' Marge exclaimed, having been rather worried as to how she would manage if there was no money coming in.

'Get Gwen to sign hers for however long she thinks she'll be away,' Lexie offered, 'and I'll give it to Leila week by week along with yours.'

'Gee, thanks!' Marge's opinion of her rose. 'Hopefully, she should be back before I . . .' Winking, she patted the area of the cushions.

Through the window, Lexie watched Marge placing her purchases into the bag behind the saddle of her bicycle. She was a fly one, every move thought out, covering up for her sister. Some woman's trouble? Tosh! What ailed Gwen Ritchie was what that soldier had put in her belly, and it was well over a year since Alistair had been home. She hadn't been in the shop for months, and nobody had seen her. Wait, though! Sandy Mearns must have seen her – he said he always got a cup of tea at Benview when he was there.

Strangely enough, Aggie Mearns walked into the shop not long after Marge had left and said, in her tinny voice, 'Was that Dougal Finnie's wife I saw biking off?'

Smiling inwardly at how fate was playing into her hands, Lexie nodded. 'She was asking if she could send a list with Alistair's kids.'

'It was aboot time she stopped comin', that track's full o' humps and muckle stanes, and it must be eight month since Dougal was hame. She coulda lost that bairn. I'm nae needin' much the day, Lexie, just a loaf, and a pair o' laces, and a packet o' envelopes.'

As she selected the requested items, Lexie manipulated the conversation to suit her. 'She was telling me Alistair's wife has to go to London for some special operation.'

'Sandy says she's a poor thing, aye sitting in a easy chair rolled up in a blanket.'

'Well, I hope the operation's a success. Now, was there anything else, Aggie?'

'No, that's the lot.'

After Mrs Mearns had paid and gone, Lexie considered what she had learned. Sandy hadn't actually seen Gwen walking about, so she could be as fat as a pig and he wouldn't know. Like most men, he probably wouldn't realize she was expecting unless she dropped the bairn at his feet.

But suspicion wasn't proof. Gwen *could* have some woman's trouble that needed a special operation, it was possible, so it was just a case of waiting to see whether one or two babies turned up at Benview in the next few weeks.

The stage had been set, but young David forestalled the final act by two days. Squeezing past his mother one morning, he muttered, 'Mum, if you and Auntie Marge get any fatter, there won't be room for both of you in this kitchen at one time.'

Marge saved Gwen's stricken face by roaring with laughter. 'It's all the country food, and the working outside gives us big appetites.'

But the boy had made the sisters think, and when they were alone, Marge said, 'I'm afraid you'll have to go today, Gwennie. I'll write out a pretend letter from Peg, saying

Mum's ill, so we'll have that to show if David or Leila ask any awkward questions when they come home from school. I'll see you on to the train at Aberdeen, so don't panic about that, and I'll carry your case down to the bus. Will you manage to walk that far?'

'Yes, I'll manage.' Gwen's mind was one big whirl. She was worried that her son and daughter might suspect the truth; she was dreading having to walk to the main road; she was scared that someone who knew her would be on the bus; she was petrified at the thought of travelling as far as Newcastle on her own in her present condition.

'It'll be all right,' Gwennie,' Marge assured her, 'but we'll have to get a move on. I'll phone from the station to let Ivy know you're on your way, and I'm sure she'll meet you at the other end.'

By the time she arrived in Aberdeen, Gwen was shivering with apprehension, and she followed Marge gratefully into the station tearoom. 'I'll go and phone Ivy,' Marge said, brightly, when she came back from the counter with a cup of tea and a sandwich. 'You'll be OK till I come back?'

Gwen nodded, afraid that the tears would come if she said anything, but she did manage to eat half the sandwich and drink the tea before her sister showed up again.

'That's all settled,' Marge said, a little breathlessly. 'I told her when you'll arrive, and she'll meet you at the station. Everything's organized, so don't look so scared. It's not your first, for heaven's sake.'

Gwen shook her head wretchedly. 'But Mum and Peg and you looked after me when I had Leila and David, and Alistair . . .' She broke off, biting her bottom lip.

'Ivy'll look after you. I'd have come with you like a shot, but we've the kids to think of. I wish there was some way we could . . . somebody we could trust to look after them, but it's best that nobody in Forvit knows what's going on.

Now, there's still two hours till the London train leaves, so why don't we go to a bank and ask if you can get some money out of that account Alistair set up for you when we came up to Scotland first?'

Gwen had made up her mind at the time that she would never touch a penny of that money, but Alistair had said she was at liberty to draw out as much as she wanted in an emergency. 'I suppose I could call this an emergency,' she muttered, 'and I *will* need cash to pay Ivy for keeping me, and for my fare home.'

This errand accomplished, they did some window shopping until Gwen spotted a clock above a jeweller's window. 'Look at the time. You'll have to get back for David and Leila. What'll they think if you're not there when they get home from school?'

'I left a note, and the pretend letter from Peg, so they think you're on your way to London because Mum's been taken ill, and if Lexie ever asks them where you are, that's what they'll say.'

'But you told her I was going to hospital . . .'

'She'll think I've told them different to stop them worrying about you. You know, my girl, you've got a dashed clever sister.' Marge gave a wicked grin. 'I've thought of everything, and I'll make ready that pram Alice said she had for Morag. It'll be all clean and sparkling like a new pin before you get back with . . . whatsisname.'

'D'you think it'll be a boy?'

'I haven't the faintest, but I'll love it whatever it is.'

Gwen had to swallow the lump which had risen in her throat at this. She had forgotten that the baby wouldn't be hers once she got back to Forvit. Marge would have to look after it otherwise David and Leila, Leila especially, would think it strange.

When they returned to the station, she said, 'Marge, I know

you're hanging about here to make sure I'm all right, but I'll be a lot happier if you just go home to the kids now.'

Not wanting to upset her sister at this stage, Marge said, 'OK, don't go lifting that case. Ask a porter to look after you when it's train time.'

Feeling anything but comfortable about the whole business, Gwen would have panicked altogether if she had known what a narrow escape she'd had from discovery. They had left Forvit at five past eleven, quite unaware that Mrs Mearns, the postman's wife, had come to Aberdeen by the next bus on her way to see a friend in Laurencekirk. She had arrived at the station while they went to the bank and, when the gates opened to let passengers in, had found a seat in a carriage near the engine because she was always afraid that the back end of the train might stop short of the platform.

Only five minutes later, the porter helped Gwen into the first empty compartment they came to, unwittingly enabling Gwen to escape detection.

The meeting on the platform at Newcastle some hours later was too much for her. Despite her abhorrence of bringing attention on herself, she burst into tears and rushed into Ivy Crocker's welcoming arms, heedless of the people milling around them.

'Hush, love,' the older woman crooned, 'hush now. It's going to be all right. Ivy'll look after you.'

When she composed herself, Gwen noticed that her old friend was looking much older. She still wore too much make-up, still bleached her hair, but there were lines on her forehead that could not be hidden. There was a sadness in her black-outlined eyes, a sadness that told how much she missed her life's partner.

Ivy was looking at her compassionately. 'All right now, dearie?'

'Yes. I'm sorry, I made a proper exhibition of myself.'

'Nobody noticed, but we'd better get on. I'll carry the case, if you can manage the bag? Won't be long now, less than half an hour on the bus, then a few minutes' walk.'

In just over the half hour, Gwen was sitting in the kitchen of an old cottage in the village of Moltby. 'Put your feet up on that pouffe till I pour you a drop of my plum wine.' Ivy pushed a squashed round pouffe towards her. 'I bet you're exhausted after such a long journey,' she observed in a moment, handing over a glass.

Gwen nodded wearily. 'I am a bit tired.'

'Your room's all ready for you, so you can have a lie down any time you want.'

'Oh Ivy, you've always been so kind to me.' Gwen's voice was trembling now, the tears perilously near the surface again. 'What must you think of me?'

Ivy stepped in before she broke down for the second time. 'Gwen, I make it my business not to mind anybody else's, and I wouldn't presume to judge you, but I would like to know . . . why?'

Knowing that Ivy had thought the world of Alistair, Gwen did her best to explain, in low, shamed monotones, beginning with Ken taking Marge and the bicycle home from the 1941 Hogmanay Do.

'Sexual attraction,' Ivy said, when the tale ended. 'That's what it had been, because you were both vulnerable to your emotions. I don't condone what you did, but I do understand. I had my own moments, you know, I wasn't always this old and this ugly.'

'Oh, Ivy, you're not ugly, and I don't know what I'd have done if . . .'

'That's enough of that. I think you're being very noble letting Marge have the baby.'

'I'm not being noble. I'm only thinking of myself – I could lose Alistair if he found out. That's another thing I'll always worry about. I can't tell lies without blushing, or giving the game away somehow. So how will I manage when Alistair and Dougal come home? One slip, and I throw a spanner into the works and burst up two marriages.'

'You'll have to harden yourself. Think of it as Marge's, right from the start . . .'

'But I'll be feeding it and caring for it for the first two weeks . . .'

Ivy leaned forward and gripped her hand. 'We'll sort something out. Have you seen a doctor, or anything?'

'No, I couldn't let anybody in Forvit know.'

'I'll get Tilly Barker to check you over tomorrow. She's our local midwife, and she's been a good friend to me. When it's born, we'll put it on the bottle, so you won't get too fond of it.' Gwen's frown made her add, 'Believe me, it's best. If you're not suckling it, you won't bond with it. You must look on it as something you're doing for your sister. A sacrifice, if you like, to please her and Dougal.'

Gwen sighed, but did not reply to this, and Ivy carried on, 'I had a baby, you know, before I met Len, and he loved that boy like it was his own. We both doted on him, maybe too much . . .' Her voice faded, her eyes misted.

Gwen leaned across and took her hand. 'What happened, Ivy?'

'Our little Billy was taken from us when he was just three and a half. The doctors never said what it was – I don't think they knew – but one day he was running about, laughing and tossing his curly head, the next, he was fighting for life in a hospital bed.' She stopped for a moment, then said, 'Two days later, he was dead.'

'Oh, Ivy, how awful. I don't know how you could have got over that.'

'I don't think we ever did, not really. Len was in the Navy at the time, so I was mostly on my own, and it was really bad for a long time.' She straightened her back abruptly. 'But it's surprising what you can survive if you have to.'

'Maybe I shouldn't have come,' Gwen murmured, unhappily. 'It might upset you . . .'

'No, dearie, I'm as hard as rock, I am. Nothing upsets me nowadays.'

'I was very sorry about Len . . . and your sister. I bet that upset you?'

'Ah, yes, that did upset me, but I'd been expecting it with Len. He'd had two slight heart attacks, you see, so I knew it was coming.'

In Ivy's back room that night, Gwen wondered if Alistair would have accepted Ken's baby as his if she'd given him the chance, like Len Crocker had done. But . . . Len hadn't been married to Ivy at the time of her pregnancy, so he had nothing to forgive, whereas she had committed adultery while Alistair was fighting for his country, worse, while he was a prisoner of war. There was no comparison.

Ivy and Marge were both right. It was better this way. She, Gwen Ritchie, was the only one who would suffer, but that was as it should be, since she was the one who had sinned.

Chapter 20

Gwen was shocked out of her misery and self-condemnation by her old friend as they sat by the fire one evening. She had just said, for the umpteenth time, that she deserved to be punished for the awful thing she had done and Ivy had burst out, 'Good God, girl! I'm sick of hearing you running yourself down like that. You surely don't think you're the only wife in this world that's ever had a little bit of fun on the side? Wives all over the country are doing it, and quite a few of them have landed the same as you. It's natural to miss the loving when your husband's away, and it's hard to resist if another man lights a spark in you. You're just one of the unlucky ones, that's all – too fertile. You had two children by the time you were two years married, remember?'

Scarlet-faced at what she took for implied criticism, Gwen hung her head, and Ivy went on, softly, 'I'm not getting at you, I'm trying to make you see things in perspective.'

'You can't understand. You were never unfaithful to Len, were you?'

Ivy rose to put some coal on the fire, then observed, 'I'll likely regret telling you this, but, after my Billy died, I felt life was passing me by. Len was away in the Navy, and I took a job as a caretaker in a block of offices, for the company as much as the money, and there was a basement flat that went with it.' She hesitated and then went on, 'I was only sixteen when I had Billy, and seventeen when I married Len, so I missed out on an awful lot. I didn't realize it at the time, of course, for I loved Len, but he was away so much.'

'What made you change?'

Ivy shrugged. 'Nothing really. I still loved Len, always have, but when young Mr Gerald, the boss's son, put his arm round me in the passage, I didn't push him away.'

She stopped again, smiling. 'He was so handsome, and I'd gone all wobbly at the knees any time he as much as looked at me, but he didn't take advantage of me. It was me – and it went from kissing in the corridor, to cuddling, then downstairs to my flat, and that's when it happened . . . as I wanted.'

Gwen gasped in astonishment. 'You planned it?'

A little sadly, Ivy said, 'He was only a boy, maybe seventeen, and I was well over twenty. It only happened that once, but I never forgot him, and I never regretted it. *And* it never made any difference to how I felt about Len. Can you understand that?'

'Oh yes,' Gwen breathed. 'It was the same as me, in a way, not love, just . . .'

'Just a need,' Ivy finished for her. 'It wouldn't have happened if Alistair had been at home, any more than if Len had been at home with me, but I was lucky. I don't know if his father suspected anything, but he sent Gerald off to their branch in Edinburgh, and I never saw him again.'

'Did you ever tell Len?'

'Gwen, I might have been a fool, but not as big a fool as that. He had accepted Billy without a murmur, but I couldn't expect him to forgive that.'

'And he never suspected anything?'

'Why should he? So, Gwen, dear, if you're thinking, as I believe you are, of telling Alistair the truth, put it out of your head. Marge wants to give Dougal a child he thinks is his, and Alistair will be none the wiser, so why upset the apple cart? And clear the shame and guilt right out of your system before you bring this child into the world.'

Trying to do as Ivy said, Gwen assured herself that, if there hadn't been a war on, she would never have . . . She wouldn't have *met* Ken Partridge in the first place. It was this awful war that was to blame, yet . . . if she hadn't been worried about Alistair . . . if Ken hadn't been leaving the next day for good . . . if Marge hadn't encouraged them . . .

She drew in a long breath and let it out slowly. She must forget all the ifs. She was the only one to blame, no matter what anybody said. Ivy was made of different stuff . . . but maybe it was losing her son that had made her start painting her face and bleaching her hair . . . and seeking affection, if not love, outside her marriage. Gwendoline Ritchie didn't have any excuse. Ken Partridge had treated her like a lady, of course, done things for her and made her feel ten years younger, so was that why? She wished with all her heart that she could look back on her time with him as a pleasurable interlude, not the shameful incident which was overshadowing everything else.

'Do you ken what kind o' operation Alistair Ritchie's wife's getting?'

Lexie shook her head. 'No, Aggie, I'm sorry. Dougal's wife just said it was some woman's trouble she had.'

'But naebody's seen her for months,' Mrs Mearns persisted.

Doodie Tough, waiting to be served and ever anxious to winkle out the last drop of any gossip or scandal, said now, with a touch of sarcasm, 'Your Sandy musta seen her.'

'Sandy? A magenty horse wi' a sky-blue tail and purple wings could knock him aff his bike and he'd never tell me.

I couldna get a thing oot o' him, except she aye sat in a chair rolled up in a blanket.' Aggie picked up her change and left.

Lexie weighed her next words carefully. 'That seems a bit queer, don't you think?'

Sensing something of interest, Doodie's eyes glittered. 'What d'you mean?'

'I wouldn't think you'd need to sit about in a blanket if it was just woman's trouble.'

Not particularly quick-witted for all her garrulity, it was a few seconds before Doodie got the meaning of this. 'You think she's expectin'?'

'Oh, I never dreamt it was anything like that, Doodie.' Not wanting it to be known that the idea had come from her, Lexie was glad that the woman had figured it out with so little prompting. 'Though now I come to think about it . . . I suppose she could be.'

'But . . .' Mrs Tough pursed her mouth and lowered her brows in thought, and at last she whispered, 'But Alistair hasna been hame for . . .' Her eyes dilating, she stopped with a satisfied smirk. 'She musta took up wi' ane o' they sodjers afore they was shifted.'

Lexie's face registered shock. 'But she was so quiet, not like her sister.'

'Still waters run deep,' intoned Doodie, narrowing her eyes now to emphasize this, 'but I must say I'd never . . . she's a dark horse, right enough.'

'We'd better watch what we're saying, though. We've no proof.'

'What else could it be, an' her needin' a blanket to hide her belly?'

Wondering if she had gone too far by implanting the suspicion, Lexie now did her best to erase it. 'We're letting our imaginations run away with us, Doodie. She must have something far wrong if she needs special equipment they haven't got in Aberdeen.'

Susceptible to anything, Mrs Tough digested this new concept with the same intensity as before. 'Aye . . . we'd best gi'e her the benefit o' the doubt.' She paid for her purchases and went out, clearly trying to decide which of the two versions she should pass on.

Lexie felt a little uncertain herself now. She had been so sure that Gwen Ritchie was expecting, but voicing it to somebody else had raised doubts in her own mind. Maybe the woman was *really* ill – but she *had* been with a soldier, there was no getting away from that. Yet . . . how would she have met him? That was the sticking point.

Gwen's labour started one afternoon only days later, three weeks early. 'Is a premature baby less likely to survive?' she asked, anxiously, during a pain-free interval.

Ivy pulled a face. 'They used to say a seven-month baby was all right, but an eight-month wouldn't have any nails – old wives' tales. Anyway, you're into the ninth month, and we'd best get Tilly. I'll ask Mona next door to go, she's quicker on her feet than me.'

Both in their thirties, Gwen and Tilly Barker, the midwife, had taken to each other as soon as they met, and had gone walking together in the cool of the evenings, when Ivy was too tired to go out. Gwen had even told Tilly the truth about her pregnancy, which the other woman had laughingly shrugged off. 'It's happening all over, lass.'

It hadn't been as bad as Gwen remembered, and it was a boy, which should please Marge, although she had always said she didn't care one way or the other.

'He's all right, isn't he?' she asked, while Tilly was cleaning him.

'Oh, you mothers,' the neat little woman smiled. 'Why wouldn't he be all right? He's perfect, got all his important little bits. Look.' She held him up for inspection.

His face was a bit redder than either of her other two had been, Gwen thought, and his tiny mouth was screwed up like he had a pain somewhere, but he was still lovely. Only one thing jarred. His head wasn't bald like David's had been, nor covered in fair down like Leila's. He had bright ginger hair! Like Ken Partridge's! Would this make Dougal start wondering, when he came home? Could two dark-haired people make a red-headed baby? It would be a problem for Marge and her, at any rate; for it would always remind them of who his father had been.

Marge was delighted to get Gwen's letter saying she'd had a boy. He had come early, all to the good, and mother and child should be fit enough to travel in a couple of weeks. Once she held the infant in her own arms, she'd feel that the Finnies were a proper family at long last. She read the letter again, smiling a little because her sister seemed worried about the colour of his hair. Any couple could have a red-headed child whatever theirs was . . . couldn't they?

She took out the letter Gwen always enclosed, to be sent to their mother. Mum would have wondered what was up if she didn't get a letter from her eldest daughter for over a month, and although the place where it had been posted wasn't supposed to be franked on an envelope in wartime, maybe they did in the cities. That would put the cat among the pigeons with a vengeance. Mum would go on her high horse and demand to be told why Gwen was in Newcastle, and what was all the secrecy about?

After addressing an envelope for her own letter to her mother, Marge laid them both down on the ledge in the front porch, ready to give to the postman next morning. Thank goodness the final stage of her plan would soon be in motion, because Sandy Mearns was always saying, 'Not long now, eh?'

He had no idea that she wasn't really pregnant, which was why she couldn't have a doctor or midwife coming to the house, not that he'd have known that. She had told him, so that he could pass it on to anyone he liked, that she was going to have the baby in a hospital in Aberdeen. She had already provisionally booked a hotel room for fourteen days, so she'd have to confirm it now she knew the exact dates it would be used. She'd been a bit worried about this end of the procedure, she hadn't really planned it properly because she hadn't been sure if Ivy would agree. She needn't have worried.

'Gwen wouldn't manage taking her case and bag on and off the train, as well as the baby,' Ivy had written, 'and I'll be delighted to see her all the way back to Forvit. I can stay for a week or two, if you need me, I wouldn't mind a little holiday.'

Ivy was going to save their bacon, Marge gloated. She had been really worried in case her sister got too attached to the baby, but Ivy had said that she had been doing as much as she could to prevent any bonding. Gwen would have less than two days in the hotel on her own with it, then maybe another couple of days letting her sister get accustomed to looking after it.

Marge's plan was carried out. Ivy saw Gwen settled into the hotel with the baby, and followed her instructions on how to get to the bus terminus. Marge met her at the end of the track, and insisted that she take a rest before Leila and David came home from school.

When they did, of course, they were overjoyed to see their Auntie Ivy again, and she invented a little fib to set their minds at ease about their mother. 'One of my friends in London went to see your Grandma and she says she's looking much better. It shouldn't be long before your Mum's home.'

That night, when the youngsters had gone to bed, much happier because of what Ivy had told them, Marge said, with a broad grin on her face, 'I didn't realize what a good liar you are. Almost as good as me.'

Ivy pulled a face. 'Only when it's necessary.'

Her expression sobering, Marge said earnestly, 'Me, too.'

The only sticky moments came when they went to the hotel next day. Although Gwen had agreed to it, she wasn't happy at having to hand the baby over to Marge, who was determined to take over right from the start.

'You'll have to get used to it,' Ivy sympathized, 'so just let him go. Look, I'll have to leave, can't keep that car waiting any longer.'

When she had gone, Marge said, 'She insisted we took the car the Bankside garage hires out. She said it would look better than me going by bus when I was supposed to be in labour. I suppose she was right, at that. Now, let me see my little darling.'

Once the ball had been set rolling, things went relatively smoothly, although Gwen was quite tearful when her sister refused to let her even hold the baby.

'Look, Gwennie,' Marge pointed out, softly, 'you have to give him up some time, and I have to learn how to deal with him as long as you're here with me.' She paused for a second, then said, 'Have you given any thought to a name for him yet?'

'If you're so determined to have him right now,' Gwen said, miserably, 'you'd better choose it yourself.'

'Dougal and I used to discuss names . . . before we realized we'd never have a family, and it was to be Nicholas for a boy and Louise for a girl.'

'Nicholas? I like that.'

'Good, then Nicholas it is.'

Marge considered that little Nicholas was an absolute darling. At just over two weeks old, his face was no longer wrinkled and red like Gwen had said it was at first, and his hair, a beautiful, thick, gingery auburn, had a little curl in it already. His infant-blue eyes would likely change to brown, the same colour as Dougal's and hers, which would allay suspicions from all directions – though there shouldn't be any after the trouble she'd taken to pull the wool over innocently inquisitive and downright nosy eyes.

After three days of togetherness, Marge told her sister that it was time she went back to her own children, a turn of phrase which she saw had upset her, but it was how it had to be now – Gwen only had two children, Nicholas wasn't hers any longer.

Thus it was that Gwen returned to Forvit alone, and sat with Ivy waiting for David and Leila to come home from school. She knew they would ask how their grandmother was, to which she could answer, honestly, that Grandma was as fit as ever.

'You'll have to be careful,' Ivy warned her. 'They're going to be all over you since you've been away so long, and you're still in a post-natal condition, so you won't have to let your emotions get the better of you.'

'Yes, I know, and I think I can cope.'

She coped very well. David let out a whoop of delight when he came in, and almost knocked her over with the force of his bear hug. Leila was less exuberant, but Gwen knew that her relief at having her mother back was just as great.

'Auntie Marge has gone away to get a baby,' David confided loudly, when they were all seated at the table. 'I don't know why she wants one, though. They're noisy smelly things, aren't they?'

Gwen summoned up a smile. 'Not all of them. Some of them are really beautiful . . .'

'Auntie Marge's will be beautiful,' Leila observed dreamily. 'I'm looking forward to when she brings it home. A real live baby'll be better than a doll.'

'Soppy!' David glowered at her. 'All girls are soppy! All they think about's getting married and having babies. Yeugh!'

Ivy chuckled as she stood up to clear the table. 'You'll change your mind about things when you're a bit older. Once a boy really falls in love, all he wants is to marry the girl and have babies with her.'

'Not me! When I'm grown up we'll be back in London and I'm going to go in for motor cycle racing. Vroom! Vroom!' He turned the throttle on his pretend steed and looked defiantly round the others.

Deeming it best not to rise to the challenge, Gwen said, 'I hope you behaved for Auntie Marge while I was away?'

'I always behave!' He looked put out that she could doubt it.

'He did behave, Mum,' Leila put in. 'She wasn't feeling well enough to bike to the shop, so we've been getting the groceries for her. Miss Fraser said we were very good messengers, but Auntie Ivy did the shopping on Monday.'

'I wanted to see the village,' Ivy explained, not wanting to admit that it had been the shopkeeper she had wanted to see, having heard about her from Marge. 'It's quite a nice little place, and I love this house, but it's a bit far away from everything for my liking.'

'When we came here first, Marge said it was at the back of beyond,' Gwen smiled, 'but you get used to it.' And it had been ideally situated for the conspiracy that was now taking place, she thought. But it would soon be over, and things would be as they were before . . . with the addition of a new baby.

When Marge's allotted fourteen days were up, Ivy went to Aberdeen to collect her and her 'son', and Gwen, to take her mind off it, cycled into the village. 'My aunt's gone to fetch Marge and the baby,' she informed Lexie.

'They're all right, are they? Dougal'll be pleased when he comes home. I bet he'd given up hope of having any children. It's twelve years since they married.'

Gwen did wonder why she was so sure of that, but presumed that Marge must have mentioned it. What worried her was the peculiar way Lexie was looking at her. It was almost as if she suspected something, some wrongdoing, but surely she couldn't have any idea . . . ? No, of course she couldn't.

'Are you keeping better yourself?' Lexie enquired, suddenly. 'Your sister said you were in London having an operation. No complications?'

Having practically forgotten this reason for her being away, Gwen felt flustered, but said, steadily, 'None. Everything went smoothly, and I don't have to go back.'

'That's good. Have you heard from Alistair lately?'

'Not for a few weeks, but I suppose no news is good news.'

'So they say.'

Lexie didn't move for some time after Alistair's wife went out. The woman certainly looked better than she'd done before the operation, but she herself still wasn't convinced about that. She'd been sure it was Gwen Ritchie with the soldier at the tower, and the length of time was right for her to have had a baby, yet it was Marge Finnie who was bringing home a son.

There was something dashed fishy going on. If Gwen *had* been in London giving birth – though maybe she hadn't gone as far as London – the child would be illegitimate, and maybe she'd had it adopted? But she shouldn't get away with it. It wasn't fair on Alistair. If she, Lexie, could plant even a tiny grain of doubt in his mind when he came home from the war, she would be doing him a service . . . though Alistair Ritchie wasn't as gullible as Doodie Tough. It wouldn't be easy to make him believe ill of his wife.

Even David fell under little Nicholas's spell. 'Look at the size of his nails,' he crowed. 'His hands are so small, I wouldn't have thought there was room on his fingers for nails at all, but they're the same as everybody else's.'

'What did you expect?' Marge laughed. 'Babies *are* the same as everybody else, just a lot smaller.'

'He's so small, I'm afraid to touch him,' Leila murmured.

'You can hold him, if you like. He won't break. Just be careful.'

The girl sat down in one of the armchairs and let her aunt hand her the infant, who burped loudly. 'Is he all right?' she asked in alarm.

'Of course he is,' Marge assured her. 'It's natural for babies to burp more than we do.'

Nicholas's next breaking of wind had David doubled up with mirth. 'I didn't know he could do it from that end as well!'

'Just like you!' Leila said, dryly, which made them all laugh.

Everyone was sorry when Ivy said she had better go home. While she'd been there, Benview had been a place of love, of laughter, of a general feeling of satisfaction with life, and the sisters were afraid that her departure would change everything. But she suggested that Gwen and her children should see her on to the train at Aberdeen, and David was excited at the thought of spending an afternoon in the city. Gwen, of course, was a bit apprehensive at leaving Marge alone with Nicky, as David had called him and it had stuck, and Marge, too, wondered how she would cope, but all went well.

Life soon returned to normal, with Nicky a well-loved addition. A large bundle of letters arrived for Gwen, though they contained little but assurances of love for them all. Marge got letters from Dougal at irregular intervals, and it was several weeks before she received the one saying how he could hardly bear to wait to see his son.

'I thought we'd never manage,' he wrote, 'but we must have done something right that last night we were together.'

Marge showed her sister this letter. 'I said it would be OK. He's sure Nicky's his.'

Gwen nodded, but remained uncertain. Once Dougal saw the bright ginger hair and green eyes, would he be so sure?

Chapter 21

Life in Benview was not quite as joyful as it might have been. The two older children were, naturally, delighted that the war looked to be almost over and they would soon see their father again, yet the prospect of leaving the friends they had made at Forvit School was quite depressing. As for Gwen and Marge, they were becoming more and more apprehensive about their return to London, although neither admitted it to the other. Their personal D-Day would soon be upon them, or, as Gwen had come to regard it, her Armageddon. As soon as hostilities were over, they would have no excuse to hibernate in this isolated cottage, and their mother, with the uncanny knack of knowing when they were keeping something from her, would do her best to ferret it out.

The summons came at the end of April. 'This is it, Gwennie,' Marge observed as she folded up Rosie's letter ordering them home and asking what they thought they were playing at staying away when there was no danger now. 'Last hurdle coming up!'

'Not the last,' Gwen sighed. 'After her, we've still got to face Dougal and Alistair.'

'We don't have to worry about them. Dougal's going to be hooked on Nicky the minute he sees him and he'll spoil him rotten, and Alistair's not likely to question my son's parentage, is he?'

'No, of course not.' Gwen tried to sound positive.

Marge went to bid Lexie Fraser goodbye before they left.

They owed her that for the help she had provided. 'We really enjoyed our stay in Forvit,' she gushed. 'It was so peaceful after the bombing in London, but Alice and Sam will want their house back. Besides, my mother's desperate to get all her chicks under her wing again.'

Trying not to show her sadness at the thought of not seeing him again, Lexie said, 'But will Alistair not want to come back to the peace of Forvit?'

'I've no idea.' Marge shrugged then held out her hand. 'It's time I was going, but thanks once again for all you did for us.'

Lexie smiled. 'You'd a pretty rough time for a while, what with you expecting and your sister having to go to London for whatever kind of operation it was.'

Marge had to do some quick thinking. She had blithely mentioned some woman's trouble at the time without specifying which, and the village gossips had likely spent hours speculating over it. None of them had ever gone out of their way to be friendly. She had even heard one calling them 'stuck-up Cockneys', but she hadn't bothered to correct her, and perhaps she and Gwen *had* kept themselves too much to themselves. They had never really felt as if they belonged, that was the trouble.

'Gwen didn't want anybody to know,' she said at last. 'It was an ovarian cyst, as big as a melon, the surgeon told her. It wasn't cancerous, thank goodness, but she still hasn't recovered properly.'

'I hope she improves once she's back with her mother. Say goodbye to her and the bairns from me. I got quite fond of Leila and David, you know.'

As Marge cycled back to Benview, she congratulated herself on remembering what had happened to one of her neighbours in Woodyates Road a year or so before the war started. Etta Smith had been a widow for many years, so when a bump appeared on her stomach, the rumour went round that she'd been having a secret affair with a married man and been left to have the baby on her own. The bump had grown as the months passed, as such bumps do, and when Etta's sister Vi turned up to look after the house and feed the cat, the sniggering gossips told each other that Etta had gone to hospital for her confinement. Then Vi had mentioned one day that her sister was having an ovarian cyst removed, which had made them all feel rotten. It would be best, Marge decided, not to let Gwen know the story she had spun about *her* 'operation'. This final, unnecessary lie would only worry her.

Lexie couldn't help wondering about Marge's version of her sister's trouble. She had seemed a bit put out at being asked, and she'd obviously had to invent something on the spur of the moment . . . not all that convincing, either. Gwen Ritchie wouldn't have had to go to London to have an ovarian cyst removed when the Royal Infirmary in Aberdeen was classed as among the best in Britain. She had definitely had a baby, but it was anybody's guess who was the father, and whether it had died at birth or been adopted. Still, Lexie mused, what did it matter now? It was a shame, though. Alistair would go back to London when he was repatriated, to the wife he believed had been faithful to him, and live in happy ignorance for the rest of his life.

Poor Alistair!

That evening, probably as a result of the frustration of her earlier thought, Lexie was beset by a memory she had done her best to ignore any time her mind touched on it, but this time it refused to go away. It had happened a few months ago, and was the last time she had gone out with any man. Ernie Paul was an old schoolmate, a cheeky devil, he'd once put his hand up her knickers when they were climbing the wall bars in the gym. He'd been quite keen on her, but at the time, she'd only had eyes for Alistair Ritchie. Ernie had got a job in Aberdeen as soon as he left school, and some years later, like most of the other young men she knew, he'd been called up.

He had come into the shop once or twice on each of his leaves, the same bantering lad he'd always been, but there had been a change in him the last time he was home . . . more serious, more intense about things, although there was still the occasional twinkle in his eyes. She had found herself warming to him, and when he asked her out, she had agreed to meet him after she shut the shop. He had taken her by bus to the Capitol Cinema in Aberdeen, and though she half-expected him to slip his hand up her leg while they were watching the film, he had been a proper gentleman, even when he saw her home. He wasn't cheeky any more, and it was only after their third date that he kissed her good night at her door.

Completely at ease with him now, she had asked him in the next time he saw her home, and as soon as she closed the door behind them, he put his arm round her waist and drew her towards him. This kiss was different from the first, a kiss that made her whole body quiver. He had pulled her down on the sofa beside him, and she had given herself up to the thrill of his caresses. His kisses had become more urgent and she hardly noticed that one of his hands had slipped down until she felt his fingers touch her most private part – she grew hot at the memory of it. Then for some inexplicable reason – for she had wanted him to go on – she had shoved him away and burst into tears and screamed at him as she jumped to her feet. 'Get out! Get out! Get out!' She couldn't stop herself, and had even lashed out at him with her feet.

'Good God, Lexie!' he had shouted, standing up and stamping to the door. 'I wouldn't have touched you . . . honest, but I thought you wanted it.' He had slammed out.

Ernie had been the only one who had ever got as far as that. She had never let any of the others, over the years, touch her in an intimate way . . . not even Alistair. She had encouraged *him*, yes, but if his hands wandered below her waist it was as if she froze with fear – and what had she to fear from him, for goodness' sake? From anybody, for that matter? It was only natural for men to try, and for girls to try to stop them. But her reaction wasn't natural. It was violent, intended to hurt. Why?

A tiny sliver of what may have been a possible explanation shot through her, but it was gone before she could make anything of it, and in any case, she wasn't sure that she wanted to understand, after all. It was quite obvious that something so bad had happened to her at one time that she couldn't bear to think about it. It had crossed her mind before that her father might have interfered with her and run away because of shame, but she couldn't remember him ever touching her where he shouldn't, not even accidentally. He had loved her as a father should love a daughter, nothing else. Yet there was still this awful sense of an impending revelation that would turn her world upside down.

Rosie couldn't get over how tall Leila and David had grown in the four and a half years they had been away, and she was moved to tears at the sight of little Nicky exploring her living room on his tottery podgy legs. 'When Dougal came to see me last,' she told Marge, 'he said he wished he had a child to leave behind if he was killed, and now it's all over bar the shouting, and he's got a son! You girls will never know how often I prayed for your husbands to come home safely and for these three houses to escape the bombs.'

'Yes, I know you had it pretty bad, Mum. I felt really guilty that I was up there when I'd no kids to worry about.'

Rosie grinned puckishly. 'But if you hadn't been up there, you wouldn't have had Nicky, would you?'

Marge felt her stomach heave at the truth of this. 'N . . . no, that's right, of course.'

Noticing the peculiar glance Marge gave Gwen, and knowing her daughters inside out, Rosie was sure that they were hiding something. What had happened in Forvit? Had one or both of them been misbehaving? No, she couldn't think that of Gwen, but Marge had gone dancing there, and she must have met lots of servicemen. Had she had a fling? No, she loved Dougal. She wouldn't have put her marriage in jeopardy. All the same, something was definitely not quite as it should be, and she would have to persevere until she found out what it was.

Over the next week or so, Rosie watched and listened to her daughters, trying to pick up even the slightest hint that would put her on the right track, but although Marge talked freely about their time at Forvit, the gossips in the little shop, the strange way the people spoke, Gwen scarcely said anything, especially about the last year of their stay. She clearly found it too painful to speak about.

Increasingly unsettled, Rosie puzzled over it constantly; positive that she wasn't making something out of nothing. Then one afternoon, when the house was quiet – the family, including Alf, having gone to the Heath – it struck her, like a bolt of lightning, so devastating that she felt faint. She shied away from it and tried to read the morning paper, but the print jumped all over the page and nothing registered, so she gave herself up to considering the awful suspicion.

Was it possible that Dougal was not Nicky's father after all? Had the monotony of Forvit made Marge have more than just a fling with another man? That must be what was wrong with Gwen. She wouldn't have approved what her sister was doing, but even if she had tried to stop her, Marge wouldn't have listened.

Rosie found herself latching on to stronger evidence. Marge and Dougal were both dark-haired and brown-eyed, but little Nicky's hair was the brightest red she had ever seen, his eyes a piercing green, both of which were highly unlikely in the normal run of things. She didn't know much about that kind of thing, of course, so it could be possible, though she doubted it in this case.

She kept her thoughts to herself when her family returned, and it wasn't until the following morning, when Peggy came in to see how she was, as she did every morning before going to work, that she decided to test the waters. 'Peg,' she asked, carefully choosing her words, 'does Nicky's colouring strike you as odd?'

'His hair, you mean? I think it's a lovely colour.'

Rosie lay back against her pillows with a sigh. Peggy wasn't all that perceptive, so it wasn't surprising that she hadn't twigged.

When she went downstairs at just after ten, the children were playing in the garden and Gwen was tidying up. Rosie decided that this would be a good time, with Marge still in her own house, to ask a few pertinent questions. 'I expect you and Marge were bored up in Scotland, with Alice's house so far from the village?'

'It wasn't too bad.'

Gwen's face, however, had a definite pink tinge, further proof to her mother that she wasn't comfortable speaking about it. So there was something! 'What did you do for entertainment?' she pressed on, but at that moment, with Gwen clearly struggling to think of an answer, Marge opened the back door and took in the situation at a glance.

'We ought to take the kids out for a while,' she said, giving Gwen a warning look. 'We'd better make the most of this lovely weather before David and Leila start their new school. Will you be OK on your own, Mum?'

'I was on my own for . . .' Rosie began, sarcastically, then thought better of it. 'I'll be fine. If Alf sees you going out, he'll likely pop round some time. He was very good at looking after me when you were away, you know.'

The stir over, Rosie picked up the telephone. 'Alf? Can you come round for a few minutes?'

'Delighted to. There's nothing wrong, I hope?'

'Not exactly. I want to ask your opinion on something, and I'm on my own for a while. They've taken the children out.'

'Righto, Rosie, my old dear. I'll be with you in two shakes of a lamb's tail.'

She replaced the receiver with a smile. She'd come to depend on Alf. He'd been there for her almost every evening during the air raids, making sure she and Peg went inside her Morrison shelter, while he sat by the fire if he wasn't on duty fire watching. If a doodlebug had fallen on the house, the survival of his wife and her mother would have been questionable, but there was no doubt that he'd have been a goner himself.

He was with her in no time. 'What's up, then, Rosie? I thought everything would be perfect for you now, with your brood all around you?'

She regarded him affectionately. His back was a little bowed, and he just had a semicircle of grey hair at the back of his head. His face was lined from the chest pains he suffered periodically, but he was always cheery, no matter what.

'I've got a bit of a problem,' she admitted, 'and I want to hear what you think.'

'I'll do my best, if you fill me in.'

'Do you know . . . how . . . people's genes affect . . . their children?'

A brief frown crossed his face. 'Genetics can be . . . but if you're thinking what I think you're thinking, Rosie, I'd advise you to forget it.'

'So you've spotted it, too? It's his colouring.'

'His hair's a lovely colour.'

'But it's his eyes, and all. I didn't think two browns could make green.'

'I know you're in deadly earnest, but put it out of your mind.'

'But it's not fair to let Dougal think . . .'

'Rosie dear, please don't say anything. It will only cause trouble. Even if it's true, I'm sure Marge regrets it now, and Nicky's a permanent reminder. Don't you think her guilt will make her suffer enough without you making it worse for her?'

She heaved a shuddering sigh. 'I know you mean well, Alf, but I can't overlook the fact that one of my daughters has committed adultery.'

He leaned towards her and took her hand. 'Listen, my dear sweet Rosie, I know your conscience tells you she should be punished, but try to see beyond that. What is to be gained by denouncing her? You will also be punishing Dougal and her innocent young son, and the strife will rub off on every one of us. Dougal will blame Gwen as the older for not taking better care of his wife, and even Alistair might put some of the blame on her. Leila and David are both old enough to sense if something's wrong. You would be opening Pandora's box, Rosie, stirring a hornets' nest, splitting up your family.'

Her soft sniff made him murmur, 'Don't upset yourself so,

my dear. You may be worrying for nothing. I think I read somewhere that red hair can be passed down from some generations back, and that could be what's happened.'

Rosie let the matter drop. Perhaps what he had just said was true, perhaps it wasn't and he was trying to plug a hole in the dyke, but he was right to tell her to say nothing. In order to be sure of having her family happily around her, she would have to keep her suspicions to herself. It was just a good thing Tiny wasn't here to put his oar in. He'd have muddied the waters, all right.

Alistair was home first. His camp had been freed in April, but he had to undergo some medical and other tests in Germany before he was pronounced fit to travel to Britain, and more tests on this side, so it was into December before he reached Lee Green. There was great jubilation, of course, and after about three quarters of an hour, Alf, realizing that Gwen would want to be alone with her husband, swept Rosie and all the rest of her family into his house for the afternoon. Even David, complaining that he wanted to be with his Dad, was persuaded that his parents deserved some time on their own.

Gwen had been shocked at how painfully thin Alistair looked when he walked in, how his cheekbones stood out, how grey his skin, how white his hair, so it came as no surprise when he kissed her only a few times and then muttered, apologetically, 'I'm sorry, my darling, but all I want to do now is sleep, sleep, sleep. In a decent bed with soft blankets and an eiderdown, with nothing at all to worry about.'

In a way, she was relieved, and when she went upstairs with him and watched him undress, her heart cramped at the sight of his skeletal body, she could have counted his ribs without touching him. There was no way she could ever willingly hurt him. She would have to make absolutely certain that nothing of what she had done ever leaked out, that he never learned that she was young Nicky's mother. It would tear him apart.

At six o'clock, when Marge came to say that Alf had prepared as good a feast as rations would allow, she had to explain that Alistair was sound asleep and she didn't want to disturb him. Marge, of course, teased her about tiring him out already.

'No, there was nothing like that. He was almost dead on his feet, and all he wanted was to sleep. Tell Alf I'm sure Alistair will appreciate the effort he's made, but I'm afraid we'll have to pass on it. Say we'll have it tomorrow, if it'll keep.'

So Alistair's real homecoming took place the day after he came home, and even though he was still exhausted, he did his best to enter into the celebration that his in-laws seemed to be bent on having.

That night, once again he wanted only to sleep, and Gwen lay by his side, thanking God that he'd come home safely to her, and praying that his health would soon improve.

Chapter 22

Alistair had been withdrawn and uncommunicative ever since he came home six months earlier. Marge had told Gwen repeatedly that she shouldn't try to push him. 'It must have been awful for him in that Stalag whatever, and he won't feel like speaking about it just yet. It'll take a while, but I'm sure he'll tell you all about it in his own good time.'

Gwen felt like saying that she didn't care if he never told her about the prisoner-of-war camp. He had been gone from her for so long that all she wanted was to be told how much he'd missed her, how much he loved her. Instead, he hardly spoke when they were alone together, which wasn't often, what with Marge, Peggy or their mother popping in whenever they felt like it, and Alistair himself going out every morning and sometimes not turning up again until just before the children were due home from school. What was more, he never told her where he had been or what he had been doing.

When he knew that Dougal was to be demobilized soon, however, and would be coming home, he seemed to ease fractionally out of his cocoon. 'We're lucky,' he observed one evening as he sat at the fireside with his wife, her mother and Marge. 'Dougal and me, I mean. I never dreamt . . . we'd both come through without a scratch. I thought about him all the time, you know, wondering what was happening to him.'

'Me, too,' Marge smiled. 'The silly devil could have been

volunteering for all kinds of dangerous missions without a thought to his own safety, you know what he's like.'

Alistair nodded gravely. 'Of course I know what he's like! Better than anybody! We were like brothers all our lives, we'd have done anything for each other. Like that other war song said, "Comrades, comrades, ever since we were boys," but we didn't end up the same way. The last line went, "When danger threatened my darling old comrade was there by my side," and we weren't there for each other, were we?'

'Neither of you was to blame for that,' Rosie pointed out, 'so just be glad you both survived.'

He lapsed into morose silence for about ten minutes, ignoring the conversation around him, and then mumbled, 'I'm whacked. I'm off to bed.'

Rosie patted Gwen's shoulder when the door closed behind him. 'Don't upset yourself, dear, it'll take him a long time to get over what he's been through.'

'I know, Mum, but he said he'd only thought about Dougal when he was a prisoner, and he's never said he . . .' She halted, then ended, shakily, 'He's never said he thought about me. He's never even said he missed me.' The tears she had pent up for months came out at last. 'I sometimes . . . wonder . . . if I'm being . . . punished for . . .'

Marge jumped in before her sister revealed their dark secret. '. . . for going to Scotland and leaving him? It was his idea, remember? Then he lost Manny, a man he practically looked up to as a god, and he didn't have a job any longer. He was concerned for your safety, and the kids', but he'd have joined up even if you hadn't been away. You've nothing to reproach yourself for . . . about that,' she added.

As soon as Rosie went to bed, Marge turned angrily on Gwen. 'What the devil were you thinking about? Do you want everybody to know?'

'I'm sorry, it was when Alistair said he'd just thought about

Dougal . . . He's been so distant to me since he came home, and . . . well, that got to me.'

'Look, Gwennie,' Marge's voice was softer now, 'you've got to make allowances for him. He's been through hell, things that he'll maybe never tell you about, and with nothing to take his mind off it, he can't help brooding. If he had a job . . .'

'I wish I could tell him that, but I don't want him to think I'm criticizing.'

'He's out every day, so maybe he *is* looking and can't find anything. Maybe that's why he's so down? There's so many men looking for jobs now. Dougal'll chivvy him on, though. Once *he's* home, Alistair'll soon get back to normal.'

Everyone, in all three houses, felt better once Dougal Finnie came home. His joy at holding the son he thought he would never have was 'indescribable', as Rosie told one of her friends, and even Alistair joined in the celebration round the Pryors' large table the day after this homecoming.

'I didn't fully realize how much Dougal wanted children,' he remarked to Gwen as they undressed for bed at the end of the convivial evening. 'He must have been jealous seeing us with our two every time we came to visit.'

Thankful that her husband was discussing something with her at last, Gwen said, 'I don't think Dougal's the jealous kind. He wouldn't be the slightest bit jealous even if somebody he knew won a fortune on the football pools.'

His eyes narrowed. 'You think I would?'

'I didn't say that!'

'It's what you were thinking, though, wasn't it? You believe I'm jealous because he's got everything he wants now – a wife, a son, a house he owns, a job to go back to?'

She summoned a smile. 'You've no reason to be jealous.

You've got a wife who loves you, a son and daughter who love you, a good home, your health's improving . . .'

He puffed out his breath from pursed lips as he lay down beside her. 'Yes, I've got all that, Gwen, and believe me, I count my blessings every night, but I just can't seem to get out of this . . . rut, I suppose you could call it. I want to be doing something, and I can't make up my mind what I want to do. What is there for me?'

'Alistair, darling, have you forgotten that Manny taught you how to mend clocks and watches? And what about all the jewellery he left you? And the money?' She could mention that without fear, she reflected, because she had paid every last penny back that she had used at the time of . . . her trouble. 'Maybe a pawnshop isn't what you want, but what about an antique shop, or a watchmaker and jeweller, something along that line.'

'I can't summon up enthusiasm for anything,' he admitted.

'Have a word with Dougal. He'll be able to point you in the right direction.' She wished she hadn't said it. It could be construed as meaning that she had every confidence in her brother-in-law and none in her husband, so she felt great relief when he merely nodded his agreement.

Meanwhile, in a bedroom only the width of two driveways away, Mr and Mrs Finnie were relaxing after a rather hectic half-hour of lovemaking. 'I don't like seeing Ally as down as he is just now,' Dougal observed, as he flicked his cartridge-shell lighter.

'He's been like that ever since he came home,' Marge answered.

'I felt like shaking him, but Gwen was trying to shield him from any questions.'

'She doesn't want him to think anybody's criticizing him.'

'That's a bloody stupid way to look at things. He needs to get off his backside and look for work. I could maybe get him in with me . . .'

'Don't suggest that, he'll just resent it. He needs to make up his own mind, or at least to *think* he's made up his own mind. Why don't you ask him out for a walk tomorrow? You might find out what's eating at him.'

Dougal took one last pull at his cigarette and stubbed it out in the ashtray beside the bed. 'Good idea, my precious, but why are we wasting time speaking about Alistair? We have years to make up yet. Show me again how much you missed me.'

'So, how're you doing, me old mate?'

Alistair's smile was somewhat wry at his friend's attempt to cheer him. 'I suppose Marge told you I've been vegetating since I came back?'

'She didn't have to, I gathered it myself from odd things that were said, and the way Gwen and Rosie watch you like hawks in case you get upset about something. Look, if you'd like to tell me what's bothering you, I'm willing to listen for as long as you want. On the other hand, if you want me to shut up, I'll do my best, but you know me.'

They were strolling across Blackheath in the direction of the Greenwich Observatory, but neither of them paid any attention to the view below them, where the River Thames sparkled in the sunshine as it meandered towards the sea, nor to the old sailing boats which were moored to the quay. A few moments passed before Alistair muttered, 'OK. We could have a seat on the grass, if you like.'

He smoked as he talked, lighting one cigarette after the other, and Dougal did the same while he listened, because he, too, had memories that he would never tell his wife. Thus, for the next two hours, Alistair spoke of being captured at Anzio on February 28, 1943, when the Germans made their big push. 'Some of our boys had gone to HQ for rations, but the Company Commander and all the rest of us were captured, surrounded by the Herman Goering lot. They were on the run by that time, of course, with Monty and the Yanks both at their heels, and they made us carry their wounded out on stretchers, for about eight to ten days, I can't remember exactly.'

He stopped to light another full-strength Capstan. 'We were under our own shell fire, of course. They ordered us to shove one of their trucks out of a ditch, and when we got it out, four of us climbed aboard it. We'd hoped we could escape along the way, but it went straight into German Headquarters. The driver got a right surprise when he found us in the back, and we were held in caves for . . . four, five days. We lost track of time.'

He went on to describe being taken in various modes of transport to Rome, where they were held in what had been a film studio, and then to Florence, until, at the end of May 1944, they were taken by rail in goods trucks into Germany itself, to Moosburg. 'It was a huge camp, held 40,000, Russians, Yugoslavs, all different nationalities. We stopped in a siding, and the SS guards gave the political prisoners a helluva beating. Then they took us to Bavaria, right up in the hills, to build a factory for them. We didn't know at the time, of course, but it was intended for making V2s.'

He glanced at Dougal for a moment, trying to explain. 'We'd to get the stone out of quarries and take out the foundations, no diggers, just barrows and spades and graips. The SS were running things, their secret police came up every now and then to see what was going on, but because we were always indulging in sabotage and trying to escape, that factory never started working.

'Fifty of us were working there, but we were moved out in April 1945, back to Stalag 7A, and General Patton liberated us on the 29th. Came roaring into the camp! You never saw anything like it! Some day!' He relaxed with a huge smile, recalling the thrill of it.

While Alistair had been talking, Dougal mentally filled in the gaps in the story. He could imagine the treatment the prisoners had received, the British as roughly handled as the others, if not worse in some instances. 'What about the food?' he asked.

'It was pretty poor in Italy, that was the worst. There was no Red Cross stuff coming in at all and there were German cooks and Italian, so we never knew what we were going to get. Usually it was a slice of black bread in the morning and a cup of substitute coffee, ersatz, the Jerries called it. At dinnertime, they filled your steel helmet with some sauerkraut, that was the rations. Night time, coffee again, and a bit of bread and jam, put on and scraped off again. Sometimes you got a wee drop macaroni.'

He paused, the memories inching back to him now that he had opened the gate a little. 'I was about a month there when I collapsed and they sent me to hospital. It was funny – the guardsmen who were there, big sturdy men, you know what they have to be, well, they didn't manage to stick it out as long as the rest of us. They caved in after two weeks, they must have needed more vitamins than we did. Once we were in Germany, though, we got our Red Cross parcels, which helped a good bit.'

'Did *you* ever try to escape?'

Alistair rubbed his chin. 'A few did try to get out of the film studios in Rome, but they were found and shot. Stalag 7A at Moosburg was considered 100% secure, but some prisoners tunnelled right under the wire, and the Jerries had got word of what they were up to, God knows how. They put Alsatians through from the camp side, and they waited at the other end till the men came out and shot the lot – seventeen of them. They hadn't a chance, Dougal, and I didn't want to end up dead meat, I'd my family to come home to, so like the coward I am, I never took one step out of line.'

'There's nothing cowardly about wanting to stay alive,' Dougal said firmly. 'I'd have been exactly the same.'

Alistair visibly perked up. 'Would you? Honestly?'

'Cross my heart and hope to die,' Dougal smiled, 'and I don't consider myself a coward.' Deciding to take the step Marge had warned him against, he went on, 'So what's your plans now?'

'I haven't got my thoughts together long enough yet to make any plans. I'll have to start earning something soon, but I don't know how. I went round the markets without thinking when I came back first, then one of Manny's old contacts let me work on his stall and that's what I've been doing for the past few months. I haven't told Gwen, because . . .'

'. . . because you're ashamed of being a barrow boy?' Dougal supplied. 'But how have you been living? You can't be making much, and Gwen can't buy food and clothes for the kids if you don't . . .'

'I told her I was drawing from the account I set up for her when she was in Forvit. She didn't use any of it, but . . .' He shook his head. 'Oh God, Dougal, I should make a proper effort to get a job, shouldn't I?'

'What kind of job do you fancy?'

'Would you think I was off my head if I said I'd like to carry out Manny's dream and open a jeweller or an antiques shop?'

'No, I'd say go for it! If you've got the money to start you off . . .'

'The thing is . . . I'm not happy about living at Rosie's. I'd like a place of our own and that'll take every penny I have, including what I'd get if I sold all the stuff the bank's had in safekeeping.'

'You'll have to make up your mind.' Dougal sounded exasperated now. 'Either your own house or your own shop, and I can't see your problem. Rosie's got tons of room, and she's not going to last for ever, is she? I don't mean that in a nasty way, I love the old dear, but you'll have to think ahead. She'll likely have left the house to Gwen, seeing Peg's settled with Alf and Marge has the best husband in the world.'

Alistair was too agitated to rise to this quip. 'I couldn't let Gwen accept the house. When the time comes, it should be sold and the money divided between . . .'

'When the time comes, you could pay Marge and Peg a third each of what it's worth, if it would make you feel any better, but for God's sake, man, take the plunge and get your shop.' Dougal rose to his feet, flexing his legs to get the circulation going again. 'Come on, Ally. They'll be expecting us back for dinner.'

Alistair looked at his watch in dismay. 'Oh, Lord, and I've done nothing but bleat on about myself. Why didn't you stop me? I'd have liked to hear what you'd been doing.'

'Nothing very exciting, I assure you, and, anyway, we've got the rest of our lives to talk to each other.'

Alice burst out with her news as soon as she entered the shop. 'Gwen says in her letter that Alistair's looking for premises so he can open a wee jeweller's or an antique shop.'

'Oh, aye?'

So excited herself, it didn't occur to Alice that Lexie might have other things on her mind. 'He's speaking about London, of course, or the south of England somewhere, but my Sam came up with a better idea when he read the letter. You see, he's never settled down since we came back, and now he's learned about the government offering assisted passages to Australia, he wants us to emigrate and let Alistair move into Benview. So I'm going to write and suggest he could open his shop up here somewhere. It's just a case of waiting to see what he thinks.'

Suddenly noticing Lexie's sunken eyes and drawn face, she said, 'Are you feeling well enough? You look ghastly.'

'I'm not all that good, to be honest.'

'See the doctor, then. It's stupid to let it run on. It could get worse, whatever it is.'

'I'm not sure about this new doctor we've got. I liked old Doctor Geddes, but this one's too young for my liking.'

'He's still a qualified doctor, Lexie, and you really need to get him in.'

'I'll see how I feel tomorrow.'

'Don't wait longer than that then. I'll have to go, but mind what I've said.'

Left by herself, Lexie leaned weakly against the counter. No doctor could cure what ailed her. Her trouble wasn't medical, it was mental. She couldn't stop wondering about what had happened to her father. She had spent nights trying to remember more of what happened before and after the time of his disappearance, but just when she thought she had something in her grasp, her mind always seemed to shut down, and she was coming more and more round to the idea that it might be best if she didn't remember. That was why she didn't want to see the new doctor. He might make her see a psychiatrist, and God knows what he would dig up. Over the last two days, she had done her best to keep her thoughts at bay, but she couldn't go on much longer like this.

Having made her decision, she went over to the small telephone exchange which had recently been installed by the Post Office. Before the war, there were only a scattering of phones in the whole of the parish, not enough to warrant an exchange, but the number of subscribers had more than doubled now. After plugging in, she waited for her call to be answered.

Since shortly after Dougal came home, a question had arisen in Alistair's mind, and no matter how hard he tried, it wouldn't go away. In fact, it grew stronger every day until it no longer needed to be answered. The proof was there every time he saw Dougal, Marge and little Nicky together. There was no resemblance between the boy and either of his parents, and when he had mentioned this casually to Gwen one day, she had flown up in the air. That was when it had dawned on him – two dark browns don't make a ginger, two browns don't make a green. As the old saying went, there had been dirty work at the crossroads! Had Marge been . . . ? Was Dougal not Nicky's father?

His mental health still in a somewhat fragile state, Alistair nibbled at this concept for hours, feeling sick at the thought of Marge being unfaithful to the finest man in the world. Should he tell Dougal? Was it fair to let him go on thinking . . . ? Why hadn't he seen it for himself?

Maybe he should ask Gwen? But would she tell him the truth? She had kept her silence about it. She wouldn't tell him a lie. She had never lied to him. When he put his question later, however, he wasn't so sure about that. 'Did you never wonder about Marge when you were in Forvit?' he began, and could see her go on the defensive.

'Wonder what about Marge?' she snapped, her eyes wary.

'If she was . . . being unfaithful to Dougal, for instance?'

Her eyes wavered for an instant, then held his. 'Marge

was never unfaithful! She did go to the dances, but she told Dougal and he trusted her.'

He didn't want to push it too far. 'Oh, well . . . I just wondered.'

Recalling it in bed, Alistair was nearly sure that his question had upset her. She had never told him a lie before, but she had told him one then – no doubt about it.

The more he turned it over in his mind, the more positive he became that Dougal was not Nicky's father, and watching them teasing each other the next day, lovingly like any father and son, but one so dark and the other so bright, he wanted to take his long-time friend aside and tell him the truth. The only thing that stopped him was the knowledge that it would break Dougal's heart. What worried him was that he was so upset himself that he was afraid he might let it out accidentally. There might even come a time when he wouldn't be able to keep it back any longer and would let fly at Marge, and even if it *was* all her fault, it would cause ructions between him and Gwen, and he didn't want that. It was like living on a razor's edge.

'What's up with Alistair?' Marge eyed her sister curiously. 'He's been snapping my head off lately and I can't think of anything I've said or done to . . .'

'Something's bothering him,' Gwen interrupted, not wanting to tell her what. 'Um . . . has Dougal ever said . . . has Alistair ever asked . . . ?' She stopped abruptly.

'The day they took a walk together, he spoke about what it was like being a prisoner of war. Dougal won't tell me anything more than that.'

Gwen's concern that her husband might have stumbled on the truth was so great that she had to find out, and so she tackled him that evening when they were sitting by the fire. 'Marge is wondering what she's done to upset you?'

'Is she, now?'

His tone was so sarcastic that her determination faltered a little, but she knew she had to get to the bottom of things. The air would have to be cleared. 'Alistair, I wish you'd tell me what's wrong with you. Did something happen to you in the prison camps that's made you change? I know it must have been a terrible time for you, and all I want to do is help you to forget.'

'And all I want is for you to tell me the truth,' he snapped. 'I hate to see my best pal being tricked, though if he wasn't so bloody besotted by the kid, he'd see it for himself.'

Gwen felt herself go cold, but she answered honestly. 'If you're still thinking Marge was unfaithful, you're wrong. I can swear with my hand on my heart – she never took one step out of line the whole time we were in Forvit. She was as true to Dougal as . . .'

He took up where she left off. '. . . as you were to me?' He thought nothing of her hesitation. Gwen had always found it difficult to speak from her heart.

Thankful that he hadn't noticed anything, she tried to coax him out of his mood. 'You've got a wrong idea in your head, darling, and if you don't get rid of it, it's going to cause a lot of trouble.'

'For Marge? You would stick up for her, of course, seeing she's your sister.'

'I'm sticking up for her because I know she's not guilty of what you think. Yes, she enjoyed herself at the dances, but if her own husband can look on that as innocent fun, I don't see why you can't.'

'You think I'm jealous, do you? You think I want Marge?'

'Of course I don't, that's silly.' Gwen was angry now. 'I think you're . . . twisted. You've never been right since you came home, and you've been worse since Dougal came back. No matter what you think – and I tell you you're making a big mistake – for God's sake don't say anything to him. He's so proud of his son, it would destroy him to think he wasn't . . .'

'I'm not heartless,' Alistair said, bitterly. 'That's the only reason I *haven't* told him. But I warn you, if he ever hints at having doubts, I won't hesitate.'

'But there's nothing to tell,' Gwen wailed. 'It's all in your . . . warped mind.'

'Thank you very much. It's nice to know where your loyalties lie.' Alistair stood up and walked towards the door.

'Where are you going?' she asked, anxiously.

'Out.'

'I'm sorry, darling, I didn't mean the things I said about you. I'm just upset at you for thinking Marge would . . .' She stopped and drew a deep breath to calm her ragged nerves. 'Can't we forget about it? You're not doing anybody any good by carrying on like this. Can't we get back to the way we were before the war?'

'One big happy family?' he sneered. 'With a cuckoo in the nest?'

His wife's cry of anguish made him halt with his hand on the door knob, and the ensuing torrent of tears, sounding as if they came from the innermost core of her, made him dart to her side. 'Oh, Gwen, my dearest darling, I'm sorry! I'm sorry! I didn't mean to hurt you. You're quite right, my mind must be warped, but I shouldn't take it out on you. I shouldn't have said anything. I know I'm wrong about Marge, but I couldn't help . . . Can you forgive me? Please?'

She looked up at him, her eyes still streaming, the sobs still racking her whole body. 'I do forgive you, Alistair. I can understand that what you went through in the war has changed you, but I wish . . . oh God, how I wish . . . I had my old husband back.'

Much later, as she lay cradled in his arms, their love having been re-avowed and demonstrated, Gwen wondered if she had been correct in her summing up of him. Had his suspicions of Marge and his desire to protect Dougal really twisted his mind? Could it be the result of the dreadful beatings and kickings he must have received in the POW camps? Or . . . was he going insane? Was he edging down a slippery slope towards utter madness? Was it possible for him to reverse?

Salvation for Alistair came at the end of January, with the arrival of a letter from his sister, addressed to him, not to Gwen as was usual.

> Dear Brother,
>
> You'll likely have a fit when you read this, so sit down and take it slowly. Gwen tells me you can't settle since you got home, and my Sam's exactly the same, but he's doing something about it. He's applied for us to go to Australia on this assisted passage scheme. The fare's only £10 if you agree to stay for at least two years, and he says it's too good a chance to miss.
>
> The trouble is Benview, and that's why I'm writing. You've said you want to open a jeweller's shop or something like that, so why don't you move up here? It would save us the bother of trying to sell the house. It's too far from civilization for most people, and it's really yours, anyway, remember? You could get a shop in Aberdeen, it's not that far if you have a car.

What I'm saying is, we would leave everything, furniture, etc., so you wouldn't have to worry about that. Sam says it's a wonderful opportunity for all of us, so please think about it and let us know by the end of the month.

Give my love to Gwen and the kids, and to all the rest of the folk at your end. I bet Dougal's still in seventh heaven having a son after all this time.

Your hoping-to-emigrate-soon sister, Alice

'Well!' exclaimed Gwen, after she read it. 'That's a surprise!'

'What do you think, though?'

'I haven't had time . . . and it's up to you. I'll fall in with whatever you want.'

'We'd better discuss it with the kids. It's their future, as well.'

And so, for the rest of that day, fortunately a Saturday when thirteen-year-old Leila and David, twelve, were at home, the topic was, 'Should we move up to Forvit for good?' Later, when they were joined by the rest of the clan, as Dougal laughingly referred to them, and after much deliberation and tossing around of opinions, the final consensus was that Alistair should make up his own mind.

Lexie's visit to the new doctor had a result she had not expected, although she should have known. Not that he did or said anything out of place – he took her blood pressure and pulses, tested her reflexes, then sounded her chest. 'Your trouble isn't physical as far as I can make out. Are you worrying about something? That is often . . .'

She had shaken her head – how could she tell him what she suspected? – but as she looked at him, her senses began to swim, and she felt herself going back to that awful night. 'Stop it,' she moaned, 'I don't like you doing that.'

Straining against the arms now trying to pin her down, she could again feel the pain of the object being forced inside her. 'It's too sore!' she screamed. 'You're hurting me! Stop! Please stop!'

She could see the sweat running down a horrible, unfeatured red face until, as abruptly as it had begun, the horror came to an end and she was able to stop struggling against it.

'That's better.' The voice was soft, the touch was gentle, and she smiled tremulously into the puzzled face of young Dr Geddes. 'I hope I didn't hurt you, but I was forced to hold you down, you were in such a state, fighting like a tigress.'

'I'm sorry,' she whispered, deeply ashamed. 'I was remembering something . . . I thought . . . you were somebody else.'

'Obviously somebody who terrified you half to death. Tell me about it. It happened when you were quite young?'

She was still trembling. 'Not quite sixteen, and I can't speak about it. To tell the truth, I'm not quite sure if it happened at all, or if it was just a horrible nightmare.'

'It would help to tell me, whether or not it actually happened. You need to get it out of your system. Facing up to it should stop the nightmares for good.'

'It was . . .' She stopped, shaking her head determinedly, knuckles white as she gripped the seat of her chair. 'I can't speak about it. I can't!'

'It's all right, don't force it. You seem to be at the limit of your endurance, and if you could only bring yourself to talk through it for me, I'd be better able to . . .' He stood up and unlocked one of the glass doors of the cabinet against the left-hand wall. 'All I can do, meantime, is give you some tablets to help you to sleep.'

And they had for as long as they lasted, Lexie thought now, though they weren't as potent as the ones Doctor Birnie had given her all those years before – they had knocked her out in minutes. But now that she knew what her father had put her through – for it *had* been her father – she could understand why she couldn't bear to let anybody else near her in that way.

She couldn't even think of Alec Fraser as her father now, but it was no wonder he had cleared out of Forvit. He had abused her so badly as to make her bleed, actually torn her. How could they have faced each other after that?

1947–1949

Chapter 23

Waiting in Benview's large kitchen for David to come home from school, Gwen Ritchie wondered what had possessed her to come back. She had wanted to watch young Nicky growing up, even though it pulled at her heartstrings to be powerless to claim him as her son. Yet . . . probably it was best this way. Alistair was so unstable that, if they'd stayed in Lee Green, she couldn't have trusted him not to blurt out his suspicions to Dougal, and she'd have been duty-bound to confess the whole sorry tale. She couldn't let Marge take the blame for what *she* had done.

Although the move to Forvit had not been made without due consideration, it was effected far too quickly for her liking. Rosie, of course, was against them going, and so, too, was Peggy, who would have to take on some of the responsibility for her mother. Alf Pryor had said it wasn't his place to put forward an opinion, but, when pressed, he had admitted that he wouldn't mind cooking Rosie's meals again. It would leave Marge free to concentrate on her husband and son, and it would give him something to occupy his time other than tending the two gardens. He had come down firmly, if just a little shamefacedly, on the opposite side from his wife.

Marge had been torn between the need to have her sister next door for company and relief that she wouldn't be there to criticize the way she was bringing up Nicky. Dougal, as Alistair's close friend, had no inhibitions about voicing *his* opinion, and had urged him to jump at the opportunity and not be so bloody stupid.

As for the younger members of Rosie's flock, two-year-old Nicky's unnatural silences let everyone know how much he would miss his two 'cousins', especially David, who had been teaching him all kinds of boys' games. David himself was keen to go back to Forvit, where he had left many friends and where there was space to roam around and act out the stories they read. Leila, however, was the one who astonished them. They had all expected her to prefer living in London because of the cinemas, dance halls and all manner of places where a young girl could meet the opposite sex, but when she was asked what she wanted, she said, 'I'd like to go back to Forvit.'

Her grandmother had reminded her that she would be leaving school at summer – she would be fourteen in May – and that Forvit would have little to offer in the way of employment.

Dougal had got round that. 'She can keep her father's books,' he crowed, then turning to Alistair, he went on, 'Your best bet's to look for a place in Aberdeen. More chance of succeeding there, and it's only twenty-eight, twenty-nine miles. You could do it in under an hour if you bought a decent car.'

That Saturday evening, the day after he got Alice's letter, Alistair had replied that they would take up the offer of the house, and in two days, she wrote back to say how pleased she was and not to worry about anything.

'We'll leave everything as it is,' she had continued, 'furniture, dishes, the lot, so all you'll need to bring, apart from your wife and kids (ha-ha) is clothes and any personal things you feel you need.'

'That's a blessing,' Alistair had grinned, 'seeing we've never had any household goods of our own, anyway.' Then he had looked at Alf somewhat apologetically. 'I nearly forgot. There's all the stuff you and your friend stored for us.'

Alf was an understanding man. 'That's all right. The Salvation Army's always looking for things for the needy, so I'll ask them to collect it . . . unless you want to have a look through it first, in case there's something you want to keep?'

Rosie had given a sarcastic laugh. 'There's nothing there worth a brass farthing. The furniture was second-hand when Tiny bought it.'

Three months later – the time it took for the Guthries' documents to come through from Australia House – the Ritchies had returned to Benview. The first three days were a sort of 'handing-over' period, with Gwen helping Alice to turn out her cupboards. The men made a bonfire of the useless items from the outhouses and also burned what Alice was throwing out.

The final leave-taking had not been as emotional as Gwen had feared, though she should have remembered that the Scots were not as demonstrative as the English. The brother and sister hadn't even kissed each other's cheeks, yet they must have known it was most unlikely that they would ever see each other again.

And now, only two days on, it was as if she had never been away, except that there was no Marge to keep her from getting depressed. Being on her own every day from morning until David came bouncing in from school around five was like a punishment – likely *was* a punishment, and she shouldn't complain. After what she had done, she had got off lightly.

She couldn't get over how attitudes had changed in the village, however. Only one or two of the village women had ever spoken to Marge and her in any sort of friendly way before, and now they all smiled and commented on the weather, or said how glad they were to see them back as a complete family.

When she mentioned this to Alistair, he had said, 'It's because you're here for good this time. They'd been timid of you and Marge before because you didn't belong and they couldn't understand what you were saying. When I went to London first, it sounded to me like they all spoke with a marble in their mouths and thought they were better than Dougal and me. So that's what the folk here had thought about you and Marge. No,' he added hastily, 'I know you wouldn't have looked down on them, but . . .' He shrugged off the prejudices of the country folk.

Gwen sighed – she would never understand. It was Lexie Fraser, who had always been quite friendly, who now seemed to give her the cold shoulder. She had never asked about Alistair, yet during the war, her first question had always been, 'How's Alistair? I saw you had a letter from him this morning,' or whenever. She looked much older, too, as if something dreadful was preying on her mind. It was a pity she couldn't meet a nice man. Marriage would do her the world of good.

Lexie watched Gwen Ritchie as she went out of the shop and cycled off. She didn't look as happy as she used to, but no doubt she hadn't wanted to come back to Forvit. What was there here for her, for goodness' sake? She, herself, would leave like a shot if she thought she could survive out in the big world, but she had a sense of security here, of being safe, as if something terrible would happen if she ventured out of her cocoon.

She had vowed, time and time again, never to think back, but she couldn't help it. She couldn't stop herself. It would haunt her for the rest of her life . . . or until her father came back and admitted what he had done. She had this other worry as well, now. Every time the doctor came into the shop, she could hardly bring herself to look at him, and he had done nothing wrong – that had been all in her mind. She had come perilously near to losing her sanity altogether at that time, and even if she was relatively calmer now, it wouldn't take much to push her over the edge.

Two other people she thought about sometimes were Nancy Lawrie and Margaret Birnie. She was sure that what Doodie Tough said about Mrs Birnie and another man couldn't be right, although Doctor Tom had told a few folk that she had never been totally happy in Forvit, and he had given in to her pleas to find a practice somewhere near Stirling so that she could look after her mother. She had gone on ahead of him, leaving him to attend to the sale of the house and the removal of their belongings. It had been a blow to the local community when he left, about three months after her father, and he'd been presented with a lovely gold watch in appreciation of his seven years' dedicated service.

It was a shame, really, because Mrs Birnie had been a lovely woman, a bit reserved maybe, but she'd likely just been shy. She'd been quite well-liked, had sung in the kirk choir and was president of the Guild, so folk couldn't understand why she hadn't been happy. Still, nobody knew what went on behind closed doors, did they? How a person behaved in private could be completely at odds with his or her public image.

Replacing the lid on a tin of the mixed biscuits she had been weighing out for Alistair's wife, Lexie's thoughts turned to Nancy Lawrie. She'd been so different from Margaret Birnie, a go-ahead girl, full of fun and always flirting with the boys. She wasn't the type of person Alec Fraser would be drawn to. He had been reserved and quiet . . . it was really just as unlikely that he had taken up with Nancy as that he had raped his daughter. An iciness clutching at the pit of her stomach, Lexie took a deep breath. If she carried on like this, they would haul her off to the nearest asylum and put her in a straightjacket . . .

Picking up her duster, she made a desultory attack on a side shelf. Gwen Ritchie didn't know when she was well off, that was her trouble. She didn't have a dark secret that ate at her very innards while she had to smile and pretend that nothing was wrong. Not only that, she had a lovely husband, two lovely children . . . everything that Lexie Fraser had ever wanted.

Leila Ritchie had walked past the house three times, hoping to catch a glimpse of Barry Mearns. She had always had a crush on him, from the first day he'd come to help with the garden, back in 1941 when she was just a little kid.

She wouldn't be a kid much longer, though she'd have to stay on another year at school because the leaving age had been raised to fifteen. The year after that, she would be old enough to get married in Scotland, so she had heard.

'Well, well! It's young Leila, isn't it?'

She looked round in surprise to find the postman, Barry's father, regarding her with an expression she was just beginning to recognize. Since she'd started wearing nylons, the latest in stockings, and putting a touch of make-up on, men as well as boys had begun to look at her like she was good enough to eat, and she couldn't help flirting a little. 'Yes, Mr Mearns, we're back. Dad's looking for a place in Aberdeen to open a jeweller's.'

'So he was saying when I handed in his letters the other day. Barry was asking if I'd seen you, so I'll need to tell him you're bonnier than ever. He's nearly finished his apprenticeship at

Bill Rettie's garage in Bankside, but he still does a bit o' gardening in his spare time, so if your Dad needs some help . . .'

'I'll tell him. I'd better be going, Mr Mearns, else Mum'll wonder where I've got to.'

'She'll need to keep her eye on you, or the lads'll all be after you. Cheeribye, lass.' Sandy gave her a laughing salute as he turned away.

Leila walked off feeling very pleased with herself, retrieved her bicycle from where she had set it against the gable wall of the Jubilee Hall and sped along the road. Barry had asked about her! And his father thought she was bonnie – it sounded even better than being pretty. Coming up for fourteen was a perfect age to be!

Leila was even more pleased with herself that evening. Her father had come home in a state of high excitement. 'I've found a wee place off Union Street!' he exulted. 'It's not ideal, a wee bit cramped, but it's right in the heart of the city and it'll do till I get on my feet.'

All through their evening meal, he told them his plans, so animated that Leila glanced at her mother who was looking happier than she had done for some years – even before Dad came home from the war, really. He'd been different then, not like he'd been before, and she'd been as upset as her mother about that. Of course, he must have had some bad experiences, and it would have taken him a long time to get over them, so they should be grateful that he was getting back to normal, though it had taken a long time.

They had just finished eating when someone knocked at the porch door, and Leila, being nearest, went to open it. 'Barry!' she gasped, her face flooding with colour.

The twenty-year-old was also embarrassed. 'I've come to see if your father needs any help with the garden. Da said . . .'

Curiosity about the caller had brought Alistair into the porch, too, but the youth was a complete stranger to him. 'You're a gardener, are you?'

'He's Barry Mearns, the postman's son,' Leila explained.

'I'm serving my time as a motor mechanic, Mr Ritchie.'

'He helped Mum and Auntie Marge with this garden when we were here before,' Leila said shyly, 'and he's really good, Dad.'

Feeling a sense of goodwill towards all men at that moment, Alistair smiled broadly. 'A reference already? That's good enough for me, and I shouldn't think I'll have much time myself to spare on the garden for a few years yet, so when can you come?'

Barry cast a grateful glance at Leila. 'I've been helping the doctor for the past few Mondays. He's wanting to change the whole layout of his garden, and we're digging out everything so he can start from scratch. The trouble is, he's often called away and I'm mostly on my own. Tuesdays, I tidy up at Mrs Wilkie's, and do a quick job on Lexie Fraser's wee square. Wednesdays . . .' he paused, then said, bashfully, 'it's choir night. I don't like to let the minister down.'

Alistair nodded appreciatively. 'Good lad.'

'Thursdays,' Barry continued, 'I've been giving my boss a hand to dig a foundation for a wash-bed he wants to put in, and a bigger area round the petrol pumps. That'll take another couple of months, maybe. I could manage you Fridays, though, if that's OK?'

'Fine, but are you sure? You're not leaving yourself much time for enjoyment.'

'There's not much to enjoy round here . . . up to now.' Barry shot another glance at Leila, whose face went crimson at what he was implying.

This was not lost on her father, who, however, decided to ignore it. 'So you'll be here on Friday at . . . ?'

'I stop at five, so I can manage by six, if that's not too early.'

'I probably won't be home, but you'll manage?'

'I know where everything is, Mr Ritchie.'

'Right! Shall we say . . . a couple of hours till we see how it goes?'

Alistair took the overnight train to London on Wednesday, to close his bank account and collect the items he had deposited in Manny's name but which were now his. He went to Lee Green after his business was over, to acquaint them with the progress he was making, and to find out how everyone was. Peggy and Dougal, of course, were both at work, but Marge, Rosie and Alf were delighted to see him, and interested in his plans. He resisted Marge's pleadings for him to stay over. 'Dougal's going to be so disappointed if he doesn't see you,' she wailed.

'I'm desperate to get home, Marge,' he excused his hurry. 'I can't wait to get started.'

It wasn't only his business that pulled him away, however. It was seeing young Nicky again. As he told himself after he settled into the window corner of the railway carriage, there wasn't a chance in hell that that kid was Dougal's. What was every bit as bad, as far as Alistair was concerned, Gwen must have known what Marge got up to. Pregnancy could be hidden up to a point, but not between two sisters who were living in an isolated cottage in the middle of a war.

To be fair to his oldest friend, he should make his own wife admit the truth and not let the deception carry on any longer, but . . . he had other things to concentrate on. He had a shop to set up and get running, and he should really try to get some sleep tonight, to be fit to see the solicitor in Aberdeen in the morning. There were papers to sign, advice to ask for . . . and he'd be better to open a current account at the bank. It was more businesslike to hand over a cheque for any stock he had to buy than a bulky wad of notes.

Everything accomplished that he had set out to do, Alistair came off the bus outside the shop/post office, and decided to go in and have a few words with Lexie. He hadn't seen her since he came back to Forvit, and . . . by God, yes! *She* would know if there had ever been any gossip about Marge. He was dismayed at how ill she looked when he went in, but it wasn't policy to say that kind of thing to a woman. 'Here's me turning up again like a bad penny,' he laughed.

'I thought you might have come to see me before,' she muttered, accusingly.

'I've been looking for premises in Aberdeen. I'm opening a shop, jewellery, new and old, watches, clocks . . .'

'You'd learned all that from your Jew, of course,' she said, listlessly now.

'Manny was the best teacher I could ever have had. I still miss him.'

For some moments, he asked about people he used to know, then he plucked up courage and came out with his question, the answer to which should settle the burning agonizing he'd done over the past months. 'Did you ever hear any rumours about Dougal's wife when she was here?'

Lexie's eyebrows lifted briefly. 'What d'you mean? What sort of rumours?'

'About her . . . going out with any of the men from Ardley Camp?'

'I never heard anything about her. It was Gwen I saw up at the tower one night with a soldier.' She hesitated briefly, regretting having said anything, and conceded, 'I could've sworn it was her voice, but I suppose it could have been Marge.'

He had fixed on one unsavoury sentence. 'It couldn't have been Gwen you saw, she wouldn't have done anything wrong. Why did you think it was her? She's blonde and Marge is dark. You'd have noticed which one it was, surely?'

'I could only see from their waists down . . . caught them in the act, though I didn't stand and watch. It was the voice that made me think it was Gwen, but they're both Cockneys, of course.'

'They're not Cockneys,' Alistair began, but didn't waste time explaining, 'and it *had* been Marge. I knew it! Dougal and her are both dark, and Nicky's bright red!'

'I suppose that could happen.'

'Not in this case, now I know what she'd been up to.'

'You should ask Gwen,' Lexie murmured. 'She must have known what was what.'

Alistair felt obliged to cover up for his wife. 'Marge wouldn't have let her know. She'd always have met the man away from the house.'

'But she couldn't have hidden . . . no, Al. Marge grew so big, I wondered if she was having twins, and it *was* born nine months after Dougal had his embarkation leave.'

Alistair was glad when she fell silent. Had his suspicions been groundless? They must have been. His wife would never have agreed to anything underhand, and Nicky must be Dougal's after all. Unless . . . he had never once heard Marge telling a lie, but she was far more capable of it than Gwen. She could have been carrying on with a soldier and been lucky that Dougal had been on leave about the right time, or near enough for her to swear it was his baby, and Gwen wouldn't have suspected a thing.

Lexie cut into his deliberations. 'I've just remembered.

Gwen was quite ill at the time, as well. She'd to go to London for an operation.'

'An operation?' he gasped. 'She never told me that in her letters – nobody did.'

'They hadn't wanted to worry you. You were in a prison camp, after all.'

'But I'd have liked to know. Was it serious? What if she'd died?'

'Marge said it was woman's trouble, a cyst that turned out to be benign. I was a bit worried about Marge being there on her own while Gwen was away, but an auntie came up from England in time to take her to the hospital, and Gwen was home before she came back with the infant.'

His mind in a state of turmoil, Alistair bade Lexie goodbye and walked pensively along the road, going over what he had heard. By the time he reached home, he had convinced himself that what Lexie had told him didn't prove he was wrong. It didn't prove he was right, either, that was the only thing.

'Why didn't you tell me about your operation?' he asked Gwen when he went inside.

By the expressions on his children's faces, he could tell that they hadn't known either, and he regretted not waiting until he and his wife were alone. But it was done now, so he persisted, 'Why didn't you let me know?'

Gwen's face was chalk white. 'Marge said . . . it would be best . . . not to worry you,' she said, haltingly, obviously upset at the accusing way he had spoken to her.

He took a deep breath, and his next words were more gentle. 'Didn't it occur to you I'd want to know?'

'You couldn't have done anything, Alistair, and . . . maybe I should have told you once it was all over, but . . .'

'You didn't tell us either, Mum,' David said loudly.

Leila was looking puzzled. 'Was that the time when you were supposed to be looking after Grandma?'

Gwen's sigh was a little tremulous. 'We only said that to save you worrying, dear.'

'But why did you have to go to London to have an operation?' David demanded. 'Isn't there a hospital in Aberdeen that could have done it?'

'It was . . . it was . . . how can I put it? They wanted to try out a new piece of equipment.'

Alistair's face darkened. 'They were experimenting on you?'

'It wasn't dangerous. It had been tested and tested, and I was all right, so can we just forget it? It's all over, and I'm as fit as a fiddle. Tell us how you got on in London.'

When Alistair left, Lexie wished that she hadn't mentioned Gwen in connection with the soldier at the tower – she could tell it had upset him. It would be better to let him think it was Marge, though she was absolutely positive that it hadn't been. He had suffered enough as a prisoner of war, it would be a crime to stir up trouble for him when he was getting his life back together again.

What Lexie told Alistair, however, had farther-reaching effects than she realized. Leila, who had only been ten at the time, was old enough now to put two and two together and make sense of what had gone on. Her mother had told a lie about going to London to look after Grandma, so the rest of it could have been a lie, too. It was too much of a coincidence that Auntie Marge and Mum had both grown so fat at that time. Now that she came to think back, they could both have been expecting babies. Uncle Dougal had been on leave about the right length of time before Nicky was born, so that was OK, but Dad had been away for a year and a half, if not more, so if Mum *had* had a baby, it must have been to somebody else.

Every time her mind touched on this, Leila felt sick, but there was nothing she could do. She couldn't accuse her mother, not unless she had proof, and in any case, she could be wrong.

Gwen felt she was living on the edge of a crumbling precipice and could do nothing to save herself if it gave way. If it ever crossed Alistair's mind, she kept thinking, that saying she'd had an ovarian cyst removed could be an excuse for going away to have a baby conceived in sin, he wouldn't have anything more to do with her. Nevertheless, even if he didn't suspect her of being Nicky's mother, if he ever accused Marge to her face of being unfaithful to her husband, or told Dougal that he wasn't Nicky's father, she would have to tell the truth. She couldn't let her sister shoulder the blame.

She had hoped that by moving to Forvit, Alistair would never have the opportunity to air his suspicions to Marge or Dougal, but he was speaking of making occasional trips to London to buy stock for his shop. Yet, even knowing that it was bound to come out some time, she was too much of a coward to confess unless she was forced to.

She would have to exist in this awful state of limbo until . . . the end.

Chapter 24

‘Are you feeling well enough, Alf?’ Rosie studied her son-in-law in some concern. ‘You look ghastly.’

He gave a faint smile. ‘Thanks, Rosie. That makes me feel absolutely tip-top.’

She shook her head at his sarcasm. ‘You didn’t need to cook anything for me if you didn’t feel up to it. I could easily have slapped two slices of bread round a chunk of cheese. Or Marge would have done something for me, if you’d asked her.’

‘No need, Rosie, old girl, though I don’t feel quite up to scratch, if you must know. Age catching up with me at last, I suppose.’

‘Oh, poof! I can give you fifteen years and there’s nothing wrong with me . . . apart from my stupid legs. If I got a new pair of knees, I’d be on top of the world.’

‘You always *are* on top of the world, Rosie, dear. I wish I’d half your spirit.’

‘No sense in moping like a dead duck all the time,’ she laughed.

He ate little of the steak and kidney pudding he had prepared, and not a single spoonful of the apple pie with the melt-in-the mouth pastry almost as good as Tiny used to make, but Rosie passed no comment. He’d be upset if she fussed.

She lay back in her chair when he had gone, her feet on the brown plush pouffe she kept handy to ease the pain in her legs. Should she say anything to Peggy, or would it worry her? Well, of course it would worry her, Rosie scolded herself, so she'd better see what Marge thought first.

As she always did, Marge went to check on her mother at half past three on the dot, having given her time for her afternoon nap, and Rosie, who hadn't slept at all that day, jumped straight in. 'I'm worried about Alf, Margie. He doesn't look a bit well, and he hardly ate any of the steak and kidney pud he cooked for me.'

'He loves cooking,' Marge smiled. 'You should think yourself lucky having at least one domesticated son-in-law. Dougal wouldn't know how to boil an egg, and neither would Alistair, I shouldn't wonder.'

'I wish you'd stick to the point,' Rosie sighed. 'It's not like Alf. He was so pale, and there was sweat on his brow like he had a fever.'

'Shall I go and have a word with him?'

'Have a look at him anyway, then come right back and tell me what you think.'

'I can't just look and walk out,' Marge objected.

'You can surely think of some excuse.'

The distance between the two back doors was not sufficient to give Marge time to think of anything, but as it happened, she didn't need an excuse. When she went into his kitchen, her brother-in-law was slumped over the sink. 'Oh, dear God, Alf!' she cried. 'What's wrong?' He patted his chest and, remembering that he had medication for his angina, she asked, 'Have you taken a pill?'

His nod made alarm course through her. If the pill wasn't helping, it must be bad – a proper heart attack. She helped him into the living room and, while she settled him in a chair, she said, 'I'll phone for the doctor. I'll just be a jiffy.'

Rushing through to the hall, she was glad that Alf had made them all have telephones installed. It was her mother they had feared for, of course, but it might be his life she could be saving now.

Having caught the doctor towards the end of his afternoon surgery, she was back in no time, not even popping in to let her mother know what was happening. 'He'll be here as soon as he can, Alf, so I'll wait with you till he comes.'

'It's a good thing your Mum told you to have a look at Alf,' Dougal said, that evening. 'He could have been dead by the time Peg came home from work.'

'I know,' Marge muttered, 'and I nearly didn't go. I thought Mum was fussing about nothing, you know what she's like, but . . . oh, Dougal, I thought it was all over before the doctor even turned up, and he was there in less than ten minutes and took him to hospital himself. How was he when you saw him?'

'He's not too good, but we'll have to play it down in front of Peg. She's worrying herself sick about him.'

'I'd be out of my mind if it was you. Um . . . do you think he'll pull through?'

'I wouldn't like to say.'

'Thank goodness you've the car. It'll save Peg having to take buses . . . or taxis, if the worst comes to the worst.'

Dougal frowned now. 'Take things as they come, eh? Don't look on the black side.'

The black side, unfortunately, came looking for them. At five minutes to five the following morning, they were roused out of fitful sleep by the slam of a car door, and when Dougal jumped to look out of the window, he gave a feeble groan. 'It's the police at Peg's!' he told his wife, pulling on his trousers and jacket over his pyjamas. 'We'd better get round there.'

When he left his house, his heart sank even more. One policeman was hammering on the Pryors' door while another was knocking on Rosie's. 'No, no!' he called to the nearest man. 'She's an old lady. You don't want to frighten her out of her wits.'

'We thought Mrs Pryor should have a neighbour or someone with her when we told her. Her husband has just died in hospital.'

Marge came running up now, trying to get her arm into the sleeve of her coat. 'Oh, no! Poor Alf . . . and poor Peg.' With an effort, she kept hold of her senses, and explained, 'I'm her sister and this is our mother's house, and she'll be wakened now anyway.'

'You'd better go in and tell her,' Dougal advised, 'I'll look after Peg.'

The next few hours were horrendous for the inhabitants of all three houses. While Dougal was running Peggy to the hospital, Marge was attending to Rosie, who had been rigid with fear when she went in. 'A burglar was trying to break in,' she whispered, her teeth chattering, her face grey, 'and I was sure he'd kill me if I made a sound.'

'It wasn't a burglar, Mum,' Marge soothed. 'It was one of the policemen. They came to tell Peg that Alf had . . . passed away, and they were trying to get a neighbour to be with her. They didn't know . . . you could hardly walk . . .'

'Oh, dear Lord! Poor Alf, I knew he was ill! He shouldn't have cooked lunch for me. It's my fault he's dead.'

'Don't be silly, Mum. He loved cooking, and oh, it's awful, really awful. I don't know what Peg's going to do.' Noticing then that her mother's face was an even more peculiar colour and that her breathing was so shallow she scarcely seemed to be breathing at all, Marge exclaimed, 'Mum! Take it easy! We don't want you . . .'

Marge was too late. Rosie, like Alf, had suffered a fatal

heart attack, but unlike his, hers had given her no warning.

Only David was his normal self at breakfast time, the other three were so quiet that he said, grumpily, 'Don't know why you lot are so miserable. Just think about me. Even if that blasted rain goes off, the pitch'll be waterlogged.'

Not receiving the reprimand he expected from his mother for saying 'blasted', he drained his cup and pushed back his chair. 'I'm going upstairs again. There's nothing to do down here.'

'You could help with the dishes,' Leila suggested, but he pretended not to hear her. Washing and drying dishes was women's work, not men's. His father never dried as much as one measly teaspoon, and *he* wasn't going to let the side down.

In his room, he sifted through his comics listlessly; he'd read them all dozens of times. He didn't care much for books, though he quite liked the William series, by Richmal Crompton. He gathered the *Wizard*s and *Boys' Own*s into a semblance of neatness and stuffed them back in his cupboard. He was bored, bored, bored.

Then his curiosity was aroused by something hanging down the back of the shelf; it must have been under the comics and he'd pushed it back when he put them in again, but he'd no idea what it was. He couldn't remember ever putting anything there. Stretching over the sundry items that he regarded as treasures, he pulled out a slim paper wallet. Then it came back to him.

Rushing downstairs, he said, 'Dad, I just found something you've never seen. I forgot all about them.'

Alistair turned round with a smile, and held out his hand for whatever he was meant to look at. 'Oh, it's photographs.'

'I took them when we were living here before and the packet must have got jammed at the back of the shelf.'

'*You* took them? They're really good. Are these boys still at school with you?'

'He's left,' a grubby finger pointed, 'but the others are still there. And that's Auntie Marge digging up potatoes. She was sweating. And here's one of Mum speaking to the postie. Uncle Ken took this one of us all having a picnic at the tower, and he took that one of me another day, after he'd been teaching me how to bowl. This was the last one in the film – Uncle Ken standing between Mum and Auntie Marge.'

Gwen's gasp made her son look at her anxiously. 'It's all right to speak about Uncle Ken now, isn't it, Mum? I forgot it was supposed to be a secret, and anyway, it surely doesn't matter when the war's been over for so long, does it?'

He was astonished to see that his mother's eyes were round with what looked like terror, her mouth gripped in her chalk-white face, and he knew that it *was not* all right. He switched his eyes back to his father, who was angrier than he had ever seen him.

'Why had it to be kept a secret?' Alistair asked, very quietly.

'Well, you know . . .' the boy began, then believing that his father didn't know, that maybe the rule hadn't applied to servicemen overseas or even in other parts of Britain, he gathered confidence and went on, '. . . because soldiers weren't allowed to visit other soldiers' families. He'd have got into trouble, maybe been stuck in the glasshouse.'

Alistair studied the picture once more, and when he raised his head, his eyes were icy and his voice was clipped as he addressed his wife. 'And who is Uncle Ken?'

'He was a soldier who drove Marge home from a dance one night,' Gwen muttered, through lips almost frozen with fear, then, realizing what her words implied, she added, 'He was only a friend.'

'A bloody good friend, going by the amount of times he must have come here!'

She pulled her senses together with a great effort. 'Stop it, Alistair! If you want to pick a quarrel, please don't do it in front of the children.'

His face dark with anger, he snapped, 'Go to your rooms, you two! I want to have something out with your mother!'

They were only halfway up the stairs when he called, 'David, what colour was Uncle Ken's hair?'

'Um . . . red, or ginger, or whatever it's called. Can I go now?'

Waiting until he heard a door closing, and guessing that they had both gone into the same room, Alistair's bottom lip curled. 'So that's why young Nicky's hair's red? Yet you swore to me Marge hadn't been unfaithful!'

'She wasn't! She really wasn't! Ken was only a friend. He had a wife and two children in Birmingham and he missed them something awful. We asked him here because we could see he was a decent man, not like some of the single boys who left a lot of sore hearts when they were posted away. He was so grateful to be part of our family.'

'He'd had a lot to be grateful for,' her husband sneered. 'He'd two kids on tap to replace his own, and a woman ready and willing to be a substitute wife!'

'It wasn't like that! We treated him like a brother, and he brought presents for Leila and David, and sometimes something for us from their cookhouse, and . . .'

'And you're still trying to tell me it was all above board? What d'you take me for, Gwen? A bloody fool?'

'You are a bloody fool!' Gwen couldn't help saying it. She had to protect her sister's marriage . . . as well as her own. 'You won't listen to reason, but please don't go telling Dougal what you've got in your stupid mind! You'll only turn him against Nicky . . . and Marge never did anything wrong. I swear, Alistair, swear!'

Nostrils flaring, he inhaled deeply, then said, his finger on the photograph and enunciating each word clearly, 'Do you swear that Nicky is not that man's son?'

In her desperation, Gwen would have sworn to almost anything . . . except this, and she had to fight her rising nausea before she could say, 'Marge wasn't unfaithful to Dougal. Never, Alistair. I've sworn it dozens of times and it's the honest truth. Believe me, all Forvit would have known if she had been.'

'Maybe they did! Maybe it was only you that didn't know. I promise you, Gwen, if I ever see Marge again, I'm going to have it out with her. Now, I'm going out for a while to clear my head. I need to think.'

The door slammed behind him and she turned guiltily as David ran down the stairs. 'I'm sorry, Mum. I didn't think . . . I should have remembered.'

'It wasn't your fault, dear,' she said, wearily. 'Your father's been different since he came home from the war, and he doesn't like the idea of us keeping secrets from him. Don't worry about it, David. Everything will be all right.'

His clouded eyes cleared. 'Can I go out now? The rain's just about off.'

'It might be a good idea to tidy your bedroom a bit, the cupboard, at least. I'm sure there's a lot of stuff that you've grown out of and could be thrown out.'

She was relieved that he went back upstairs without arguing, and hoped that he and Leila wouldn't start discussing what had happened. The girl was old enough to see what had caused her father's anger, and perhaps wise enough to work out that her mother was not telling the truth. To take her own mind off things, Gwen cleared the table, washed up the dishes and then wielded the sweeping brush on the kitchen floor as if repelling an army. Why hadn't she remembered about the photographs? She didn't blame David, he hadn't dreamt . . . Nevertheless, the evidence of Ken Partridge's visits was there in black and white and there was no denying that.

Her innards tight with worry, she took a duster and the tin of Jamieson's wax polish from the cupboard and attacked the floor again. Some moments later, perhaps as a result of this physical effort, her fears eased a little. Even if Alistair asked the entire population of Forvit, no one could give him any scandal about Marge, not even if he went to the shop, because Marge had done nothing to give rise to any. It was *she*, his own wife, who could have set tongues wagging . . . but not a soul could have seen her on either of the nights she had been with Ken. They had been well away from the village.

Alistair stumbled slowly down the hill. He had sat by the tower for hours, agonizing, but he needed someone to talk to, so, still shaken by what he had learned, he now took the path towards the village. He had to find out whether or not Nicky was indeed 'Uncle Ken's' son, and the only person who could – or would – tell him, was Lexie. Glancing at his watch, he was pleased to see that she would be closing the shop in five minutes.

He walked a little quicker when he reached the road, and arrived at the shop as the last customer was leaving. 'Can I have a word with you, Lexie?' he asked, anxiously.

Nodding, she locked the door and led him through to the house. 'What's up, Alistair?' she asked when they were seated. 'I can see something's happened.'

Before he could tell her about the photographs David had unearthed, someone rapped loudly on the shop door. 'Ignore it,' she sighed. 'Somebody always tries it on, and whoever it is, they'll just have to wait till tomorrow.'

But the caller, after another assault on the shop door, tramped round the side of the house, making them look at each other in dismay. 'I'd better answer it,' Lexie muttered when the heavy knock came at the porch.

'It's the bobby,' she said, unnecessarily, in a minute, ushering the tall policeman inside. 'He wants to use the phone, and I'll have to show him how the exchange works.'

Through the open door, he watched her fitting the bulky earphones on her head, picking up a lead and plugging it in and then winding the handle at the side for a few seconds. When the call was apparently answered, she handed the earphones to the constable and waited for him to end his call before unplugging and switching off. Too far away to hear what was being said, Alistair did not have to contain his curiosity very long before they came through from the shop again, both looking somewhat agitated.

'He had to report to Aberdeen,' Lexie said, her voice trembling. 'They've found a body in the moor, not far from the back of the Jubilee Hall.'

'Good God!' Alistair exclaimed. 'I did hear somebody saying there were diggers working there. What . . .'

'They're clearing a site for building new houses, but . . .' She broke off, then added, 'They say it's not big enough for a man, so it must be a woman.'

Relief coursed through Alistair. For a moment, he had feared that they had found her father. He turned to the policeman. 'Have you any idea who it is?'

'Not yet.' Magnus Robbie, from the Police House in Bankside and usually referred to behind his back as Bobby Robbie, sat heavily down on a chair. 'It'll need to be examined first, afore they can say for sure it *is* a woman and how lang she's been there.' He took out his handkerchief and mopped his brow and neck. 'I'd a right turn, I can tell you. It's my first murder, and she's nae a bonnie sight. I'd say she's been there for a good few year, though I could be wrong. They'll need to ken if any women ever went missing.'

Alistair looked at Lexie apologetically. 'What about Nancy Lawrie? You always said your father wouldn't have run away with her.'

'It . . . might be her.' Lexie sounded somewhat hesitant. 'She did disappear, but that was nearly twenty years ago.'

'I've only been up here for about ten year,' observed Robbie, 'so I dinna ken what went on afore that. Did any other women ever disappear?'

After considering this carefully, Lexie shook her head. 'Nobody that I know of.'

Robbie shook his head hopelessly. 'I suppose it could be a gypsy. I've heard they used to come to Dotterton, and that's nae far . . . five mile at the most. Less, if somebody wasna wanting to be seen and come through the woods.'

Looking a bit happier about things, he stood up. 'That's what it must be. Them gyppos have quick tempers, and . . . well, if one found his woman wi' another man, he might have stabbed her in the heat of the minute and then had to get rid o' the body.'

Alistair nodded. 'If it was years ago, you might never find out who she is . . . was.'

'No, they shift aboot like ants, but a Detective Inspector's coming up from Aberdeen, so it's nae up to me to find out who did it. I'd better get back to the scene o' the crime.'

When Robbie left, Alistair regarded Lexie in some concern. 'You're as white as a sheet. D'you want me to stay with you for a while till you get over the shock?'

She gave a semblance of a smile. 'I'm all right. I thought at first it might have been my father's body, so I was glad when Robbie said it was a woman, but it can't have been anybody from round here. Who'd have wanted to kill Nancy Lawrie? She was only about seventeen, and nobody else went missing.

Go home, Alistair, I'm OK, and Gwen's likely wondering where you are.'

He hadn't the heart to mention his own problem, not after what she had just been through, and so he took his leave, giving her a comforting pat on the shoulder as she saw him out. He didn't really believe that she was all right; he was far from all right himself. Hearing about that body had given him a bit of a shock, too. Whoever she was, the dead woman had been somebody's daughter, or girlfriend, or wife, and even if she *had* been a gypsy, being murdered and buried in a moor was no way to end up.

His mind jumping like a grasshopper, he wondered if he had made something out of nothing with regard to the snap of the man his son had obviously been quite fond of. While he, himself, had been far from home, he had accepted invitations to the homes of a few girls he had met, had been made very welcome by their parents, had felt happy to be part of a family for even a short space of time. He had done nothing out of place with any of them, so why should he think the worst of this 'Uncle Ken'? And, now that he came to think of it, he had never told Gwen about those friendships, either, so she wasn't the only one to have kept secrets. It was Marge who had betrayed her husband, and although he didn't like the idea of Dougal being cuckolded and even worse, fooled into believing he was a father, it was probably best all round for him to hold his tongue.

Gwen was still sitting by the fire when he went in, her face showing evidence of prolonged weeping. 'I'm sorry, darling,' he said, holding out his arms to her.

She jumped up and ran into them, and while he held her tightly, he told her that he had spent a long time at the tower thinking, then he'd gone to see Lexie.

'I thought that's where you'd go,' his wife said, tremulously. 'What did she say?'

'I didn't get round to asking her,' he admitted, and told her about Magnus Robbie's visit. 'He'd to report a body being found.'

'A body?' she gasped. 'Do they know who . . . ?'

'I thought it might have been Alec Fraser – Lexie's father – and so did she at first, but apparently it's a woman, and the bobby says it could be a gypsy.'

He told her about the platonic friendships he had made during the war and went on, 'So you see, I wasn't any different from that Ken, was I? It was . . . well, Marge . . .'

'I told you, Alistair,' Gwen said, relieved that he had stopped being so aggressive, 'there was never anything other than friendship between Marge and Ken. I swear it! And she never wrote to him after he was posted.'

Going by the years of the Finnies' childlessness, the colour of the boy's hair, plus the fact that Lexie had said it could have been Marge with the soldier, Alistair was more convinced than ever about her guilt, but he said, 'OK, we'll leave it at that.'

In bed that night, listening to Alistair's deep steady breathing, Gwen was thankful that he had dropped the subject, but she was well aware that he hadn't changed his mind. The problem was, although he obviously hadn't the slightest suspicion that it was his own wife who was Nicky's mother, if he ever told Dougal that *he* wasn't the boy's father, she would have to own up, and take the consequences.

Unable to sleep, Lexie was turning things over in her mind. Nancy Lawrie, out of all the women who had ever left Forvit, was the only one unaccounted for. If, as the gossips had said at the time, she had been expecting Alec Fraser's baby, had she told him about it? If she had – Lexie's blood ran cold at the thought – would he have killed her to keep it from his wife and fled in shame? It would be the natural reaction . . . but her father would never have killed anybody . . . whatever else he had done.

But . . . he *had* run away. With no clothes. No money. Not even his bank book!

Chapter 25

The funerals – Rosie being interred with her beloved Tiny, and Alf in the adjacent part of the double lair which she had thoughtfully purchased to accommodate her entire family – had been heart-wrenching for all of them, but Peggy, having lost her husband as well as her mother, was harder hit than her sisters. Dougal and Alistair did their best to comfort all three, but there were also the younger members of the family to consider.

Although no longer a child, and blossoming out as a woman, Leila couldn't stop crying. She had loved her grandmother and had missed her deeply when they moved away from her again. But she had also thought a great deal of her Auntie Peg and Uncle Alf, and couldn't bear the idea of one without the other.

David, still a boy, had tried to behave like the man he wanted to be, and had successfully hidden his grief until his grandmother's coffin was being lowered into its final resting place beside the grandfather he could not remember. Then he had to let it out, scrubbing his cheeks with his handkerchief in great mortification until he managed to stem his tears.

Nicky could not quite take in the fact that he would never see his Nanna again, nor his Uncle Alf, who had often slipped him a tanner to buy sweets, but the strained atmosphere in whichever house he happened to find himself over the past few days had effectively subdued his loud boyish treble.

At the funeral tea, Gwen was in constant dread that Ivy Crocker – who had come all the way from Newcastle on her own – would let it slip that she had been present at Nicky's birth and lay bare the secret his biological mother was struggling to keep from Alistair and Dougal, and she felt faint with relief when the seventy-year-old just clasped her hand for slightly longer than was necessary before leaving. She should have known that she could depend on her old friend not to let her down.

She desperately wanted to warn Marge that David had let the cat out of the bag about Ken Partridge's visits, but they never had a chance to be on their own. If their husbands took the children out of the way for a while, Peggy was always hovering somewhere near and she, too, had to be kept in the dark. She had more than enough to cope with already.

Gwen's worst fear, however, was that Alistair might inadvertently say something to Dougal about Ken, perhaps mention that he had ginger hair and thus sow suspicion in his friend's mind, even though he had promised not to.

Despite her sorrow, despite not wanting to leave Peggy just yet, she was glad when Alistair said, on the second evening after the funeral, 'We'd better go home tomorrow. If the shop's shut too long, customers might think it's shut for good.'

'You put a card in the door saying "Closed due to family bereavement",' Leila reminded him, 'so they'll know you'll be back.'

'But it's best not to stay away too long.'

The leave-taking was the hardest any of them had ever had to endure, the emotional kisses and long embraces seemed to go on for ever, even David lingering inside the group as if that would delay the parting, and it took the arrival of the taxi Alistair had ordered to take them to King's Cross to finally make the split.

* * *

Lying back in the carriage, Alistair closed his eyes and, because of the tension of the past few days, he soon fell asleep, and it was some time later, he didn't know how long, when he became aware of where he was and why. Reluctant to talk, however, he kept his eyes shut and let his thoughts return to Lee Green. Each time he had been alone with Dougal, he had been sorely tempted to tell him the truth about Nicky, but it would have been barbaric to inflict further heartache on the family – it would have affected every single one of them. He had tried to keep his manner to Marge as civil as he could, and even if he'd had to count to ten occasionally, they'd all been too upset about Rosie and Alf to notice.

If he'd been there any longer, though, the slightest thing could have lit the fuse of his anger at Marge for betraying her husband. It wasn't fair to Dougal to let it run on, and there would come a time when he wouldn't be able to hold his tongue, but it hadn't been possible to say anything in the circumstances. Besides, he had given his promise to Gwen.

'Mum, d'you think Auntie Peggy'll ever get over losing Alf?'

Leila's voice suddenly got through to him, and he listened listlessly to see how his wife would answer.

'She'll never forget him, if that's what you mean,' Gwen murmured, 'but she will get over his death eventually.'

'It was awful Grandma dying like that, too. Auntie Marge must have had a terrible shock.'

'Your Auntie Marge is a much stronger person than Peg. She can cope with anything, and she'll help her baby sister to get over things.'

'Baby sister?' Leila laughed. 'Auntie Peg's not a baby now.'

'Marge and I always looked on her as our baby sister, and it annoyed her. When she was still at school, she wanted to do the things we did, but our Dad wouldn't allow it.'

'Boyfriends and that, d'you mean?'

Gwen laughed softly. 'You probably won't believe it, but Marge never had a boyfriend till she met Dougal.'

'What about you, Mum? Was Dad your only one?'

After a brief hesitation, Gwen said, 'No, I did go out with another boy first, but it was all over before I knew your Dad.'

Having known this anyway, Alistair was glad that Gwen was being honest with their daughter. That was the difference between her and Marge. *She* would never tell lies, or do anything she might be ashamed of later . . . whereas Marge . . .

The low voices carried on, but it was only when Nicky's name filtered into his semiconsciousness that he listened properly, wanting to know what Leila was saying about the boy. 'He's not so naughty as he was in Forvit. Don't you think so, Mum?'

'He's that bit older,' Gwen explained. 'I thought he was going to be a ragamuffin like David used to be, but he was never as bad as that, I don't think.'

Wondering why David wasn't objecting to this slur on him, Alistair took a cautious peep out of the eye farthest from his wife. David was fast asleep, which was why his mother had said what she did.

Nothing was said for another few moments, then Leila murmured, 'Mum, can I ask you something? About Nicky.'

'Yes, dear, of course you can.'

Discerning a hint of apprehension in his wife's voice, Alistair strained to hear.

'I couldn't help thinking . . .' Leila went on, '. . . he's awfully like . . . Uncle Ken.'

'That's only because of his red hair.'

'But his eyes are the same green as Uncle Ken's, and he . . .'

What Leila was about to add was never said, because Gwen interrupted. 'Wake up, David, we're coming into York. If you're thirsty, you'll get something at the trolley on the platform.'

The boy jumped up at once. 'Are you coming, Leila?'

'No, I'm too sleepy.'

Through all the squealing of brakes, banging of carriage doors and other loud noises, Alistair still feigned sleep. What he had just heard had convinced him that his suspicions were well founded. Gwen's abrupt interruption of Leila's questioning had been too fortuitous to be coincidence. She'd been afraid of what the girl might say, and if they hadn't arrived in York, she'd have roused David on some other pretext. It dawned on Alistair now that Leila might have been old enough at the time to twig that something was going on between Marge and her soldier 'friend' – kids were a lot more perceptive than adults gave them credit for – and was only just beginning to understand what it was. But he had better not ask her anything.

It was Leila and Gwen who slept all the way to Edinburgh, although Alistair suspected that his wife was shamming, as he had been earlier, but David, his usual inquisitive self again, kept asking about the places they were passing and gave him no space to think.

Lexie's heart sank when Magnus Robbie walked into the shop for the first time since the discovery of the body. 'Have they found something else?' she asked, still not convinced that it wasn't her father. 'Are they still sure it's a woman?'

Robbie took off his hat and gave his head a thorough scratch before answering. 'They are that, and the coroner's report says she's been dead for anything from ten to twenty years, so they're putting out an appeal to find that lassie you spoke aboot.'

'Nancy Lawrie?'

'That's her. Apparently, she disappeared in 1929, so I dinna ken aboot you, Lexie, but my money's on her.'

'No, I'm nearly sure it's not her, I don't know why. It's just a feeling I've got.'

The policeman regarded his chubby fingers for a second, then pronounced, in his more official tongue, 'But the law doesn't work on feelings, Lexie. It's facts that's needed – indispupital . . . indist . . . facts that naebody can argue aboot. Proof! Absolute proof!'

She managed to ignore his lapse in pronunciation, if lapse it was; he wasn't very bright at the best of times. 'How do they expect to get proof, then?'

He looked somewhat put out at being expected to know this. 'The proof . . .' he began, stopped and started again. 'The proof is in the eating.'

'What?' Lexie took a moment to fathom out this ridiculous statement. 'Oh! It's the proof of the *pudding* that's in the eating,' she corrected, gathering that he must have been in the bar earlier. 'The proof of a crime . . .'

'The proof of a crime is the body,' he butted in, stiffly. 'A buried body suggests a murder, and murder . . . is . . . a . . . crime.' He looked at her triumphantly.

'Yes, I know, but you need . . .'

'We need proof of . . . um . . . identity. You wouldna happen to know where that Nancy's folk flitted to, would you?'

'No, they didn't tell . . .' Lexie glanced at the door as the bell tinkled. 'Oh, it's you, Aggie. Do you know where the Lawries went? Nancy's Mam and Dad? The police want to find them.'

Clearly flattered at being asked, Mrs Mearns drew herself up to her full, well-padded four feet eleven. 'No, it was like they disappeared off the face o' the earth and all. Of course, Nettie was black affronted that Nancy'd got hersel' in the family way . . .' It occurring to her who the presumptive father had been, she slid easily into another tack. 'I tell you what, though. If I mind right, somebody once tell't me Ina McConnachie up at Leyton kept in touch wi' Nettie, so you'd better ask her . . .' The policeman having already gone, she stopped in mid-sentence and turned to Lexie with a sigh. 'He's useless, that ane. I coulda tell't him that days ago if he'd asked.'

'He's doing his best. Now, what can I do for you today?'

The door opening to admit Mattie Wilkie, Mrs Mearns laid a scribbled shopping list on the counter and left the shopkeeper to get on with it. Lexie couldn't help smiling at her exaggerated version of her brief encounter with Bobby Robbie, and kept her ears open when they lowered their voices.

'It must be Nancy Lawrie,' Mattie said, in a hoarse almost-stage whisper. 'The time's aboot right. D'you think . . . um . . . *he* . . . could've . . . ?'

Aggie gave this idea, new to her, her deepest consideration for a few moments. 'It hardly seems like him, but you never ken. They said yon Dr Crippen was as nice a man as you could meet.'

Outraged at this, Lexie felt like letting fly at them, but they were customers, after all, and she had been taught that the customer is always right. Not these two, though.

Fortunately, Mattie came up with another rumour which was circulating. 'I heard ane o' them tecs saying it could be a gypsy woman.'

'Ach!' Aggie snorted. 'They're aye saying something, and they ken damn all!'

'Lizzie says she heard somebody had seen a couple o' gypsies fighting one night up by the moor, a man and a woman, aboot the right time, it was.'

'How could onybody mind what happened twenty year ago?'

Lexie gathered from Aggie's tone that the idea of it just being a gypsy's body wasn't nearly as exciting as the possibility of having known the person concerned.

Mattie gave it one last try. 'It could be onybody. If he'd a car, a man could bury a body hunders o' miles away from where he killed it. Look at that Buck Ruxton doon in England some place. He killed his wife and their maid and drove them up to Scotland to dump them in a burn.'

'They wasna lang in being found, though, and he was a foreigner, an Indian or something, nae English.' Having lost interest in the discussion, the postman's wife turned to Lexie. 'Is that it?' She handed over a pound note, then said, 'If you're nae needin' a lot, Mattie, I'll wait and walk along the road wi' you.'

They had not been gone long when Detective Inspector Roderick Liddell walked in. In charge of the case, he had been using Lexie's parlour as a makeshift incident room. He hadn't bothered her much, but she didn't think she would have minded if he had.

'May I use your phone again, Miss Fraser?' he asked. 'I expect you know we've been trying to trace Mr and Mrs Lawrie, the parents of . . .'

'Nancy. Yes, I know. Did you get anything from Mrs McConnachie at Leyton?'

'She gave us an address, but she wasn't sure if they were still there, or if they were still alive. It's some years since she was in touch with Mrs Lawrie.'

'I hope you find them.'

'Yes, I suppose you must want to know, one way or the other.'

She nodded, not actually sure that she did want to know, after all.

* * *

Gwen Ritchie was anything but contented – she was alone at Benview for most of the day and missed Marge's cheery chatter. Leila was working with her father in Aberdeen, and the shop didn't close until six. This meant making something for David, who came in from school around five and went out about half an hour later on some pretext or other, and having another meal ready at seven for herself and the 'workers'.

Leila generally hurried through hers, then gave herself a quick wash, a puff of powder and a dab of lipstick before cycling off to meet her friends. Which left her, Gwen mused, the cook, the laundress, the cleaner, alone with her husband, which was anything but comfortable for her. She could tell that something was smouldering under the surface of his overpolite exterior. He hadn't mentioned Marge, nor Nicky, nor Ken Partridge since they came back from Lee Green, but something about him made her edgy; nothing definite, nothing she could challenge him with, just the suggestion of doubt on his face at times and, more often, the almost-accusing way he regarded her.

The peculiar looks Leila gave her occasionally also disquieted her, as if her daughter was turning something over in her mind, and that, too, could only be to do with Nicky. Sure that things were building up against her, Gwen seriously considered making a clean breast of everything to her husband and facing up to the consequences – they couldn't be worse than this constant dread of an eruption that would blow everything sky-high.

Detective Inspector Liddell looked apologetically at Lexie when she opened the door to him for the second time that day. 'I hope I'm not disturbing you, Miss Fraser?'

'Is there some news at last?' she asked, anxiously.

'A bit of a setback, actually. According to the coroner the

woman was between thirty-five and forty, so that rules out Nancy Lawrie. We haven't managed to trace her parents yet, I'm afraid. They had moved from the address we were given. We still hope to get a result from our appeal for information on her, of course, even if it won't help us to identify the body. We have begun the next line of enquiry – the gypsies – but they have their own methods of punishing the wrongdoers amongst them, which do not include bringing in the police. I've the feeling that we're wasting our time there, but I'll keep you informed if anything does transpire. I'm sorry to have intruded, Miss Fraser.'

He turned to go, but Lexie said quickly, 'You're very welcome to stay for a cup of tea, Inspector, I'd be glad of the company. That is, if you don't have to go somewhere else?'

'Nowhere else tonight, but if we're to be drinking tea together, wouldn't it be more friendly to call me Roddy?'

'Only if you call me Lexie,' she smiled. Their eyes suddenly locked, but in a moment, she dropped hers in confusion and rose to put the kettle on to boil. She had felt drawn towards this man from the first time he came asking the questions he had to ask. He couldn't believe that no search had been made for her father and Nancy at the time, even when she said she'd been told it was such a common occurrence it was a waste of police time.

'You have never believed that your father was with the girl?' he asked, as she set out the cups and saucers.

It was as if their minds were on the same planet, she thought. 'Never, and I never will, unless he comes and tells me himself.'

'Maybe he will, Lexie, some day. There has been no response yet to the posters that have been put up in every police station in Scotland for information about her. They say that she went missing from Forvit, Aberdeenshire in May 1929. It's better that we concentrate on her for now,' he explained, 'because, if they *are* together, there's the chance that if we find her, we'll also find him, but if that fails, we will make a separate search for your father, in the hope that he can tell us where she is.'

Noticing how grim his expression was now, a wave of horror swept over her, and she was almost afraid to ask, 'Roddy, you think he . . . killed her, don't you?'

To her immense relief, he shook his head. 'It's a possibility, of course, but somehow I don't think so.'

The shrilling of the telephone startled her, and she ran through to the shop, the Inspector at her heels. 'It's for you,' she said, handing him the earphones.

He listened intently for some moments, then said, crisply, 'I'll be there as soon as I can.' He turned to her. 'I'm sorry, Lexie. Something has cropped up.'

He didn't say what, and she didn't like to ask.

Chapter 26

With David also working with his father, Gwen was alone from 7.15 a.m. until 6.45 p.m. five days a week, and until 1.30 p.m. on Saturdays, wondering sometimes where the years had gone. One minute, her son had been a tousle-headed, cheeky-faced podge, the next, it seemed, he was a tall, slim young man, hair slicked back with his father's Imperial Leather brilliantine, his voice varying from treble to bass. But she eventually got more or less used to the change in him and to the long days without a soul for company.

One balmy August day, she had her usual lonely sandwich at half past twelve, then went out to wage war on the weeds in the garden, and had been at it for less than an hour when she heard a vehicle coming up the track. Apart from Alistair's old Austin and the postman's van – Sandy Mearns didn't have to do his round on a bicycle any longer – this was so unusual that she stopped what she was doing and waited for it to come into sight. It turned out to be a big black car which reminded her of the one Dougal had driven when they were in London for the funerals, then her heart leapt. It *was* Dougal's Ford. Marge was in the front passenger seat, waving excitedly to her, and Nicky was in the back seat with his head poking out of the window, and . . . yes! Peggy was sitting beside him.

She rushed forward to embrace her sisters, then she was hugging her secret son close to her, smiling somewhat wryly at his, 'Are you glad to see us, Auntie Gwen?'

'Of course I am, dear. Oh, Marge, why didn't you let me know you were coming?'

'Didn't know myself,' Marge chuckled. 'We were just touring and Peggy mentioned she'd like to see Edinburgh, and being so far north, Forvit kept calling to me.'

By the time Alistair, Leila and David came home, furniture had been shuttled around, beds changed, sleeping arrangements made and – Dougal and Nicky having gone to the village for more supplies – a huge meal had been prepared.

Nothing of any consequence was said while they dined, and as soon as they finished, Leila jumped to her feet. 'I'm meeting Barry at eight, Mum, but I won't be late home.'

It was Marge who grinned, 'The postman's boy? Don't keep him waiting, dear, but just make sure you don't do anything I wouldn't do.'

'That gives her a pretty wide scope.' It had come out without Alistair thinking, and he tried to pretend he'd been joking by giving her a broad wink.

'We'll take the boys out for an hour to let you tidy up.' Dougal's voice had a tightness in it. 'That's if you haven't got a date, as well, David?'

'A date? With a girl? Who, me?' David's shocked expression made them all laugh.

Desperate to get Marge on her own, Gwen said, 'Why don't you go with them, Peg?'

'No, thanks,' Peggy retorted. 'I'd rather do dishes than plough through heather and ladder all my stockings.'

The three sisters had plenty to discuss – Rosie had left her house to Gwen, and both Marge and Peggy wanted her to persuade Alistair to come back to London. 'It would be a waste of time,' she told them, 'his shop's established now, and this is where he wants to be. He was born and brought up in this house, and . . .'

'Oh, Gwennie!' Peggy burst out. 'It would be lovely if all

three of us could be together again.' Emotional tears coming to her eyes, she murmured, 'I'd better go to bed. See you in the morning.'

Gwen waited until she heard the upstairs door being closed. 'She still hasn't got over Alf and Mum, has she? But I'm glad she's gone, so I can tell you the bad news at last.'

A crease furrowed Marge's smooth forehead. 'What bad news?'

'Do you remember Ken Partridge giving David a camera?'

'Yes of course, and he took some jolly good snaps.'

'Yes, of all of us . . . including Ken.'

It took a minute for the significance of this to sink in. 'You mean he showed them to Alistair? How awful for you. What did you . . . ?'

'He got it all wrong. He asked David what colour Ken's hair was, and he's convinced it was you and Ken . . .'

'Good Lord, Gwen! Good Lord!'

'I swore to him that you'd never been unfaithful to Dougal . . .'

'Which was the truth.' Marge's smile was a little crooked.

'But he won't believe it. He's positive . . . you and Ken . . .'

'He's not likely to tell Dougal, is he?'

'I don't know, honestly. When we were there for the funerals, he promised me he wouldn't say anything, but now they're out together, God knows . . .'

'He wouldn't say anything in front of the boys?'

'He's been so different since he came home from the war, I don't know what he'll do.'

'Well, Gwendoline, I'm afraid the only thing we can do is keep our fingers crossed. I doubt if even God would help us now, after the things we did.'

'Oh, Marge,' Gwen gulped, 'I don't know how you can be so calm.'

'Getting in a paddy's not going to change anything, is it?'

* * *

With David pointing out rabbit holes to Nicky, explaining about the lichen on the trees, showing him a badger's sett, and generally keeping well away from the two men, Alistair decided to take the bull by the horns. It was now . . . or never! 'Nicky's getting to be a nice looking lad,' he began.

'Aye,' laughed Dougal, 'nothing like his father, eh?'

'No, nothing like *you*,' Alistair said quietly, then added, 'but very like his father.'

Dougal's face darkened. 'What the hell d'you mean by that?'

'I'm sorry, but I think it's time you knew. His father was a soldier Marge met during the war. He was stationed at Ardley House and they . . .'

'For Christ's sake, man! You're mad! Absolutely raving. I was home on leave . . .'

Alistair nodded morosely. 'Round about the right time? What if you were? How long had you been married without having any children? Have you never had doubts?'

'Never. Christ, Ally, I trusted Marge. She wouldn't have been unfaithful . . .'

'Wouldn't she? I'll have to get David to show you the snaps he took.'

'Photographs won't prove anything.'

'Wait till you see them.' Alistair had heard the doubt creeping into Dougal's voice and recognized it dawning in his eyes. He didn't relish what he was doing, but it had to be done. No man worth his salt could let his best friend go through life thinking he had a son when he hadn't. He should be grateful.

Each wrapped in his own thoughts – Alistair in self-righteousness, Dougal in outraged disbelief and anger – they made the walk back without saying another word, except if either of the boys asked them something.

* * *

The minute the men walked in, both wives could tell that something was wrong between them, and when Alistair asked David to bring down his old snaps, Gwen knew that this was it for her. She sought for Marge's hand to reassure her that *she* had no need to worry, but when Dougal went to the bathroom and Alistair's attention was on David, who had brought down the photographs, her sister managed to whisper, 'Leave all the talking to me, Gwennie.'

Waiting until Dougal came back, Marge said, brightly, 'May I see those snaps after you, please? David took them during the war and I'd completely forgotten about them.'

Gwen held her breath. Dougal's expression had lightened, but Alistair's was darker than ever, and he said, harshly, 'I'm surprised you forgot about your lover.'

Marge laughed gaily. 'My lover? Ken Partridge? He was never my lover. Yes, he came to the cottage nearly every week when he was stationed at Ardley, but only as a friend. He told us about his wife and family, and we told him about you two. And he was ever so good with Leila and David, giving them presents and . . .'

Trying to dispel the unpleasantness he could sense but couldn't understand, David butted in. 'He taught me how to hold a cricket bat properly, and how to bowl, and . . .'

His father turned on him angrily. 'Stay out of it, David! You don't know anything about this, so go upstairs and keep Nicky from coming down.'

The boy blanched and spun round, giving a last appealing glance at his mother before slamming the door behind him, but before she could say anything, Marge, who had been flicking through the photographs, held up the one which had caused all the trouble. 'Is this what's bothering you, Alistair?'

He seemed uncomfortable now. 'Well, do you see how he's looking at you? Like you were the only person in the world to him?'

'We were playing the fool for David,' she laughed. 'I said something funny and Ken was laughing at me, that's all.'

Alistair scowled. 'That maybe explains the photo, but it doesn't explain . . .' He broke off to take a deep breath. 'Can you deny that *he* . . .' he jabbed his finger on the shiny black and white card, 'is . . . Nicky's . . . father?' He turned desperately to Dougal. 'Look at it, man. Can't you see the resemblance? And David says *he* had ginger hair, as well!'

Gwen could stand it no longer. 'That's enough,' she said quietly. 'You're absolutely right. Ken *was* Nicky's father, but it's not Marge you should be accusing, it's me.'

Her husband whipped round to face her, the wounded shock in his eyes tearing at her heart. 'You? What in God's name are you saying?'

Marge stepped in again. 'Don't listen to her, Alistair! She's covering for me, but I admit it! Ken Partridge *was* my lover!'

'It's not true!' Gwen cried. 'It was me!' She gulped and ended, 'I'm Nicky's real mother, and . . . Ken Partridge is his real father.'

The two men exchanged utterly shocked, perplexed looks, obviously wondering which of the women to believe, then Alistair said, bitterly, 'Gwen's telling the truth, Dougal. She wouldn't tell a lie like that.' His head drooped for a few seconds before he addressed himself to his sister-in-law. 'I can't tell you how sorry I am for causing you all this trouble, Marge, but I honestly did think . . .'

'It's all right,' she told him, 'I can see why you made the mistake, but Gwen wasn't to blame for what happened. I made Ken take her out for a walk, and I should have realized they were both too vulnerable. He was going home on embarkation leave so it was his last night here, and . . . well, she was upset about not hearing from you for so long, and surely . . . you can understand . . . and forgive?'

He glared at her and spat out, 'I can neither understand, nor forgive. The pair of you have made a fool of me all this time, and . . . oh God!' He shot a look of what might have been apology at his old friend and barged out.

Dougal regarded the two women with distaste. 'What am I supposed to do now? I've just learned that my son's not my son, and my wife isn't even his mother.' He glowered at Marge. 'That *is* true, I take it?' Her mute nod made him continue, 'Am I expected to carry on as if nothing had happened? Or am I meant to hand the boy over to Gwen? Damn it all, Marge! I love that kid! I can't just turn my back on him because you two played silly games when he was born. If Alistair hadn't seen that snap and stumbled on the truth, he wouldn't have been any the wiser, and no more would I.'

'That's true,' she admitted. 'And don't blame Gwen for that, either. It was my idea that she should hand her baby over to me – in fact, the whole plan was my idea.'

'I'll leave you to explain everything,' Gwen interrupted. 'I'd better go after Alistair.'

Guessing where her husband would be headed, she went up the rough track. She had been relieved when Dougal said that he loved Nicky – it meant that he wouldn't need much persuading to take the boy back to London – and she was almost sure that he and Marge could sort out their differences. After all, *she* hadn't been unfaithful. Her only sin lay in claiming that the child was hers and Dougal's.

Gwen had to go all the way up the hill before she saw Alistair, squatting on the stony ground beside the tower. 'I'm so sorry,' she muttered, stroking the crown of his head.

'Don't touch me!' he growled, jumping up and pushing her. 'How could you let me go on believing it was Marge, when all the time it was you! You and a ginger-headed soldier!

Get out of my sight, for I don't want you anywhere near me! Ever again!'

He gave her another shove, and knowing that any argument or attempt at explanation would be useless, she turned and retraced her steps. She deserved his scorn, his disgust. She had known all along, right from the night it happened, that Alistair would never forgive her if he found out.

She would have to face up to life without him . . . and probably without her children, too. All three of them.

Chapter 27

Lexie was on her way to lock the shop door when a woman with a vaguely familiar face walked in. 'My goodness!' the incomer exclaimed. 'It's not Lexie, is it?'

'Yes, I'm Lexie Fraser, but . . . ?'

'You likely won't remember me. Nancy Lawrie . . .'

Her legs buckling, Lexie grabbed at the wooden counter. This was something she had never imagined, not in any of the various scenarios she'd played over in her mind. Was she about to learn where her father was?

The other woman was looking at her in some concern. 'Are you all right? I heard the police want to talk to me, but I wanted a quick word with Alec first. Is he handy?'

With a low moan, Lexie slid to her knees and, Nancy, running round the counter in consternation, half-lifted her on to the courtesy chair. 'I don't know what's wrong, but . . . look, I waited till nearly closing time, so what if I lock up and make some tea for you?'

Not waiting for an answer, she stepped back to turn the key in the lock, and then led her charge through to the house. While the tea was being made for her, Lexie took stock of her visitor. Nancy's figure was fuller than when she was a girl, but she still had the same almost jet black hair, with just a few silver strands showing in it, although it had been cut into a neat bob instead of hanging loose to her shoulders. Her face was rounder than Lexie remembered, her cheeks not quite so rosy, but her brown eyes were still as dark, with perhaps a hint of sadness in them now. That was natural, Lexie mused, for this must be the first time she'd come back to the village which had once been her home, and twenty years was a long time to be away, however well she was wearing.

'Are you feeling any better?' Nancy asked, handing her a steaming cup.

'Yes, thanks. I'm sorry I was . . .'

'It was my fault, a ghost from the past, but I only want to see your father.'

Lexie's mouth went dry again. 'He's not still with you?'

'Still?' Nancy was clearly puzzled. 'He never *was* with me, you should know that.'

Trying to swallow the bitter bile burning her throat, Lexie whispered, 'Didn't he run away to be with you?'

'Me and Alec? What on earth made you think that, Lexie?'

'They all said you were expecting to him, and that's why . . .'

'So the gossips got it cockeyed as usual. I *was* expecting, that was right, but not to Alec. He's the finest man I ever knew.'

This was not how his daughter regarded him, Lexie thought. He had abandoned his wife and child, whoever he had gone off with. There was still something she wanted answered, however, although she could scarcely bring herself to speak. 'But . . .,' she croaked, '. . . who was the father?'

Her face flushing, Nancy murmured, 'Tom Birnie.'

'The doctor?' Lexie gasped, unable to believe this.

So the story was told of how a forty-year-old doctor had taken advantage of a naïve seventeen-year-old girl, had sworn that he loved her, and she had believed every word.

'A month or so after I told him I was pregnant,' Nancy went on, 'he rented a room in Edinburgh for me, and said he'd come to see me as often as he could. He promised to marry me and buy us a decent house after his wife divorced him.'

'Did he keep any of his promises?'

'He came to see me once, then his wife's mother took ill, and she went to Stirling to look after her, so he wrote saying he couldn't tell her about me till the old woman was better. That was the last I heard from him.'

'I wouldn't have thought Dr Birnie would be so . . . after he said he loved you?'

Nancy blew a derogatory raspberry. 'Some men swear they love a girl to get their evil way with her, but I was lucky, in a way. Tom had paid three months' rent for the room, and I got a job at the sheet music counter in Princes Street Woolies – that paid my keep and let me save a wee bit every week. The landlady, Mrs Will, was really good. When I'd to stop working, she let me have free board for helping in the house – she had other lodgers, you see – but she didn't really need help. She was a wee ball of energy.'

The tale went on and Lexie learned that when the baby was born, Mrs Will had looked after it so that Nancy could take another job. 'Was it a boy or a girl?' she asked.

'A boy. I called him Alexander, after your father.'

Lexie's heart, and her stomach, plummeted rapidly. If people knew that Nancy had called her son Alexander, they would be in no doubt as to who the father had been, but Nancy had noticed her discomfiture. 'I didn't know what to do when I found out I was expecting,' she explained, hastily. 'Tom swore it couldn't be his and I knew Ma and Da would wash their hands of me if they knew, so I was at my wits' end. Alec noticed I was crying one day and when he asked what was wrong, I just came out with it. He took me to Tom's house and threatened to tell his wife if he didn't take responsibility for what he'd done. That's what made

Tom get me the room, and I want to let your father know that things didn't turn out too badly for me, after all.'

'But he's not here!' Lexie burst out. 'He never came home from choir practice the night after you disappeared. That's why we all thought he'd gone to be with you.'

'But . . . but . . .' Nancy floundered, 'I didn't know. You've never heard from him?'

'Not a word, and it was really the finish of my mother. She was never very strong, if you remember, and after Dad went away, she just pined and pined. She'd nothing left in her to fight the cancer.'

A silence fell between them as her words dried up, each trying to find a reason why Alec Fraser had left his family, and two full minutes had passed when a loud rapping on the porch door made them both jump. 'I can't speak to anybody now,' Lexie whispered.

A second knock was followed by a man saying softly, 'Lexie?'

'It's the Detective Inspector,' she said in relief, rising to let him in.

Roddy Liddell came straight to the point when he saw her companion. 'You're Nancy Lawrie, I take it?'

'How did you know . . . ?'

'Someone told Constable Robbie that she had seen you going into the Post Office, so I came to make sure there was no mistake.'

'No mistake.' Nancy's smile, however, was somewhat forced. 'I can't think why the police want to see me, though, not after twenty years.'

'Yes, a search for you should have been instigated at the time,' he admitted.

With no prompting, Nancy launched into a brief outline of her story, after which he leaned back, sighing. 'I originally thought it was your body we'd found.' Nancy's strangled gasp made him add, 'I'm sorry. You obviously don't know about that.'

'I hadn't got round to telling her,' Lexie defended herself, 'and I always hoped it wasn't Nancy's, because it could have meant my father had killed her.'

Nancy took hold of her hand before saying, 'Alec hadn't it in him to kill a spider, let alone another human being. Your father was a gentleman, Lexie, a truly gentle man.'

Liddell politely refused Lexie's offer of tea, his mind too occupied with solving the crime. 'I wonder . . . ?' He looked at Nancy speculatively. 'Would there be any likelihood of the doctor – Birnie? – paying Lexie's father a large sum of money to keep his mouth shut and leave Forvit altogether?'

'I wouldn't put it past Tom to have tried,' Nancy said, 'but I can't see Alec taking it.'

'He wouldn't have taken money from anybody,' Lexie agreed.

'I remember you telling me that he hadn't even taken his bankbook with him,' the Inspector pointed out, 'and no money was missing from the shop or the church. Does that not suggest that he'd had ample funds to live on for some time? Of course, there's another side to the coin. Alec Fraser himself may have seen an opportunity to make some money. He could have blackmailed Birnie, threatened to get him struck off the medical register . . . a very lucrative, ongoing . . .'

He broke off, regarded the two outraged faces for a moment, then shook his head. 'I can see you don't think much of that idea, but you must agree that my best bet now is to find Birnie, and get the truth out of him.'

'If you're lucky,' Nancy put in. 'He doesn't know what truth is.'

Liddell turned to Lexie. 'We will keep up our appeal for information on your father's whereabouts . . .' He pulled pensively at his ear lobe. 'The thing is, twenty years on, it's going to be difficult, especially if he doesn't want to be found . . .' He got to his feet. 'I'll keep in touch, Lexie, and if either you or Miss Lawrie hear anything that could be of use, please let me know. No, don't get up, I'll see myself out.'

'He's nice,' Nancy remarked after he was gone, 'and he fancies you.'

'Don't be daft,' Lexie mumbled, but her blush revealed that she quite fancied him. 'It's getting late, you won't get a train back to Edinburgh from Aberdeen tonight. I'll make up a bed for you here, if you like.'

'No, it's all right. With that Inspector coming, I didn't get time to tell you the end of my story. After Alexander was born, I got a job in the office of a big furniture store, and . . . well, I married the manager a year later.'

Lexie clapped her hands. 'You're still together, I hope?'

'Still together and still in love . . . even after nearly eighteen years. We had a daughter – she'd have been fourteen in three weeks if she'd lived, but she died at three months.'

'Oh, Nancy, I'm so sorry.'

'It was hard at the time, but we got over the worst of it, and we had Alexander. Greig has been a wonderful father to him, and put him to George Herriot's and then on to St Andrews' University. He's studying law now, and seems to be doing very well.'

'So you're Mrs Greig . . . what?' Lexie wanted to know.

'I'm Mrs Greig Fleming, and proud of it.' Nancy gave a slightly embarrassed laugh. 'He's waiting in the hotel bar. He took me to Oldmeldrum to see my mother before we came to Forvit. You see, I started buying the *Aberdeen Press and Journal* to keep up with the north news, and I saw my father's death in it a few years ago. I took a note of the address, but I couldn't pluck up the courage to write to

Ma. Then, when I heard the bobbies were looking for me, Greig said we could do the two things in one go.'

'What did your mother say when she saw you?'

'She broke down, Lexie, and everything's just fine between us again. She asked us to go back and spend the night there.' She swallowed then continued, 'I'll only need to find out where Alec is to make my happiness complete.'

'The police are doing all they can.'

'Aye. Anyway, I'd better get going. Cheerio, Lexie, and I'll keep in touch.'

Of the six persons in Benview that night, one slept soundly, three somewhat fitfully and two didn't even try. Nicky was completely ignorant of the trauma which had laid bare the true facts of his birth, David and Leila suspected that trouble was brewing and Peggy had been aware before she went to bed that something was not as it should be. She would have been horrified to learn that her sisters had sat up all night wondering when their men would return, and, as time went on, *if* they would return at all.

'I'm nearly sure Dougal won't hold anything against me,' Marge observed at one point. 'He'll come round once he's got over the shock. He loves Nicky like he *was* his father, and that won't change.'

Gwen shook her head. 'Did you see Alistair's face when I said . . . He'd been so sure it was you who . . .' A sob came into her voice now. 'He thought it was his duty to let his old friend know the truth, and he didn't consider how Dougal would feel.'

'He knows how it feels himself now, though,' Marge said, somewhat drily. 'If only I hadn't interfered. I should have guessed what would happen. Both you and Ken in an emotional state and being paired off like that . . . it *had* to come. Don't blame yourself, Gwennie. If it had been me, I'd likely have done it months before.'

Gwen dabbed her eyes with the tight wad of damp handkerchief. 'I know you're trying to make me feel better, Marge, but it's not helping. There's no excuse for what I did and I'll have to take my punishment for it.'

'But it was me who made you hide it,' Marge burst out. 'I made you play along with a stupid plot that couldn't possibly stay hidden for ever . . .' She paused, then added, with a glimmer of a smile at her lips, '. . . though we might have got away with it if David hadn't kept those dashed snaps.'

'No, that wasn't what did it. Alistair has suspected for a long time that Dougal wasn't Nicky's father, but he never had any doubt about you being his mother. He . . . he trusted me, that's why he's so upset.'

Raising her eyebrows, Marge asked, 'Would you rather we hadn't pretended? Would you have preferred if I'd let you write to Alistair to tell him you'd had a baby to another man? Or would you have waited and sprung it on him when he came home?'

'I don't know. It would have hurt him just as much whenever I told him, wouldn't it?'

'Since we're being honest, I guess you're right. On the other hand, maybe it hit him harder because he practically found out for himself. The only difference I can see is that if you'd told him at the time, he might have learned to accept it before he came home. Time does blunt . . .'

'But he was a prisoner of war and I couldn't . . .'

'You didn't know he was a prisoner. You just hadn't heard from him for a long time, then you were told he was missing and you thought he might have been killed. Maybe you hoped . . .' She clapped her free hand over her errant mouth. 'I'm sorry, Gwennie, I didn't mean that.'

'I never wished him dead, if that's what you were going to

say, but I . . . did sometimes wish the baby wouldn't live. I know I wouldn't hear of an abortion, but now you know.'

Marge looked her straight in the eye. 'I'd better tell you that I often wished the same thing, so now *you* know, too.'

Needing both shaking hands to steady the glass Marge had given her some time ago, Gwen took a good gulp of the neat whisky, hoping that it would give her the strength to survive this terrible ordeal. Not being a drinker, however, the fiery liquor almost took her breath away, and a few seconds passed before she managed a hoarse, 'Marge, do you think Alistair will ever forgive me?'

'I'd love to say yes, but I doubt it. Maybe you should come back to London with us for a while, to let him . . . you know, start missing you. That might do the trick.'

Gwen mulled this over for a few moments, then shook her head. 'I'd rather not leave him, not in the state he's in. Mind you, I wouldn't be surprised if he throws me out when he comes back, but I don't want to depend on you and Peg.'

'Are you forgetting Mum's house is yours now?' Marge's voice now became sharply sarcastic. 'You can settle in there and brood for as long as you like.'

They sat back, thoughts running on much the same lines, although one was confident that her husband would forgive her for her part in the deception, while the other was equally positive that hers would not.

Dougal picked up a stone and flung it as far as he could. 'What are you thinking, Ally?'

'What d'you think I'm thinking? God Almighty, man, you've no idea how it feels to find out my wife's had a son to somebody else when I was rotting in a prison camp!'

'I do know, Ally. The same as I felt when you told me it was Marge – like the bottom of my stomach had fallen out, like somebody had stuck a dagger in my bloody guts and was twisting it round and round to dig out my heart. That's it, isn't it?'

Alistair's head-shake was an agreement. 'I never thought how it would affect you. I was positive it was Marge . . . and I thought you should know. I'm sorry. I wish to God I hadn't opened my big mouth. Your life would have gone on as usual and I'd have been glad it wasn't my wife that . . .'

'Stop tormenting yourself, Ally. Things were different during the war. Didn't you ever have a wee fling yourself?'

'Never. Did you?'

'A bit of flirting. I did go all the way once, but we'd both been soaking up the drink like sponges and it didn't mean a thing.'

'I'm not like you,' Alistair said, morosely. 'I never let myself get in a position to be tempted.'

Shrugging at this, Dougal picked up another stone and sent it flying down the hill. 'We'd better get back. They'll be wondering where we are.'

'Before we go, are you going to . . . the boy, now you know he's not yours?'

Dougal's head swivelled round abruptly. 'Why? Do you want him?'

'God, no! I'll never be able to live with Gwen again, never mind her . . . bastard.'

'Come now, Ally, that's a bit much. You're not going to leave her, are you?'

'Why should I leave? She's the one who did wrong.' Alistair reflected for a short time, then said, 'You go on back. I've still a lot of thinking to do.'

Dougal got to his feet reluctantly. 'You're not going to do anything stupid, I hope?'

'I'm not that daft. Go on, and say I want to be on my own for a while.'

Listening to the steadily diminishing sound of Dougal's feet, Alistair knew that he should make a decision, but his whole body was ice-cold and his brain was frozen solid. New thoughts were an impossibility. All he could do was go over what had happened a few hours ago . . . though it felt like a lifetime.

Recalling it only increased the ache in his heart, brought nausea and a desperate wish for oblivion. He couldn't cope with this. What was he supposed to do? Gwen couldn't really expect him to forgive her. Conceiving another man's child was bad enough, but letting her sister pass it off as hers was a thousand times worse. It was the deception that stuck in his craw, and the years they'd kept him in ignorance, made a proper fool of him.

Small flecks of light in the sky foretelling imminent dawn, he stood up stiffly, flexing all his joints to get them to move. He couldn't go home. He couldn't face any of them. He wouldn't be able to face anybody ever again. After a few tottery steps round the tower, he took up his stance at the other side, looking across at the dark silhouettes of the mountains in the distance, the bens he knew and loved, waiting for some sign of what he should do.

Dougal shook his head when he returned to Benview. 'You'd better get some sleep, Gwen. He said he needed time to think, and I doubt if he'll come back tonight.'

'Tonight's past already,' Marge muttered. 'It's nearly five tomorrow morning.'

He turned on her angrily. 'Trust you to make a joke at a time like this. And you'd better go to bed as well, because I'm going out again, and I probably won't come back till some time tomorrow either – later on today,' he added, to make sure she understood.

Outside again, shivering, he took his coat from the boot of his car, but in the act of putting it on, he wondered if he should go back inside to take one for Alistair, who was also out there in the cold, coatless. But if he went in again, he might say things in his bitterness that he would later regret, though both women deserved all the venom he could hurl at them.

As he stumbled up the uneven path again, it occurred to him that he should be thankful that it wasn't *his* wife who'd been unfaithful, but the thought didn't ease the aching void inside him. The circumstances had been such that Gwen's adultery was understandable, if not excusable, but what Marge had done had taken hours of planning. She had calmly plotted out a way to deceive not only her sister's husband but also her own, and would have got away with it if it hadn't been for some old photographs.

He could hardly believe how gullible he'd been. Fancy believing he'd managed to father a child after all the years he'd tried ... but Marge wasn't Nicky's mother, either. If he was sterile, she was barren. What a combination! Yet ... he was sure that she loved the boy as much as he did. They couldn't give him up, even if Alistair was willing to accept him, which wasn't likely. There was, of course, the inevitable doubt. Could *he* still look on Nicky in the same way as before? Could he maintain the same relationship with his wife? Wouldn't the thought of her scheming always come to the forefront of his mind, to cast up if she did anything to displease him in future?

He looked up, expecting to find his friend sitting by the tower, but there was no one there. In any case, would they still be friends, or would Alistair cut himself off from all further contact? The only way to find out would be to ask him, but where was he?

For God's sake! Where was he?

Chapter 28

Nancy Lawrie had left hours ago, yet Lexie Fraser still couldn't get over the shock, a double shock, in fact. Her first thought was that she would learn where her father had been all those years, that he was alive and well, and it had been a terrible disappointment when the woman couldn't tell her. Despite having always voiced her belief that he hadn't run off with a young girl, as Nancy had been then, it was worse to have it proved and not to know why he had vanished so abruptly . . . so completely.

After striving for some time to find an acceptable answer, it had crossed her mind that he might have been involved with a woman nearer his own age, but it couldn't have been anybody from around Forvit – nobody else had ever gone missing. The thing was, he had hardly ever gone anywhere, just a day in Aberdeen now and then on business. He could have met somebody there, of course, but it didn't seem likely – he had never stayed away long enough.

Lexie had convinced herself once more, however, that there had been no other woman. There must be some truth in her nightmares, but why had he raped her? Had his wife's illness affected her before they knew she was ill? If she'd been refusing him his rights, would his growing frustration have culminated in turning to his daughter? He had always been a loving father, had cuddled her much more than her mother ever had, had only stopped taking her on his knee when she left school at fourteen. She had accepted it as natural, but now she came to think about it, none of the other girls had ever said *her* father still took her on his knee. Her stomach lurching, Lexie mentally scolded herself for being so naïve, and for so long. She was thirty-six now, for goodness' sake, and it should have dawned on her years ago.

Another possible reason for his disappearance struck her now – more sinister but less hurtful to herself. When Roddy Liddell learned that Nancy was alive, he had jumped to the conclusion that the body unearthed by the excavators must be one of the travelling people, and working on that might be worth a try. Her father had been a compassionate man, so if he'd come across a gypsy girl in some sort of trouble, he would have tried to do something to help her, and it was well known that gypsy men were jealous-minded and fiery-tempered. If one of them found his woman with another man, no matter how innocently, that could have been enough to make him kill her.

Lexie took in a shuddering breath. That would explain the female body, and it was just possible that the man might have . . . she'd heard of people being abducted by the gypsies. Or they could have threatened to kill him, which would explain him running away. Trying to moisten her lips, she discovered that her tongue was just as dry, but she was sick of tea; she must have drunk gallons over the past few hours. She needed something stronger.

She never kept spirits in the house – Roddy Liddell wouldn't drink on duty and he was the only man who came to see her nowadays – so she made her way through to the shop on legs that felt as if they were attached to her body by pieces of elastic. She switched on the light and was so engrossed in choosing between Glenfiddich or 5-Star Cognac that the imperative knock on the shop door almost made the two bottles slip through her fingers. Her nerves were in such a state that she couldn't face speaking to anyone – whoever it was shouldn't expect to be served in the middle of the night even though she was behind the counter – but a hoarse voice hissed through the letterbox, 'It's Alistair, Lexie.'

Her hand shook as she turned the key in the lock, and he barged right past her and through to the house before she could utter a word. Locking the shop door and switching off the light again, she supposed that he had heard what had happened and had come to discuss what it meant to her.

'Oh, God, it's awful!' he moaned, when she joined him in her kitchen.

'I still can't take it in properly,' she agreed, before she noticed how strangely he was looking at her. 'How did you find out?'

His expression hardened. 'How long have *you* known?'

'Since just before six, and when the police inspector came . . .'

'Police?' he exclaimed. 'What have the police got to do with it?'

'He thought the body was Nancy Lawrie, so when somebody told him they'd seen her coming here . . .' His stunned expression made her say, sharply, 'You didn't know about her turning up again? What did you come for, then?'

He seemed to search for a reply, then, his voice hoarse and strained, he put forward another question. 'Didn't your father come with her?'

'You'll never believe this . . .' she began, but before she could tell him anything, her knees gave way and she thumped down on the sofa.

'Lexie, I'm sorry,' Alistair muttered. 'I wouldn't have forced my way in if I'd . . .'

Her attempted smile didn't reach her eyes, 'I need a drink. That's why I was in the shop . . . will you get the bottle of brandy I left on the counter?'

He dashed through to fetch it, took two glasses from the

cupboard she indicated with her hand, and sat down beside her. 'Has something happened to Alec – is he ill? Is that why she came?'

She took one good sip to fortify her, and let it swirl around in her mouth before swallowing it with a grimacing shudder. 'He was never with her. He never had anything to do with her. It wasn't his baby she was having, it was Doctor Birnie's.'

His own troubles fading, Alistair's eyes widened in disbelief. 'Doctor Tom? All I can remember about him was he was tall, and kind of good-looking, and he surely wouldn't have needed to take up with a young lassie. His wife was a right bonnie woman, though she was middle-aged. Her hair was a lovely wavy chestnut, and her eyes were dark brown and looked at you as if you meant something to her. I'd a bit of a crush on her when I was about thirteen or so.'

Stuck for something else to say, he added, 'Maybe she wasn't as old as that. I suppose everybody over twenty was middle-aged to me at that age.'

At that moment, someone knocked on the kitchen window and, noticing Lexie's apprehension, he asked, gently, 'Will I open the door, or . . . ?'

'It's Dougal Finnie, Lexie,' came a deep voice. 'Is Alistair there?'

Alistair rose and went to the door, but to save Dougal blurting out what had happened at Benview earlier, he said, as he let him in, 'Lexie's had a bit of a shock. Nancy Lawrie came to see her today and Alec didn't run away with her, after all.'

'My God! So where did he go?'

Her mind and emotions in utter turmoil, Lexie accepted Dougal's presence without question and answered him herself. 'She thought he was still here. She wanted to speak to him. I was just going to tell Alistair . . .'

The two men listened, spellbound, as the sorry tale

unfolded, not saying a word in case they dammed the flow, but when she finally said, 'And that's all I know,' Dougal murmured, 'It's a funny business, isn't it? You've no idea what made your father . . . ?'

She related what had been going through her mind during the hours she had been sitting alone, but when she mentioned the likelihood of him being threatened by an angry gypsy, Alistair soothed, 'No, Lexie! Your father wouldn't . . . there must be some other explanation. Maybe he *did* meet a woman in Aberdeen . . .' He stopped abruptly. 'You said the police inspector had been here last night again. What did he have to say?'

'They're going to start a proper search for him, but I don't think they'll ever . . .'

Dougal gave a slightly anxious cough. 'Ally, I think it's time we were going. We've still some things to sort out ourselves.'

Alistair scowled. 'We can't leave Lexie in this state.' He turned to her solicitously. 'We'll stay as long as you want.'

'Your wives'll wonder where you are.'

The two men exchanged cautious glances, then Dougal said, 'There was a wee bit a row, that's why we came out, and they won't expect us till we show up.'

'No, off you go,' she murmured. 'I'll be OK. I'll have to open the shop in a couple of hours anyway for the newspapers. The van'll be here any time now.'

Alistair was not particularly keen on returning to face the music, but he bowed to Lexie's wishes and left quietly, for which she was truly grateful. She was glad she'd had someone to talk to, more than glad that it had been Alistair and Dougal, but was relieved that they had gone now. She had to open the shop soon; she couldn't let her customers down.

She busied herself tidying up the kitchen and giving the room a perfunctory sweep and dust before she went upstairs to wash herself and change her clothes. Downstairs again, she felt a bit peckish and made a couple of slices of toast and a cup of cocoa to wash them down. It was while she was rinsing her dishes that the question arose in her mind. Why had Alistair come to see her? He hadn't known about Nancy Lawrie, and Dougal had said something about a row. But who had the row been between? Not Alistair and Dougal, they had still been very friendly. Gwen and Marge?

Come to think of it, though, it was Dougal who had been most eager to get back to Benview, so maybe the quarrel had been between him and Marge. Maybe he'd walked out on his family, just like her father had walked out on his twenty years ago? Maybe poor Marge was crying her eyes out right now. But that wouldn't have made Alistair come to see her . . . unless he and Gwen had fallen out about it.

Everything tidy, she went to the mirror to give her face a light rub of pancake make-up and apply a touch of lipstick before opening the shop. Whatever had happened in the past, she reflected as she turned the key in the lock, all she could do now was to wait and see if anything came of the police search for her father.

'Look Ally,' Dougal observed as they walked along the road, 'I know you feel sorry for Lexie, but you'd better steer clear of her. You've your own life to sort out.'

'Aye.'

'What are you going to do about Gwen?'

'God knows.'

'It's not up to Him, though, it's up to you! Either you let things go and carry on as you were, or . . .'

'Or?'

'For any sake, Ally! Do you want me to make your mind up for you? If you can't bring yourself to understand how it happened and forgive her, you'll have to leave her, or tell her to get out. Gee yourself, man!'

Alistair stopped walking and looked pathetically at his friend. 'I can't forgive her, Dougal, and I'll never forget what she did.'

'Nobody's asking you to forget, but if I can forgive Marge for telling me lies . . .'

'That's a different thing! She didn't have another man's child.'

'Granted, but telling me I was the father of another man's child was just about as bad, wouldn't you say?' Dougal stretched out his arm to pat his friend on the back. 'Let it go, Ally. Don't ruin your children's lives as well as your own and Gwen's. Be . . . what's the word? Magnanimous, I think. Try, I know it'll be hard, but it's the best way.' Getting no reply, he deemed it wise to leave Alistair to work it out for himself.

As it happened, the decision was taken for him. When they went into the house, a row of cases and bags was sitting in the porch, and the three women were silent and tearful.

'What's going on?' Dougal asked Marge.

'Gwen's coming back with us . . . and no arguing!'

He turned to Alistair, waiting for him to plead with his wife to stay, but he snarled, 'Good! That saves me throwing you out!' Then he spun round and stalked through the door again.

'It's OK, Dougal,' Gwen muttered, 'he's made it plain that he wants me to leave. I know what I'm doing, and Leila and David will be all right. Their lives are here. Now there's no more to be said, but if you want some breakfast before we go . . . ?'

'I'm not hungry.'

'Let's get the car packed, then. That's if . . . will it be too tight a squeeze with an extra passenger and more luggage?'

'We'll manage.' Dougal's voice was gruff.

Everyone was upset by the time the car was loaded, including little Nicky, who could sense the drama around him, and as they drew away from the house, even the four adults had to fight back the tears.

Chapter 29

In bed by herself for the first time since Alistair had come home from the war, Gwen lay staring at the ceiling, the ache in her heart too great for sleep although she was physically exhausted. She would have liked to forget the past twenty-something hours – or thirty-something or forty-something, whichever it was – to expunge them from her memory for ever, but she couldn't. It was like having a cavity in her tooth and, in spite of the pain it caused, being unable to keep her tongue from probing inside, or, when she was small, like picking at the scar of an earlier injury and making it take all the longer to heal.

After trying everything she could to make her change her mind, Marge had conceded that it was Gwen's choice and let the subject drop, and Dougal had carried the bag out to his car. He, too, had been against her running off, urging her to wait until she had talked things over with her husband at least one more time, but she couldn't bear the idea of having to face Alistair again. And, unable to budge her on this, Marge had made her family's breakfast before rousing Peggy.

Their youngest sister had been horrified at what had gone on while she was asleep, but her fury was directed at Gwen for what she had done, not at Alistair for not trying to understand. The quarrel which had ensued had wakened Leila, whose face had blanched when she heard the reason for it. 'When I saw Nicky at Grandma's funeral, I said he was like Ken. I told you on the train home, remember, Mum?'

Recalling it, Gwen felt worse than ever. She had never dreamt that her daughter suspected anything, but, bless her heart, Leila hadn't turned against her. Through her tears, she had said, 'If it wasn't that I don't want to be hundreds of miles away from Barry, I'd come with you.'

At this, Dougal had pulled a face. 'There wouldn't have been room for you, Leila. It's going to be hard enough to pack everybody in as it is, plus all the luggage.'

By the time two cases had been strapped to the roof rack, and as many of the bags, cases and parcels as possible in the boot, the two boys had appeared, and Leila, guessing that the adults wouldn't want Nicky to hear anything, took him upstairs again to make sure he hadn't left any of the comics and toys he had arrived with.

It had been left to Gwen to tell David, and her fragile composure had almost snapped at the sight of his stricken face. 'I don't know if you can understand why,' she ended, 'but I'm going back to London to live in Grandma's house. She left it to me.'

'Yes, I understand.' His voice, beginning to deepen anyway, had cracked. 'But what about us? Leila and me? Where are we going to live?'

'I'll let you make your own choice,' Gwen had said, her own voice perilously near breaking. 'You both work in Aberdeen, so . . .' She had been unable to go on.

Because the car was packed to capacity and more – Gwen's travelling bag ended up sitting on the floor with Nicky's feet resting on it, and both she and Peggy nursing large carrier bags – the choice did not have to be made immediately, and Leila and David stood at the gate, white-faced and forlorn, as they waved goodbye.

They met Alistair halfway down the track, but he kept his head down even when Dougal drew his car to a halt. 'Drive on,' Gwen whispered, her heart so full she had nothing to say to her husband on perhaps the last time she would ever see him.

Dougal, however, obviously wanted to make Alistair squirm. Rolling down his window, he called, 'Your wife's in my car, man, heartbroken at having to leave her home and her children. I hope you're pleased with yourself.'

The other man making no sign of having heard, Dougal continued, 'Damn you, you selfish son-of-a-bitch!'

He had driven on then, his face scarlet, and they had soon left Forvit far behind, but cramped as they were, only young Nicky ever complained. They made the whole journey, all five hundred plus miles of it, in eighteen hours – including the stops due to the call of nature and to buy some sustenance to keep them going – with only a modicum of conversation between them.

Turning to her other side now, Gwen wondered if the pain in her limbs would ever go away. They had almost seized up when Dougal helped her out of the car, and no doubt Peggy would be the same. Her youngest sister hadn't spoken to her since they set out, and, quite possibly, Marge, too, would start resenting her for upsetting their lives. It was going to be hard on all of them with her living in the middle house, and how was she going to cope with seeing young Nicky every day and his carroty nob reminding her of who his father had been?

Marge had said they would leave her alone if that's what she wanted, and right now that's exactly what she wanted. She would have to come to terms with herself before she could face anyone else, and that was going to take some time. Then! What then? She couldn't expect Alistair to send her any money, so she would have to get a job of some kind, and she had never gone out to work before.

Dougal had made a stop in Lewisham to let them stock up on provisions, so she rose to make a cup of tea. She wasn't hungry, but she needed something to refresh her mouth. Looking at the little clock her mother had always had on the bedside table, she found that it was still only two o'clock – five hours short of two days since she left home. No, she corrected herself, home was here now . . . but her thoughts were still in Forvit. Alistair would be getting up in a few hours, and Leila and David, breakfast would be the usual rush, without her to make sure they had everything, then they would all get in the car . . .

She would have to stop this. She would never get over things if she carried on like this. Gulping down the lump of self-pity in her throat that threatened to choke her, she came to the conclusion that she would never get over anything anyway, not on her own. She couldn't appeal to Marge or Peggy for sympathy or advice, so who . . . ? Dear old Ivy had died over a year ago, and now there was absolutely nobody.

Then it struck her – Tilly Barker! After delivering Nicky, the midwife had become a good friend, and they had exchanged Christmas cards ever since. She had also written when Ivy died. Yes, Tilly would help her, Gwen decided . . . if she had remembered to take her address book with her. Grabbing her handbag, she rummaged inside, casting aside letters from Marge as well as old electricity and gas bills. It flitted across her mind that Alistair would have to look after those now, but it didn't put her off her search. Just as she was thinking that she must have forgotten to put the little book back after she wrote her cards last Christmas, her fingers touched its imitation leather cover.

The decision made, she deemed it best to leave before the households on either side of her were stirring, and so it was that, if anyone had been in Woodyates Road ten minutes later, he or she would have seen her closing her house door very carefully to prevent any noisy click, creeping furtively down the garden path and being equally cautious opening and closing the gate. Then, carrying the travelling bag she hadn't yet unpacked, she strode purposefully towards Burnt Ash Road and the railway station. She would be in King's Cross in no time, and even if she had to wait hours for a train to Newcastle, at least she wouldn't be seen there.

Alistair studied his son and daughter as they ate the toast he had made for them. By the look of them they'd had as little sleep as he had. Although he had found out, only by asking a direct question, that they knew everything, they hadn't mentioned their mother again, not even to condemn her or take her part. What was more, they had neither accused him of being cruel nor agreed that he had done the right thing. It was difficult to know what they were thinking, where he stood with them.

When he'd arrived back in the cottage two mornings ago, he could see that they were very upset, but they had kept themselves under control, even David, who was normally quicker to air his true feelings than Leila. They had both expressed their desire to go to work as usual, and he'd had to wait until evening before Leila told him that they were going to stay with him until they made up their minds what to do.

'I'm going steady with Barry Mearns,' she had told him with no sign of shyness, 'so I don't really want to leave, and David's in Forvit football team, so . . . well, we'll just wait and see what happens.'

And that was it – she wouldn't say another word. That evening, she had gone out to meet her lad as soon as she had tidied up the supper things, and David had gone out with his friends, so he himself would have been free to go to see Lexie, but it didn't feel right. It wasn't that he didn't want to see her, because he did, more than he had ever done in his whole life, but he was just managing, by the skin of his teeth, to keep himself under control at the moment, and it would only need one word of encouragement from her . . . If she gave way to her emotions and all, anything could happen, and he wasn't ready for any more complications in his life.

Of course, Lexie didn't know yet about Gwen, but no doubt it would soon get round the place that his wife had left him, and he'd have to make it known that *he* was the innocent party and had wanted her to go. It made no real difference, of course, for either way, they would know that another man was involved. He could practically hear Lizzie Wilkie's mother and her cronies. 'That's what comes o' takin' up wi' they English dirt.'

And the reply would be, 'Aye, they're nae like Forvit lassies.'

But surely at least one of the women would stick up for Gwen? Say something like, 'But Alistair Ritchie's wife wasna as flighty as her sister.'

That was what kept niggling at him, eating away at his self-esteem. Gwen had always been content to sit at home every night with her husband and children, both before and after the war. She had never looked at another man . . . so what had been so special about 'Uncle Ken'? It probably hadn't been all her fault, of course, the man could have put pressure on her. Knowing how genuine she was, he could have set himself out to push down her barriers, to get her to fall for him. Making up to her children would have been the first step, and sympathizing about not hearing from her husband, until, being the kind of person she was, the liking had turned to loving and she'd have been putty in his hands. That was how it had been, and nobody could tell him they'd only been together once. Marge was as bad, of course, thinking up lies to cover up for her, and spinning absolute whoppers after the child was born. He still couldn't understand Gwen agreeing to a deception like that.

Yet . . . if she had written and told him instead of letting him find out for himself, would he have forgiven her? He didn't think so. He'd have been taken prisoner before he got such a letter, as low as he could be, so what would that have done to him? He'd have felt like doing himself in, that was what – so he should be grateful that she hadn't mentioned it. What if she had told him after he was repatriated? How would he have felt then? He would have arrived home a physical wreck to a wife he hadn't seen in three years to find her holding a two-year-old kid. It might have taken his befogged brain a few minutes to figure out it was another man's child, but once he did . . . Christ! He'd have felt like doing *her* in!

His hands had been tied by the way it happened – to learn a thing like that in front of your best friend and his wife, in front of your own kids! Oh, he'd yelled at her, but if they'd been on their own it would have been different. He likely *would* have killed her, he'd been so angry. Any man would have been the same, especially when he had kept on the straight and narrow himself before he was sent overseas and captured.

God, what a bloody mess!

Having been half expecting Alistair to put in another appearance, Lexie answered the door with a smile which slipped a little when she saw Roddy Liddell. His visits were beginning to disconcert her, in more ways than one. 'I'm sorry to be bothering you so late,' he said, 'but there's something I must ask you. May I come in?'

She wondered what on earth he wanted to find out, for she had told him everything she knew, which wasn't much, but she didn't want to make him feel he was intruding. He had been a bit stiff towards her lately, for some reason.

When he was seated, he said, 'I know I've made a nuisance

of myself already, but I was going over the information we have so far, when something struck me.'

'Yes?' she ventured.

'When the body was found, the constable recorded that you were very shocked, that before he told you it was a woman, you thought it might be your father.'

'Yes?' Her deepening apprehension was evident in her voice.

'Had you any reason to think that it could have been your father?'

'Not really, but . . . he disappeared the day after Nancy, and everybody thought . . . but it wasn't my father's child she was carrying, it was the doctor's.'

'Yes, I remember – Tom Birnie.' Liddell rubbed his left hand across his mouth. 'Could there possibly have been anything between Mrs Birnie and your father?'

'Oh no! They knew each other, of course. He was choirmaster at the kirk, and she was one of the contraltos, but that was all. There was never any gossip about them, and she went to Stirling to look after her mother.'

'So her husband made out, but he wouldn't want it known that she had left him.'

'No, I'm positive my father wasn't carrying on with Mrs Birnie.' Gulping, she went on, 'I wish I knew where he was and why . . .' She broke off, too overcome to continue.

'I didn't mean to upset you,' the man began, 'that's the last thing I'd want to do, Lexie.'

'Is it Roddy?' she managed to whisper, her heart hammering against her ribs.

'Yes,' he replied, and then his manner changed abruptly. 'I must get to the bottom of the mysteries surrounding this murder. I must keep an open mind. I hope you understand.'

When she locked the door behind him a few minutes later, she sat down at the fire again. She did understand.

She, too, felt that the slate would have to be wiped clean, otherwise there would always be a restraint, a barrier, between them.

Gwen hired a cab to take her from Newcastle to Moltby, praying as it took her out of the city that Tilly hadn't moved. Her limbs were trembling as she pressed the doorbell, but Tilly's smiling welcome, astonished but warm, dispelled her fears. 'Gwen Ritchie! Oh, my dear, what's happened? I can see there's something.'

Despite feeling that what she was about to confess could turn Tilly against her, too, Gwen told her everything, the tears coming in fits and starts as she spoke, and she was grateful that her listener did not interrupt. 'I don't know what you think of me now,' she ended. 'I'll understand if you tell me to leave.'

'Leave?' Tilly cried. 'Why would I do that? You told me at the time that the baby wasn't your husband's. Quite a few of the children I brought into the world during the war were mistakes, and . . .'

'But the lies I'd to tell?'

'I can understand the need for them. I was lucky, you know. I got involved with an American marine not long after you went home. He was a real film-star type, and it was his voice that got me – such a gorgeous drawl, deep and sexy.' She laughed at the astonishment on Gwen's face. 'I met him at a dance, his name was Grover, he must have been six foot five or six, and I fell for him like I was a teenager again, and me in my thirties.'

'But you didn't . . . ?'

'Lots of times, but, like I said, I was lucky, which was a blessing. I couldn't have passed a child of his off as Fred's.' She stopped, then finished with a twinkle in her eyes and a huge grin all over her round face, 'You see, he was black.'

'Oh, Tilly!'

'That shocked you? I bet you don't feel so bad now about your little affair, eh?'

'I can't believe you actually . . . Don't you feel guilty at all?'

Tilly pulled a face. 'I did at first, but Fred was a warden and often out all night, and in any case, I discovered . . . well, to put it bluntly, it had put a bit of ginger into my relations with Fred. So, good came from . . . I was going to say, from evil, but I never felt I was doing anything wrong.'

'What I did was a lot worse. It was the lies that got to Alistair, the not owning up to Nicky being mine. I was scared to tell the truth in case I spoiled my marriage, but in the end, I destroyed it completely, and very nearly Marge's, as well.' She fell silent, then, after a few moments, she asked, 'Did your Fred never suspect anything? Didn't he wonder why . . . like you said, there was more ginger in your relationship?'

'If he did, he didn't say anything, just enjoyed it.'

Gwen managed a weak smile. 'Tilly, I hope you don't mind, but . . .'

'Yes, you can stop here for as long as you like.'

'How did you know . . . ?'

'I'm not psychic, it was just a matter of logic. You hadn't anywhere to go when your husband put you out . . .'

Gwen told her about the house in Lee Green and went on, 'But I couldn't stay there with my sisters so close, and Peggy wasn't very friendly, and I needed somebody to talk to . . . but what will Fred say?'

'Fred won't say anything. He's not a bad old stick, though he sometimes goes down the pub and comes back smelling like a knocking shop. You're welcome to stay here till you sort things out.'

'I don't know if they'll ever sort out,' Gwen muttered.

'It don't matter,' Tilly beamed. 'You can move in altogether if you like.'

Lexie wasn't surprised by the phone call from Nancy Lawrie – she'd never be able to think of her as Mrs Fleming – but she *was* surprised by what she said.

'I've just thought, Lexie . . . oh, you'll likely say I'm off my rocker, but it's worth a try.'

'But . . . but . . . ? I don't understand.'

'Listen. Why don't I put an advert in one of the Scottish papers for information as to the whereabouts of Alec Fraser, at one time resident in Forvit, Aberdeenshire?'

'But the police haven't had any reply to their appeals.'

'That's the point! Some folk are scared to have anything to do with the police, but they might answer a newspaper ad. D'you see what I mean?'

At a loss to know what to think, Lexie said, miserably, 'I'm not sure.'

'You don't sound very keen. Don't you want to find your father?'

'I do, but . . . shouldn't we leave it to the police?' Lexie couldn't understand what was wrong with her. Was she afraid to know the truth? Was that why she was holding back?

'They haven't done very much so far, have they? Look, I'll put in a full description. Somebody must know where he is, even if he's changed his name.'

She couldn't catch Nancy's enthusiasm. She *wasn't* keen on finding her father . . . not after what he had done to her . . . or what she thought he had done to her. She had read once that a dream meant the opposite of what had happened or was going to happen, so maybe her nightmares didn't mean a thing. She had never actually remembered a face, or anything definite, and she could be wrong. She had taken a sleeping tablet, and it could all just be her imagination. 'All right, Nancy,' she mumbled.

'You want me to go ahead? I'm sure it'll work, Lexie, I know somebody's going to get in touch with me, and I'll let you know the minute they do.'

Disconnecting the line, Lexie guessed that Nancy would have carried out her plan whether or not it had been agreed on. As she had said, it was worth a try, and no harm would be done if nothing came of it.

Chapter 30

If she hadn't left a note saying that she was going away and didn't know when she would be back, Marge Finnie and Peggy Pryor would have been extremely worried about their sister. As it was, they couldn't understand her reason for it.

'What does she mean she needs to get some peace?' Peggy wailed. 'We weren't going to pester her.'

'She should have known that. I told her we'd leave her alone, if that's what she wanted, and we didn't go near her.' Marge looked pensively at the small sheet of paper. 'Should I let Alistair know she's gone?'

'It's up to you, but I don't think he'd care – not the way he was when we left.'

'He's had time to think, though. He'll blame us if anything happens to her.'

Peggy scowled at this. 'It's not our fault. She's thirty-six, for goodness' sake . . . old enough to look after herself.'

'That's just it.' Marge shook her head sadly. 'She's never had to look after herself. She'd Mum and Dad at first, then she'd Alistair, and it was up to me in Forvit.'

Casting her eyes heavenwards, Peggy sneered, 'You didn't make a very good job of it, did you? You said yourself she wouldn't have gone out with that Ken Whatsit at all if you hadn't made her.'

Stung by her younger sister's sarcasm, Marge spat back, 'Well, if you're going to start casting things up, there's no more to be said, is there?'

They flounced back to their own homes and tackled their household chores with much vigour but little awareness of what they were doing, and it took Marge only about ten minutes to think better of her high-handed attitude. Gwen had every right to be alone if she wanted to; she certainly had a lot to think about, and she probably felt hemmed in having a sister living on either side of her, not that they would have pressurized her in any way, Marge assured herself. But it was easier for her. She had come off lightly, after all. Dougal was still a fraction cool towards her, but she was practically sure that he would understand the reason for what she did and would come round soon. He hadn't discussed it with her yet, of course, hadn't even mentioned it, but it was early days, and at least he hadn't changed towards young Nicky. That was the main thing.

As she so often did, Marge made an abrupt decision. What was the point of falling out with Peggy when they couldn't do anything about anything? What was done couldn't be undone, as their Mum used to say. If Gwen didn't want advice from her own sisters, that was that! They'd have to let her take her own time to come to terms with herself, wherever she was . . . which was a mystery, for she didn't have Ivy to run to now.

Marge was about to pick up the telephone when it rang, making such a pang of guilty fear shoot through her that her hand hovered in the air for a second before she lifted the receiver, and she had never felt as thankful as she did when Peggy's voice said, 'I've just made a pot of tea . . . are you coming round?'

Alistair's mind could cope with only one thing, and no matter how many angles he viewed it from, he couldn't bring himself to excuse his wife for what she had done. If only he'd had more time to talk it over with Dougal . . . though Dougal was bound to be biased. Gwen's adultery had given him the son he had longed for, so he wasn't likely to condemn her. He hadn't even condemned his own wife, in spite of her trying to shoulder the blame . . . and she *did* have a lot to answer for, both before and after the event, which, of course, could only be laid at Gwen's door.

A customer interrupted his thoughts at this point, and he gladly entered into a discussion about the watch she had brought in for repair. 'It hasn't varied a minute in the three years since my mother gave it to me for my twenty-first,' the smart young woman told him, 'and it just stopped with no warning, and I didn't overwind it. I've always been very careful about that.'

'It could be a speck of dirt,' Alistair suggested. 'That's the usual reason for a watch stopping. Or . . . what line of work are you in? It might be . . .'

She gave a wry laugh. 'You've probably hit the nail on the head, Mr Ritchie. I've only been teaching for six months, but I suppose it could be the chalk.'

Alistair forced a reassuring smile. 'Quite a few teachers come in with their watches clogged with chalk dust, and it's easily remedied. I'll give it a good clean and blow out and you can collect it in . . . say thirty minutes?'

'I'm on my dinner hour, so is it all right if I come in after school?'

'Yes, of course.'

'I'll be here about ten to four, then. I say, I like what you've done to your shop. It's much brighter now. See you.'

With the click of the door closing, his smile faded, and he looked around him with little interest. It was Leila who had gone at him for weeks about the front shop looking dingy. Neither he nor David had noticed; men didn't set the same store by appearances. The fittings were as they had been when he bought the place – previously a small wool shop – a solid wooden counter, wooden shelves on the walls, and it really had been dingy compared with what it was now.

It had all happened so quickly. Less than a month ago, a customer had happened to mention that another jeweller was about to retire and was letting all his glass cases go cheap for a quick sale. Leila had bullied him into buying the lot, and Barry and his cousin, an apprentice joiner, had worked the miracle. After painting the doors and walls, making the place look 100% better already, they whipped out the old wooden counter and shelves and fixed up their replacements over one Saturday evening and Sunday morning, and stayed all afternoon to help get all the glass cases spotlessly shining. Mickey, the cousin, had then gone off, whistling, to meet his girlfriend, but Barry had helped to set the stock of timepieces and jewellery out on display. It was a great improvement, Alistair conceded now, though it was a pity Gwen had never seen it.

He was kept fairly busy for the rest of that day, so it was not until he was home in Benview, and both Leila and David had gone out, that he had the chance to get back to his problem ... though he didn't look on it as a problem. Problems needed to be worked out, answers had to be found, decisions had to be taken, but ... he had already taken the decision, which was why he was sitting by himself in this remote cottage, sick to death of his own company and wondering if there was any point to life. Maybe he should have a night in the bar, drink until his brain was so pickled it wouldn't be able to think at all. But it probably wouldn't help. Nothing would help. That was the bloody awful thing!

He kept brooding for some time. He needed somebody to talk to, somebody who would listen and sympathize, somebody who could be objective, but he wouldn't find anybody like that in the bar. There was always Lexie, of course, but had she got over the shocks she'd had herself recently? In any case, wouldn't this give her the chance to sneer at him? His beloved wife giving herself to another man as soon as his back was turned?

But was it true? Marge had said she was the adulterer, and Gwen, being the older, had wanted to shield her. That was it, wasn't it? That was the kind of thing Gwen would do, and Marge had always been . . . the flighty one, going dancing, having a good time. Marge wouldn't have pleaded guilty just to save her sister's marriage.

It was over an hour later, his mind having gone round and round so many times that he hardly knew what to think or what to feel, before it touched on something he should have remembered before. He hadn't long come back to Forvit to live, he had gone to the shop for cigarettes, and Lexie had flung it at him that she had once seen Gwen lying with a soldier up at the tower. When he refused to believe it, she had quickly said it might have been Marge, but he knew now. It *had* been Gwen.

He'd been a bit annoyed at Lexie for telling him at all, had put it down to yet another attempt to get him back – that was why he had buried it as deeply as he could – but she had only wanted him to know the truth about his wife. So that was it! No more touching on the possibility that she was innocent and he should ask her to come home; no more dreaming of a loving reconciliation; only the prospect of a long, lonely life without her.

He banked up the fire with dross, put on his jacket then remembered that he should leave word for Leila and David to let them know he had gone for a walk . . . in case they got home before he did. If he came home at all.

* * *

Downhearted because she had heard nothing from either Nancy Lawrie or Roddy Liddell for a couple of days, Lexie wondered if the latest rumour she'd heard was true. It all stemmed from the postie claiming to have seen Dougal Finnie and his family early one morning that week in a car going towards Aberdeen. This in itself was strange, since Dougal had told her himself, when he came to buy some groceries, that they'd be here for the last week of his holidays and they'd brought Marge's other sister with them. What was even more peculiar, though, was what else Sandy Mearns had told his wife.

'He says there was twa cases strapped to the roof,' Aggie reported, 'an' the door o' the boot was held doon wi' string, so it had been packed that full they surely couldna shut it. Dougal's wife was sitting in the front, an' the youngest sister was in the back wi' Dougal's laddie in the middle, atween her and . . .' She gave a quick glance round to make sure that no one else had come into the shop before whispering, with obvious delight at having such juicy news to impart, '. . . atween her and Alistair Ritchie's wife.'

She paused to give her listener time to digest this, then added, 'Sandy says she could hardly see ower the top o' the bag she had on her knee, so me an' Lizzie Wilkie thinks she's left Alistair . . . for good.'

She had waited expectantly for a reaction, and then, disappointed at getting none, she had dropped her purse into her shopping bag and left, no doubt to pass on her gossip to the first person she met. But, Lexie thought now, it couldn't be true. Gwen wouldn't leave Alistair, and she certainly would never leave her bairns. Besides, if the car was as packed as Sandy had made out to Aggie, they couldn't be going as far as London; they wouldn't have room to move. Dougal must have been giving Gwen a lift to Aberdeen to do some shopping, that was all. As Nancy had complained the other day, gossips – and in particular, Forvit gossips – nearly always got things twisted.

The whole business was queer, though. Why would Dougal leave so soon? He had mentioned a row the other night – between him and Alistair? It couldn't have been the sisters, not when they were all squeezed in the car together. Had Alistair found out about Gwen's supposedly-non-existent baby and thrown her out? It was the only thing it could have been, and Marge had made Dougal take her back to London with them . . .

Lexie was mulling this over – she'd always been sure it was Gwen she had seen with a soldier – and feeling sorry for Alistair, when someone came to the door. With him uppermost in her mind, she jumped to the conclusion that he had come to confront her about what she had said, and wondered if she should let him in. There would likely be no reasoning with him, he might attack her. He might . . .

Her old nightmare returning, her heart palpitated wildly. She was back in that awful night, when another man – about the same age as Alistair was now – *had* raped her. That was why she couldn't bear anybody to touch her.

She didn't push the half-memories away now. She mentally laid them out and confronted them. She had to know all the whys and wherefores, but it was so long ago, it was difficult to separate fact from imagination. She had been in bed, that was fact. She had been naked . . . but was that imagination? It had seemed to her at the time that there were dozens of hands, touching, poking, prodding . . . then that thing . . . No, face up to it. She was old enough now to know what had been rammed inside her, that was fact, also the excruciating pain she had suffered. No one could imagine that!

She still couldn't picture a face, because she hadn't been able to open her eyes. Recreating the scene, she closed them now, and that was when she heard the hoarse whisper.

'The sins of the fathers shall be . . .' She couldn't make out the next bit, but it had ended, *'until the third and fourth generation.'*

What did it mean? Had her father been chanting about the sin he was in the act of perpetrating at the time? He'd certainly known the Bible inside out.

A chill seemed to settle over her; it wasn't only her limbs that were trembling. She pulled her cardigan closer round her and huddled nearer to the fire but still felt cold, and when she heard another knock, she had to suppress a scream of terror. Unable to make any move, she couldn't tear her eyes away from the door handle as it turned, and flung her arms over her head as the door itself was pushed open.

'Lexie! I'm sorry if I've scared you. I did knock a few times. What . . . ?'

She lowered her arms with relief. 'Roddy! Thank God it's you.'

He hurried forward as if to take her in his arms, but her stony expression halted him in his tracks. 'What is it, my dear? What's happened?'

He sat down at the opposite side of the fire while she told him why she'd been afraid to open the door, ending by saying sorrowfully, 'But Alistair's not really like that and I don't know what came over me.' She couldn't possibly tell this man about the loathsome memories that had flooded back to her. 'I was just being stupid.'

He kept looking at her so enquiringly that she burst out with it. 'I was remembering the night my father went away . . .'

Slowly and painfully, he got it out of her, not interrupting in case the confidences dried up, but when she stopped speaking, he said, gently, 'You can't be sure it was your father, though?'

'It must have been, and he ran away because he was ashamed of what he did.'

Roddy's mouth twisted. 'We've had no luck with our search for him.'

She wondered fleetingly if she should let him know that Nancy had already sent letters to two Scottish newspapers, the *Scotsman* and the *Daily Record*, but decided against it. Time enough if anything came of it. 'Are you any nearer finding whose body it is?'

'No, but that reminds me. We did find a ring just below where the body was lying – that's what I came to tell you.'

'What kind of ring was it? Wedding? Engagement?'

'Just a plain signet ring, but it has an inscription inside, which should help us to identify her. The initials M.M.McL, and the date 30.6.1906, which may be a special birthday or anniversary of some kind. Whoever buried her may have removed any other rings but had, perhaps, not known about this one.'

To enable her to pass on the information to Nancy, Lexie made a mental note of the initials then offered her visitor a choice of tea or something stronger to drink, but Roddy pleaded pressure of work and left shortly afterwards. With peace to think, she tried to remember if there had ever been anyone living in the neighbourhood with the initials M.M.McL., but the only two she could think of had to be ruled out. Old Maggie McLennan had died a natural death about fifteen years ago at the age of eighty-three, and Molly McLaren had been killed in one of the air raids on Clydebank during the war. It was a terrible tragedy, for she'd only been eighteen and just started her training as a nurse.

When Lexie called Edinburgh to tell her about the ring, Nancy had important news of her own to pass on. 'I've just finished speaking to a Mrs Chalmers in Aberdeen, and I'm still all excited. She saw my advert and said she wanted to ask me some questions about it. She wouldn't tell me anything, but she must know your father, or she'd known him at some time. She's coming to see me tomorrow forenoon, and I'll give you a call as soon as she leaves, and let you know what's happened.'

Lexie did not hold out much hope of learning anything from such an unlikely source, but she urged Nancy not to forget to mention the ring that had been found, in case there was some sort of connection.

When Roddy Liddell walked into the shop the following morning, she felt somewhat annoyed – she wouldn't feel free to talk to Nancy if she phoned while he was there – but what he had to tell her left her reeling with shock.

'We're on to something at long last. I've just heard from Glasgow that a Thomas Birnie has contacted them.'

'Doctor Birnie?' She could scarcely credit it. 'But why? He wouldn't know where my father is.'

'He told them that his wife had run off with another man many years ago, and he'd been shocked when he called at Police Headquarters yesterday to ask about an attaché case which had been stolen from his car, and saw a photograph of this same man on a Missing poster. "Alec Fraser ran off with my wife," he told the desk sergeant.'

Lexie's gasp was genuine. 'I don't believe him. He told Nancy and everybody here that his wife went to Stirling to look after her sick mother, and she forced him to give up his practice and move down there to be with her.'

'Like I suggested once, he was too ashamed to let people know she had left him, and he spun that story when a patient said she hadn't seen his wife for a few weeks.'

Lexie leaned forward so that her midriff was supported by the counter, then looked accusingly at the detective. 'He'd been pulling the wool over their eyes, the Glasgow police, I mean. Nancy said he could make his lies sound like the gospel truth. Mrs Birnie wasn't the kind to run away with anybody, and no more was my father. They knew each other, of course, she was in his choir, but that was all.'

'That may have been all anyone knew about, but there could have been more.'

'No, not here, not in a wee place like this. Whatever anybody does, however much they try to keep it secret, somebody else always gets to know about it.'

She hesitated for a moment, then said, 'D'you know what I think? Nancy said Tom Birnie wasn't pleased at my father for making him admit to fathering her child, so I'm nearly sure this is just a story he's made up to get back at him.'

'What good would it do Birnie, though?'

'I don't know, just the satisfaction of blackening my father's character, I suppose. In any case, whatever he said, it hasn't taken you any nearer to finding my Dad, has it?'

Roddy smiled wryly. 'No, it hasn't.'

He had only been gone from the shop for five minutes when Nancy rang. 'Take the chair round from the end of the counter,' she ordered. 'You'll need a seat when I tell you the latest.'

Stretching as far as she could, Lexie managed to hook her toes round a leg of the chair provided for elderly customers and pull it towards her. 'Right, hurry up and tell me, for I've got something to tell you, and all.'

'OK. You know that woman from Aberdeen I spoke about? She's Mrs Birnie's sister. She says she didn't know Alec Fraser, but according to Tom, he was the man Margaret ran away with in 1929. She has never heard a word from her since.'

The wind having been taken out of her sails, Lexie mumbled, 'I still don't believe it.'

'What d'you mean still? Has somebody else told you the same thing?'

'Roddy Liddell's been in to tell me the doctor contacted the police in Glasgow and told them that same story, but you said yourself he was a liar.'

'Oh.' There was a wealth of meaning in the word, then silence.

Lexie waited for a few moments, then said, 'Are you still there, Nancy?'

'Yes, I'm thinking, and you're right. I wouldn't trust that two-faced swine supposing he'd a halo and wings – though he's more likely to have horns and a tail. Anyway, Mrs Chalmers gave me her mother's phone number – she was going to Stirling to see her after she left me – so I'll give her a tinkle there in the afternoon and ask if her sister ever divorced Tom. I wouldn't put it past him to have lied to me about her refusing, as well. He could have been free to marry me and never let on . . . though I'm glad he didn't, as things turned out.'

'Did you remember to tell Mrs Birnie's sister about the ring and the initials?'

'Oh, damn! I clean forgot, I was so surprised at what she was telling me. I'll mention it when I phone her at her mother's, though. I'll speak to you later.'

Lexie was kept busy that afternoon and old Mrs Wilkie came in just on six to complain in her best English, 'All yon biscuits I bocht yesterday was broken, and I'd to crummel them ower my stewed rhubarb. You'll need to replace them . . . free.'

Fly to all Lizzie's mother's tricks, Lexie said, firmly, 'If you haven't taken the other packet back, Mattie, I can't replace it, I'm afraid.'

The old woman stamped out in high dudgeon at being refused, and Lexie was locking up for the day when the telephone shrilled. Presuming that Nancy would only be ringing to vent her fury about Tom Birnie, whose wife had probably divorced him and thus left him free to marry whatever paramour he had by that time, Lexie plugged listlessly into the small exchange. Her eardrums were assaulted by the shrill voice.

'Oh, God, Lexie, I wanted to ring you hours ago, but I knew you wouldn't have peace to listen. I've nearly bitten my fingernails right down to my knuckles waiting till you shut the shop.'

Knowing Nancy well enough by now to realize that she was excitable and prone to exaggeration, Lexie held little hope of hearing anything of importance. 'If you'd stop yapping,' she said, quietly, 'you'd be able to tell me now, whatever it is.'

Nancy's voice slid several points down the vocal scale as she held her emotions in check. 'D'you know what Margaret Birnie's mother's name is?'

'I've no idea, but I bet you're going to tell me.'

'She's Mrs Tabitha McLeish.'

'And . . . ?'

'She had two daughters – Mary, the oldest one, married a Bill Chalmers, and Margaret married Tom Birnie. Do you get it?'

Lexie felt quite exasperated by this guessing game. 'Yes, I realize that Mrs Chalmers is Mrs Birnie's sister, and their mother's a Mrs McLeish, but . . . ?'

'Mrs McLeish's maiden name was Martin, and both daughters have that as a middle name. Mrs Chalmers was once Mary Martin McLeish. Now do you get it?'

'Mary Martin McLeish?' Lexie repeated it slowly, taking time to consider what it signified, and then light dawned in a blinding flash. 'Oh, I see now! Mrs Birnie would have been Margaret Martin McLeish! M.M.McL. It's her ring! Her body they found!'

'The penny's dropped at last! Now, Mrs Chalmers said she would get on to Aberdeen police as soon as she stopped speaking to me, and arrange to go and identify the ring when she got home, which would have been around five. So you can expect a call from your friendly Detective Inspector some time this evening. Look, I'll have to go. Greig'll be home in a few minutes, and I've nothing ready for him to eat. I've been too excited to cook, so it'll be fish and chips, I'm afraid. Give me a tinkle as soon as you can, to let me know what's happening.'

Leaving her telephone exchange ready for other calls, Lexie went through to the house and tried to think how this new development would affect her. If the body did turn out to be Margaret Birnie, it meant that she had never left Forvit at all. She hadn't run away with any other man. The doctor had told lies about that, though he'd pretended it was to save his own face, so . . . was it possible . . . had he killed her? He must have!

Lexie was still going over and over this possibility, when Roddy Liddell arrived. 'I suppose Nancy has told you what was going on?' he asked, plumping down on the vacant armchair. 'It is . . . was . . . Margaret Birnie's ring. Apparently both sisters were given a signet ring on their eighteenth birthday, and according to Mrs Chalmers, Mrs Birnie had to wear hers on the cranny of her right hand when she was older. I believe that whoever killed her had removed her wedding ring, but hadn't known, or had forgotten, about the other one.'

'She could have lost it herself . . . how can you be sure it's her body?'

'Mrs Chalmers told us that her sister had broken her left leg just below the knee and her left arm just above the wrist in a cycling accident when she was about fourteen, and our surgeon has confirmed that it is definitely Margaret's body. All we have to do now, is to pick up the doctor.'

Without warning, a horrible thought struck Lexie. 'What if it wasn't him?'

Roddy regarded her in some surprise. 'Who else could it have been?'

Swallowing nervously, she muttered, 'Suppose she *had* been having an affair with my father and he'd made her pregnant? Suppose he got angry when she told him?'

The detective stretched across the fireplace and patted her hand reassuringly. 'From what I've heard of him from you and Nancy and other people I've spoken to, he was definitely not an aggressive man.'

'But, he might have wanted to stop her telling anybody, my mother, or the doctor, and he could have killed her. Then he'd have had to bury her, and he wouldn't have been able to face my mother, and that could be why he disappeared.'

Her visitor sighed deeply. 'Do you honestly think he had it in him to murder another human being?'

'He hadn't meant to kill her. He could have given her a push or a shake that knocked her off her feet and she hit her head on a stone, or something like that.' She halted, then shook her head. 'But if he hadn't meant to kill her, he wouldn't have buried her. He'd have reported it . . . wouldn't he?'

'I'm sorry, Lexie, but I must point out that people who kill without premeditation, accidentally or otherwise, become so agitated that all they are concerned with is how to dispose of the body. Once they've left the scene of the crime and can think rationally, they are too scared to go back and own up to it.'

'But . . .' Lexie's face puckered up and she held out both arms to the detective as if appealing for comfort.

'Don't upset yourself, my dear,' he murmured, rising to pull her to her feet and then holding her tenderly. 'At the moment, we're still guessing, and we can do nothing more until we hear what Doctor Birnie has to say.' He glanced at the clock. 'I thought I'd have heard by this time. I gave them this number.'

Right on cue, the telephone rang, and dropping one arm, he pulled her through to the shop. She made the connection for him then stood by his side, her eyes following every movement of his lips.

'What? Oh, no! For God's sake! It proves he did it, though, doesn't it? I take it the heat's on to find him? Let me know as soon as you hear anything.'

'Birnie's vanished,' he announced as they walked back to the kitchen. 'His wife says he told her he'd found somebody else, and went out on his round next morning and never came back. She says she doesn't know where he is, but they think the other woman was just a blind and that she's protecting him. Still, it's a good thing for us that he did take off, for it proves he's guilty. We'll find him, don't doubt that, Lexie.'

Her feelings having seesawed so much over the past hour or so, she couldn't hold back a sob of relief. 'Thank goodness it wasn't my father.'

Liddell's arms went round her again, more purposefully than before. 'My poor, poor Lexie. I had hoped the case would be finished tonight, everything solved, but . . .' He lowered his head towards her and brushed her lips with his. 'I won't rest till Birnie's under lock and key, but I wish I could find your father for you. I'll do all I can to trace him, believe me.'

'Roddy, you've been so kind . . .'

Her voice was so tremulous that it came as no surprise to him when she burst into tears, and his arms tightened round her. 'Let it out, Lexie. It'll do you good.'

He held her until she calmed, and then looked deeply into her eyes. 'Will you be all right on your own tonight, or would you like me to stay with you?'

Not having the nerve to say she would prefer if he kept her company, she assured him that she would be fine.

'Lock the door behind me,' he instructed, as he took his leave, 'then try to get some sleep, though I know that's easier said than done at a time like this.'

Rising to obey his first order, she thought she may as well go to bed when she was at it, but before she reached the bedroom someone knocked at the outside door. Knowing it couldn't be Roddy, her legs shaking, she turned and shouted, 'Who's there?'

'It's Alistair, Lexie.'

'Go away! I don't want to see you. I'm going to bed.'

'I've something to tell you.'

'If it's about Gwen, I know she's left you.'

'You were right, Lexie. It was her you saw with the soldier. I need somebody to talk to and there's nobody else.'

His last three words were his undoing. 'Leave me alone. I'm not letting you in!'

She held her breath until she heard his feet going round the side of the house, then she relaxed, but she couldn't help thinking how much things had changed. At one time, she'd have rushed to let him in. She had practically offered herself to him more than once . . . but that was before she had remembered being raped. If she had let him do what he wanted the night before he went to London, would the awful memory have come back then, or would he have obliterated it for good? And all those other young men she had stopped after egging them on, had it been stirring in her mind then too? Had she been scared, though she didn't know why?

Well, now she knew why . . . and who . . . and it was awful, unbearable. Alec Fraser hadn't run off with Nancy Lawrie, or Margaret Birnie, or any other woman, and the only explanation was his shame at raping his daughter.

Having walked for hours trying to think straight, and getting no respite at Lexie's house, Alistair's walk back to Benview was slow and laboured. It was maybe just as well she hadn't let him in, he mused, with a sob in his throat. He was still upset by what Gwen had done; the showdown had taken him by surprise, his heart still felt leaden. Coming to a smooth stretch of grass at the roadside, he sat down to have a breather. Everything was going wrong for him. Every-bloody-thing in his life. He'd been away from his wife and family for five years, two of them spent in a prisoner-of-war camp, and round about the time he was captured, his wife had been consoling herself with another man. Ken Bloody Partridge – it was a name he would never forget.

He fished in his jacket pocket for his packet of Capstan, and couldn't stop his hand from shaking as he snapped his lighter, but the first long draw of the cigarette did help him. The pain in his heart eased a fraction, the obstruction in his throat disappeared – maybe the effects would only last as long as the cigarette itself, but at least he was getting some benefit from it.

Chapter 31

Two weeks on, Alistair was no nearer to forgiving his wife, despite recalling what *he* had almost done while she was giving birth to their daughter sixteen years earlier. There were times when he came close, but he always excused himself on the grounds that the circumstances had been entirely different. His lapse had come of a weakness, weakness born of heightened emotions and pique at Lexie's negative reaction.

The atmosphere at Benview was still distinctly chilly; Leila in particular making it clear that she held him responsible for breaking up the family, which was ridiculous since he had done nothing wrong. Life wasn't fair. It never had been. Not for him.

He was beginning to realize, however, that such self-pity could not continue for ever. His business was suffering because of his lack of concentration and that was bad. He would have to pull himself together and face up to being an unattached man. Not that he wanted to be attached again, but he should at least try to lead a more or less normal life. He wasn't the only one whose wife had borne a child to another man while he was away. The damned war had a lot to answer for, though it was no excuse for being unfaithful . . . for a woman or for a man, though just as many husbands as wives had done a bit of philandering . . . more probably.

That evening, as he sat down with his children to their evening meal, Alistair decided that it was time to make them understand how deeply their mother had hurt him. He had never defended himself to them, and they needed to be told. Waiting until David had finished his second helping, he motioned to them to remain where they were.

'But I'm in a hurry,' David pouted. 'I'm going out with my pals.'

Leila scowled at her father. 'I'm meeting Barry, and I don't want to be late.'

Impatient at their self-absorption, he barked, 'What I'm going to say to you is far more important than pals or lads.'

They glanced at each other, silently apprehensive, yet obviously resentful, so he went straight into the little speech he had planned. 'I know you both feel I was too hard on your mother, but let me give you my side.' He started by relating his experiences in the war, the deprivations of being part of an invading force in alien territory even before he was caught and put behind the barbed wire of an Italian prison camp. Then had come the transfer to the first of several German Stalags, and the long hazardous treks from one to the next, with only the thought of his loving wife and children to keep him sane when there was no food, no kindness, and seemingly, no hope.

'I loved your mother,' he told them, 'and I prayed that it wouldn't be long till I'd be going home to her again. I trusted her to be faithful to me because I stupidly thought she loved me just as much as I loved her.'

'She did, Dad,' Leila burst out. 'She did. She just made one silly mistake.'

Alistair shook his head mournfully. 'Young Nicky was the result of that one silly mistake, and that kind of thing can't be hidden, Leila, though she and her sister did their best.' He looked at each of his listeners in turn now. 'I don't suppose you know how they managed to pull the wool over everybody's eyes?' Their blank expressions telling him that they didn't, he detailed the plot Marge had hatched, and was pleased to see his daughter's eyes widen, her expression soften a little.

'I never knew,' she whispered.

'That's what I can't forgive,' he admitted. 'If she'd confessed to me at the time, I'd have been hurt, naturally, but I could have coped with it like I learned to cope with all the other things fate threw at me. But learning like I did, years after . . .' He ran his hand across his perspiring brow. 'Right from the minute I saw him, I knew Nicky couldn't be Dougal's, but I thought it was Marge who had misbehaved, and your mother let me carry right on believing that.'

'It was all my fault, wasn't it?' David muttered suddenly. 'If I hadn't let you see the old snaps, you'd never have . . .'

'No, that wasn't what did it. They just proved to me I'd been right about Marge. I never dreamed that . . .' He swallowed before going on, '. . . that it was your mother.'

'Auntie Marge was willing to take the blame,' Leila reminded him, 'and Mum didn't need to tell you the truth. You'd never have found out if she hadn't.'

'Truth will always come out, and I had the right to know, hadn't I? My heart was ground to dust that day, and I've only been half a man since. It was like a part of me had been taken away, a part I needed to keep me alive.'

'Dad,' Leila said, gently, 'I can imagine how badly you feel, but Mum does love you and if you loved her as much as you said, you'd have understood that she didn't mean to do it, it just happened. Ken and her . . . their feelings, emotions, were all upside down, and their bodies needed each other. Don't you see? I've got to go, but think about it.'

She grabbed her coat from the back of the chair where she had thrown it when she came home and ran out, and David, his face red because of the nature of the conversation, stood up. 'I'm late, as well, Dad, but I think Leila's right. Not that

I know about feelings and emotions,' he added hastily, 'but it makes sense . . . doesn't it?'

Left alone, Alistair wondered if he should have resisted the urge to make them see things from his point of view. He had uncovered something else for him to worry about. Had his sixteen-year-old daughter been speaking from experience? Had Barry Mearns been . . . ? It was agony to think that the postman's son's rough paws had touched her, caressed her, knowing it would arouse her passions as well as his own.

'I'm surprised we haven't heard one word from Gwen.' Marge eyed her husband warily, because she sensed that he didn't like speaking about her older sister now. 'She's been away for well over a week.'

Dougal drained his teacup and got to his feet. 'She'll be all right. Don't fuss!'

'It's not like her, that's all.' But she said no more about it, and kissed him before he left for work, Nicky running out to wave him goodbye as he drove off.

When her son came in again, Marge said, 'Mummy has to go to the dentist this morning, remember, so be a good boy for Auntie Pam.' The courtesy title was given to Pamela Deans, who lived in the other half of the semi-detached villa. She was a widow who lived alone, but she had brought up a family of three and knew how to amuse little boys, even little boys as active as Nicholas Finnie.

'Auntie Pam found a box of tin soldiers in her attic,' Nicky observed, fidgeting with impatience to get his hands on them. 'She says they're her Frank's, but he's in Australia. Her Frank must be a funny man if he played with soldiers, what d'you think, Mummy?'

Marge couldn't help smiling. 'He'd just have been a boy

when he played with them. He was grown up when he went to Australia.'

'Where's Australia, Mummy?'

'On the other side of the world, darling – a long, long way from Lee Green.'

'When I grow up will I go to the other side of the world, Mummy?'

'I can't tell you that. It depends on a lot of things. Now stop asking questions and put on your jersey.'

It was one of Dougal's busiest days. They'd had a long weekend off because of the Bank Holiday, and there was a mountain of paperwork to catch up on. He had told the girl in the outer office that he didn't want to be disturbed, so he glared at her when she gave a timid knock and walked in. 'I told you I didn't want . . .' he began, but stopped, his face paling, when he saw the uniformed man behind her.

'I'm sorry to disturb you, Mr Finnie,' the policeman said, 'but . . .'

Dougal held his hand up. 'It's all right, Jane, you may go.' Only one explanation had jumped to his mind, so when the girl shut the door behind her, he said, 'I suppose this is about my sister-in-law? What has she done?'

The other man turned an embarrassed pink. 'No, Mr Finnie, it's not about your sister-in-law, it's . . . about your wife. There has been an accident . . .'

Dougal could feel the blood draining from his face. 'An accident? How bad is she? Which hospital did they take . . . ?'

'I'm afraid . . . she died on the way to hospital. It seems she was standing at a junction speaking to another lady when an articulated lorry carrying sewage pipes took the corner too quickly, and . . .' The young policeman licked his dry lips. 'The load slipped and . . . it all happened in a matter of seconds, according to witnesses.'

'Where is she? I have to go . . .'

'Look sir,' the uniformed man looked most uncomfortable, 'I know how anxious you must be, but another ten minutes or so won't make any difference, and I really think you should give yourself a little time . . . to steady your nerves.'

'I'm perfectly all right!' He couldn't help being curt.

'If you say so. Your wife's identity card was in her handbag, that's how we knew where she lived. There was no one in when we called there, but a little boy was playing in the garden next door . . .'

'That had been my son,' Dougal managed to croak. 'Mrs Deans was looking after him to let my wife go to the dentist.'

'So I believe. Your son said his Mummy had gone to the tooth man, and Mrs Deans gave us your office address. Is there anyone I can contact for you, Mr Finnie, someone to give you some support through this dreadful time?'

'Will you please notify my sister-in-law? Mrs Pryor.'

'Would she be the lady you were referring to earlier?'

'No, there are . . . were . . . three sisters. Gwen, the one who went away without leaving any address, Marge, my wife, and Peggy, the youngest, Mrs Pryor.'

As he and Peggy sat by his fireside, Dougal couldn't remember half of what he had done that day. 'It's been a nightmare,' he groaned, 'and I kept wishing I'd wake up.'

'I was the same,' she admitted. 'I still can't believe it.' She looked at him pensively, noting how grey he looked, how absolutely done in. 'Do you want me to phone Alistair? You might feel a little bit better with another man to lean on.'

'I don't know if he'd want to come.'

'Because of . . . Nicky, you mean? But surely he'd put all

that out of his mind at a time like this? I'll tell him Gwen's not here . . .' Peggy broke off, her eyes misting. 'I wish I knew where she was, though. She'd want to know about Marge. She'd want to be here.'

Dougal patted her hand. 'I'm truly sorry she's not here for you. I've been so wrapped up in myself . . . but you've lost a sister. You likely think you've lost them both, but I'm sure Gwen'll come back.'

A little of the hopelessness left Peggy's eyes. 'Do you really think so?'

'I do, Peg, but are you sure you've no idea where she could be? Marge couldn't think of anybody she'd have gone to, not with dear old Ivy gone, but maybe you can remember somebody else she'd been close to.'

'I've racked my brains, Dougal, and I just can't think of anybody else.' She stood up wearily. 'I think I'll go home and phone Alistair from there. He should know . . . about Gwen, as well as Marge.'

She had to get away for a few minutes. The pain in Dougal's eyes, the change in him from a bright, upright, healthy man to a bowed, haggard wreck with stubble on his chin and upper lip, his hair uncombed since he'd gone to work in the morning, was too much to bear on top of her own grief. She needed a short respite, to charge her batteries.

Once inside her hallway, her hand trembling, she dialled the number and glanced at the clock while she waited for an answer. Good grief! She hadn't dreamt it was half past nine already. Thinking that everyone at Benview must be out, she was on the point of laying down the receiver when a rather weary 'Hello?' came over the line. 'Alistair?' she said, huskily, 'it's Peggy.'

'What is it? Is something wrong with Gwen?' She was gratified to hear a touch of anxiety in his voice. 'Nothing's wrong with Gwen as far as I know, but Marge was . . . killed in an accident . . . this forenoon.' It wasn't easy for her to say. It turned the prolonged nightmare into stark reality.

'What?' His gasp was followed by a short silence, then he murmured, 'No, no, Peg, say that isn't true.'

'It is true.' Peggy fought down the lump in her throat. She had to keep calm, she couldn't let herself go to pieces on the telephone. 'I can't talk any more, Alistair, I'm too upset, but Dougal needs you.'

'Tell him I'll be there as soon as I can. Wait! What did you mean nothing was wrong with Gwen . . . as far as you know?'

'We . . . don't know . . . where she is.' The tears spilling out, her throat constricting, she put the instrument back on its rest, and sat down to give way to the sorrow she'd had to deny in front of Dougal.

On the early morning train to London, Alistair couldn't help feeling as upset about Gwen being missing as about her sister's death, but he tried to concentrate on what Peggy had said. An accident? She might have explained and not left him wondering? Had it been anything to do with Dougal? Had he fallen out with Marge over young Nicky? Had he finally let out the fury he must have nursed since her deceit was uncovered? Had he lost control . . . and killed her? Oh God, not that!

The noises in Edinburgh's Waverley Station brought him reluctantly out of the exhausted sleep he had succumbed to. He didn't want to remember, but he couldn't banish the memory of the awful event in Benview he couldn't remember how long ago – sometimes it felt like for ever, at others it was as if it had only just happened. He drew in a ragged breath. The pain Gwen had caused him was still too raw to dwell on. Maybe, like the pain of bereavement, it would ease with time, but he didn't think so; the deception she had played was far worse than any bereavement. He had blamed Marge, as well, at the time, but . . . oh, Lord, how he wished now that he had made his peace with her.

Roddy Liddell didn't relish what he had to do. Lexie was distressed enough already, but it was better that she knew. 'I'm sorry,' he said softly, when she let him in, 'it's more bad news, I'm afraid.'

She motioned him to a chair. 'You'd better tell me.'

The resigned acceptance on her face made him revise what he had said. 'It's not all bad, a sort of mixed bag, actually. The good news is that we managed to trace Doctor Birnie for the second time, purely by accident. One of his patients happened to be in another part of Glasgow yesterday, at the opposite side of the city, when she recognized him going into a small villa. Word having got round her own area that he was wanted by the police, she gave the address to her nearest police station. The Investigating Officer presumed that he'd been visiting another patient, but it turned out that Birnie hadn't had time to find another practice.'

'So that's it?' Lexie, breathed. 'You've got him?'

Roddy shook his head angrily. 'No, he's too clever by far, and here's the bad news. He professed deep sorrow on hearing that his first wife's body had been found in Forvit, but swore that he knew nothing about her death.'

'He would say that, wouldn't he?' Lexie muttered.

The detective nodded. 'It would be only natural, whether or not it was true. On the following day, however, he contacted the DI and told them that, after much deliberation, he had concluded that . . .' He stopped. 'Oh, Lexie, I don't think I should go on.'

Steeling herself, she whispered, 'Whatever it is, you'd better tell me. You can't leave it at that.'

Standing up, the detective moved swiftly to sit beside her on the sofa. 'Yes, you're right. It would be insensitive of me not to tell you now. Birnie said that he had been thinking, and it had occurred to him that Alec Fraser, the man he thought Margaret had run away with, must have killed her, possibly she'd been pregnant and he hadn't wanted anyone to find out. Birnie also said he had probably buried her there to cause most heartache to him, her husband.'

'Oh, Roddy!' Lexie burst out. 'That couldn't be true ... could it?'

Taking her hand, he clasped it reassuringly. 'I doubt it. It sounds to me more like the invention of a desperate man ... a guilty man. Please, Lexie, don't distress yourself.'

'I'm all right,' she whispered, but she obviously wasn't. 'Did he say anything else?'

'When he was told there had been no evidence of pregnancy, he shrugged it off and said they must have quarrelled. He made a point of saying that his wife was an even-tempered woman, but hinted that your father could be "quite volatile if he was angered."'

This was too much for Lexie. 'Nancy said he was a liar,' she sobbed. 'You don't believe him, surely?'

'Absolutely not!' Wishing that there was more he could do to put her mind at ease, Roddy added, 'If Birnie thinks he's got away with it, he has a nasty shock coming to him. The case is not closed, not by any means.'

'They didn't let him go?'

'With no proof of his guilt, we have to presume him innocent, but he's obviously on the run, and we *will* get him!'

When Lexie recovered her composure, Roddy said he had to report at HQ that night, and although he did feel guilty at leaving her, she vowed that she was perfectly all right.

* * *

It was almost nine the following night when Alistair rang Dougal's doorbell. At one time, he would just have walked in, but their last parting had not been on the best of terms and he was feeling uneasy about this meeting. Peggy let him in, and he was relieved that she, at least, had no reservations with him, giving him a kiss and a warm hug before he went into the living room.

Dougal, his eyes puffy and red-rimmed and surrounded by dark circles, jumped to his feet and came towards him as though they hadn't seen each other for years. 'Oh, Ally, I'm right glad you're here.'

Alistair could tell that every word was heartfelt, and his own emotion was such that he could hardly speak for a second or two, then he flung his arms round his old pal and held him, their cheeks running with tears, and Peggy, her own eyes streaming, withdrew to the scullery.

Scarcely noticing when their sister-in-law excused herself and went home to bed, the two men sat for hours, reminiscing about the early, happy, days of their marriages, of the hotel in Guilford Street, of Tiny and Rosie, even of Manny Isaacson, who had also been a big part of their lives at that time. They avoided talk of the war and the years following, afraid to come anywhere near to the 'trouble' and having to skirt around it, which would draw more attention to it.

It had to come, of course, and with one careless slip, Dougal uncovered it. 'Marge and Peg were both worried about Gwen . . .' Too late, his hand flew to his mouth. 'I'm sorry,' he mumbled, 'I forgot . . . you haven't asked about her, so I thought . . .'

'I didn't know what to say,' Alistair interrupted. 'I don't want to see her, but I didn't realize there was a problem.'

Dougal filled him in about his wife's disappearance then said, 'I think they were fussing about nothing. She said she wanted peace to think, and I can understand that.'

Surprised at the alarm that came to him, Alistair muttered, 'So you think she's OK?'

'I can't be sure, of course, and it's nearly two weeks since she . . .'

'Two weeks?' A light cramping had started round his heart . . . as it would do for anyone he knew who had just walked away from her home and sisters. 'She couldn't have been here long when she . . .'

'Not more than a couple of days, and the thing is,' Dougal explained, 'we don't know where she is. We can't think of anybody she'd have gone to now she doesn't have Ivy.'

Alistair extracted the last cigarette from his packet, snapped his lighter and leaned back to think. No Manny, no Ivy, the two people Gwen had been closest to at one time. She'd never been as friendly with anybody else, not that he knew of. Then the answer hit him square on, making an iciness shoot through him and settle in his very bones. 'Ken Partridge!' he said, harshly. 'I bet that's where she'll be. He's the only one she *could* go to. Did Marge ever mention where he came from?'

'Not that I can remember. Don't you know?'

'No, and I don't want to.' Alistair's lips pressed together, and no more was said on the subject.

'What's on your mind, Tilly?' Gwen asked suddenly. 'Something's been on the tip of your tongue for ten minutes at least, so you'd better come out with it, whatever it is.'

The woman heaved a sigh. 'Don't get me wrong, Gwen, love, I don't want rid of you, and I know you've had a bad time, but . . . you should be with your husband and children.'

'But Alistair doesn't want me. He wanted me to leave.'

'It was what he'd wanted at that specific moment, any man would after what you'd just told him, but he's had time to think. He's had two whole weeks of coming home to an empty house, having to cook his own meals and do his own laundry . . .'

Gwen felt her hackles rising at the criticism. 'He'll have Leila doing everything for him, or . . .' She gave voice to a thought that had been niggling at her ever since she left Forvit. '. . . or he'll get Lexie Fraser to do it. She was his girlfriend before he ever came to London, and I think he still loves her.'

Tilly shook her head. 'I doubt that very much. I don't know him, but from what you've said about him, I wouldn't think he was the kind of man to . . .'

'You'd have said I wasn't the kind of woman to be unfaithful, either, but I was, though I'll regret it to my dying day. If only I'd stood up to Marge and told her to mind her own business, I wouldn't be in this mess now.'

'You did what you did, love, and you can't change things by wishing, but it's time you did something to sort out your life. For a start, why don't you write to one of your sisters to let them know where you are, they must be worrying, then I think you should write to Alistair. Don't ask him to take you back, just ask how he is and how Leila and David are. Leave it up to him to tell you how he feels, don't force him.'

Pulling a face, Gwen said, 'It's too soon. Is it all right if I wait till I've been away for . . . say two months?'

'You're welcome if that's what you want. Maybe you're right about it being too soon. Another six weeks might be best.'

The funeral had been an ordeal for the three chief mourners. Both Dougal and Peggy had been inconsolable, and Alistair had been hard pressed to stop his emotions from getting the better of him. He had been truly thankful that he hadn't had to see much of young Nicky. Mrs Deans, Dougal's next-door neighbour, had kept him until they came home from the service, and he'd gone to bed about eight, asking for his Mummy, which had upset them all over again.

Back at his own fireside again, Alistair wondered what was going to happen about the boy since Dougal wasn't his real father, he hadn't liked to ask his old friend about it, but Peggy seemed to think he would keep him, which was a blessing. *He* certainly didn't want him, reminding him of his wife's faithlessness. His mind refused to veer from the subject of his wife now, and he wondered where she was. He had asked David and Leila if they knew where 'Uncle Ken' lived, but neither of them could tell him, and anyway, what did it matter? If that's where she was, he didn't want her back.

Chapter 32

Lexie felt she had no one to confide in now. She could talk quite easily to Roddy Liddell these days – they were quite close now – but how could she tell him that she didn't believe her father was a murderer, just an incestuous rapist. Just? she thought, grimly. Incestuous rape was every bit as bad as murder . . . worse, for the person at the receiving end, at any rate.

She was almost certain that this was the reason for her father's disappearance. Whatever had made him do it, the shame and guilt had been too much for him to bear, for he was a decent man at heart, everybody had said so. One thing she was absolutely sure of was that he hadn't been having an affair with the doctor's wife, no matter what Tom Birnie had told the police. And there had been no evidence of pregnancy when they did an autopsy on the body, so that was another of his lies exposed.

Constantly wondering if she would ever learn the truth, Lexie was quite glad when Nancy Lawrie phoned her one evening to ask if there had been any further developments. 'Not a thing,' she told her, morosely, 'and the waiting's getting me down.'

'Well, I've been thinking.' Nancy's voice held a hint of excitement. 'Do you know if the police ever asked Margaret Birnie's mother if she'd heard from her at all since she left Forvit? Mrs McLeish, wasn't it? She must be in her eighties, I'd think, and if they didn't ask her, she likely wouldn't have thought it was important.'

Lexie had to be perfectly honest. 'But we know where Mrs Birnie is . . . was.'

'That's where she ended up, but maybe she'd come back to see *him* before he got everything sold up and he killed her in a temper. Now d'you see?'

'I can't think properly, Nancy.'

'Sorry. What I'm getting at . . . maybe the old lady can tell us where your father is . . . or was at some time. If we got his first address, we could maybe trace him from there.'

Lexie's spirits lifted for the first time in weeks. 'I suppose . . . it's possible. At least we know Mrs McLeish is still alive. Will I tell Roddy . . . the Detective Inspector . . . ?'

'Ah-ha! So it's Roddy now, is it? But no, I don't think we should involve the police just yet. Leave it to me. Greig's taking me to Stirling on Sunday to see her.'

'I wish I could do something. I'd love to go with you, but I'm not free on Sundays till dinnertime – I've to open for the papers, you see – and that wouldn't give me time.'

'No, I'm afraid not, but don't worry. I won't upset the old lady, and she'll maybe be glad to speak to someone about her daughter . . . and her son-in-law. You never know, I might learn a few interesting things about him. Any family scandals would have been swept under the carpet at the time, but she mightn't be so discreet now.'

'Let me know what happens as soon as you can. I'll be all on edge.'

'It could turn out to be a waste of time, Lexie, but it's worth a try, isn't it?'

'Oh, yes, and thanks, Nancy. At least you're doing something. I feel so useless.'

She had only just hung up when Roddy Liddell appeared. 'Nothing new to report,' he began, looking slightly embarrassed, 'but I thought I'd come to see how you were.'

'Not too bad.' She found it hard to disguise the hope that Nancy had raised in her.

'I should have come before. Did you think we'd stopped bothering?'

'I knew you'd tell me if you'd found out anything.'

'Police all over Scotland are trying to trace your father, and nothing's turned up.' He eyed her uncertainly. 'I'm trying to persuade the powers-that-be to give the builders the go-ahead to excavate the whole of the site.'

The hope disintegrated. 'You think *his* body's there as well?'

'It's a possibility, Lexie.'

'Oh, but . . .' This was a new idea to her, loathsome, alarming, and despite wanting to appear composed in front of this man, she couldn't stop the tears from edging out.

He handed her his handkerchief. 'Don't you think it would be best for you to know, one way or the other?' he said gently, his eyes holding deep compassion. 'The answer is either that he's been murdered, or that *he* was the murderer. I realize it's not much of an option, but there doesn't seem to be anything in between.'

'I suppose not.' Her knees were shaking as she contemplated telling him the option Nancy had put forward, but she thought better of it. He might be glad of the suggestion, might even have it followed up, but speaking about it might bring bad luck, and she didn't need any more of that. She needed to believe she was on the verge of finding her father and learning the truth of what had happened all those years ago.

'D'you want some brandy?' He was even more solicitous now.

'No, I'm OK . . . Oh, I'm sorry, Roddy, I should have offered you something . . . ?'

'No, I'm OK.'

Wondering why the corners of his mouth had twitched, it

dawned on her that he had repeated her own words. Poor soul, he was doing his best to cheer her, and she was making his job harder by persisting in feeling sorry for herself. She attempted to make amends. 'It's good of you to call to tell me yourself, Roddy. You don't have to, you know.'

'I know I don't, I just want to. You don't mind, do you?'

His appealing eyes – as if he were afraid of being rejected – and his attractive boyish grin were enough to tell her he meant it. 'No, you can come as often as you like, you know that. I'm always pleased to see you.'

'Are you? Are you really, Lexie? I sometimes get the feeling you'd rather I didn't . . .'

'No, it's not you,' she interrupted. 'It's worrying about what you might have come to tell me.'

He grinned again. 'Will I arrange a signal? I could give three taps on the window and say, "Me . . . friend . . . open sesame." How would that do?'

She had to laugh. 'Oh, Roddy, you're so good for me.'

'I aim to please.' The teasing light left his eyes. 'I'd like to be . . . your friend.'

'You *are* my friend, a very good friend.'

'Good. I mean . . . to tell the truth, Lexie, I'd . . .' His face colouring, he stopped short and stood up. 'Now, remember, I'll never let this investigation drop. I'm as anxious as you to get to the bottom of it, so you'll tell me if you think of anything that might help us, won't you? Promise?'

Crossing her fingers, she muttered, 'Yes, of course.' She couldn't look him in the eye and make a solemn promise, not when she knew she would break her word if Nancy's visit to Mrs McLeish paid off. They didn't want the bobbies jumping in with their size thirteen boots and spoiling everything. In an attempt to pacify her protesting conscience, she jumped to her feet. 'Thank you for what you're doing, Roddy, you really are a true friend.' She pulled her hand out of his clasp, and added, breathily because her heart was racing. 'And you'll let me know the minute *you* hear anything?'

'Definitely, and that's a promise, too!'

Mrs Deans had offered to look after young Nicky during the days in order to let Dougal go back to work, and Peggy came in every evening to give him his bath and see that he got to bed at a decent time, because his father seemed to have lost interest in everything, including the clock. The passing weeks, however, had made the boy more and more fractious, demanding to see his mother although all three of the adults attending him had tried to break it to him in their own different ways that he would never see her again – not in those basic words, of course.

It came as no surprise to the other two, then, when Mrs Deans said she was leaving to stay with her son in Southampton. 'I'm sorry, Dougal,' she went on, 'but I'm wearing on for seventy and I can't manage him when he goes into one of his tantrums, and Gordon's been telling me for years I should sell my house and go and live with them. I feel I'm leaving you in the lurch, but, honestly . . .'

'Don't feel like that,' Dougal assured her, his stomach slowly returning to its normal position. 'You've your own life to lead and I'll easily find somebody else.'

When she left, he grimaced to Peggy. 'I knew that would come, but I didn't expect it just yet, and who on earth's going to look after an uncontrollable five-year-old?'

His sister-in-law, however, having also known that it would come some day, had a solution ready for him. 'What would you say to a thirty-five-year-old widow who knows him and loves him in spite of all his going-on?' Seeing the perplexity on Dougal's face reddening to comprehension, she gave a little chuckle. 'It makes sense, doesn't it?'

He shook his head. 'It might make sense, but it's not practical. You can't give up your job to look after my child.'

It crossed neither of their minds that Nicky wasn't Dougal's biological child, nor even his late wife's, and Peggy said, very firmly, 'I don't have to work, you know. I could live quite comfortably on what Alf left me.'

'No, Peg, I can't expect you to . . . you've a life of your own to live, as well.'

'. . . to do with as I choose,' she grinned, 'and if I choose to look after a little boy who only behaves badly because his heart is aching for his Mummy, that's my own business.'

Burying his head in his hands, Dougal groaned, 'Oh, Peg, I can't let you . . .'

'And there's another thing,' she stated. 'This little boy has a Scottish father who's as stubborn as a mule, and he needs looking after, too.'

Dougal's head jerked up. 'Oh now, wait a minute! I'm maybe no great shakes at seeing to Nicky, but I can look after myself.'

'Can you cook? I haven't seen any evidence of it.'

'I never get the chance. You've made all our meals since . . .' He swallowed before going on, '. . . since Marge died, and Mrs Deans baked cakes and biscuits for Nicky, but I'm sure I could manage.'

Peggy shook her head. 'I despair of you. Why can't you just be grateful and accept my offer? You can pay me what you paid Mrs Deans, if that would make you feel any better, but it's just as easy to cook for three as for one, easier in fact.'

Taking one of her hands, he pressed it hard to show his gratitude, then swung away from her to hide his tears, and knowing how mortified he was at crying, she just said, 'I'll start the day Mrs Deans leaves. See you in the morning.'

As she strode past what was now Gwen's house, still empty, Peggy wondered when all the worry and upsets would end.

She had definitely lost one sister, and it looked as though the other one was lost to her, as well, whether by choice or by some accident. If only she knew what had happened.

Tilly made up her mind to give it one last try. The longer Gwen stopped on there, the harder it would be for her to go back. No matter if what happened had been her fault or her sister's, her Alistair should have done the proper thing and forgiven her. Of course, she still loved him, that was quite obvious. She was always making excuses for him, that he was a changed man when he came home from the prison camp and had never got back to his old self again, but, surely he still had some of the milk of human kindness in him?

Gwen's woebegone face when she came down to breakfast almost made Tilly change her mind, but she drew in a deep breath to give her strength and said, 'Now, I hope you won't be offended, love, but I do think it's time you went home . . . for your own sake.'

'Home?' Gwen's voice was listless. 'I don't have any home . . . except here.'

'This is not your home, Gwen, and if you feel you can't go back to Forvit, you should go back to London. Your sisters must be out of their minds worrying about you.'

'I left a note telling them I needed peace to think . . .'

'That was nearly four months ago. Write to them to let them know you're all right.'

Gwen gave a resigned sigh. 'I suppose I should write, but I can't go back . . . not yet.'

'Don't fret, then, lovie. If that's how you feel, I won't throw you out. You can stay here for as long as you need me. Fred won't mind.'

Listening to Gwen trailing upstairs to tidy her room, Tilly banished all thoughts of lazy evenings by the fire with her husband – Fred hardly spent any time at home these days – or an early night when they felt like it, even a late morning if *she* took it into her head. It looked as if they had a lodger for life.

Giving herself a mental shake, she went to the kitchen for her carpet sweeper. What was she going on about? Gwen helped with the housework. She was good company . . . most of the time. It wasn't so bad. It was just that Fred . . . well, he was just being Fred and hinting that he could do with a bit of peace and quiet in his own home.

Chapter 33

David Ritchie couldn't get home fast enough. He and his pals had been, not exactly rampaging through the woods between Forvit and Bankside, just giving vent to their youthful high spirits by racing about and yelling at the tops of their voices. That, of course, had led on to acting out a Tarzan film they'd seen – there had been a film show every Friday and Saturday in the village hall for a few months now. The boys took it in turn to be the hero, yodelling, or trying to, the famous call as he swung on a low branch, while the others were either 'baddies' or apes . . . or, most reluctantly, Jane.

None of the fourteen/fifteen-year-olds wore watches, but being winter, the onset of dusk told them when it was time to go home, and they made their way back to where they had left their bicycles. This was the point at which they split up and went in various directions, David and his best friend, Eddie Mearns, younger brother of Barry, wheeling their bikes back to Forvit. They preferred to walk to Eddie's house, because it gave them time to talk over anything they felt was worth discussing, just the two of them. As soon as their friends had left them this particular evening, Eddie said, 'They've dug up another body.'

This was much more interesting than the usual kind of titbits he gleaned from his father, whose job as postman let him in on many little secrets, and almost dropping his cycle in surprise, David asked, 'Do they know who it is?'

'One of the workmen told my Dad it's Alec Fraser, Lexie

from the shop's father. He run off with a young girl, or somebody else's wife, years and years ago . . . or everybody thought he run off, but he couldn't've, could he? I'm nae supposed to tell anybody, mind, for the police havena made it public yet, so you'd better keep it to yourself.'

It was a meaty topic, however, and the two boys made the most of it, speculating on why this man – a man who had disappeared long before they were born – had been killed, and more exciting still, who had done the dirty deed. By the time they came to Eddie's house, they were agreed on one thing – the murderer must be somebody from the village or quite near to it. Who else would want to kill the man who had just been the local shopkeeper? But neither of them could come up with any kind of motive.

'My Mam says Alec Fraser was a decent man,' Eddie remarked, as they stood at his gate for a few moments, 'and my Dad says he was well respected, for he took the kirk choir and that, but there musta been something bad about him afore somebody'd want to murder him.'

'That doesn't follow,' David pointed out. 'He could have found out something bad about the murderer, and he got killed to stop him telling the police.'

'It's like that picture we saw a few weeks back. James Cagney, or was it Raymond Massey? I canna mind the name o' it, though.'

'Neither can I, and I'd better be going, Eddie, or my Dad'll be yelling his head off at me for being so late. See you on Saturday, usual time?'

'Aye, it's a Western wi' Joel McCrea, and it's a Boris Karloff next week.'

'Good, I like creepy pictures better than Westerns.'

As David swung his leg over the bar of his cycle, his mind returned to the more fascinating business of the murder . . . a real murder! This, then, was the reason for his haste as he pedalled hell for leather along the road in his anxiety to get home and tell his news. He hadn't actually promised Eddie that he would keep it to himself, and his father was friendly with Lexie Fraser, so he'd be pleased to hear the latest about her father.

Throwing his bicycle down, he burst into the house. 'You'll never guess, Dad!'

His father and sister had been reading quietly by the fire, so Alistair looked up in some annoyance at the noisy intrusion. 'Must you come barging in like that? And you haven't left your bike outside, have you?'

Only then remembering the strict instructions he'd been given when he got this new Raleigh three-speed for his birthday, David dashed out again to put it under cover in the shed. It didn't look like it was going to rain, but he didn't want to chance it getting rusty. In his excitement, his fingers fumbled with the lock before managing to get it back in the hasp and snapping it shut, then he darted back inside to impart his red-hot scoop.

Closing the door quietly behind him, he said, as nonchalantly as he could, to see what the effect would be, 'They've dug up Alec Fraser.'

His father's first reaction did not disappoint him. Leaping to his feet, Alistair cried, 'What? When? Who told you?'

'One of the workmen told Eddie's Dad . . .'

Before David could give any further details, not that there were any more to give, just his and Eddie's speculations, Alistair was hauling on his jacket and going through the door. 'Poor Lexie, she'll need me.'

In another few moments, brother and sister heard an engine being started and the noise of the car's tyres crunching down the stony track. 'Is something going on between Dad and Lexie?' David asked sadly, wishing that his father had at least stayed long enough to pass some kind of comment on what had happened – his bombshell had fizzled out.

Leila shook her head. 'I don't think so. They've been friends since they were at school, that's all it is.'

'But he goes racing off to her every time anything goes wrong. He went there after the row with Mum, remember? That's where Uncle Dougal found him, and there's been other times.'

'He needs somebody to talk to.' Although only a little over a year older, Leila could look on things from an adult point of view, whereas her brother's outlook was still that of a child. 'Mum always said he was never the same after he came home from the war. We were too young to remember how he was before, but she said he was even-tempered and full of life whereas after he came back she never knew how he'd be, fine one minute and grumpy and short-tempered the next. Mind you, after what he told us he went through as a prisoner of war, it's not surprising he changed. I'm sure there's nothing between him and Lexie Fraser, though. He still loves Mum, I know he does.'

Neither of them feeling the need of anything to eat or drink, Leila made David tell her exactly what Eddie Mearns had said, and felt somewhat let down when he couldn't tell her anything more. They went to bed about a quarter of an hour after their father had gone out, but when, in their separate rooms, they heard him coming in just minutes later, they each decided against going down to ask him why he was home so soon.

Earlier that same evening, Lexie Fraser was making herself some cheese sandwiches as she listened to the end of the six o'clock news on the wireless, but she was interrupted by the bell shrilling on the shop's small telephone exchange. Laying down the knife, she ran through, plugged in and put on the headpiece. 'Forvit Post Office.'

'It's Nancy, Lexie. Listen, this is going to warm the cockles of your heart. You know I told you Mrs McLeish said she never reported Margaret missing because Tom had said she'd run off with another man? And you said that's what he'd told the police, as well, but now they're looking for him again?'

Utterly mystified, Lexie murmured, 'Yes, I know all that, but what . . . ?'

'Well, I've just had a phone call from Mrs Chalmers in Aberdeen, the other daughter, remember, and speak about blinking coincidences!'

'Nancy!' Lexie felt exasperated by the other woman's habit of spinning out any information she had to give. 'Will you just tell me what she . . .'

'Sorry, I get carried away. She's just back from a touring holiday on the west coast, and on their way back, they stopped in Inveraray to take a look round, and who do you think they saw coming out of a shop? This is where the coincidence comes in – it was Tom Birnie himself – he's her brother-in-law, remember. She said her first thought was to confront him there and then, but she knew he'd have bluffed it out and spun her some weird story, so she went into the shop and asked where the nearest doctor lived, because her husband had cut his foot on a piece of glass.'

'But . . . but . . .' Lexie was absolutely mystified. 'That wasn't true, was it?'

'Of course it wasn't true. She made it up on the spur of the moment, and I think it was pretty clever of her. Anyway, the shoplady said that Doctor Balfour had been in just a few minutes ago, and he was on his way home, so she gave Mrs Chalmers his address.'

'So it wasn't Tom Birnie . . . ?'

'Lexie, would you use your brains?' Nancy sounded disappointed with her. 'He must have moved from Glasgow after the police spoke to him that second time, and changed his name to make it more difficult for them to find him again. He'd likely have got away with it if Mrs Chalmers hadn't been in that particular place at that particular time. It was fate, Lexie, and don't you see? Tom Birnie must have something to hide, or he wouldn't change his name and hide away in a wee place like Inveraray. And now I'm surer than ever that we'll find Alec, even if he's changed his name, and all. Somebody's bound to see him somewhere and recognize him.'

Despite her head still being in a whirl, it occurred to Lexie that Nancy had omitted one vital factor. 'What'll happen now, then? Has Mrs Chalmers given Tom's address to the police . . . ?'

'I asked her not to. I thought you'd like to tell your detective friend yourself.'

'I don't know when I'll see him.'

Hearing a trace of wistfulness in the words, Nancy said, 'Friend Birnie won't be going anywhere – he doesn't know he's been spotted – so a few days' wait won't matter.'

A sudden strength surged up in Lexie now. 'I'll tell him as soon as I can, he comes in quite a lot. Um, Nancy, do you think Tom Birnie would know where my father is?'

'He might, but don't bank on it, Lexie.'

'I won't. I don't suppose he'd tell anybody, anyway.'

'Not likely. Now, you'll let me know what happens?'

'Of course I will, and thanks for what you've done, Nancy.'

'My pleasure. I'd like to see that lying devil get his comeuppance for what he did to me, and to other girls, as well, for all I know. Speak to you soon.'

Lexie had just got back to her sandwich-making when Roddy Liddell knocked on her kitchen window, and she signed to him to come in. 'I've got news for you . . .' she began, but stopped when she saw how grave his face was. 'Has something happened? What have you come to tell me?'

'Let me get you some brandy first, Lexie.'

'No! Tell me now! It's about my father, isn't it?'

'I'm truly sorry. The excavators turned up another body first thing this morning, but I was under strict orders not to tell you until we learned a bit more about it. The police surgeon's report on his first examination was that it's male, probably about five feet eleven in height and around forty years of age . . .'

'Oh, God! It *is* my father, isn't it? Will I have to . . . identify him?'

Liddell's eyes rested on her pityingly. 'There's little hope of positive identification, as you might understand after so long, but they kept searching for something that could either point to it being your father, or rule him out altogether, and they were ready to stop for the day when one of the men saw this.' He took a gold pocket watch from his pocket and held it out to her.

She took it with trembling hands, opened the back with some difficulty and looked at the inscription through a mist of unshed tears. 'To AWF with all my love CRS, and the date 18.6.1907,' she read out. She gulped to hide her emotion, but her voice broke several times as she added, 'My mother gave it to him on their wedding day. His full name was Alexander William Fraser and . . . he was twenty at the time. Her name was Caroline Ross Shewan and she was nineteen.' She stopped to clear her throat, but was overcome with the tears she could contain no longer.

Gathering her into his arms awkwardly, he let her weep, murmuring gentle words of comfort against her hair, and when the dreadful heaving sobs eased, he kissed her cheek, the salt taste of her tears making him ache with pity for her.

'I feel as if I'd betrayed you, Lexie,' he murmured. 'If it had been up to me, I'd have come straight here when I was told they'd found him, but my Super was there, and God knows who else, and they watched me like a hawk so I couldn't slip away. They said they weren't sure whose body it was, but I knew right from the start, and I'm so sorry, my dear.'

Her thoughts were so concentrated on the news he had given her that the endearment was lost on her. 'It's all right, Roddy. I know it wasn't your fault, but I'm so mixed up I don't know what to think about anything.'

The exhaustion of her torrent of weeping sounded in her voice, and he said, 'Don't think about it yet, Lexie. Wait till you're . . .'

'I can't help thinking about it. I'm glad they found him, it proves he didn't kill Mrs Birnie, but on the other hand . . . well, he's my father, and he's dead, and . . .'

'Isn't it better to know for sure than to keep on wondering? At least, as you said, we know he's innocent, but we still have to find Birnie. He's the only suspect now.'

Her head snapped up. 'I forgot! That's what I was going to tell you. Nancy Lawrie rang up and gave me his address.'

He listened, amazed, as she told him how Mrs Birnie's sister had accidentally run him to ground, and then he said, 'Well that's good news. Thank goodness we've got something positive on him at last. We'll get the bugger now. I'm sure it was him. I felt it all along. May I use your phone to let my Super know?'

'I'll put you through.'

Once she connected him, she left him to pass on the most important piece of information they'd had so far, and went back to sit by the fire. It was a mild evening so she wasn't cold, but the heat gave her some comfort, and as her feelings metaphorically thawed out, she was ashamed for having broken down so completely in front of Roddy, though he'd been like a rock to her. She wouldn't have been able to stop crying at all if he hadn't been there.

She felt a little shy with him when he came through from the shop again, beaming as he sat down beside her. 'Well, that's the last stage set in motion, but I'll stay on with you for a while, till you get over the shock a bit. The Super understands how upset you must be, and said I can stay for as long as you need me. I parked the car at the other end of the village, so the neighbours won't have any cause to gossip. How are you feeling now?'

'Much better, thanks to you. I'd have gone to pieces if you hadn't . . .'

'Lexie, I know this isn't an appropriate time, but I have to know if . . .' He looked away in some embarrassment, and his voice was barely audible as he went on, 'I need to know if there's any chance for me. If there's not, don't be afraid to say, and I'll never mention it again.'

It took a moment for her to understand what he meant, and it was surprise as much as shyness that held her back from throwing her arms round his neck. 'It's OK, Roddy,' she said, cautiously, 'I've been hoping you'd . . .'

Taken abruptly into his arms, she gave herself up to the thrill of his kisses, but they ended just as abruptly. 'No, Lexie dear,' he murmured, as she tried to kiss him again, 'now I know how you feel, this can wait . . . till we get Tom Birnie safely behind bars.'

As usual while driving down the track, it took all Alistair's concentration to avoid the sharp stones which could slash his tyres, so he was on the road before he could do any thinking. If it really was Alec Fraser's body that had been found, everything pointed to Tom Birnie being the killer.

There was nobody else it could have been. Poor, poor Lexie. What a state she must be in.

It didn't take long for him to reach the village, and he drew into the little side lane some distance from the shop. The only other vehicle in sight was the little red Post Office van at Sandy Mearns's gate, and he didn't want Aggie or Doodie Tough or any of the other scandalmongers, to see his A40 outside the shop and make something out of nothing. It wouldn't be fair to Lexie.

He closed his car door quietly and walked along to the opening through to her house. It was getting quite dark, yet her light wasn't on and he hoped that she hadn't gone out, though she would be needing company after what she'd been told today. As he stood uncertainly, wondering what to do, he could see the flickering of the fire through the curtains, so she couldn't have gone far. She had told him once that she didn't lock her porch door if she wasn't going to be out long, so she likely wouldn't mind if he went in to wait for her.

In case she was inside sleeping off the effects of long bouts of weeping, he made no sound as he turned the handle with great caution, stepped gingerly over the threshold then closed the door carefully behind him. The door into the kitchen was half open, and there she was on the couch . . . but not asleep. For a few moments, transfixed by the sight of the detective with his arms around her, Alistair stood with his mouth agape, until a weird sensation started in his innards. If he had loved Lexie, he'd have sworn it was jealousy, but he didn't, so it wasn't – it couldn't be? It was just shock at seeing her being kissed so ardently by a man . . . especially this man.

The pair were so absorbed in each other that they weren't aware of his presence, so he backed out on tiptoe, took time to close the door silently again and stumbled to his car on legs that felt as heavy as tree trunks. Then he plumped down in the driver's seat to start the engine. He had to think, but not here – not so near.

Arriving back at Benview, he went straight to bed to consider what he had seen. It was strange, really, that Lexie hadn't met somebody long before this. But that 'tec? He wasn't a good choice. What could she see in him? Had it been reaction to what he'd told her? Or had he taken advantage of her vulnerability?

Alistair stretched out to the chest of drawers for his cigarettes and lighter, but as the flame ignited, it dawned on him that, although he had never actually loved Lexie, he had always been sure that she loved him. Was that why he felt so betrayed?

David was surprised to hear his father's car coming back after just twenty minutes. What had happened at Lexie Fraser's house? If only Mum was here. If he knew where she was, he'd write and beg her to come home. She wouldn't know about poor Auntie Marge, of course, and she'd be terrible upset when she did.

Oh, this was awful! How could he sleep with all these thoughts jumbling round in his head? Maybe he should try reading? He'd read all his comics, though, and Mum had made him put all his books in the cupboard on the landing on the shelf under hers and Dad's. He might as well take a look. There might be one he hadn't read.

Jamming his feet into his slippers, he crept across his bedroom and inched the door open to save it squeaking, then stepped along the landing to the next door, which was a bit trickier. He held his breath at the three long creaks it gave before he got it open, but nobody shouted at him so he felt for the flashlight Mum kept there because there wasn't an electric point. The weak beam wavered along the row,

Treasure Island, *Huckleberry Finn*, *The Last of the Mohicans*, *Children of the New Forest*, two of the *Biggles* series. He'd read them all . . . two or three times. Looking up at the shelf above, he didn't fancy any of Dad's books, Dickens and that crowd would be dull and boring. C.S. Forester's *The African Queen* sounded a bit more promising, though, at least it looked action-packed.

Settling down in bed again, he pulled out a bookmark and wondered why Dad hadn't finished the book. Then he remembered seeing Mum reading it. She probably hadn't finished it when she went away, and Dad must have put it back in the cupboard.

The bookmark however, wasn't a bookmark, he discovered. It was a letter from somebody called Tilly to his mother, dated 1 March 1948, telling her that Ivy Crocker had died. It ended, 'Remember, if you're ever anywhere near Newcastle, Fred and I would love to see you again.'

The name Tilly was vaguely familiar, and he pondered over where he could have heard or seen it before. She lived near Auntie Ivy . . . where Mum had gone when she had the baby. Did Tilly know about that? He hadn't known himself at the time, not till Dad had told him and Leila what had happened. He still couldn't fathom out all the ins and outs of it, some things still puzzled him. Was Nicky his brother, for instance? They had the same mother, but apparently Uncle Ken was Nicky's father. That's what had caused all the trouble.

Out of nowhere, it suddenly struck David where he had seen the name Tilly before. She sent Mum a Christmas card every year. 'Love from Tilly and Fred', she always put, the same as the letter. His heart skipped a beat. Was that where Mum was? Dad said he had no idea, nobody had.

A warm excited glow began to spread through the boy's rapidly-cooling body. If he could trace her and get her to come home, it would make up for being to blame for the burst-up in the first place. If he hadn't shown Dad those snaps . . .

Yes! It was all up to him now.

Chapter 34

Roddy Liddell had spent an almost sleepless night, but it wasn't the murder investigation which had kept him awake. Yesterday had been quite a momentous day for him, apart from the unearthing of Alec Fraser's body. He had more or less told the dead man's daughter how he felt about her, and wonder of wonders, she had said she felt the same. Perfect result, despite the bad timing.

But he'd have to put it on a back burner meantime. For now, he had to concentrate on tracking down that damned murdering doctor, whatever name he was calling himself. He had contacted Mrs Chalmers first thing this morning, and was inclined to believe, from the way she spoke, that it really was Tom Birnie she had seen, and that she wasn't one of the cranks they sometimes had to put up with. She had understood that she would be called as a witness at the trial, and said she would be happy to let the whole world know the kind of rotter her brother-in-law had been and obviously still was.

Of course, Liddell warned himself, the case might never come to trial if the man was as accomplished a liar as it appeared. Mrs Chalmers' evidence was only second-hand; it was her deceased sister's word against a desperate Birnie's. It would be impossible to make people believe that a doctor as well respected as he had been in Forvit, and likely in Glasgow and Inveraray too, would have illicit associations with young girls. He would deny it, no doubt about that, and look suitably horrified that his wife's sister would even think such things about him. What Nancy Lawrie could say would be more effective, if she was willing to testify, although, again, the swine would probably deny everything, and accuse her of telling lies out of spite because he had rebuffed her advances.

In any case, would she be capable of describing to a crowded court what he had done to her? Could he put her through such an ordeal . . . even for Lexie's sake? Infidelity was not enough to convict a man for murder, nor was fathering a child on a woman not his wife, nor was breach of promise. The whole investigation was liable to collapse, with not even the smallest piece of circumstantial evidence to go on. What could anybody expect after twenty years? Tom Birnie's method of killing his two victims and his reason for so doing were likely to remain his secret for evermore.

Since Nancy Lawrie had miraculously appeared again, the Forvit women had reversed their opinion of Alec Fraser. Yesterday afternoon, he'd been hard pressed not to laugh out loud.

'I never thought Alec Fraser would've run off wi' her.' This was the postman's wife.

The one they called Doodie had almost nodded her head off. 'Me, either. Didn't I say, Mattie? I said no, no, nae Alec. He's a decent man and he would never've ta'en up wi' a lassie young enough to be his dother.'

Mattie had added, 'As for him and Mrs Birnie! Well, there was nae wey there would be ony scandal aboot them. They was pillars o' society, baith the two o' them.'

Not that that was conclusive, Roddy mused. Pillars of society had been known to stray, even to commit heinous crimes, they were only human, after all, with human feelings and failings.

Glancing at his alarm clock, which he had set for six

but switched off at five thirty because he was wide awake, Roddy was astonished to see that it was now almost quarter to seven. Good God! He'd planned to collect Gaudie and be on the way to Inveraray before seven, and it would take him all his time to be ready for half past.

First telephoning to tell his sergeant that he was running late, Liddell gave himself the quickest wash and shave he'd ever had, rummaged in his chest of drawers for a clean shirt and uncrumpled tie till the kettle boiled, and drank his cup of tea while he dressed. It was twenty-nine minutes past seven when he went out to his car, his brown wavy hair flopping over his eyes because he'd forgotten to brush it, two small pieces of toilet paper attached to his chin to staunch the blood where the razor had nicked it.

Alistair's thoughts were so tangled when it was almost time to get up that he knew his work would suffer. Maybe he should just lie there in the hope that exhaustion would overcome him eventually and he could sleep for a few hours?

He had more or less decided that what he felt for Lexie now stemmed from pity rather than love, but he still couldn't make up his mind about his wife. What he felt for her wasn't so easily defined. This not knowing where she was had blunted the earlier hatred and resentment for the pain she had caused, and what was left was an aching anxiety to know that she was safe and well. What she had done while he was a prisoner of war still rankled, and he wasn't sure if he could ever forgive her, but his children needed their mother and for that reason alone, he would ask her to come home. The thing was, where the devil was she? She had made it quite clear to her sisters – just Peggy now – that she wanted to be on her own, but that was almost six months ago. Surely she had done all the thinking she needed by this time.

Oh, hell! He couldn't carry on like this, going round and round and getting nowhere. He'd be as well going in to work to take his mind off it.

After a quick wash and shave, he came out of the bathroom and called, 'Come on, troops, time to get up,' before going downstairs.

The first meal of the day had deteriorated into a cup of tea and a slice of toast each, but neither his son nor his daughter had complained . . . so far. A flurry of raised voices overhead made him smile. David would be accusing Leila of sneaking into the bathroom before him, and she would be retaliating by saying she couldn't let him go first because he splashed soapy water all over the floor and left the basin in such a mess. But they were good kids, and David seemed to have a talent for repairing old clocks and watches. Leila, of course, wasn't quite so dedicated. She appeared to be serious about Barry Mearns, so she probably had her mind set on marriage and babies, not a career in a small watch-maker/jewellery shop in a side street.

Leila came downstairs first. 'David thinks Mum's with the Tilly Something who sent her a card every Christmas.'

Taken aback, he stammered, 'I . . . I never knew her.'

'Are you going to get in touch with her? She lived beside Auntie Ivy, so it must be in or near Moltby somewhere.'

'But she might have moved . . .' The accusation in his daughter's eyes made him get to his feet. 'I'll tell you what. If you and David clear everything up when you're finished, I'll go and phone Auntie Peggy. I'm not saying she knows that address, but she could possibly find out for us.'

* * *

As David grudgingly dried the dishes, his ears were fine-tuned to catch what his father was saying on the phone in the little porch at the front door, but, unfortunately, all he could hear was an odd phrase here and there, and only one side of the conversation.

'... I should know myself ... yes, yes ... paid more attention ...'

David nudged his sister. 'Auntie Peggy's getting on to him for not remembering himself.'

'What? ... Gwen's address book? ... I don't know. I think she kept it in her handbag.'

'She doesn't know either,' David muttered in disgust.

'She didn't know Mum ever went to Auntie Ivy's ...' Leila stopped speaking at David's imperative 'Ssshh!'

'Yes? ... it doesn't matter ... but I'd be grateful if you or Dougal remember anything ... Yes, I know he wasn't at home, but Marge could have said something in a letter ... OK, thanks anyway.'

He came back into the kitchen, shaking his head. 'She doesn't know. Well, that's it, I suppose.' Alistair gave a long sigh and shook his head again. 'Look at the time! The shop won't be opened at eight o'clock this morning.'

'Nobody ever comes in as early as that, anyway,' Leila consoled.

'This'll be the day somebody does,' her father said, dolefully. 'Have you both got everything, now?'

David gave an annoyed exclamation. 'No, I've forgot a hankie. Just be a tick.'

With his father and sister on their way to the car, he ran to the sideboard and extracted a sheet of notepaper and an envelope from the left-hand drawer. He wasn't going to be stumped because he didn't know exactly where this Tilly lived. He was desperate to see his mother, and the only way to find her would be to write ... to any sort of address. He was often left on his own in the little back workshop, and surely he'd have a chance to scribble a few lines, and Dad wouldn't miss a stamp if he took one.

'Thomas Birnie?'

The tall, white-haired man frowned, then gave a light laugh. 'No, I'm sorry, you've got the wrong man. My name is Charles Balfour and I've never heard of this . . . what was it you called him? Birnie?'

'I am Detective Inspector Liddell from Aberdeen City Police, and this is Detective Sergeant Gaudie. There is no mistake and we are taking you to the Police Station here . . .'

'Are you arresting me? On what charge, may I ask?'

His insolence got under Liddell's skin. 'No charge . . . yet. We are merely taking you in for routine questioning.'

'Questioning? About what? A robbery, a paternity suit, ha ha? You've got the wrong man, I tell you. I have committed no such crimes, Inspector.'

Having to hold himself back from punching the man in his supercilious face, Liddell said, 'It is nothing like that. Fetch your coat, please, and come with us now.'

'Am I allowed to tell my wife where I am going?'

Gaudie's restraining hand on his sleeve made Liddell take a deep breath, and he managed to keep his voice steady. 'Yes, of course.'

Birnie disappeared into what they took to be the kitchen, and came back in a few seconds, followed by a brown-haired, pleasant-faced woman who looked to be in her late forties, much younger than her husband, if he was her legal husband, which was doubtful. 'What's wrong, Inspector? What is Charles supposed to have done?'

The soft, lilting Highland tongue made Liddell feel even

more sorry for her. Poor soul, he thought, she's in for a shock when everything comes out. 'We want to question him regarding his first wife, Ma'am.'

Her unlined brow wrinkled. 'His first wife died many years ago.'

'Yes, Ma'am, we know. Are you ready, sir?'

With a sneering smile at Liddell, the doctor kissed her cheek. 'I'll be back before you know it, my dear. There's been some terrible mistake, but I'll soon clear it up.'

They hadn't far to go, and within minutes, the three men were seated at a table in a small room in Inveraray Police Station. Giving his sergeant time to produce his notebook and pencil, Liddell regarded his suspect. The man must know he was about to be accused of murder, but his eyes – a startlingly bright shade of blue – held no indication of worry or apprehension, and his hands were as steady as a rock when he took out a packet of cigarettes. 'May I?' he asked, as he extracted one and fished in his pocket for his lighter.

Silently, Liddell pushed the ashtray over to him. 'If you're ready, we can begin. As your present wife mentioned, your first wife died some years ago. Is that correct?'

The silver head nodded, the mouth turned up briefly in a sad little smile. 'Yes, that is so, Inspector. Sadly, Margaret caught a chill one night, which developed into pneumonia. She'd had a bad chest since she was a child, I believe, and I did advise her not to go out that night, it was so cold and damp, but she wouldn't listen.'

'She was, perhaps, going to choir practice at the church?'

Liddell thought he could discern a flicker of anxiety now, but Birnie said, quite calmly and with a sarcastic smile on his long lean face, 'No, Inspector, Margaret had a voice like a corncrake. As I told you before, you have the wrong man.'

'No, sir, I think not. You have been definitely identified by a witness as Thomas Birnie, medical practitioner.'

'A case of mistaken identity, Inspector.'

'She swears ...'

'She? Oh, Inspector, never, never trust a woman's judgement. If you ask any woman if she has seen a certain man, of course she will say yes. It is part of their nature.'

'Is it part of their nature to provide that certain man's address?' Liddell was growing increasingly irritated by the doctor's attitude. 'Furthermore, this lady had not been asked anything about you. She did, of course, know that we were trying to trace you, but she came to us of her own accord to tell us where she had seen you, and how she discovered where you lived ... under an assumed name.'

'I am afraid your witness picked me at random, Inspector. I had never heard the name Thomas Birnie until you mentioned it to me earlier. Where, if I may dare to ask, does your witness live?'

'She and her family were on holiday in Inveraray from Aberdeen when she spotted you. She knew you very well at one time, and I have every faith in her. She made no mistake.'

'I have never known anyone from Aberdeen, Inspector. I cannot understand this.'

Liddell was pleased to detect a tremor in the voice now. Birnie was getting edgy, though he would still brazen it out. 'How long have you been practising in Inveraray?'

There was a slight pause. 'Um, we moved here only a few weeks ago, on account of my wife's health. Prior to that I was almost twenty years in the heart of Glasgow.'

That could be true, Liddell thought; since he left Forvit, but it would have to be checked. 'And before that?' This was the crucial period.

'Dunoon. From the time I qualified until Margaret died . . . almost eight years.'

'Not Dunoon, Doctor. Well over a hundred miles from there, wasn't it?'

'What are you getting at, Inspector?' The mask was beginning to slip, the voice was sharper, higher. 'Where am I supposed to have been?'

'Do you know Aberdeenshire at all, Doctor?'

'No, I have never been as far north as that.'

The questioning went on for hours, over and over the same details, with Birnie obviously trying to remain calm, but there was an odd second or two when Liddell knew that perseverance would pay off. The man would crack . . . if they kept at him.

It was almost midnight, with all three men on the verge of collapse, when, after Birnie had again denied ever being in Aberdeenshire, Liddell said, wearily, 'So if we take you to a small village some miles to the north of Aberdeen tomorrow, you will be confident of not being recognized?'

At this, Birnie jumped to his feet, his face crimson with anger. 'Can't you get it into your thick police skull that I have never – ever! – set foot in Forvit?' His colour draining, he thumped down on his seat again.

Almost simultaneously, Gaudie threw down his pencil with a smirk on his face, and Liddell himself leaned back with a tremendous feeling of satisfaction. He had known Birnie would put his foot in it eventually.

Tilly was smiling as she came in with the post. 'It's for you, Gwen, but just look at how it's addressed. Mrs A. Ritchie, care of Tilly and Fred, Somewhere in Moltby, Near Newcastle, and somebody in the post office has written, "Try Barker, Jasmine Cottage." Just as well, or you mightn't have . . .'

Grabbing the letter, Gwen gasped, 'It's David's writing. Oh, God! Maybe Alistair's ill, or Leila.' Her nervous fingers made a sorry mess of the envelope, but at last she drew out the single sheet. '"Dear Mum,"' she read out, '"if you ever get this letter, please come home as soon as you can. Your loving son, David." Oh, goodness, something must be far wrong up there.'

Tilly shook her head. 'David must be missing you, he's still very young.'

'He knows I can't go back. His father as good as threw me out.'

'Alistair likely didn't want to climb down, so he let David do the pleading.'

'D'you really think that's it?' A note of hope came through the question.

'It's how it looks to me.' Tilly's brow suddenly furrowed. 'But Alistair knows where you are . . . doesn't he?'

'I never told Marge or Peg where I was going,' Gwen muttered, guiltily.

Gasping, Tilly said, 'No wonder nobody's written before. They must be frantic with worry, and it's high time you got in touch. Go and phone right this minute.'

It was with some reluctance that Gwen went upstairs for her purse, but she was down in seconds pulling on her coat. 'I'm not going to be bulldozed into going home, though, if I don't think Alistair wants me.'

The nearest telephone kiosk being in the village proper, Tilly knew that she would be gone for at least twenty minutes, and busied herself by sweeping the flagged kitchen floor, sluicing down her back doorstep and emptying the teapot on to the rose bush under the bedroom window. Then she went back inside, filled the kettle and put it on the stove.

Gwen would likely be glad of something to heat her when she came in out of that cold wind.

Gwen timed it perfectly, running in, her face ashen, as the kettle started to warble.

'What's up, love?' cried Tilly, jumping up to take her in her arms.

'Marge is dead! And I didn't know! Oh, Tilly, it's awful!'

'There, there, my lovie. Don't upset yourself.'

'But I didn't know, that's what hurts. A big pipe fell off a lorry and hit her, and she died on the way to hospital, and Peg said they'd all been worried stiff about me.' She took in a deep gulp of air and went on, 'Alistair had phoned Peg to ask your address, but she'd never heard of you, and I took my address book away with me.'

'You should have phoned his shop when you were at it. I'm sure he'd have dropped everything and come to you.'

'I just had the two pennies, but Peg said she'd ring him and tell him I'd be at Lee Green. She wants me there as soon as I can . . . to talk about . . .'

Tilly's sympathy metamorphosed into brisk efficiency as she organized her soon-to-be-ex-lodger and looked up the LNER timetable. 'There's a train at ten past two, so you'll need to catch the 12.45 bus from here. You'll just have time to get your things together and have a bite of something to keep you going.'

Gwen was glad that she'd have no time to brood over her sister's death, although Marge's cheery face still flashed into her mind occasionally.

Their leave-taking was harrowing, because Tilly, as close to Gwen now as Ivy had been, couldn't hold back the tears, which set her off, too. Everything bad, as well as good, comes to an end, however, and at last she was sitting on the bus with her bag at her feet and her hands clenched.

She was on her way to Lee Green again, but even though Peggy had said she would tell Alistair to drop everything and come to London, too, it would be anything but a happy homecoming.

Chapter 35

The welcome in Lee Green was even more traumatic than the farewell in Moltby. Hours were spent in the telling of, and the mourning for, Marge's death. Over the months since it happened, Peggy had learned to hide her sorrow, to profess acceptance, but the fragile veneer was scraped away by the depth of Gwen's grief. 'I should have been here,' she sobbed. 'I can't bear to think she died and I didn't even feel something inside me.'

Peggy put extra pressure on the hand she was gripping. 'It wouldn't have made any difference, Gwennie. She never regained consciousness. She wouldn't have known that none of her family was with her at the end, only two ambulance men.'

And so it went on, the tearing apart of one heart and the desperate struggle of the other not to let the wound open again, and when Dougal came home from work it began all over again, with him doing his best to console his wife's sisters while he, the bereaved husband, was equally in need of comfort – even more so, in fact.

It was almost time for bed when Gwen remembered. 'Where's Nicky? Who's been looking after him?'

'You remember Eth Powell, three doors down? I asked if she'd take him today and keep him overnight, till I saw how you were.' Peggy glanced at Dougal now and, a slight nod telling her it was all right, she continued, 'Pam Deans looked after him at first while we were at work, till one of her sons persuaded her to go and live with him and his wife. Then . . . well, I gave up my job and took over.'

'And *you* bath him when you come home, and put him to bed?' Gwen asked Dougal.

'That's how it was for a while,' he answered, carefully.

'But not any more?'

'Let me tell her.' Peggy regarded Gwen apprehensively. 'For the first few weeks, I went to my own house as soon as Dougal came in, but it seemed so silly to be burning two lots of electricity and gas, so . . . I more or less talked him into letting me move in here.'

Dougal took up the explanation. 'Gwen, I can see by your face what you think, but it wasn't like that. We stuck to the rules and slept in different rooms, but we had all our meals together, and sat together in the evenings, remembering things Marge used to say and do, and . . . we gradually began to feel closer to each other. I suppose it was inevitable, really, two lonely people brought together by one vulnerable little boy. We still sleep in separate rooms, Gwen, we haven't done anything wrong. We were hoping and praying you'd come back, because we want your blessing on us getting married in another six months or so. It's the only way it would feel right for us.'

She looked down at her hands, uncertain of how she felt. It seemed awful that Dougal was thinking of taking a second wife so soon, yet . . . why shouldn't he? He was a decent man. He hadn't jumped straight into bed with another woman, and if he did feel the need of somebody else, he couldn't do better than Peggy. Gwen lifted her head again, and her heart went out to the two people waiting so anxiously for her verdict. She had been on her own for months now, yet she had always cherished a faint hope that she could go back to Alistair one day. They didn't have that – Alf and Marge were gone for good.

The thing was, if Peg was wrong about Alistair, it would be difficult to live where she would see Nicky every day. She would have to keep her distance, be an aunt not a mother . . . which was probably just as well. If Alistair ever did want her back, he wouldn't want Nicky thrown in.

'Dougal,' she began, 'don't think I'm against you two getting married. It's just I'll have to get used to the idea – it's been quite a shock on top of . . .'

'We discussed it night after night,' Peggy said, quietly, 'and we've decided to put both houses on the market and move to another district altogether.'

'Either that,' added Dougal, tentatively, 'or . . . my mother's getting on now, and I'd like to see her and my sister again. Once we sell up here, we could easily afford a holiday in America for the three of us, and there's always the chance I could get a better job and settle over there. What do you think?'

'It's up to you.' Gwen's throat had tightened. She was happy for Nicky that Dougal was including him in their plans, although, if they remained over there, she would never see her younger son again, and her last sister would be lost to her, as well.

Seeing how their news had affected her, Peggy said, 'Leave it just now, Dougal. She still hasn't got over Marge.'

'None of us'll ever get over Marge,' he said sharply, 'but you're right. It's too soon for us to be making definite plans.' He paused, then said, 'Peg, did you remember to phone Alistair?'

'Yes, just after I phoned you, and he said he'd get here as soon as he could. They've all missed you, you know, Gwen.'

'David and Leila probably have, but I'm not so sure about Alistair.'

'He's had time to cool down and think,' Peggy said hastily,

to avoid the subject being dragged up and dissected again. 'I'm almost sure he wants you to go home.'

'I'll believe that when he tells me himself. Being a prisoner of war changed him, you know. The old Alistair would have been shocked at what I did, but he'd have got over it. This Alistair broods over things, and . . .' She broke off with a sigh. 'I'll just have to wait and see what happens.'

The phone call put Alistair into a state of flux. He didn't know whether to be glad or sorry that Gwen had materialized again. He had been out of his mind wondering if she was all right, yet he couldn't forgive her. She apparently wanted to come back, but it was all very well for her. She wasn't the one who had been betrayed. It wasn't her heart that had come within a hairsbreadth of being ground to dust. She wouldn't have to cope with nightly images of her spouse making love with somebody else.

What worried him more than anything, though, was the fact that David had felt driven to write to his mother. If the boy missed her as much as that . . . ?

'Who was that on the phone?' Leila was looking at him in some concern.

'Your Auntie Peggy. Did you know David had written to your mother?'

'Where did he get her address?'

'God knows.'

'What are you going to do, Dad? Are you going to let her come home?'

He gave a doubtful shrug. 'Do you and David want her home?'

'Of course we do. Don't you?'

He avoided her eyes. 'I don't know, Leila, and that's the

truth. She . . . no, I still can't speak about it, not yet and especially not to you.'

'Don't be too hard on her, Dad. She's been punished for what she did – she must have spent years wondering when the axe was going to fall. She's not a bad person.'

'I know that, but . . . no, you can't understand, Leila.'

'Maybe I can't, but . . . please, Dad, make her come home.'

He raised his head again. 'I said I'd go to speak to her, and we'd see what happens. Will we shut up the shop for a few days, or will you two manage to keep things going till I come back?'

'We'll manage.'

'Just take a note of anything I need to do, and I'll attend to it when I get back. I'll have to go and pack a few things, so you and David will have to take the bus home.'

'I bet he would crawl home on his hands and knees if it would bring Mum back.'

Her trill of laughter was music to his ears; neither she nor David had so much as smiled for some time, and his own heart lightened a little as he went out to his car.

On his way to Forvit, he decided that he might as well tell Lexie that he was going to see Gwen. Whatever she said, even if she told him he was being a fool, it wouldn't make him change his mind, but it was best that she knew.

It proved difficult to speak about personal matters in the shop. He was forced to stop each time a customer came in, and he had only got as far as telling her how David had worked out where to contact his mother, when they were interrupted again.

This time, it was Detective Inspector Roddy Liddell who walked in, his face so grave that they both knew he had something seriously bad to impart. 'I'd advise you to shut the shop, Lexie,' he began, then looked at Alistair. 'I'm glad you're here, too. She's going to need somebody and I'll have to get back after I say what I have to say.'

Noticing that the blood had ebbed from Lexie's face, Alistair took it upon himself to walk across to the shop door, turn the key in the lock and push down the snib. 'What is it? Has there been a new development?'

Liddell was already shepherding her through the connecting door to her house, his arm protectively round her waist, and all thoughts of going to London flew out of Alistair's mind as he followed them. Whatever the 'tec had to tell Lexie, he appeared to be quite sure that it would knock her for six.

In the kitchen, Liddell sat on the sofa with her, taking her hand between both of his, but Alistair, waiting to hear the bad news, remained standing.

'I wish I didn't have to do this,' Roddy said, after a moment. 'And I don't know where to begin.'

'It might be a good idea to begin at the beginning.' Alistair couldn't help the sarcasm.

'Yes, of course. Yesterday, my sergeant and I went to the address in Inveraray given by Mrs Chalmers. The man who answered the door denied that he was Tom Birnie, but we took him in for questioning anyway.'

With both his listeners' attention riveted on him, he told them of the long hours of questioning before the man made his fatal slip and his interrogators knew for certain that he *was* the man they were after.

An important question occurred to Alistair. 'If he hadn't shot himself in the foot, so to speak, would you have let him go?'

Liddell gave his head a firm shake. 'No, I was one hundred per cent positive that we had the right man and we'd have kept on and on at him until he did crack. He gave the game away by naming Forvit, which we had avoided mentioning, so we brought him up to Aberdeen to get his full statement, and believe me, once he started, he didn't want to stop. He boasted about all the young girls he had seduced – that was the word he used, but we did get him to admit that in most cases it had been rape – and then he came to Nancy Lawrie. I'll read a bit of my sergeant's notes. He's good, got it almost verbatim.

'I'd actually grown quite fond of the girl, but when she collared me one day and said she was in the family way and what was I going to do about it, she got me on the raw. I thought she was trying to trap me and I got really angry. I said it wasn't mine, and I could take no responsibility for it. She had got herself into the mess and she could bloody well get herself out of it.'

At this point, Lexie spoke for the first time. 'Nancy said he promised to marry her when his wife divorced him, though he never did, but he got her a room in Edinburgh.'

The detective nodded his agreement with this. 'That came later. At first, she was so upset by the doctor's attitude, and scared that her parents would find out, that when your father asked her why she was crying, she burst out with the whole sorry story.'

'Yes, she told me all that, and Dad went to Tom Birnie and threatened to tell his wife what he'd done if he didn't support Nancy and the child.'

Liddell hesitated before saying – softly wary and obviously ready to stop if Lexie's reaction was too strong – 'This is when it turned really nasty, I'm afraid. He fooled Nancy into believing that he would marry her when his wife divorced him, but he says he never had any intention of leaving her. It was she who had the money, you see, and he didn't want to foul his own nest by admitting what he had done.

'Unfortunately, he hadn't fooled Margaret. She had known for years the kind of man he was and hadn't been particularly worried because she knew he wasn't serious about any of them . . . until Nancy. So she tackled him one night and they'd had a ding-dong row that went on for hours, he said, and was still raging when they went up to bed. She had thrown every bad name she knew at him, and at first he laughed it off, but when she started to say foul things about Nancy, he lost his temper and hit her to shut her up. It didn't stop her, though, and she kept on, pummelling into him while she spat out more filth and . . .'

Liddell glanced briefly at Alistair before he went on, 'He says he didn't mean to kill her, but he lost control altogether, and one of his punches knocked her on to the bed and he lifted a pillow without thinking and suffocated her.'

Lexie rendered speechless by this, it was left to Alistair to say, 'You can't suffocate somebody without meaning to, though.'

'No, it was definitely murder, but probably unpremeditated. At any rate, he panicked, and sat for a while wondering what to do, till he realized that the longer he waited, the worse it would be for him to shift her – rigor mortis sets in after so many hours. Of course, it disappears again after about another twenty-four hours, but he couldn't wait that long to dispose of the body. So he wrapped it in the bedspread, bumped her down the stairs and through the kitchen, but unluckily for him . . .'

Liddell's voice had begun to waver before he stopped speaking, and now he put one arm round Lexie's shoulders. 'This is the worst bit for you to hear, my dear, and I should probably have told you this first, but . . .'

He looked round at Alistair, who said, 'Aye, it was my fault you didn't. But go on, tell us now, for God's sake. Has this something to do with Lexie's father?'

'Yes. I'm afraid so. Birnie said that when he opened the back door, Alec Fraser was standing on the step with his hand raised ready to knock. He said he'd come to ask if Margaret was well enough, because she hadn't turned up for choir practice that night, then, according to Birnie, Alec looked past him and saw what he shouldn't have seen. A strand of Margaret's hair had worked its way out at the top of the bedspread.'

Roddy paused with a sigh. 'I'll give you his account of what happened next, if I can find the place. Ah, here it is.'

'Fraser froze with shock, but I couldn't chance him recovering and running off to report me, so I punched him in the solar plexus and knocked him out. Then I ran up to the bedroom and got the pillow . . .'

Out of consideration for Lexie, Liddell stopped there, but she muttered, 'No, Roddy, I want to know everything. What did he do after he smothered my father?'

'He wrapped him in a sheet and had two bodies to dispose of. He was telling me all this without batting an eyelid, boasting about it, but he admitted he'd had quite a struggle to drag them, one at a time, through the back door. He wondered if he should put them in his car and hide them somewhere miles away, until it struck him that the handiest place would be best, the nearest, the one it would be least likely for anyone to look, even if the police did make a search for them as missing persons. At the other side of the wall was a moor which had been shown on maps as early as the sixteen hundreds, an ideal burial ground, although it needed a Herculean effort to get them over the wall.

'I'll quote here – "*I didn't bury them in the same grave. I couldn't have Fraser lying on top of Margaret for all eternity, but I had to get rid of the sanctimonious bastard.*"

'That was how he put it,' Roddy said apologetically. 'The hue and cry went up next day about Alec Fraser having disappeared, but Mrs Birnie wasn't missed until one of her friends realized that she hadn't seen the doctor's wife for some time and asked him if she was well enough. That was when he put out the story about her going to Stirling to look after her sick mother, the story he'd had time to manufacture.'

Roddy waited for a moment to see if Lexie wanted to say anything at this point, but she seemed to have sunk into some kind of morose reverie, so he went on, wanting to get it over. 'The day after the murders, Birnie was called in to attend to your mother, and he went back that night with the excuse that the two of you needed something to help you to sleep. What he gave your mother had her out like a light in minutes, he told me, so he took you through to your room, Lexie, gave you the same sleeping potion or whatever, and waited to see if it took effect. Of course, we know now that he was easily aroused by young girls' bodies, and as you took off your clothes it occurred to him how he could get his revenge on your father for interfering in things that didn't concern him.'

Only then did Lexie give a start and her eyes darkened as she exclaimed, 'It was the doctor that raped me?'

'Yes, it was Tom Birnie, adulterer, seducer, rapist and murderer . . . and liar, of course. Accomplished liar. You weren't the only one, Lexie, just one of many.'

'That doesn't make much difference to me, though.' She made a loud gulping noise and then muttered, 'No, I'm wrong. It does make a difference. I can think of my father as a decent man now, after all the years of hating him for what he did to me.'

'You can be proud of him,' Liddell pointed out. 'He wasn't afraid to do what he felt needed to be done. He did what he could for Nancy Lawrie, and if he'd arrived at the doctor's house half an hour earlier, he'd likely have tried to help Margaret Birnie. As it was, he didn't even get a chance to accuse her husband of murdering her.'

'Everybody always said Alec Fraser was a gentleman,' Alistair put in here. 'People could hardly believe he'd run off with anybody, never mind a girl like Nancy, but that was how it looked, and I'm glad his name's been cleared at last.'

Lexie released a shuddering sigh as Liddell got to his feet. 'Don't leave me, Roddy.'

He bent down and kissed her brow. 'I have to, Lexie, my dear. I've overstayed the time I was allowed, as it is.'

'She'll be all right,' Alistair stated, firmly. 'I'll stay with her . . . all night if necessary.'

'Thanks, I hate having to go like this, but my Super wants me back right away. I'll come back as soon as I can, Lexie, but I can't promise any definite time . . . or day, even. There's still a lot of work to be done before we get things properly tied up.'

'I understand, Roddy.' She was plainly trying to keep her voice steady, but she couldn't disguise its slight tremor. 'I'll see you when I see you.'

She controlled herself until his footsteps faded, and then the floodgates opened. 'Oh, Lexie,' Alistair begged, 'please don't cry like that. I know how upset you must be, but it tears me apart hearing you . . .'

She stretched out a hand and pulled him down beside her, and he had no option but to take her in his arms – not that he didn't want to, because he felt more genuine love for her at that precise moment than he had ever done before. Over the past few weeks, too, he had found himself recalling, with deep fondness, the evenings they had spent together in the shadow of the tower when they were young . . . before her father . . . before she thought Alec had abandoned her. Not only that, it had just transpired, she had thought that it was shame at raping her which had made him leave, and that wasn't true either. But it explained her peculiar behaviour. That was why she'd been like she was, why she had suddenly started fighting him off after making him believe she wanted him to make love to her, after she'd succeeded in making *him* desperate for it. But it was no wonder she had changed. Being raped at sixteen would be bad enough, but thinking it was her own father . . .

How could any doctor, in a position of trust, take advantage of young female patients like that? It was . . . despicable, though that word wasn't really strong enough, and there was no excuse for it. And then, to top it all, he had killed his wife in a fit of rage, also an innocent well-meaning man . . . Christ Almighty! How low could a human being sink?

It dawned on him now that Lexie's almost hysterical sobbing had eased. 'Do you fancy a drink to steady you?' he asked her.

She drew in a long, quivering breath. 'I'll go through and get a bottle of brandy from the shop. Roddy and I finished one the last time he was here.'

He let her do it. It was something to occupy her for a wee while, but it gave him, unfortunately, time to imagine what she and the 'tec had got up to after finishing off a whole bottle of brandy. Had she let *him* go all the way? But maybe the bottle hadn't been full when they started? He sincerely hoped not, for even if Lexie wasn't a young girl any longer, she had kept her figure. Of course, she hadn't borne any children, so it had been easier for her than for Gwen, whose waist was thicker than it had once been, and her breasts more flabby.

A lead ball hit him in the gut. With everything that had happened, he had forgotten all about Gwen. She would be sitting in Lee Green tomorrow on her own waiting for him to show up. Of course, she might spend the night in Peg's house, or Dougal's, though that wouldn't make it any easier for her. But he couldn't help it. He had promised to look after Lexie tonight, and he couldn't let her down. He couldn't even phone Dougal to explain. If Lexie knew he had promised to go to Lee Green, she would make him go.

He raised his head with a smile when she came back with a bottle of Five Star Cognac, and watched while she took out two goblets and almost filled them. Then, after sitting down beside him again, she murmured, 'I don't know what I'd have done tonight without you, Alistair, d'you know that?'

'I'm just glad I was here, though I'm sure Liddell wouldn't have gone back on duty if you'd been on your own.'

She gave a tremulous smile. 'I wouldn't be too sure of that. Doesn't duty come first, last and always with a cop?'

'Do you . . . is it serious between you?'

Shrugging sadly, she said, 'I wish I knew. I don't know what's wrong with me, but I always pick men who can't make a definite commitment to me.'

He took this as a hit at him. 'Lexie, we were far too young . . .'

'Forget what I said, I'm not thinking straight. You know, you don't have to stay with me all night. I've got over the worst, and I'll be all right.'

'No, Lexie, if I leave now, you'll go over and over things in your mind till you're in a right old state.'

She looked at him cautiously. 'I need to go over it again, Alistair. I want to remember how it happened. Now I know it wasn't my father, maybe other details will come back to me. As a matter of fact, just a few minutes ago, something that man said came into my head. It was while he was . . . actually doing it, and he must have thought the sleeping pills he gave me had taken effect, but if he'd only realized, he was keeping me awake with the pain he was causing.'

'I think you should try to forget,' Alistair muttered, uncomfortably.

'No, Al, I have to remember everything that happened that night, to lay it all out and see the truth of it, before I can let myself forget. Please don't try to stop me.'

His heart aching with pity for her – or could it be that love was blossoming after all this time? – he put an arm around her and pulled her against him so that her head was resting on his shoulder. 'Get it off your chest, then, but remember, I'm here to catch you if you feel you're falling into a bottomless pit.'

She fished for his free hand and gripped it tightly, reassuring herself and drawing comfort from him before she began. She told him how happy her childhood had been, how her father had been everything a child could wish for, how he had given her a love of music. 'I'm sure he was disappointed that I couldn't sing for peanuts, but he never said anything. He was always loving towards Mum and me, and she was quite happy for him to be helping people out of little troubles they couldn't see a way round themselves, men as well as women, and girls. Mum trusted him, that's why it came as such a shock when he just went off. He hadn't told her about Nancy, I don't know why. If he had, things might have turned out differently. As it was, she couldn't bring herself to believe he'd run away with a young girl, but there wasn't any other explanation.'

Lexie suddenly twisted round to look up into Alistair's face. 'That's really what killed her, you know, the thought of him betraying her and the nagging suspicion he could have been carrying on with other females for years.'

Her lovely blue eyes were pleading, her trembling lips only inches away from his as he looked down on her, and he was overcome with love for her, but he knew better than to kiss her – not yet. He had to let her work out the sequence of events, had to listen if she wanted to describe every move the evil doctor had made. 'I'm sorry, my dear.' It was all he could say.

She *did* go into every last detail which had flooded into her reawakened mind, describing Birnie's lascivious face – although she said 'drooling' – as she undressed after taking the sleeping tablets. 'He even unfastened my bra because my fingers wouldn't work. I don't think he put my pyjamas on for me. I think he wanted me naked . . .' She shuddered. 'Wait, though, something else is coming back . . .' She closed her eyes for a few moments then whispered, 'He was gripping my . . . breasts and moaning, not words, just sounds, then he muttered something about the sins of the fathers. It was after that, when he was fastening his trousers, that he gave a horrible, cackling laugh and said, 'That's paid you back for sticking your nose in where it wasn't wanted, you interfering slimy bastard.' I thought it was me he was calling names and I was too young to understand what they meant, but now I do.'

Alistair felt really uncomfortable at hearing what Lexie had gone through, but he had promised to listen and he supposed it was good that she could talk about it. Luckily for him, having satisfied herself as to what had been done to her and by whom, she didn't want to go any further down that particular path.

For the last minute or two, she had been looking into the fire, but she swivelled round once more. 'Maybe now you'll see why I couldn't let you do what you wanted, nor any of the other boys I went out with, locals and boys from Ardley Camp during the war. Not only that, I couldn't forget you, Al, you were always there in my mind. Even after you got married, I still believed I could get you back. After I met

Gwen, though, I knew I'd just been fooling myself. That reminds me, have you heard from her yet?'

He shook his head vehemently. It was true – he hadn't heard from Gwen. He'd only heard of her through Peggy when she phoned. 'Since she went away, I've been thinking more about how things used to be between us, Lexie. I think I did love you, but . . .'

'But I was too eager?'

'Aye, that was it. We . . . I've wasted a lot of years, Lexie . . . darling.'

She gave him no encouragement – he had to lift her chin with his thumb – but the minute their lips touched he believed that he could sense the electricity between them. 'Oh, Lexie,' he groaned.

Strangely, he didn't even think of going any further than that. It wouldn't have been fair to her after what she had learned earlier, and he was content just to hold her in his arms and stroke her fine blonde hair.

They stayed like that until the fire died down. 'Will I put on more coal?' he asked.

'It's hardly worth it. It's ten to ten.'

'Yes, it's time you went to bed. I'll sleep on the couch, if you look out a couple of blankets for me.'

She propped herself up on one elbow and looked deep into his eyes. 'I don't want you to sleep down here. Come upstairs and just be there for me – if that's all right?'

He wasn't too sure of the wisdom of this – in such a situation wouldn't he be tempted? – but if that was what she wanted, he would do his best.

Later, lying on top of the bedcovers while she slept in fits and starts in the crook of his arm, he thought of his wife, who would be expecting him in the morning; of his children, who would believe that he was on his way to London until Peggy or Gwen phoned to let them know he hadn't arrived. But he resolutely put all thoughts of them out of his mind. What did anything matter? He had been reunited with Lexie and she would never, ever, let him down.

Chapter 36

Chilled to the bone despite the electric fire which Lexie had switched on so that he wouldn't be cold, Alistair regarded it doubtfully; he could just make out the faint glow of the spiralled strip of its single element; there didn't seem to be any heat coming from the damned thing. Shouldn't it be brighter than that? Lexie must be warm enough, though. Astonishingly, despite what she had learned last night, she was fast asleep, not, however, an altogether peaceful sleep. Her body was restless, moving, jerking involuntarily every now and then.

Poor lass. She hadn't had an easy life, especially with that awful suspicion about her father at the back of her mind for so many years. Thank goodness she knew the truth now, which, he had to admit, much as it went against the grain, was entirely due to the efforts of Detective Inspector Roderick Liddell. Still, there was no need to be jealous of him now. With the case solved, he wouldn't be bothering Lexie much longer. She'd be free to get on with her life, a life that she had dreamed of for twenty years, a life with her first and only love.

Alistair's sigh came out louder than he intended, so loud that his companion stirred and opened her eyes. 'Are you OK, Al? You look cold.'

'I'm not too bad,' he fibbed. 'Go back to sleep. You need all the rest you can get.'

'I haven't really been asleep, just dozing off and on. I've

been conscious of you there all the time, thank goodness. Come under the blankets and speak to me.'

Ignoring the warning bell ringing in his head, he hoisted himself up then slid in beside her. 'You *are* cold!' she exclaimed. 'You're shivering. Come closer till I see if I can get some heat into you.'

She moved over and he obediently lay in the spot she had vacated for him, his temperature shooting up with the heat of her as she snuggled against him. Good God, he thought, that wasn't bad going – from well below zero to well above boiling point in a couple of seconds – but he said nothing, for fear of breaking the spell.

'I've something to tell you, Al,' she murmured after a while.

His limbs feeling as if they belonged to him again and wouldn't cut off her circulation if they touched her, he put an arm round her and ran his hand gently down her back. He wanted to show that he loved her, too, that he had come to his senses at long last. Her little intake of breath showed that the caress had pleased her, but he wanted to hear her say what he was sure she was going to say. 'Yes? What is it, my darling?'

She kissed him first. 'Oh, Al, my dear, dear Al. All my life it was you I wanted . . .'

'Yes,' he breathed, 'and you've got me now.'

'But that's just the point,' she whispered. 'Now I know I can have you . . .'

His kiss was tender. It wasn't time yet for passion. 'There's no need for you to worry, my darling. I know what you're trying to say.'

'Do you?' She sounded surprised. 'How could you? You can't have guessed?'

'Yes, it wasn't difficult, all the signs were there.'

'But we tried to keep it a secret till . . .'

This wasn't going as he thought. In fact, his mouth had dried up, the chill had settled on him again. 'We? You and who else? Oh, no!' The understanding almost crushed him. 'Don't tell me that bloody 'tec's been at you, got you fooled.'

She pulled away from him. 'Alistair, that's not fair. Roddy's been very good to me, very considerate, and I love him . . . more than I ever loved you.'

He didn't believe her. He had caught her on the raw, and she was trying to get back at him by saying that. 'You hardly know him. How long is it since you met him?'

'Long enough. It doesn't take long to fall in love, and it doesn't take long to be sure if the other person loves you back.'

'You can't know that for sure.' Alistair was fighting against the intrusive feeling that it wasn't only Gwen who had betrayed him. 'I bet he's married and you're just a bit on the side for him.'

Her open hand slapped his cheek, and as he jumped back, she spat out, 'Thank you for those kind words!' Her voice was icy. 'But let me tell you, his wife died over five years ago, and I would trust him before you, any day! Get out of my house, Alistair Ritchie, and I don't want to see you ever again!'

Needing no second telling, he leapt out of bed, scuttled down the stairs and slammed out of the house. His mind was in such a state of torment that he completely forgot parking his car at the shop door the day before and walked in the other direction . . . and carried on walking, sheer instinct alone guiding his feet. All he was conscious of, apart from the jagged pain of rejection, was self-pity, an overwhelming deluge of self-pity. Why did all these bad things have to happen to him? What had he done, for God's sake, that he had to be punished for it? Hadn't he fought for his King and country? Hadn't he endured over two years in a prisoner-of-war camp? Hadn't he worked his gut out to run a business successful enough to keep his family in a decent style?

And then he'd been felled by learning that his wife had cheated on him while he was away, that she had filled her lonely hours with another man, that she had even let this other man make love to her and plant a child inside her. All that of course, according to her, was Marge's fault, and God had certainly punished *her*. One smack with a sewage pipe and poof!

Poof? Why did that remind him of something? Somebody? Somebody who said 'Poof', and snapped his fingers? *His* fingers. Yes, it had been a man. *Manny!* Manny Isaacson. Oh, if only those happy days could come back again. If only there had never been a war. If only he had never made Gwen take their children to Forvit. If only he'd never left Forvit in the first place. He would likely have married Lexie, and they'd have been happy ever after. *She* wouldn't have broken her marriage vows.

Alistair had no control over his thoughts, which were leading him to ridiculous heights of improbability . . . nor over his feet, which were taking him towards the tower, his old trysting place with Lexie. They were averse to going home, where, his subconscious mind told him, lay decisions to be taken, explanations to be made, neither of which he was capable of at the present time.

There was a light layer of frost on the stony path, making his footsteps crackle as he made his way up the hill, and the scrub and clumps of heather on either side of him seemed to be ghostly, uneven, white shapes in the dim light of the half moon. When he reached the track which branched off to the right, the way to his own house, he stomped past it, firmly set now on getting to the old tower which had deteriorated even further since he was a youth, to the place where he could be sure of peace to think, to confront whatever it was that had been bothering him, ripping him apart.

Reaching his goal, he sat down on the far side, leaning against the crumbling stone wall, drawing his feet up and putting his arms round his knees. Why was he in such a state? What had happened to him? He felt completely and utterly lost, with no friends, no family, to guide him. Oh, Manny, if only you were here. You would advise me. You would keep me right. You would help me to make my decision.

What decision, though? That was the point. The ache inside him was growing angrier at the thought of having to make it. Clearly, whatever choice he made would not be a happy one. Nothing in his life would be happy now. Nothing could be even the least little bit happy any more. It was to do with . . . two women. That was it. One woman he loved, and the other woman he . . . also loved?

He sat up with a start. Where was Lexie? Why had she left him up here on his own, with these big boulders all round him. What if more bits fell down? Would anybody care if he was hurt, or killed? Nobody!

Gradually, however, as he sat regarding the surrounding stones with distaste rather than fear, a picture of two small children returned to him. Two fair-haired children – a boy and a girl. But there was another child's face intruding – a face topped with bright ginger hair, an appealing face but one he didn't want to see.

He closed his eyes, and tried to conjure something else up, and thankfully it was Lexie who came into his inner view. But where was she? Something was wrong somewhere, something far wrong. He had to find her . . . as soon as he could, before she . . .

Rising unsteadily to his feet, he skirted the debris and set off down the hill again, his feet, this time, scarcely taking time to touch the ground. But it wasn't dark now. It was morning, early morning. His mind on what he knew was an urgent quest, he broke into a desperate run, gaining further momentum on the last steep slope before the track joined the road.

He didn't see the single-decker bus coming, and even if he had, he would have been unable to stop.

'Something could have happened. Why don't you phone the shop and find out . . . ?'

'No, Peg, I know exactly what's happened,' Gwen interrupted. 'He's changed his mind. He's had time to think, and he still can't forgive me.'

'Go home, anyway,' her sister pleaded. 'For David's sake, and Leila's.'

Shaking her head, Gwen murmured, 'It's for their sakes I'm not going back. Alistair can be very nasty, as I found out, and there would likely be another big scene. I can't put them through that again. In any case, he probably wouldn't let me in.'

'Haven't you got the doorkey with you?'

'I didn't think . . .'

'I don't suppose it matters.'

After a few minutes' silence, however, Peggy suddenly said, 'Don't you love him any more, Gwennie?'

She didn't have to think about this. 'I've never stopped loving him, but it's obvious he doesn't love me now, so what's the point?'

'The point is,' her sister said brusquely, 'that you are his wife, and not only that, you have two children to think of.' She paused, then went on, cautiously, 'Yes, just two. It's easier all round if you forget . . . Once we take Nicky to America, Alistair might come round.'

'Do you think so?' A trace of hope appeared in Gwen's eyes.

'It's possible.'

* * *

'It's funny Dad hasn't phoned yet,' David said, as he and his sister were walking down to catch the bus. 'He should have got to Lee Green by now.'

'Maybe Mum and him were too busy talking to notice the time,' Leila comforted. 'One of them'll likely phone the shop this forenoon.'

'Leila, what if she doesn't want to come home?'

'She's probably still getting over Auntie Marge. She wouldn't have known anything about that, remember.'

'No, I forgot. But Auntie Peggy could have let us know what was going on?'

'She won't want to interfere. Mum's got to make up her own mind.'

'I'd have thought she'd be desperate to see us.'

'You're still too young to understand, David. Come on, we'd better hurry or we'll miss the bus and we'll have to wait an hour for the next one.'

He dutifully speeded up, but his face told of his inner dissatisfication with the way things were turning out. They waited at what was recognized as a courtesy bus stop, but the bus didn't arrive on time, and they argued for some minutes over whether to go home and come back in an hour to get the next bus, or, as David wanted, to start walking in the hope that this bus had been held up and would catch up with them. Leila had finally given in, and they were twenty minutes on their way when a car drew up alongside them.

They knew the driver by sight and he explained that the postman had told him there had been an accident about a mile and a half back. 'Somebody apparently ran on to the road in front of the bus. Goodness knows how long it'll be before you'll get one, so you'd better hop in and I'll give you a lift into town.'

They accepted gratefully, and while they were speeding

towards the city, he said, 'You're Alistair Ritchie's two, aren't you? I was at school with him, a year younger – Sid MacConnachie.' Gathering from their animated faces that they would be interested in hearing about their father's boyhood, he told them of the mischief Dougal and Alistair had got up to, but he changed the subject when they came to the outskirts of Aberdeen. 'I was sorry to hear about your Auntie Marge. I only met her once or twice – at the dances for the boys at the camp during the war – but she was full of fun. I wasn't called up for service, you see . . . graded 4F at my medical.'

'4F?' asked David, his curiosity aroused. 'What was that?'

'Well, you know what A1 means?'

'The best there is?'

'Right, and they graded you down from that. 4F was the lowest, practically branding you ready to kick the bucket.' MacConnachie gave a throaty chuckle. 'They failed you for deafness, flat feet, asthma and that kind of thing . . . and I had the lot.' He grinned at Leila through the mirror after negotiating the intricacies of Queen's Cross, a meeting of five streets. 'Where do you want me to drop you? I turn down Holburn Street.'

'That's fine,' she smiled. 'Let us off when you come to Holburn Junction. We haven't far to go from there.'

As soon as the car stopped, David started to run, anxious in case his mother or father phoned to tell them what had been decided, while Leila hurried behind him.

It was, however, almost noon before the telephone rang, but when David dived to answer it, it was Lexie Fraser to tell them that their father had been in an accident with the early morning bus and was in the Aberdeen Royal Infirmary, although she was so upset that the boy had difficulty making out what she was saying. 'Lock up the shop,' she instructed, after obviously pulling herself together, 'and get a taxi to the hospital, you and Leila. Tell the driver I'll pay when you get here.'

David looked at the receiver for a moment after she rang off, and Leila asked, 'Well? It was Mum, wasn't it? What did she say? Is she coming home?'

He burst into tears now. 'It was Lexie. Dad's in hospital . . . it was him that was in that accident . . . but how could it be? He's in London with Mum, isn't he?'

'How is he?' Leila asked Lexie, thankful that the woman had appeared quickly, because the man at the door had been most unwilling to let them in without visiting cards, and the taxi driver had displayed obvious disbelief that he would be paid.

'He's still unconscious, but I thought you should be here in case he comes round.'

'Have you told my Mum?' David wanted to know, finding his voice at last.

Lexie looked puzzled. 'I thought nobody knew where your Mum was.'

'She's back in Lee Green,' Leila cut in, to avoid David going into a long explanation.

'Do you know her telephone number?'

'I know the three of them,' Leila said proudly, her voice trembling just a little. 'Should I go and find a phone?'

'If you don't mind. I'll wait with David till you come back.'

Leila had rung her grandma's number and her aunt's before she found Gwen at Dougal's, but it was Peggy who took control of the situation when she heard what had happened. 'Leila, is anybody there with you . . . an older person, I mean?'

'Yes, Lexie Fraser's here. I don't know yet how she found

out about the accident, but it was her that phoned us. We're all at the hospital, and Dad's still unconscious.'

'I'll let Dougal know, and he'll likely want to take your Mum up on the train. I'll stay here with Nicky, and I won't leave the house at all, so phone me the minute there's any change in your Dad.'

When Dougal and Gwen walked into the hospital waiting room the following day, both Leila and David looked ready to collapse, but stood up to hug their mother. Then Lexie rose to shake her hand.

'I'm glad you're here, Gwen,' she murmured, 'and you, too, Dougal, but we'd better leave the explanations till . . . later. I'll take you along to see Alistair, but I'd better warn you, he's not a pretty sight.'

All five of them remained in the hospital for the rest of that day, taking it in turns to go to the small tearoom for a cup of tea and a biscuit, while the others kept vigil in the corridor outside Alistair's ward. Dougal sought out one of the doctors to find out how hopeful they were of the patient's recovery, and the elderly man, utterly worn out as he appeared to be, spent several minutes talking to him and Gwen.

'He seems to think Ally should come round any time,' Dougal observed cheerfully, when the doctor had left. 'They can't do much about anything till he does, so we'll just have to wait to find out how the injuries will affect him.'

Lexie insisted that she should take Leila and Dougal home that night, but it was three days later before Alistair regained consciousness and was pronounced out of danger, and another few hours before Dougal could persuade Gwen to leave the hospital.

Not until they arrived at Benview, however, did she let her thoughts touch on the accident, and why Alistair had been in that particular spot at that particular time, a time when both Leila and David were under the impression that he had gone to Lee Green to fetch her home. 'I'm sure Lexie Fraser knows something,' she said to Dougal, when they were seated by the fireside. 'She said explanations could wait, so . . . d'you think Alistair had been with her all night?'

'Don't torture yourself, Gwen. Look, why don't I go and ask her to come and see you as soon as she can? It's Sunday, and the shop'll be shut by now. I'll take Leila's bike.'

He had just tucked his trouser legs into his socks when they heard a vehicle drawing up outside. 'It's our car,' Gwen muttered, looking out of the window. 'Sandy Mearns is driving and Lexie's coming out. So Alistair must have left the car there for some reason.'

'Don't upset yourself. Wait till you hear what she has to say.'

They had to wait a further few minutes, Barry arriving to take his father back, before Lexie told them anything, and even if some of her story bordered on the unbelievable, it did go a long way to allay Gwen's fears, though there were still a few things that niggled at her.

'I wouldn't have got through that night if he hadn't been there with me,' Lexie assured her. 'Roddy had to go back on duty, so he was glad Alistair could stay. Look, Gwen, nothing went on between us, absolutely nothing. I don't know why he came to see me, he didn't get a chance to say because Roddy came to tell me they'd arrested Tom Birnie. He's admitted to killing both his wife and my father, and as you can imagine, I was in such a state, I think Alistair was scared I'd do something silly . . . and maybe I would have, if he hadn't been there.'

Gwen still looked puzzled. 'I understand all that, but why

was he coming down from the tower at that time of morning? That's what I can't understand.'

'To be honest, neither can I.' Lexie met her eyes squarely. 'Maybe he was trying to make up his mind about taking you back, and he'd decided he would. That would explain him rushing back . . . to pick up his car.'

This bolstered Gwen's flagging hopes of reconciliation with her husband.

Roddy's face told Lexie that something dreadful had happened, and he burst out with it as soon as he closed the door. 'Tom Birnie committed suicide last night! Poisoned himself! We don't know exactly what it was he used, we'll have to wait for the autopsy report.'

'But where would he have got poison? Wasn't he searched?'

'You're as bad as my Super. He was stripped and searched, and nothing was found on him or his clothes, but he left a note . . . to rub my nose in it.' Roddy's long-suffering sigh told of the scorn his superintendent had heaped on him. 'He said he had always known he was bound to be caught some time, and he had taken the precaution of making ready for it. He'd hollowed the heel of one of each pair of shoes he bought over the years, hidden a capsule of poison in the cavity then fixed a rubber heel on top.'

'He'd been doing that for twenty years?'

'It would always have been at the back of his mind, though nobody noticed anything odd about him. His wife says he was the kindest of men. She's totally shocked, can't believe the things he confessed to. He even boasted he'd married her bigamously, after running out on his second wife.'

'Poor woman!'

'It's her I feel most sorry for, and all the other poor women he brutalized, including you. How are you, now, my dear? Have you got over . . . ?'

'I didn't have time to think about that for days . . . but you don't know, of course.'

She told him about Alistair's accident, about him still being in hospital in Aberdeen, then continued, 'He stayed with me all night, you know, after you told us you'd arrested Tom Birnie.'

Roddy looked at her questioningly. 'You said he was running down from the tower and came out on to the road in front of the bus. What had he been doing up there?'

Lexie took a moment to answer. 'We'd had a disagreement, and he rushed out . . .'

'A disagreement? Good God! At a time like that? What was going on, Lexie?'

Having resolved to keep nothing back from him, she murmured, 'I told you he never felt the same about me as I did about him when we were younger, but that night . . .'

'You mean . . . he tried something on . . . after what I'd just told you?'

'No, no, it wasn't that. He wouldn't believe that I didn't love him, and he said I was a fool for . . . he said I was just a bit on the side for you, so I slapped his face. He wasn't stable, you know. Being a prisoner of war changed him, and then Gwen leaving him . . .'

Roddy bit his bottom lip. 'I always had the nasty feeling there was still something between you.'

'There wasn't, just . . . a girl always has a sort of soft spot for her first love, no matter how he treated her. But he was mad at me for hitting him and he just slammed out.'

A rather uncomfortable silence fell then, while she frantically thought of some way to change the subject. 'Does Nancy know about Doctor Birnie?' she asked, at last.

'Last time we talked to her, she was told that he'd been arrested, but she doesn't know that he killed himself.'

'Oh, Roddy!' Lexie burst into tears now, and as he held out his handkerchief to her, he said, 'I know how you feel, my dear. You wish he hadn't been such a coward. You wish he'd lived to be hanged for what he did. Am I right?'

She nodded, but after a moment, she said, in a contrite little voice, 'Is that bad of me?'

'Not in the slightest. He was a monster, and even if he could turn on the charm and be a model husband, like this last "wife" says, it doesn't excuse the anguish and agony he put his victims through, including his first wife. You should think of yourself now, put the past behind you.'

Her heartbeats speeded up, but she couldn't say what she knew he wanted her to say. There was still something holding her back, still the fear of being manipulated into something that would end in tears.

'What's wrong, my darling?' His arms stole round her, and his eyes, and his voice, softened. 'Is it still too soon for you? If it is, it's all right. I love you, my darling, and I'm willing to wait.'

She shook her head sorrowfully. 'Oh, Roddy, I'm sorry.'

'No need to be sorry, Lexie. As usual, I've jumped in with my size thirteen boots and made a muck of it.'

'No, no! It's not you . . . it's me . . .'

There was something in his face now, a quirkiness that banished all her fears. This man could never hurt her. She would be safe with him . . . wouldn't she?

As if he sensed that the love blossoming within her was still quite fragile, his lips touched hers reverently, brushing, lingering, until, with a soft sigh, she gave herself up to the magic of his kisses, the magic of him.

'Lexie,' he murmured after a minute or so, 'I want you to be quite, quite sure, before you commit yourself . . .'

'I am,' she whispered into his ear, 'quite, quite sure.'

With a quick intake of breath, he took her face between his hands. 'Isn't it about time you told me how much you love me?'

Needless to say, it was some hours before Detective Inspector Roderick Liddell left the house behind the general store-cum-Post Office, during which time everlasting love had been sworn, a proposal of marriage had been made . . . and accepted.

1950

Chapter 37

After going over and over it in her mind, Gwen decided that she'd have to tell Alistair about Lexie and Roddy Liddell. Once he started going out again, he would hear it for himself, and it was better that it came from her. The trouble was, he was so unstable, how would he take it, and when would be the best time?

She waited until afternoon. She generally sat with him for a couple of hours after lunch was over and her housework was done, and before she had to prepare the evening meal. It was a peaceful time, a time to discuss what was in the newspaper and on the wireless, a time to talk about anything she was sure would not upset him. Even after six months, he was still fragile, in mind as well as body, and had to be treated with kid gloves.

'The new man's taking over the shop today,' she began, carefully.

'Aye,' he said, in his usual expressionless voice, so that she could never be certain if he had actually taken in what she said. 'Sandy Mearns told me this morning.'

The postman had been a lifeline to Gwen. He had arranged that their delivery be the last of his morning round, which let him have half an hour or so to sit and speak to Alistair over a cup of tea and a biscuit. Perhaps it was because he was older, on the verge of retirement, that he was the only one who seemed to get through to him. Not even David, nor Leila who was his favourite, could hold his attention for more than a few minutes, yet he chatted away to Sandy all the time he was there, which gave her freedom to do things she couldn't get at otherwise. If she was out of Alistair's sight for longer than it took to go to the bathroom, he was shouting for her.

Dragging her thoughts back to the matter in hand, she said, brightly, 'I'm glad for Lexie. She waited a long time, and she couldn't have picked a nicer man than Roddy.'

Alistair's brow wrinkled. 'Roddy? The 'tec? But he hasn't taken over the shop?'

She couldn't help wondering, not for the first time, why he seemed to have such a down on the man, but she let it pass. 'No, it's a Bill Munro, and I don't know where he comes from. I meant . . . Lexie's marrying Roddy on Saturday in Aberdeen and I wish I could go and see her. She'll make a lovely bride.'

Her husband was silent for so long that she wished she hadn't raised the subject after all. Lexie was one of his closest friends, and besides helping Leila and David at the time of their father's accident, she had stayed at his bedside until his wife managed to be there with him. Had there been more than friendship between them? Had the romance of their childhood carried over into adulthood, or had it lapsed when he went to London and been revived again when he returned to Forvit? There had been other occasions when she had been suspicious, had felt jealous of Lexie, but it had always blown over. Not this time.

Yet . . . if he loved Lexie, why had he been so upset when he learned about . . . his wife's one and only slip? It would have been an ideal let-out for him, a perfect reason to file for divorce, but he hadn't taken it. That was why she had always hoped . . .

'Aren't you happy for Lexie?' she asked, wanting to get at the truth once and for all. In his present state, he wasn't capable of carrying off a downright lie. 'You thought quite a lot of her at one time, didn't you?'

His eyes, when he turned them on her, were accusing, as if he knew exactly what she was up to. 'Yes,' he said, slowly and very deliberately, 'I've always thought quite a lot of Lexie, and if Dougal Finnie hadn't whisked me off to London, I'd likely have married her. Is that what you wanted me to say?'

Disappointment almost choked her. She'd wanted him to tell her that it had only been puppy love between him and Lexie, that it was his love for *her* that was the real thing, the true love, but she had been deluding herself all these years. 'So . . . you're not happy for her?' she got out with great difficulty, laying herself wide open to further heartache.

At that moment, the telephone rang, and she jumped up, relieved yet angry at being interrupted. He watched as she listened intently for a few seconds, and then without having said a word herself, she held out the receiver to him. 'It's Dougal,' but held her ear as near to it as she could.

'Before I tell you anything, Ally,' came the loud metallic voice – unnaturally loud with the possible intention of letting her hear, too? – 'I hope you're a lot better than when I left you. Gwen's letters say you're coming on nicely, but I want to hear it from you, and I want the truth, mind.'

'The truth is I'm fine, so you'd better hit me with whatever it is you're hedging about, for I know it's nothing good.'

'Depends how you look at it, Ally boy. I don't know if Gwen told you, but I made up my mind to emigrate to America . . .'

'No, she didn't tell me.' Alistair's voice was clipped, Gwen noticed, his face closed.

'Well, I filled in all the forms, and everything's cut and dried. We're ready to leave now for Southampton and we sail tomorrow.'

'We?'

'Oh God, did she not tell you that, either?'

'She thinks she's shielding me from getting hurt.' Alistair sounded bitter, now. 'So . . . who's we?'

'Peg and me, of course. We didn't know if I could marry my sister-in-law in this country, and we didn't have time to make enquiries, so she changed her name to mine by deed poll, and we're travelling as man and wife. If it's possible, we'll make it legal when we get to the other side. If not . . . well . . . it won't matter.'

Alistair glanced at Gwen, who gave his hand a reassuring squeeze. 'What about . . . ?' he whispered to her, his hand over the mouthpiece.

'It's all right,' she whispered back. 'Just listen to what he's got to say.'

'If you're wondering about Nicky,' Dougal continued, 'we're taking him with us. He is our son, after all.'

Seeing the haunted look in her husband's eyes, Gwen took the instrument from him. 'Thanks for telling him yourself, Dougal, but I think he needs time to digest it. He's still not quite . . . you know. Bon voyage, dear.'

'Thanks, Gwen, but somebody else wants a word.'

'Hi, Gwennie, it's your baby sister. How are you coping?'

'Better for hearing you. Oh, Peg, America's such a long way off.'

'We'll keep in touch.'

The sound of a slight scuffle came across the wire now, then a treble voice piped, 'It's me, Auntie Gwen. Isn't it exciting? Dad says we'll be going on a great big boat all the way across the Atlantic Ocean, and I've to make up my mind not to be seasick.'

'That's good,' she breathed, her raw emotion scarcely letting her speak. 'You won't forget me when you're over there, will you?'

'Of course I won't. I'll write as often as I can, but I 'spect I'll be awful busy for a good while.'

'I 'spect you will,' she managed to laugh. 'Never mind, drop me a note any time you can manage it.'

'Can I say goodbye to Uncle Alistair, please?'

She turned round. 'Nicky wants to say goodbye.' She didn't know what to expect, a tantrum perhaps, or hurling the telephone across the room, but she didn't flinch, and after a very slight hesitation he took the instrument from her. She could still hear both sides, the boy's voice coming across loud and clear.

'Is that you, Uncle Alistair?'

'It's me, Nicky. You're ready to go, then?'

'Our luggage is all sitting ready for the cab to take with us to the station, and I can hardly wait, but I couldn't go without saying goodbye to Auntie Gwen and you.'

Alistair's eyes searched his wife's now. 'I haven't known you very well, Nicky, but I know she's going to miss you. I hope you have a good journey; I bet you're looking forward to it, aren't you?'

'Not half! I didn't sleep last night for thinking about it. I'll have to say cheerio now, though. Mum wants to speak to you, too.'

'Goodbye . . . Nicky.'

'Hi, Alistair. This is it, then.'

'Yes, this is it. Um . . . Peg, you'll take good care of the boy, won't you?'

'You don't need to ask. He's in good hands.'

'Yes, I know. Sorry for . . .'

'It's all right, I understand. Look after yourself, Alistair, and we'll write and keep you up to date with . . . everything.'

'Thanks, Peg, and . . . safe crossing.'

'Bye, Alistair.'

He laid the receiver back in its cradle. 'Gwen, would you mind if I went out for a wee while? I need space.'

'Are you sure you're fit to be out by yourself? Would it

be better if I went out instead? I could bike to the village and get another magazine for you. It would give me a chance to see the new man.'

'Well . . . if you don't mind?'

She was on her way in minutes, glad of the fresh air and the light wind fanning her cheeks. She did feel a bit anxious about leaving him alone, but she could understand his need to think. In addition to Lexie's marriage, he now had to cope with the thought of his wife's illegitimate son being whisked across the Atlantic out of her reach. What would he make of it all?

Lexie Fraser, of course, was not in the shop. She had spent a week with the new owner to help him get to know the customers, but she had stopped working on Saturday. So that was that, Gwen thought. She'd have liked to tender good wishes for the future, but maybe it was just as well she wouldn't have the chance, feeling as she did about Alistair's relationship with her. After exchanging a few remarks with Mr Munro about the way prices were going up, she paid for the *Titbits* she had bought for Alistair and the other items she had purchased and went outside. As luck would have it, she was still putting her groceries into the basket of her cycle when a bus stopped beside her and Lexie Fraser stepped off.

'Thank goodness I've seen you, Gwen,' she smiled. 'I didn't want to leave without saying goodbye, but I didn't want to come to Benview in case it upset Alistair. Come on round and have a cup of tea. You'll have to excuse the mess. I'm still packing.'

Feeling trapped, Gwen followed her. 'I thought you'd moved out already.'

'No, the removal van's coming on Friday to take my things to Edinburgh. Roddy put in for a transfer. He thought it would be best for me to be away from . . . Forvit, and the house he's bought isn't far from where Nancy Lawrie lives. I told him not to go to the expense of buying furniture. What's here is in reasonable condition, because I replaced my mother's stuff bit by bit over the years.'

Lexie unlocked the house door and ushered Gwen inside. 'Sit down if you can find a decent place to park yourself, and I'll put on the kettle. How's Alistair keeping?'

Shifting a large carton on to the floor, Gwen sat down in one of the easy chairs. 'He's coming on nicely, still a bit unstable, you know, but not too bad, considering.'

'How are you keeping yourself, though? You've been going at things like a beaver ever since you came home.'

'I have to keep busy, otherwise I'd . . .' Gwen stopped with a little sigh. 'I don't mind doing everything for him, if only he wouldn't . . .' She halted again, then continued with a smile. 'No, you don't want to hear me moaning.'

Sitting down at the opposite side of the fire, Lexie stretched out her legs. 'If you want to moan, Gwen, carry on. It's time I thought of somebody else for a change.'

'It's all right. I'm making a mountain out of a molehill. I get so tired at times I feel a bit resentful, if you understand.'

'I should think you would. How long's that now? Nearly six months, isn't it?'

'It won't be for much longer, he's well on the way to recovery. The doctors were very pleased with him when he had his last checkup.'

'I'm glad. You know, when I saw him that first time . . . I thought he'd had it.'

'I'll always be grateful for what you did at that time, Lexie. I don't know how Leila and David would have coped without you.'

'I was glad to be able to help.' Lexie got to her feet again as the kettle lid began to dance. 'They're nice kids, and I've always thought a lot of them.'

'And Alistair?' It was out before Gwen could stop it.

'Yes, Gwen, and Alistair,' Lexie murmured, filling the teapot. 'I loved him once, or thought I did. After what had happened to me, I needed him, though I didn't realize why, and then my mother died, and I clung to him in my mind. It was like an obsession, and it wasn't till I met Roddy that I fell in love properly.'

Watching her take a second mug out of a box – she had kept only one out for her own use, presumably – Gwen said, 'I know I asked before, Lexie, but have you any idea what Alistair did after he left your house that morning . . . the morning of the accident? Where he went? Why he was coming down the hill on to the road?'

'I'd say he'd been up to the tower to do some thinking.'

The other woman's eyes refused to meet Gwen's now, so she persisted, 'What did he have to think about, that's the point? He was with you all night, wasn't he? Did he do something he shouldn't? Don't be afraid to tell me – he'd thrown me out before that.'

Lexie waited until she was seated again before answering. 'You know, Gwen, he never loved me, not really, but he took it for granted that I'd always loved him, and he turned a bit nasty when I told him I loved Roddy. He said I was fooling myself, that I was only a bit on the side for Roddy, so . . . I slapped his face and he stormed out.' She paused momentarily, then went on, 'I suppose I should have gone after him in case he did anything silly, but I was in such a state myself it never crossed my mind.'

'Oh, I'm not blaming you for anything. I just wanted to know.'

'But you've got to believe me, Gwen. He never loved me, never ever. It was you he loved, and it was pride that held him back from trying to stop you leaving, and pride that wouldn't let him write and ask you to come back. It's a good thing that young David took the initiative. He could be a detective some day with his powers of deduction.'

'Yes, it was all down to him that Alistair took me back, and I suppose we'll manage to get over things eventually and learn to live in peace together.'

'Listen, Gwen, and don't take this the wrong way. I'd really like if you could persuade him to come to the wedding. I've asked Nancy Lawrie to be matron-of-honour because I didn't have anyone else, and she's the only one on my side apart from her husband if you two aren't there. I couldn't ask any of my customers, because only a few people are allowed in Aberdeen Register Office, and the ones I didn't ask would be offended, so . . . please Gwen? Take David and Leila, as well. You're . . . my family.'

'I'll see what I can do, although I'm not sure if he's well enough to . . .'

'You've been taking him on the bus to Aberdeen for his checkups, haven't you?'

'It's not the travelling I'm worried about. It's his mental state.'

'Trust me, Gwen. I'm sure it'll make him see sense and get over everything.'

On her way home, Gwen mulled over Lexie's last statement. Was she right? Would seeing his first girlfriend, the woman he still had a soft spot for if nothing more, being married to another man straighten all the kinks in Alistair's mind? Wasn't it more likely to send him off the rails altogether? But she had better ask him and let him decide whether or not to put himself through this fresh torture.

It had taken some persuasion, but the Ritchie family caught the second bus on Saturday morning to give Gwen and Leila time to buy clothes suitable for a wedding. David, chattering unceasingly, and Alistair, strangely silent all the way to the city, already had decent suits to wear, although as they all trooped into Falconer's store, Gwen detailed her husband to go to the men's department and buy a more presentable tie for each of them.

'We'll meet you in the restaurant about half past ten,' she instructed. 'We can have a cup of tea and a scone or something before we go to the Registrar.'

The ties were chosen in less than five minutes, so Alistair suggested that having a look at the harbour would fill in the remaining fifty-five minutes before they had to meet their womenfolk. It was a cold day, but quite pleasant as long as they kept moving, so they stepped smartly down Market Street towards Regent Quay, where there was always some activity going on, the loading or unloading of the large cargo vessels.

David, however, had other things on his mind. 'Dad,' he began, as they passed the Labour Exchange and rounded the corner, 'are you going to let Mum stay with us once you're right better?'

Alistair's eyebrows shot up. 'Do you think I shouldn't?'

'I think you should! I know what she did wasn't right, but if you love her, you'd be able to forgive her.'

Evading the implied question, Alistair said, 'Look, there's a Norwegian boat. It's likely brought in some timber – pine, possibly.'

His son wasn't to be sidetracked. 'Don't change the subject. Is it Mum you love, or Lexie? Why have you come here today? Are you hoping to stop the wedding?'

Alistair felt a sudden spurt of anger. How dare his son say things like that to him? Where on earth had he got the idea that . . . ? God Almighty! How many other folk had got that impression? Had Leila? Worse still, had Gwen?

'Dad? I'd like an answer.'

'Leave it, David. I can't think properly just now. We have to get back.'

While they completed the rest of what was a rectangle – along Regent Quay, up the even steeper Marischal Street, along Union Street back to Falconer's – Alistair turned the question of what he felt for his wife over and over in his mind. Gwen probably did know how he felt about Lexie, yet she had almost forced him to attend the wedding. Was she hoping that he would give up on his first love when he saw her marrying the 'tec?

He didn't care about anything these days, so why the hell had he come? He hadn't had the strength, the willpower, to refuse, that was why. Gwen had said she would like to see the wedding, but she wouldn't have gone and left him on his own, so it had been easier to agree. Yet . . . was that all it had been? He could remember now how he had briefly felt ashamed of himself, not so much for being a burden to her – which he was – but for resenting her getting her own way, when she'd had precious little to be grateful for over the past few months. He'd had everything his way.

He and David had only a few minutes to wait on the store's top floor before Gwen and Leila joined them and they all went into the restaurant. His wife looked at him anxiously as they sat down. 'Are you all right, Alistair?'

'Perfect,' he said, sarcastically, because he was absolutely done in. It wasn't just the effect of the physical exercise, it was all the concentrated thinking he was having to do.

He knew that his brain wasn't anything like back to normal – it might never be – but surely he knew what was what? No, even that was debatable. Unable to banish the picture of his wife with that Ken Partridge, he had put her through hell since she came back. Would he ever be able to forgive her?

Unaware that she was watching him, he gave a slight start. Would he *ever* be able to forgive her? He usually thought that he would *never* be able to forgive her. It must be a step forward? He did feel that bit different today. Lexie had apparently sat with him during his first few days in hospital, but it was Gwen who had tended him day and night since he was discharged, Gwen who had comforted him when his darkest demons were tormenting him, Gwen who smiled even when he was shouting for attention. Only a woman whose love was unshakeable could have put up with him..

It had been some time after he was home before he started wondering about his accident, and why he'd been coming down from the tower so early that morning. It had been like trying to dig up an irremovable stone, however. Maybe it was better for him not to know, just to accept things as they were. He should praise Leila and David for coping so well in the shop without him, instead of resenting that, too. Life would be much easier for all of them, himself included, if he mended his ways. He stood in danger of losing his wife if he carried on the way he was doing.

Testing his feelings further, he decided that he could live quite happily without Lexie in the background, but he couldn't visualize spending the rest of his life without Gwen. The question he should be asking himself was, *Would she ever forgive him?*

In the Register Office, part of a row of granite buildings with shops at street level, the wedding party was shown into a drab, uninspiring room, where sat an elderly gentleman with a high, Victorian-type collar. He gave them a weary, harassed smile as he motioned to the main participants – bride and groom and their attendants – to come forward, and to the Ritchies and the only other man to take a seat.

Noticing how drawn Alistair was looking, Gwen wished that she hadn't made him come. Was he stable enough to watch Lexie Fraser marrying Roddy Liddell? Was he planning to do something to stop the wedding? He was obviously deep in thought, and she primed herself for the explosion she was almost sure would come, but everything went smoothly. The vows were affirmed, the ring placed on the third finger of the bride's left hand, and the ceremony was being brought to a close.

'I now pronounce you man and wife,' the registrar intoned, constant repetition of the words over many years depriving them of any real meaning. 'You may kiss the bride.'

It was then that Alistair jumped to his feet, taking everyone by surprise, even his own wife, but it was nothing like she had feared. 'I love you, Gwen,' he said, articulating each word in a loud clear voice that rang round the room, 'and I always will!'

The registrar's head jerked up, Lexie and Roddy whipped round grinning; Nancy Fleming was beaming when she turned; Leila, although scarlet with embarrassment, wore a beatific smile of sheer happiness. The best man, another police inspector, and Greig Fleming, Nancy's husband, not understanding the poignancy of the statement, were both staring at Alistair as if he had taken leave of his senses.

David seemed to be the only one to have retained the power of speech. Barely able to contain his excitement, he chortled, 'Atta boy, Dad! Close your mouth, Mum, so he can kiss you, and all.'

The House of Lyall

Doris Davidson

Young Marion Cheyne comes from a humble background in a remote village, but her heart is full of ambition. When her employer leaves a plate of gold sovereigns in full view, she is unable to resist the temptation to help herself on the way to a better life. Seizing her chance, she escapes and sets off for Aberdeen. Here she changes her name to Marianne, but her character remains courageous and determined – and unscrupulous when necessary.

Fortune smiles, and a dream she thought impossible is fulfilled when she marries the heir to Castle Lyall. Marianne understands it is a business arrangement, but though she is a woman of strong passions she will not allow love to interfere with social elevation. Life as a lady of the glen suits her. She is popular with the workers and servants and Marianne in turn vows to do everything in her power to protect the Lyall name.

Through the trials and triumphs of two world wars, Marianne will stop at nothing to guard her hard-won position. But there are many secrets in her past that refuse to stay safely buried. Nothing in the small community of the glen can remain hidden for ever . . .

Praise for Doris Davidson's novels:

'Compelling' *Aberdeen Evening Express*

'Absorbing' *Manchester Evening News*

ISBN 0 00 651321 2